Butterflies &

VICIOUS LIES

USA TODAY BESTSELLING AUTHOR

KAYLEIGH KING

This is a work of fiction. Names, characters, businesses, places, events, locales, and incidents are either the products of the author's imagination or used in a fictitious manner. Any resemblance to actual persons, living or dead, or actual events is purely coincidental.

Cover Design: Cat Imb at TRC DESIGNS

Copy Editing: Ellie McLove MY BROTHER'S EDITOR

Copy Editing: Amanda Rash DRAFT HOUSE EDITORIAL SERVICES

ISBN: 979-8-9863360-3-9

BLURB

I told her my secrets and she told me gilded lies. The words that dripped from her lips like honey were nothing but empty promises.

Her betrayal blindsided me.

Posie had been my constant. My anchor. My calm. Until she wasn't.

Now she's my enemy.

Before I could even the score, she fled to the other side of the country where she thought she was safe from my wrath.

She was wrong.

It didn't matter how far my butterfly flew, I always knew where she was. All I had to do was wait and prepare for her return.

After six years, Posie has flown back into town, and I have her cage waiting.

A NOTE FROM THE AUTHOR

TRIGGER & CONTENT WARNING - Please Read

Triggers include but are not limited to: Drug and alcohol addiction, overdose, suicide, child abuse, sexual assault, questionable consent between MC's, drugging, car accident, grief, parent suffering a stroke, strong language, and sexually explicit scenes.

If you need further details or explanations of any of these listed TW/CW, please email kayleighkingassistant@gmail.com. We'll be happy to answer any questions.

For those who love even when it hurts.

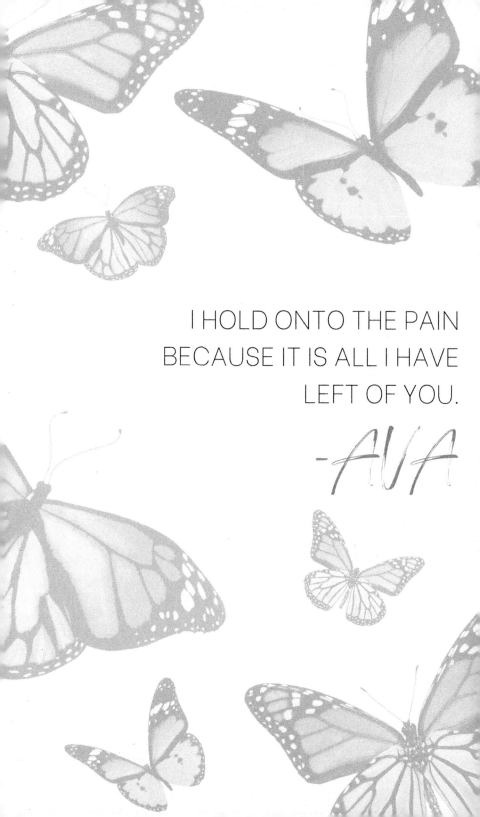

I HOLD ONTO THE PAIN
BECAUSE IT IS ALL I HAVE
LEFT OF YOU.

-AVA

PLAYLIST

LISTEN HERE: spoti.fi/3ImLVtq
Edge Of The Dark - Emmit Fenn
Youth - Daughter
While You're At It - Jessie Murph
I Don't Hate You - Kyla La Grange
Where You Gonna Go - Gregory Alan Isakov
Let Me Hurt - Emily Rowed
Mum - Luke Hemmings
Love Like This - Acoustic - Kodaline
There's Something Dark - Dustin Kensrue
My Eyes - The Lumineers
Lie - Sasha Alex Sloan
Cold Feet - Callinsick
Death of Me - PVRIS

PROLOGUE
POSIE

I HEAR those three little words at night when I sleep. I hear them in my dreams as I relive that night over and over again. Sometimes, I swear I can still feel his breath on my cheek when he leaned in close to whisper them in my ear. My heart still jumps at the memory, my palms still get sweaty.

Three little words that changed everything.

The passion that burned in his eyes as he stared at me on that dark street, flashing police lights bouncing off the houses, still makes my skin burn. The way his voice cracked as he spoke still makes my chest ache.

Three little words that broke my heart into a million sharp pieces. Three little words that hold so much weight, they're almost suffocating.

I know what you're thinking. I know exactly what three words you think I'm referring to, but you're wrong. I wish on shooting stars to this day, wishing that night could have ended differently.

Instead, I was left with nothing but three little words and a broken heart.

I hate you.

This is our story, one that started in love but ended in hate.

That line between love and hate? I'm here to tell you that it's not as thin as you've been told. It's an impenetrable steel wall.

It doesn't matter how many stars I wish on; Rafferty Blackwell will always hate me.

My lies made sure of it.

ONE
RAFFERTY

WHEN YOU'RE INJURED, they ask you to rate your pain on a scale from one to ten. One being something as simple as a splinter, ten being a gunshot to the abdomen.

If anger was rated the same way, I would say that I live at a constant five. It's a persistent ache just under my skin. Some days, like today, it's more prominent, but for almost six years now, the continuous rage has been my shadow. It clings to me, following me wherever I go.

Coming home to a house full of drunk and high coeds isn't helping. Especially after I'd told Paxton just this morning that I didn't want anyone at the house this weekend.

My brother has his own reasons for wanting the house full of people, and that's the only reason I didn't send everyone packing the second I walked through the front door. Instead, I weaved through the sweaty bodies, ignoring the people shouting my name and removing the grabby hands of overzealous females from my body, and escaped through the glass sliding door at the back of the house.

The only company I have out here in this quiet solitude are the ever-present thoughts in my head and the cigarette between my fingers. It's a habit I've harbored for years, and at this point, I wonder if quitting is worth the misery. I figure my body is already full of poison and darkness, I might as well breathe it into my lungs too.

My eyes are locked on the glowing orange embers, the only source of light in this dark corner of the yard. As if hypnotized by the small flame, and completely consumed by the unwanted memories swirling around in my brain, I watch it burn. The ash breaks off and falls to the stone beneath the chair I sit in. The wind carries it off, washing away any evidence it had ever fallen. If only it were that easy to wipe the slate clean. I've found it takes a little more effort and tedious planning.

The sliding door opens, and the sound of footsteps follows. I don't have to look up to know who it is. Only two people are dumb enough to disturb me when I'm in this kind of headspace, and Rome had a mandatory family event tonight.

Pax sprawls into the wooden chair across from me, leg casually hanging over the arm of it. He doesn't say anything, just sits there with the bottle of scotch dangling from his tattooed fingertips. Like always, his fingernails are coated in chipped black nail polish.

Putting the cigarette to my lips, I look at my brother through the cloud of smoke. The darkness that resides in his blue eyes is the same I see in myself when I look in the mirror. I tried so fucking hard to shield him from it all, but I failed him. It took one night for everything to fall apart around us and for the darkness to invade Pax's soul.

And there's no one to blame but *her*.

Pax blinks and his head shakes, just barely, as if he's finally been pulled back from the haunted place he'd found himself in. Turning his head, he looks at me. "Today was her first day back, but I'm sure you already know that."

I drop the cigarette onto the ground and stomp it out with my booted foot. "I do."

It doesn't matter how far away my butterfly flew; I always knew where she was. She may have thought she was out there free from me but she was always ensnared in my net. I was just waiting for the right moment to draw her back in. Five years of waiting patiently, and it's finally time.

"She seems to be settling in okay."

I'll give her a few days to fall into a false sense of security and comfort. She should savor every moment of peace and rest she can get because when I get my hands on her, both will be sorely lacking from her life.

When I don't respond to his comment, Pax sits straighter in his chair and sighs. "What are you going to do to her, Raff?"

I'm going to clip her wings and, like the end of my cigarette, I'm going to burn her until there's nothing left but ash. Bit by bit, she'll float away into nothingness, and I'll finally regain what she stole from me.

"Nothing that she hasn't earned."

TWO
POSIE

LIFE HAS a way of knocking you down and then laughing at you as you sit there on the ground with bloody hands and knees. It finds enjoyment in your discomfort, like a sick masochist. Like right now, I swear, I hear the joyous cackling in the branches of the tree I sit under in the quad.

The unease I've felt since stepping foot back in this town —*this state*—only gets worse the longer I spend on campus.

I never intended on moving back to Washington, but the other thing about life is it enjoys fucking up your best-laid plans. There was a set course I was steadily on. I'd been working toward it for as long as I can remember, and things were really looking like they'd turn out my way.

My first life-altering event almost knocked me off track, but with some fighting and a shit-ton of therapy, I regained whatever remained of my balance. I wasn't so lucky the second time life decided to fuck shit up for me.

The events of last fall had me completely reeling, and no matter how much I tried, I couldn't recover. My path changed and my options became limited, and that's ultimately how I ended up in the state I literally fled from nearly six years ago.

7

I simply had nowhere else to go if I still wanted to earn my degree.

Not getting a diploma isn't an option. Never has been. The importance of a college education has been engraved into me since I was too young to understand what an undergrad was. I should be thankful for the opportunity to finish my degree at Olympic Sound University but being here feels like I'm constantly teetering on the edge of disaster. It's only a matter of time before my judgment day is before me. I can only outrun it for so long.

The mocking wind blows the corner of my stationary up off the textbook I'm using to write on. It's the same pale-yellow paper that I write on every time. Sending handwritten letters is such a thing of the past, but I enjoy writing one to him every week. Even though I never get one in return.

I miss you every day and wish I could be with you. -Love, Posie.

I sign the letters the same every week, and each time I scribble those words across the yellow paper, my chest constricts painfully and my eyes burn. Many times, I've sent a letter to him with the black ink smudged from my tears. In my heart, I know we're doing the right thing, but it still hurts like hell, and I miss him more than anything. It hurts more knowing how close to him I am now. Yet, we must be kept apart.

Like I said, life loves to revel in your misery.

Neatly folding the paper, I put it in the matching envelope and scribble the address that is forever committed to my memory.

"Writing a letter under a tree? I feel like I'm intruding on your Disney princess moment." The voice comes from behind me, making me fly off the ground and to my feet. Zadie's pixie-like features twist in confusion and green eyes scan around us for danger. "What the hell? You've been jumpy all week. Are you sure you're doing alright? It's like you're hiding from the boogeyman or expecting him to come around the corner at any given moment."

"I'm not hiding," I correct. It's true. I'm not hiding from *him*, but I'm sure as hell not going to go out of my way to announce my presence. Though, I'd bet money he already knows I'm back. Before I left town, he had an uncanny ability of knowing everyone's business. I'm sure he's only found new and more clever ways at obtaining secrets. "I told you, I like to keep a low profile."

The irony that I went from thriving in the spotlight on a stage to whatever this new cagey behavior of mine is, isn't lost on me.

"*Yeah* ... I know that's what you said, but I'll be honest, I'm not sure that's going to work for me." Zadie exaggerates a fake grimace to match her teasing tone. "There are so many places to go and things to do around here, and I'm going to feel bad going to all of them while you're hiding away in the apartment like a hermit."

When I got the notification about the apartment listing on an Olympic Sound Student Facebook group, I thought it was too good to be true. Zadie was desperate for a new roommate after her original one transferred schools at the last minute. The rent she was asking was just in range of what I can afford with my part-time job at the dance studio, and since I'm without a car, the location was ideal. It's within walking distance of all the places I'll need to be. I responded to it immediately, and before I knew it, I was signing the lease agreement.

Moving back here is arguably one of the hardest things I've ever had to do, and everything about it has been rushed. I've been incredibly fortunate so many of the pieces have fallen into place with surprising ease.

In the five days that I've lived with her, I've discovered Zadie Hill is the epitome of a social butterfly. There hasn't been one person we've passed on campus she hasn't known, or at the very least, known through someone else. She's doing her best to tell me everyone's names and she gives me bits of information on each of them. I'm trying to retain the information as best I can, but it's all going in one ear and out the other.

Every night this week, Zadie's dolled herself up and left to go to different parties. She gets back just before sunrise and crawls into bed. I'm not sure how she does it, but she's always up before ten a.m. and looks completely refreshed. For all I know, she's made a deal with the devil to avoid hangovers. If that's the case, I need her to give me his contact information because I'm in need of his services.

"*Again*, I'm not hiding," I stress, tucking the textbook and envelope into my bag. "I've just been busy with moving in and starting my job this week, I haven't had time to go out with you. Plus, I'm not a huge party person anymore."

There was a time that I was at a party every weekend. I enjoyed every second of them, soaking up the energy of the loud music and flowing alcohol, but a lot has changed since then.

Zadie doesn't believe me and instantly calls my bluff.

"Didn't you say you're off this Friday?" she asks, leading me across the concrete walkway toward the coffee cart we'd agreed to meet at before our next classes. "There's a party that night and you're coming with me."

"*What?* No, absolutely not."

We stand in line at the cart, and I bounce nervously on my toes while searching the surrounding area. The clock is running out, and sooner or later, I'll come face-to-face with one of them. Or worst-case scenario, both of them at the same time. Part of me wants to get it over with, like ripping off a Band-Aid, but the wound the bandage is covering isn't small or healed. It's a fatal stab wound, and I'm fairly certain I'd bleed out immediately. And if by some miracle I survive that, he'll find another way to kill me.

I've done the best I can to keep those ugly memories at bay, but I know the second I look into those blue eyes, there will be no containing them. They'll tear apart all the repair work I've done on myself these past years.

Zadie ignores my comment and sidles up to the coffee cart. She knows my order because she was appalled when she learned I only drink black coffee. I had to explain that I don't drink coffee for the taste. To me, it's the magical elixir that will get me through the rest of my day. After drinking it like this for five years, I no longer notice the bitterness of it. Meanwhile, she gets the sugary drink filled to the brim with whipped cream.

"Look," she starts, spinning back to me after paying for our caffeinated beverages. "I know we're not really at a place in our friendship yet where we're divulging deep dark secrets. *I get it.* We're still at the *peeing with the door closed* phase. But I'm going to real-talk you a little bit because I think we're on a high-speed train to best-friend-ville, and I want to give you a little taste of what it's like to be my friend."

This should be good.

"I don't have deep dark secrets." Pausing to think over everything else she said, I quickly add, "And I get stage fright. So, I don't know if we'll ever have an open-door policy. I can't even go when someone is in the stall next to me."

Silently, she gestures for me to move to the other side of the cart with her so we can wait out of everyone's way.

"I don't know who the monster under your bed is, but I know they're here. I wouldn't need to be a psychology major to notice your weird-ass behavior."

The fact Zadie speaks softer than her usual *"look at me"* volume shows how sincere she's trying to be. She's not trying to point out my flaws, but in her own way, she's trying to help. She just hasn't figured out there isn't any helping me with this. The damage was done long ago. There wasn't any coming back from it when I made that choice. I knew it then and I know it now.

"You mentioned that you used to live in Seattle, so my guess is you have some lingering history here that you're still trying to outrun."

Unable to help myself, I shift anxiously on my feet and push my long hair behind my ear when the wind blows it forward. "Zadie, it's a really long story and I—"

She holds her hand up, cutting me off. "I'm not asking you to tell me about your demons, Posie. Like I said, I haven't earned the privilege of hearing about those yet. We'll get there, but for now, I'll keep shutting the bathroom door and not pry for information you're not ready to give." Zadie gives my forearm a reassuring squeeze. "What I will tell you is you shouldn't allow your past to ruin the opportunities you could have here. You only go to college once. I don't want you to look back on these days and regret hanging out at home when you could be having fun."

I already live with so much regret—like a suffocating amount. Adding more sounds unbearable, so I relent. "I'll think about it, okay?"

"Posie, that's not the answer I was looking for."

"Yeah, well, it's the best I can do for you right now."

Zadie's face scrunches before she huffs out a breath. "Fine, but no promises I won't have Lark help me drag your ass out of the apartment."

Within the first three minutes of meeting Zadie, she was talking to me about Lark like I knew her myself. With a little bit of patience and a few key questions, I finally pieced together Lark is a senator's daughter and they've been friends since freshman year.

Their friendship makes me long for the ones I'd made in New York. Having to leave Juilliard like that was humiliating. The fact I fucked up my dream is embarrassing. While my aunt tries to argue that it's not my fault, I know it is. I shut down and couldn't handle everything. It would be hard to face those people again knowing they know I tossed away a once-in-a-lifetime opportunity.

"Okay, well, it's only Tuesday, so that means I have a couple days to think it over."

"Will you actually think it over?"

"Of course."

The barista calls out our orders and I scurry over to collect them before she can try to guilt me anymore.

She takes the cup from me and narrows her eyes at me in suspicion. "I can't tell if you're lying to me or not."

Bringing my coffee to my lips, I conceal my sly smirk. "And you never will." I bump her with my shoulder playfully before starting to walk toward the building my next class is held in.

I get about five feet when she calls after me. "Don't walk away like you're all *proud* of yourself. Lying is a very bad skill to excel at."

Turning, I walk backward a few paces while shrugging nonchalantly. "We all have to be good at something, right?"

THREE
POSIE

THE HALLWAY LEADING to the auditorium my art history class is held in is packed full of students. People weave around the groups of people who have decided the middle of the hallway is an excellent place to catch up and talk about weekend plans. I bite my tongue when I walk past them so I don't make some snarky remark about their complete disregard for their surroundings.

This is the one building I didn't tour when Zadie walked me around campus the other day. She said the auditorium is at the end of the long hallway, but this building is shaped like a misshapen 'T' and there are *two* long hallways here. And both lead to opposite sides of the building.

Getting up on my tippy-toes, I try to see around everyone. My shorter stature makes it hard to see if there are any signs posted on the walls to help get my bearings.

Frustrated with the students who keep blocking my path, I let out an annoyed huff when I shove around another group of them.

Coming out the other side, I search the hallway.

My world tilts as my eyes land on the figure.

I've barely had a chance to fully comprehend who I'm looking at as my feet turn into pieces of concrete and I come to an abrupt stop. All the oxygen leaves my body, and my lungs burn when I fail to inhale another breath.

It's like everyone but the two of us is moving in fast forward. They turn into colorful blurs while we remain perfectly still, staring at each other, and the obnoxious chatter turns to soft, incoherent buzzing. For all I know, I've lost the ability to breathe *and* hear.

It's been years, but I'd recognize him anywhere. The boy that I remember has turned into a man. It makes me wonder if I look as grown up as him. I don't feel like I've changed, but I know I must have. Five years is a long time.

He looks exhausted with dark, almost purple, circles under his blue eyes. The smile that I remember so fondly is void from his angular face. Any signs of his adolescent features are gone, and before me stands a man I never thought I'd get to meet in person.

Paxton Blackwell is now a man.

That sadness residing in his gaze makes my heart crack like a fragile piece of glass, and just like I expected to happen, memories of the pain we shared between us come roaring to the surface.

Of the two brothers, I'm glad it's Pax I'm seeing first. It hurts, but I know seeing his older brother will be excruciating in comparison. Sometimes, heartbreak never heals, no matter how much time passes. With each beat, it demands that you remember what you lost.

I want to go to him, but the second my foot lifts off the ground, Pax's head slowly shakes. The move is so subtle I almost miss it. It's like a silent warning, but I'm not exactly sure what he's alerting me to. As a precaution, I look around me for danger but don't find anything.

With his name on the tip of my tongue, I turn back to him,

but as if in a puff of smoke, Pax has disappeared. The same longing I've fought for years overcomes me. For as long as I can remember, the Blackwell brothers were my constant, and even with how badly things ended for us, I missed them every day I was gone.

Against every instinct in my body, and my original plan to avoid them, I rush down the hallway after him. For so long, I dreaded the day I'd see him again, but in a turn of events, the brief glance I got wasn't enough. There are a million questions I want to ask him. Mainly, I just want to bury my face in his chest and hug him like I used to. And I really want to know if he's okay. It's a silly question, given the circumstances, but I still want to hear his answer. And I want to be able to look him in the eyes when he does. The truth always sat in his eyes, even when we were all too blind to realize it.

I don't bother with saying excuse me as I follow down the hallway after Pax. He couldn't have gotten that far ahead of me, but every time I lift onto my toes, I can't see his tall frame anywhere. He must have grown six inches since the last time I saw him. It's a sad reality that the boy who used to be my best friend now looks like a stranger.

Frustrated, I pause and look in all directions for him. I go as far as peeping into a few of the classrooms with open doors, but still, I come up empty.

Dejected, I give up and reluctantly turn back toward the direction I'd come. One good thing came out of this, and it's that I know for sure the auditorium I need to go to is on the other side of the building.

Staring at my shockingly shaky hands, my fingers clench and unclench as I try to soothe the nerves the fleeting encounter caused. Starting back down the hallway, I get no more than three feet when I'm abruptly pulled backward into the dark classroom I pass.

I try to fight the sudden grip on me, but the hands holding me by my upper arms are unrelenting. All my training has made me strong, but I'm no match for their brute strength. Without looking at them, I know they're much taller than me. The hallway is so busy with people lost in their own conversations and dealings that my blatant abduction goes unnoticed. The second my lips part to yell for help, a hand slaps down on my face and painfully silences any of my attempts at being rescued.

My heart slams against my ribs almost as hard as the door slams after we enter the room. I don't have time to inspect the dark classroom before I'm violently whirled around and the front of my body slams into the white wall.

Fighting against the hands gripping me, I try to turn my head to look at the person holding me hostage. My head barely turns an inch in their direction when their hand leaves my mouth to thread through the strands of my hair and the side of my face is pressed harshly into the wall. The unyielding pressure on my skull instantly makes a headache form, and I worry if I'm held like this for too long, bruising will form on my face. The logical side of my brain knows I shouldn't be worried about something as insignificant as a bruise right now. I should be more worried about my *life*.

Panic begins to take over as adrenaline shoots through my veins. With their hand gone from my mouth, I could scream, but I'm too stunned to make a noise. I always said if I ever found myself in a situation like this, I would fight like hell. Instead, I find that the fear is making me freeze in place. My limbs are heavy and there's a high-pitched ringing in my ears.

"Please..." My plea is a barely audible choked sob. I'm trying to fight the urge to cry, but my eyes are already burning as tears begin to form.

Chills of uncontainable terror run down my spine when they shift their body closer and their head drops down to mine. The chills only amplify when they finally speak.

"I knew he'd try to warn you," he whispers darkly into my

ear, so close I can feel his breath against my cheek. "He's always had a soft spot for you. I suppose there was a time that we both did." His other hand brushes the wild strands of my hair off my face with a tenderness I know is a lie. I'd almost prefer if he hurt me more. The softness of his touch holds the unspoken promise of pain. "Isn't that right, Posie?"

Hearing him say my name after all this time is like a hot blade slicing through my soul.

It's taken five years, but I've finally been reunited with the boy I gave all my firsts to. I gave him my heart, and in return, he gave me his. In the end, I looked him in the eyes while I broke it along with all the promises I made him.

I can't remember the last time I allowed myself to say his name out loud. It became something like a bad omen or reprehensible swear word. But when I choke out his name, it feels as familiar as it used to.

"Rafferty."

It feels like coming home even though I know it's an illusion.

I'm not home. I'm in enemy territory, and there are whispers of war in the air.

FOUR
RAFFERTY

I'VE KEPT tabs on her over the years. She may have deleted her
social media when she fled from me, but I found ways to stay
up-to-date on what Posie Davenport had been up to. I know all
the ways she's changed her hair over the years, and I know the
names of each of the ballets she's performed in. I know the
names of the friends she left at Juilliard, and I know the names of
the men she kissed after me. Even if there were only two.

All my calculated planning made me ready for this moment.
I was *prepared* to come face-to-face with her after all this time.

Or I thought I was.

No amount of planning could have prepared me for what it
would be like to be in a room with the girl that destroyed my life.
The anger that rages in my soul flares and the flames burn just
beneath my skin. There is a plan—*my plan*—in place for her, but
I'm so close to saying *fuck it* to all of it and dealing with her
now.

The thing that stops me is knowing that it would be too fast.
She needs to feel the pain she caused for herself, and she needs
to experience the same kind of havoc she inflicted on me. *On my
family.*

I want to see her break just like she broke me.

She's shorter than I remember her being, but then again, I've grown not only in height but in muscle mass since we were last in the same room together. She's also thinner than she ever was, but her lean muscles felt defined under my hands when I pulled her in here. The intense training and dedicated workout routines have made her strong.

Her straight, light-brown hair has more blonde at the ends than I remember, and it's several inches longer than she used to wear it. I'm not complaining, the long strands make it easy for me to hold her in place, and the harsh traction on her scalp keeps her from fighting too much.

The one thing that hasn't changed is the sugary citrus scent that clings to her skin. It fills my nose, assaulting me with memories of our tainted past. There were times I would dream of her and her betrayal and wake up smelling it faintly in the air.

I never tried to forget her or force myself to move on. Instead, I clung to those memories and used them to fuel me. They were like kerosene for my anger. While it raged on, it pushed me to work harder and become what I am today.

And that's why I laugh when she says my name like she still has any idea who I am. She doesn't know me. Posie doesn't know the man she forced me to become. This version of me wouldn't exist if it weren't for her treacherous actions.

"I've waited so long for this," I growl, taking in a deep lungful of her intoxicating scent to stoke my flame-like fury. "What did I tell you that night on the street?" *The night everything changed.*

My hand increases pressure on her skull, pressing her harder into the drywall. The small whimper of pain delights me, encouraging me to keep going. When she doesn't immediately answer me like I want, I decide to do just that. With my free hand, I twist her arm behind her back and manipulate it as far as I can without popping it from its socket.

Posie cries out louder this time, tears running from her pale honey-colored eyes and down her cheek.

"What did I tell you?" I grit out.

"That you ... hate me," she chokes between broken sobs.

I laugh at this. "Of course, that's the part you'd fixate on." She was supposed to be the one person I could never hate. Instead, she's become the one thing I despise the most. "What else did I tell you, Posie?"

Her tongue swipes out, wetting her bottom lip, while she takes strained, panting breaths. *That's it. Breathe through the pain, Butterfly.* It's a skill I'm well acquainted with myself.

Finally, she repeats, word for word, the threat I'd spoken that night while surrounded by police cars and rain soaking through our clothes. "That I better enjoy the time I have away from you, because one day you were going to find me and I was going to pay for what I did."

Releasing the hold I have on her, I spin her and force her spine to press against the white wall. The panic and dread in her eyes satisfy the sadistic monster purring inside of me. I feel alive staring down at her, something I haven't felt in so long. Her terror awakens the pieces of me I thought were long dead.

My head dips toward her and her chin tips up, as if on muscle-memory alone. This position is so familiar, but it doesn't feel like it used to. The air that crackles between us is full of sinister intentions and hatred.

"You're out of time, Butterfly. Welcome home."

The nickname I'd given her early in our youth no longer holds sweet sentimental value as I say it. It's said with venom and a deadly promise. Taking hold of her jaw, my fingers dig into her skin as I force her to remain still. She tries to pull out of reach as my tongue wipes away the salty tears on her cheek. *"Delicious,"* I praise. "Your tears now mean more to me than you ever did."

The pain shines across her pretty face, and when she tries to look away from me again, I allow it. "Raff, you don't have to do this…" Her voice is scratchy as emotion continues to fill her throat. "I know you don't want me here, but I have a year left of school and then I'll be gone. You never have to see me again. I'll stay out of your way, you won't even know that I'm here."

I tsk her and take a step back from her small frame. She wipes at the cheek I just licked, like she can remove the invisible burn left there.

"Bargaining isn't a good look on you. It's also a waste of both our time." In the fray of getting her inside this classroom, her leather shoulder bag had fallen to the ground. Her things are scattered around our feet. The toe of my well-broken-in leather boot kicks a yellow envelope across the tile floor. "And who says I don't want you here? You're precisely where I need you to be."

Her eyes widen at this. She has no idea the strings I've pulled to put all this in motion. And each one was so worth it. I'd call in all the favors I've collected over the years to have her right here with waves of fear seeping from her pores.

"I'll be in touch soon, Posie," I promise darkly. "But in the meantime, be a good girl and stick to yourself. After all, you're not here to make friends or enjoy your time."

The stubbornness and strength I remember so clearly settle in her flushed face as she glares at me. "Who the fuck do you think you are telling me what I can or can't do? You have no right to order me around, Rafferty."

Charging forward a step, reclaiming the space I'd just allotted her, I slam my fist against the wall beside her head. "I know exactly who the fuck I am, and you're about to fucking learn yourself." Eyes flicking over her once more, I back away toward the door. "Just one last warning before I go; stay the fuck away from my brother. You've caused him enough pain."

Posie's actions had many repercussions but watching what it's done to my brother has been the hardest part of all this.

While that night changed me, it destroyed the person my brother once was. It made him an empty shell of a human.

I have no interest in hearing her speak anymore, so before she can argue, I spin around and exit the room. Excitement and rage create a dangerous mixture in my bloodstream as I leave the building.

FIVE
POSIE
FIFTEEN YEARS OLD

I'M SO proud of my dad for getting his dream job but switching schools in the middle of my freshman year of high school is less than ideal. With Dad's newly-appointed title of police captain comes a lot of new connections. Like the Mayor. He himself pulled strings to get me enrolled in the best private school in Dad's new district.

My dad is ecstatic about the opportunity while I'm still coming to grips with it. Henry Davenport has always lectured the importance of a good education, and I'm thankful I am lucky enough to receive a scholarship to Hemlock Hill Academy but walking into this school feels like I'm walking into a wolves' den.

That is if the den were a state-of-the-art institute made of overpriced marble and glass.

We live a very comfortable life, and I've never wanted for anything, but compared to the affluent families who send their children to this school, my dad makes pennies.

Pulling up in my dad's police-issued SUV makes me feel like I don't belong. Every car in this parking lot is flashy and expensive. I'll never understand why teenagers need to drive luxury imports. Many, if not all of them, drive newer and more luxurious cars than the teachers and staff.

A group of girls walks by our car, each of them with a high-end bag over their shoulder and red-soled heels on their feet. Everyone here wears variations of the same black, white, and navy-blue uniform, but it's accessories like theirs that differentiate them from the scholarship kids like me.

"Dad," I gripe, sinking lower into the leather of the passenger seat. "Why couldn't I have just stayed at my school?"

He sighs, hand shifting on the steering wheel. "P, we've been talking about this for two weeks. This will be good for you and look amazing on your applications for college. It might also help your chances of getting into that fancy school in Massachusetts you want to attend."

His last point is why I'd reluctantly agreed to transfer schools —not that I really had a choice in the matter.

My goal since I was in my very first ballet class was to attend Juilliard. I've dedicated my life to dance and have done everything in my power to boost my chances of achieving my dream. The performing arts boarding school located in Massachusetts has given many students just like me a leg up in being accepted to Juilliard. The application process is competitive, and my chances of getting in are slim, but I haven't given up hope.

The director of my current ballet academy has gone as far as to reach out to her contacts in the industry in hopes of having them write recommendation letters for my application. Now it's just a waiting game, and I could be waiting up to a year to hear from them.

"I just... I don't know these people." The students at the public high school I should be attending are the same students I went to elementary and middle school with. I may not have been extremely close to any of them, but there was at least mutual history between us.

Dad moves up in the drop-off line we're waiting in. With

each inch we move closer to the front of the impressive building, the harder my heart pounds with nerves. I can stand in front of a theater with hundreds in attendance and not blink an eye but walking into this new school is making my skin crawl.

"You're not going to be alone." Dad gives my shoulder a reassuring squeeze. "The boys are here. They'll show you around."

I don't know about that.

We've known the Blackwell family for as long as I can remember. I'm pretty sure Paxton and I took our first steps together. With Dad's long shifts at the station, I've spent a lot of time at the Blackwells' house. Hell, one of their spare bedrooms has practically been given to me since there are a lot of nights Dad can't make it to pick me up. Their mother, Mollie, is the closest thing I've had to a mother since my own left when I was two.

Pax was more than excited when I told him I'd be transferring to his school. Rafferty got quiet and didn't say anything. His cold blue eyes raked over me before he had silently left the room. I don't think he liked the idea of me intruding on his world any more than I already do.

Sometimes, the look on his face makes me think he just barely tolerates my existence, that my just breathing the same air as him is somehow offensive. Other times, his intense blue stare examines me like he's slowly uncovering every inch of me. Like he knows every secret and piece of my soul. It makes my heart thud and palms sweat. Sometimes, I don't think he realizes that he's looking at me in such a way. When he catches himself, the change is almost instant—like flipping a switch. If you blink, you could miss it entirely.

I wish I could read his mind and know what he's thinking when he looks at me like that, but Rafferty Blackwell has always been good at keeping his emotions close to the vest.

"Yeah, I guess."

We finally reach the front of the drop-off line and I undo my seat belt. Dad pipes up again just as my fingers brush against the door handle. "Don't forget that I'm working late tonight. Mollie will be here to pick you guys up after school, and when my shift is over, I'll pick you up from their house."

I laugh at this. "By Mollie, you obviously mean her driver, right?" Mollie Wilde-Blackwell doesn't drive herself. It's just another mundane task she hires staff for. I'm not fully convinced she brushes her own teeth.

Dad's face pinches behind his reflective sunglasses. "Yes, I suppose I mean her driver."

My dad might be surrounded by crazy-rich families like the Blackwells, but he's retained the hard-working, blue-collar views he was raised with. Their way of life is as foreign to him as this school is to me.

"Have a good first day, honey." He waves at me while I climb from the car. "See you tonight."

The Suburban drives away and I'm officially left to face this all alone. I have no idea where Paxton is, and I don't want to look weak by texting him to meet me out here.

It's just school, Posie. You made it through Mrs. Vasilisa's advanced pointe class and her harsh critiques unscathed. You can make it through a basic day of school.

Forcing myself to fake the same level of confidence I have while I'm on stage, I lift my chin and start up the front steps of my new school.

The entire time I walk down the main corridor to the wing where my locker is, I feel eyes on me. People look at me and whisper to their friends. The students that attend this school come from families that all know each other. It's not very often that 'outsiders' like myself become new students here.

The same group of girls that walked past our car are leaning against a set of blue lockers. Their judgmental gazes rake over me, looking for flaws or evidence that I don't belong here. I know they've found something when the gorgeous redhead in the middle smirks and whispers something to the girl next to her.

Grinding my teeth together so I don't turn around and say something I'll regret, I force myself to keep walking. My only goal for today is to stay as far under the radar as possible and confronting them is a surefire way to obliterate that plan.

It's not until I reach my locker that I relax a little. Stashing my canvas backpack inside, I grab my class schedule I printed out last night and the books I'll need for my first class. Of course, it's math. I suck at math. The idea of writing three back-to-back essays for English is more appealing than taking one algebra final. I'll never understand why they felt the need to put the *alphabet* in *math*. It was an unnecessary and rude move if you ask me.

With the things I need in hand, I begin to close the metal door, but my hand retracts almost instantly when it's shoved closed by the person who's appeared at my side.

Startled, I step back from them. This action only makes the cocky smile on the blond guy's face grow.

"A little skittish, huh?" he muses, dark brown eyes exploring my face. "Don't worry, fresh-meat, we'll make you feel welcome here in no time." The cluster of his friends that stand behind him laughs at this, only further boosting his *clearly* out-of-control ego. *Fucking rich pricks.* "Where's your next class? I'll show you the way."

He reaches for the printed schedule in my hand, but I tuck it behind my back before he can grab it.

"That's okay." If he'd bothered to look closer, he'd find how unimpressed I am by his behavior, but I don't think this dude often looks past himself. "I can find my own way. Thank you for offering…" I trail off, not knowing his name.

"Bryce Fitzgibbons." He says his name with such pride, and his eyes examine me as if they're waiting for me to have some kind of *reaction* to hearing it. Like I should automatically fall all over myself at this information.

Meanwhile, all I can think is *Bryce* sounds like a name perfectly suited for an absolute *douche*. Which means his parents really manifested their son's attitude when they put it on his birth certificate. Let's be real, it's almost as unflattering as *Chad*.

Not about to further assist his inflated ego, I keep my indifferent expression firmly in place. "*Cool.*" I nod once. "Well, Bryce, I'm going to go find my class now." My attempt to walk past him is halted when he slides in front of me again.

"I didn't catch your name." The grin on his face reminds me of one a slimy politician would wear. Disgust bubbles in my stomach at the sight of it. "And I'm very interested in knowing it, seeing as you're the goddamn prettiest scholarship kid that's ever walked through those doors. I bet your name is as pretty as the rest of you."

Like a storm moving in, a dark shadow falls over us. The postures of the students standing about instantly stiffen and the energy becomes tense, like they're bracing for impact.

"You don't need to know her name." A voice comes from behind me—one I would recognize anywhere. "You don't need to concern yourself with a fucking thing when it comes to her, Fitzgibbons."

While everyone else around us is shying away, I step closer to his body but don't dare touch him. It doesn't matter how long I've known him, it doesn't feel like it's something that's allowed. He put an invisible boundary between us, and I definitely won't be the first one to cross it.

Bryce holds his hands up in mock-surrender. "Hey, I was just trying to welcome her to the school." That stupid cheeky smile remains in place. "Just consider me Hemlock Hill's very own welcome wagon."

"Go welcome someone else. Your services aren't needed here."

The preppy douchebag's face hardens. "I just wanted to be nice and lend a helping hand to our newest student. I don't see why you felt you needed to interfere, Rafferty." Frankly, I'm not sure why Raff is interfering either. I was under the impression he'd feed me to the wolves the first chance he got. "Had I known I'd be stepping on toes, I never would have approached her. If you want the poor scholarship girl for yourself, just say so."

My dad has raised me to be compassionate but to also have a backbone. I don't let people talk to me or about me like that. I begin to step forward, prepared to put this asshole in his fucking place, but I barely get my foot off the ground before Rafferty shifts around me, putting himself between us.

He's sixteen, but Rafferty holds himself in a way that makes him appear bigger and older. I've seen grown men look at him with caution in their eyes.

When I said that Rafferty holds his emotion close to the vest, I meant it, but on the rare occasion he decides to show how he feels, it's never in a good way. It's *always* anger. He never shows the good, only the bad and ugly.

The smiles that have graced his handsome face as of late haven't been genuine ones. The ones I have seen have been cruel or taunting. He's always had a chip on his shoulder, but it's started to grow over the past year.

"Do you really want to piss me off?" Rafferty's voice is so low and steady it sends chills down my spine. But not in fear. It's something … *else*. "You and I both know what an unwise choice that is, but if you really feel like going there, that's fine with me."

Bryce laughs at this, and he shrugs it off like he's not nervous. The way his eyes dart around, looking for a teacher or administrator to help gives away his false bravado though.

Rafferty laughs at this blatant move. A cold, menacing sound. "You think they'll come to your rescue and stop me? No one will stop me. They wouldn't fucking dare. Know why?"

Bryce's friends have all dispersed and taken several steps away as a precaution. "Because when I say my name, it fucking means something. You think you're someone because your car-salesman daddy came into a little money when your grandma croaked? That name you're so goddamn proud of means nothing. No one here gives a shit about the *Fitzgibbons*." His chin nods ever so slightly in my direction. "And *she* certainly doesn't give a fuck who you are or what your name is."

Still not backing down, Bryce forces a smirk to stay on his face. "Yeah? Had you not interfered, I'm sure I could have made her care. Would have been easy enough. Girls like her are easily impressed."

Under his school-issued black button-down, the one he wears with the sleeves rolled up and his required tie and blazer nowhere in sight, Rafferty's spine stiffens. I've seen this happen before and expect him to charge Bryce, but he remains firmly placed in front of me.

"The next time I catch you prancing around her, boasting like a fucking peacock, I will remind you just how inconsequential you really are. Like an ant under my shoe, you'll remember where you stand on the food chain."

Point expertly made, Rafferty decides he's done here. Without looking at me, his hand reaches back and locks around my wrist. With a harsh yank, he pulls me away from the gawking students and faculty and past a now-pale Bryce. The look on his face would be funny if Raff hadn't just ruined my plans. This isn't how I wanted to start my first day at this new school. My wish for a low profile has effectively gone out the goddamn window. Before the end of this period, everyone in the building will know that *Rafferty Blackwell* stood up for the new scholar-ship kid.

And they'll be just as confused as *I* am.

Rafferty charges through the hallways, not bothering to get out of anyone's way. Like an incoming bullet train, people jump out of his way to not get run over. My attempts to yank my wrist free are futile and I'm forced to jog awkwardly behind him.

"Raff..." I try to get his attention, but my soft call to him goes unheard in the bustle of the hallway. People stare at us as we pass, brows furrowed and mouths slightly agape. All he's doing is furthering the whispers and rumors that will be said about me. Needing to put a stop to this, and try and do some damage control, I yank harder against his grip. "*Rafferty.*"

Finally, he comes to a stop and whirls around toward me.

"What the hell was *that?*" I try to ask, but the harshness I find on his face tells me that I won't be getting an answer.

The iciness in his eyes isn't new to me. It reminds me of the glaciers in the arctic. They're just as cold and uninhabitable. "You need to stay away from him."

Wrist now free of his bruising hold, I coddle it in my other hand and hold it against my chest.

"I'll try my hardest, but I make no promises. You know that polo shirt and boat shoe-wearing douchebags are *totally* my type." My attempt to lighten the mood completely fails and Raff's face only grows darker. More threatening.

"You think I'm joking?" He takes a step toward me and his chin tips toward his chest so he can continue to hold my gaze captive. "Stay the fuck away from him, Posie. Actually, stay away from all of them."

Irritation flares in my chest, and the lighthearted smile I'd been wearing falls and a scowl takes its place. "From *all* of them? So, what, Raff? You don't want me to make *any* friends while I'm here?"

"You have Paxton."

I hide the slight flinch that he's only including Pax and not himself. It should be something I'm used to by now, but somehow it still hurts. I don't know what I ever did to make Rafferty so standoffish and bitter toward me.

"Pax and I only have two classes together. We don't even

share a lunch period." The idea of sitting alone in the lunchroom makes my stomach drop.

There isn't a glimmer of sympathy on his face. His expression remains completely passive and his posture rigid. "Do what I say and go to class, Butterfly."

Rafferty has no idea what kind of reaction my body has when he calls me that. It's like by simply speaking the word into existence, he summons a swarm of them to erupt in my stomach. Their wings beat violently against my ribs, demanding I acknowledge them. He's the only one who calls me Butterfly, and even if he only uses the moniker on rare occasions, the intensity of my reaction is always the same.

Feeling ballsy, I lift my chin and plant my feet. "Why do I have to do what you say?"

I don't know if it's the lingering agitation from the confrontation with Bryce or the fact that I just challenged him, but *something* flickers in his eyes. Without a word, he takes another step forward and claims more of my personal space as his own. The boldness I'd been feeling just seconds ago evaporates into thin air from his nearness.

His voice lowers as he challenges, "Do you really want to find out what happens if you don't listen to me?"

One question is all it takes for me to lose the ability to speak. My stunned silence is precisely the answer he wanted, and with one last lingering examination of my face, the corner of his mouth lifts in the faintest hint of a smirk.

"That's what I thought."

With that, he spins on his heel and stalks down the hallway with his usual arrogant nonchalance. He walks away like what just happened was *normal* when it was anything but.

SIX
POSIE

THE SECOND THE door to that dark classroom closed behind him, I collapsed to the ground in a shaky ball. I stayed there until I could breathe normally and get my legs to support my weight again. The professor of my class that day was less than amused by my tardiness, but I couldn't very well explain to him what had happened. Not when I was struggling to understand it myself.

It's taken me the last three days to finally wrap my head around it, and even then, it still feels like a bad dream.

I knew my reunion with Rafferty wasn't going to be a pleasant one, but I foolishly tricked myself into believing there was a chance it wouldn't be *that* bad. That every horrible situation I've made up in my head was simply a worst-case scenario. I knew Rafferty wouldn't ever move on from what happened, but I couldn't help but hope that while I was away on the East Coast trying to heal, Rafferty had been here doing the same.

All it took was one look in his cold eyes to know he hasn't healed at all. The same pain and anger that was on his face the night everything happened remains there now. It's a sight that is as heartbreaking as it is terrifying.

The scenarios I'd concocted didn't come close to how our

reunion actually played out. I've seen Rafferty inflict physical pain on others many times. I naively believed I was never going to be one of his victims. That I may be the recipient of his wrath and anger, but never his bruising touch.

It was a harsh lesson to learn that not only am I his enemy, but I'm also going to be one of his victims.

I'm the person that struck the match and burned everything down around him. The rules we used to play by no longer exist. Rafferty has had five years to come up with a new rule book, and my tender temple and aching shoulder are proof there aren't any lines he won't cross.

I'd be lying if I said I wasn't terrified of what my future looks like. I've had all this time to prepare myself for it, but I know without a doubt that I'm not ready.

For the first two days after our encounter, I let the fear and anxiety control me. I woke up from my fitful sleep covered in sweat, the terror still working through my veins like a virus. My stomach was in constant knots, and I felt like I was going to throw up. The jumpiness Zadie had noticed before had multiplied tenfold, and I truly did act like a monster was going to come around the corner at any given time.

This morning, I woke up in a similar state, but the exhaustion has brought on another emotion. Irritability. And right now, I'm letting that take over, and I'm savoring the fact it's briefly numbing my fear and unease.

Everyone in the campus dining hall is talking too loud, and every two minutes, it seems like someone is bumping into me or my chair. The Styrofoam cup that holds my coffee is covered in crescent-moon dents from me digging my fingernails into it. I'm lucky I haven't poked a hole in the damn thing at this point.

Shifting in my seat made of hard plastic, I pull the well-worn Yankees baseball hat farther down my forehead. I'm wearing it for two reasons. One, I was too tired to wash my hair this morning, and two, I'm hoping it's helping hide the dark circles my concealer is failing to fully disguise.

"Did you decide if you're coming to the party tonight?" Lark's soft voice pulls me from the dark fog swirling in my head. Completely out of it, I hadn't realized she'd sat down across from me with her signature green juice in her hand.

Lark Holloway is the only college student I know who shows up to class looking like she walked off the runway or off an Instagram model's feed. While most of us look like we barely crawled out of bed in time for class, she looks pristine. There isn't a blonde hair out of place or a single fleck of lint on her black lace-trimmed camisole or white flowy pants. The four-inch heels that constantly sit on her feet are what really get me, though. Olympic Sound isn't a huge university, but I wouldn't be caught dead walking across campus in *heels*.

"I don't think it's a good idea," I offer, Rafferty's parting threat playing in my head. *You're not here to make friends or enjoy your time.* "Actually, I'm fairly certain it's a terrible idea. I know Zadie really wants me there. She's been like a broken record talking about it."

While I've been reliving the worst period of my life, my roommate has been planning her outfit for this party and relentlessly pestering me about going with her.

"This party has kind of become a tradition for her. Well, for all of us I guess since we've gone to it every year." While Zadie talks loudly and dramatically waves her hands about, Lark is soft-spoken. Everything about her is calm and gentle, and I find that her energy puts me at ease. Which is something I need right now. "It's the campus's unofficial back-to-school party, and since the guys that host it are graduating this year, Zadie wants everyone there." A small smile pulls at her lips as she takes a sip of her juice. "You may have noticed she takes these things a little too seriously."

The sound that comes from me is a mix of a laugh and a

scoff. "Oh, *really*? No, I hadn't put that together until now. I just thought she liked to occasionally show me every article of clothing in her closet," I joke, glancing at the entrance. "Where is she anyway? She said she was going to meet us here before her next class."

Lark's manicured hand gestures to the back of the room toward the hallway that leads to private study rooms. "She's over there talking to Rome and Rafferty."

My chest hurts as the heart that used to belong to him constricts. I choke out his name before I can stop myself. "*Rafferty?*"

Turning my head, my eyes zero in on Zadie and the pair of tall figures she talks to. The one I don't recognize, Rome, nods along to whatever she's saying but his focus is really on the phone in his hand. Rafferty at least looks at her while she speaks, but the bland look on his face is one I recognize. It's one he's always worn, and I know it means he couldn't give a single shit about what my roommate is telling him.

When things shifted between us in high school, he stopped looking at me like that. It made me feel *special* that he cared about what I had to say. He used to make me feel a lot of things. Now all he makes me feel is scared and anxious. And so fucking *guilty*.

I hate it but know I must bear it. Choices were made, and Rafferty's wrath was always going to be the price for them.

"Zadie knows Rafferty?"

It's none of your business, Posie. Stop asking questions about him. The answers will only make it hurt worse.

"You've probably learned by now that Zadie knows every-one." Lark laughs, turning her attention back to me. "Zadie and I were in the same dorm freshman year, and I introduced her to Rafferty. He transferred to my high school during the start of his senior year, and we had some friends in common, so we got to know each other."

An ugly and uncontrollable surge of jealousy rushes to the surface and my muscles grow tight. It's like an automatic reflex that's been programmed into me. There isn't a single logical reason I should still feel this way, but no matter how much time has passed or how much pain I've endured for him, it's still a habit I can't seem to break.

Trying my best to recover from my unwanted physical reaction to Lark's comment, I nod my head and take a drink of my now cold coffee. "That makes sense. I'm convinced Zadie could make friends with a rabid raccoon."

"I'm pretty sure that she'd succeed too, but I wouldn't go as far as to say that she's friends with Rafferty. Don't get me wrong, she's tried, but he and his brother don't really let people get close. They can be kind of ... *standoffish*. Guarded."

Pax was always more on the shy side, but he had a group of friends at Hemlock Hill that he hung out with. It makes me sad he's become reclusive like his brother.

On their own accord, my eyes drift back to where Raff stands. Zadie is laughing at something, and as she does, she reaches out and places her hand on his forearm. Like he can sense me watching this interaction, his gaze slices into mine. I don't know what I'm expecting him to do—or *hoping* he'll do—but like a cold impassive statue, he simply stares back at me.

Rome says something and nudges him with his shoulder, but Rafferty is unmoved. Something in my gut tells me he's daring me to look away from him—to run from him and whatever sinister intentions he has for me. I want to run, and *know* that I should, but like I said earlier, I'm tired and I'm irritated, and I don't feel like giving him the satisfaction. Not yet anyway. I know what's coming my way, but that doesn't mean I have to make it easy for him.

Lifting my cup, I nod my head once in a silent greeting. Once his face darkens and his lips flatten into a tight line, I look away from him. It was a small act of rebellion, but it made me feel more in control than I have in three days.

It's also a move that doesn't go unnoticed by Lark.

Her perfectly shaped eyebrows rise in confusion and her doll-like sapphire eyes widen. "Do *you* know Rafferty Wilde?"

It's not a lie when I shake my head. "Nope."

I know Rafferty *Blackwell*, but he's not here. He's dead, and I was the murder weapon.

Any further conversation on the topic comes to a screeching halt when Zadie skips back to the table with Rome and Rafferty following a step behind. Like I'm watching a violent storm roll in, my bones brace for impact.

While Rafferty's expression is cold and threatening, Rome's lips are curled into an arrogant smirk, and his posture is relaxed and nonchalant.

He's about the same height as Raff with similar broad shoulders and trim waist. I wouldn't be the least bit surprised to learn they spend a lot of time working out together. Where Rafferty's dark hair is longer and the messy waves fall to his forehead and curl around his ears, Rome's almost-black hair is shorn short. Raff's always been pale, but Rome's skin has a natural olive tone.

Even with these differences in appearance, you can tell with one look that they were cut from the same cloth. One of them just doesn't bother hiding behind a casual mask. He lets everyone know that he's not to be fucked with.

Zadie tugs on the long strands of my stick-straight hair before plopping down in the white plastic chair beside me. "Hi, babes."

The blonde across from us opens her mouth to return the greeting but stops when Rome comes to stand directly behind her. With his hands on the back of her chair, he leans his head down next to hers.

"Hello, princess."

There's a split second that I believe there's something going on between them, but as Lark's perfectly symmetrical face twists into utter disgust and she whirls in her seat to shove him away, I discover I'm in fact *very* wrong.

"Back the hell off, Valentino," she snaps with a harshness I didn't know she was capable of. "What did I say about calling me *princess*?"

Rome's smirk only grows at this and his brown eyes light up with mischief. "And what did I say the last time you put your hands on me like this?" He twists a honey-blonde strand of her hair between his fingers, and she immediately slaps his hand away. "I said if you want to hit or shove me, that's fine, but at least put some *effort* into it. Put some fucking *weight* into. I like it rough. Make it hurt, princess."

"You're impossible," she seethes as she flies up from her chair and swings her bag over her shoulder. "Zadie, I'll see you tonight at the party, and Posie, I hope I'll see you there too, but don't let her pressure you into it. You can say no. She will find a way to get over it. Isn't that right, Zadie?"

Zadie blinks up at Lark. "Um, *false*. I will one hundred percent hold a grudge until the day I die if she doesn't come to this party."

I can feel his eyes on me. With each pass of them over my skin, it's like blades are slicing into my flesh, adding to the invisible scars he's already left there. He's waiting for me to give in, to look up at him, but I keep my focus on my roommate and new friend.

Deciding not to push the subject since she knows it's a loss cause, Lark shakes her head and looks at me sympathetically. "Good luck."

"*Good luck?*" Zadie repeats loudly as Lark walks away from us. "Why the hell does she need good luck? It's one fucking party. I don't know why everyone's making such a big deal out of it." Turning her attention back to me, she jabs a finger into the tabletop as she all but orders, "You're going and you're going to have some goddamn fun. Got it?"

My rebuttal is on the tip of my tongue but admitting that attending isn't a good idea in front of Rafferty feels like letting him win. He doesn't want me here, and he sure as hell doesn't want me to enjoy a single second of my time here. So instead, I lift my shoulder and lean back in my chair with false bravado.

"Maybe I should go," I offer. "It could be fun."

Do you know the expression *playing with fire*? Well, I'm juggling flames knowing full well I'm going to get burned.

Zadie bounces in her chair and the many bracelets she wears chime together as her hands clap. "Yes! *See*, was that so hard?"

Lifting my chin, I finally look into Raff's intense gaze. My heart thuds painfully against my chest and a shiver runs down my spine, but I still don't shy away. "No, it wasn't. I really don't know what I was so afraid of."

Rafferty used to be one of the few people on the planet that really knew me. He could know what I was thinking just from the way my brows pulled together or my posture shifted. And I could do the same with him.

I wonder if he can still see through me and if he knows I'm lying through my fucking teeth.

I don't look away from him even as Zadie says her goodbyes and kisses me on the cheek. It's not until she's fully walked through the exit does Rafferty speak.

"This is your last warning." His words are low and flat, lacking all emotion. "Don't go to the party. Stay home."

My arms cross stubbornly, and I make sure to keep my hands safely tucked against my body to hide the way they're trembling. I can pretend I'm brave all I want, but my body knows the horrible truth. I have every reason to be afraid, and Rafferty has every reason to be angry at me.

Standing from my chair, I grab my half-full cup of coffee and step around the table, preparing to leave. This move brings me closer to him and causes him to bristle. It's the complete opposite reaction he used to have when I'd get near him. There was a time I was the only one who could calm him. It's just more tragic proof of how things have changed.

"You've always had a terrible habit of telling me what to do, Raff."

"Had you listened to me back then, we could have avoided all of this," he bites. "You have no one but yourself to blame now."

My throat burns as I nod once. "I know."

It was never a question of *if* I'll pay for what I did to Rafferty. It was a question of *when*. I'm officially out of borrowed time.

SEVEN
RAFFERTY

ONCE UPON A TIME, this house was a firehouse. It was filled to the brim with first responders who put their lives on the line every day to save others. Now, it's frequently full of drunk college students that use the two-story high fireman's pole to perform uncoordinated—and unsolicited—pole dances. I'm not saying I don't enjoy a good pole dance or striptease, but so far, none of the girls who've attempted to put on a show have impressed me with their so-called *skill*.

Their desperate act for attention isn't a complete loss as there's always some frat boy willing to take the *graceful* coed home with them. As they like to say, one man's trash is another man's treasure.

Like right now, the horny sophomore that has no business being here is staring at the girl twisting around the brass pole with hearts in his glossy eyes. She was putting on a show for anyone who would pay attention to her, but when she finds him observing her like a lovesick puppy, her demeanor shifts in an instant. She now looks at him like she was doing it for him and only him. Coming to an unsteady stop, she smirks as she teeters on her heels toward him. When she's close enough, she throws her arms around his neck and, without any preamble, has her tongue down his throat.

"I watched her puke in the street ten minutes ago," Rome says, coming to lean against the kitchen island next to me with a beer bottle in his hand. He has the night off from family obligations and it looks like he plans on making the most of it.

"I don't get the impression that he cares."

Tearing my eyes away from the drunken public display of affection, I shake my head. You can call me a lot of things, but outwardly affectionate isn't on the list. The way I see it, when you touch your girl in public, you're *claiming* her. Making it clear to everyone else that she's not to be fucked with.

There has only been one girl I've kissed or touched in public, and that was because I simply couldn't stop myself. Stranger or friend, I needed everyone who looked at her to know that she was *mine*. Failure to understand this always led to my hands getting bloody. If someone's eyes lingered on her just a little bit too long for my liking, I was breaking their face in and threatening to pluck their eyeballs from their skull with a pocketknife. That was the extent I was willing to go for her because *that* was how much she meant to me.

Had I known that she would be my downfall and my greatest regret, I would have let them stare at her like the whore she is. Would have saved me a lot of fucking pain and time if I had.

"He's on a track to get his dick wet tonight. Of course, he doesn't care." Rome chuckles, still finding entertainment in the sloppy train wreck in the middle of the crowded room. "Get it, my man! That's right, show her who's boss." His hands cup around his mouth as he shouts across the room, and to really drive his point home, his hips grind the air.

My friend finds humor in things that most would deem inappropriate. Like funerals or autopsies. Normally, it's a trait I can appreciate, but tonight, I'm not in the mood for his antics.

48

Tonight is the night that everything finally falls into place. All I have to do is wait for her to fly through my front door.

It doesn't matter how many years we've spent apart, I still know Posie Davenport. The only time she took kindly to an order from me was when my cock was in her. She'd enthusiastically do anything I asked with a smile on her pretty face. On any other occasion, a command from me, or anyone else, would have her bristling and telling us to go fuck ourselves.

Now isn't any different. My instruction not to come tonight will be a challenge to her. *A dare.* She'll show up to prove her misguided point. *You don't own or control me.*

What she has yet to realize is I'm mere hours away from doing just that. By midnight tonight, Posie will be mine again, but in a different way than before. This time, I will be able to control her because I hold all the cards. One wrong move from her will have her paying a price that will not only affect her but also the ones she loves most.

Teeth grinding with impatience and irritation, I glower at the people loitering about. "I'm so over this shit. The dancing, the drinking, the random people fucking on my couches and countertops. All of it. When I graduate and move away from this town, I'm never inviting anyone over again. No more strangers in my goddamn space."

The novelty of these parties wore off long ago. All through high school, it was my house people came to, and once I got to Olympic Sound, it was no different. How could it be? The people I went to high school with are the same people I will be graduating with in the spring. I'm condemned to run in the same social circles the rest of my life. Even if I wanted to move away and start anew, that wasn't a choice I was granted. It was written in permanent black and white that these people and this state are my forever.

Rome, of course, laughs at this.

My brows rise. "What? You think I'm kidding? I'm dead

fucking serious. I won't even let you come over. I've done my time. A little silence and solitude are all I want."

"You and I both know the silence will make you go crazy. The only thing to keep you company will be your thoughts, and those will always be your worst enemy. You'll be begging me to bring a case of beer over long before I miss your broody company."

Rome has known me through all of this. There's no fooling him. He was the first friend I made when I was forced to switch schools my senior year. He saw me through all the stages of my rage, and he's the only person who knows the true depths of my fury. He's also the only person who supports my plan.

Paxton hasn't said it aloud, but I can see it in his sad eyes that he doesn't approve. I've tried to make him see the truth about Posie, but he's still clinging to those memories they shared. The loyalty he has for his childhood best friend is blinding him. I can only hope that one day he'll see the truth just as I have.

Dark eyes cutting to the front door, his chin nods in that direction. "If you were capable of silencing those thoughts of yours, we wouldn't be dealing with *her*, now would we?"

She's here. *Finally.*

As always, you can hear Zadie before you can see her. She's a flourish of bright color and sparkly bracelets. A neon sign that reads *look at me* could be above her head and I would still be drawn to her more subdued roommate that follows behind her like a quiet shadow.

Posie didn't put the same level of effort into her outfit that Zadie did, but still, she has a way of capturing the attention of the people she passes as they walk farther into the house. It's always been that way, and she's always been naively unaware of the stares. Instead of the cropped black-long-sleeved top and jeans she wears, she could be wearing a burlap sack and people's heads would still turn. It's never been about the clothes she wears or the way she styles her long straight hair. Posie has a presence. One even I couldn't resist.

I know the truth now.

She's a siren whose song pulls people in. Once they're close enough, she wraps her arms around them, and while they're blinded by her pretty lies, she drowns them. They won't know it's happened until it's too late.

Her entrance reminds me of her first day at Hemlock Hill. Just like they were then, people are curious about the new girl. She's like a drop of blood in a piranha tank. Fresh meat for them to pick clean. Little do they know they won't get the chance to get a *real* taste. I plan to devour her whole. Bit by bit, I'll take pieces of her until there's nothing left but bones.

If they still want her when I'm done, they're more than welcome to enjoy my leftovers. Like vultures on a carcass, they can have whatever remains of her.

"She showed up." Rome follows my lead when I push away from the counter and stalk forward a couple feet. "You were right."

"Of course, she did. There was no version of this plan where she didn't." Knowing your enemy is always key in war, and there's no one who knows her better than I do. She's fighting with two hands tied behind her back because when I stand before her, I look like the boy she fell in love with at fifteen, but I'm a stranger.

Hell, there are days I hardly recognize myself in the mirror.

About ready to burst with impatience, my foot lifts off the ground to move forward, but before I can finish the step, Rome's hand lands on my shoulder.

"Raff, you're positive this is what you want to do? What you *need* to do?" My glare has him holding his hands up in surrender. "*Hey.* Don't look at me like that. You know I'm with you to the end, and I'll do whatever you ask me to do. I just want to make sure this is the path you want to go down. Some things just can't be undone, brother."

"There are a lot of things I regret, Rome." I regret ever trusting her with my secrets, and I regret that I didn't see her betrayal coming sooner. If I had, I could have cut the wires on the bomb she detonated on my family. Loving her blinded me and stopped me from saving the ones who needed me most. "This won't be on the fucking list."

This is how I heal from the wounds she inflicted. This is how I get even.

EIGHT
POSIE

AS FAR AS bad ideas go, this one is up there. Like, I'm sure breaking into the zoo and trying to pet a lion would be a better idea than this. At least when the lion mauled me to death, it'd be relatively fast. One look into Rafferty's cold eyes tells me he plans on drawing this out as long as he can.

I'm tired of speculating what his plans are, and I'm exhausted from the constant fear of him jumping out of every dark shadow. At this point, I just want to get the show on the road. Once I know what he intends to do to me, I can deal with it from there, but this guessing game might be the death of me.

So, like a lamb knowing they're about to be slaughtered, I walk into his house with my shoulders back and my chin high. It's nothing more than a brave facade. Underneath the courageous face is a heart that feels like it might explode as it slams against the cage it's kept in, and with each beat, dread spreads in my veins.

The sensation only grows as the scent of him wraps around me. There are fifty people crammed into this old firehouse, but I can still sense Rafferty first. The same expensive spicy cologne he's worn since he was fourteen clings to every inch of this place along with the smoky scent of his cigarettes. It's a habit I always hated, and for a time, he quit, but it seems he's picked it back up. I'm no more than five feet into the house when the hairs on the back of my neck stand on end. He spotted me before I found him because, *of course,* he did. He's been waiting for me to show up. Since the night police pounded on his front door with an arrest warrant, he's been anticipating the day I'd walk back into his cage. The sad, or depending how you want to look at it, *funny* thing about it, is he didn't have to trick me or trap me. I did it voluntarily.

It takes everything in me to not seek out the source of danger. There was a time that I searched for him in every room I walked into because I couldn't wait to be near him. Now the idea of his touch has my stomach rolling.

Keeping my attention firmly ahead of me, I watch my room-mate as she is greeted by the masses. Zadie, dressed in a pink top that ties around her boobs and a short skirt, floats inside, not a single care in her word. She's completely in her element. Meanwhile, I'm certain I'm in one of the many circles of hell and the devil is waiting around the corner to collect his debt.

In thirty seconds flat, Zadie has drinks in our hands and she's secured her place in the middle of the makeshift dance floor. The White Claw freezes my fingers while I stand silently beside her as she chats up people like they're all her long-lost best friends. Like a fish out of water, I feel completely out of place. Do I dance? Do I introduce myself to the people standing close by and try to strike up a meaningless conversation?

This awkwardness is ridiculous. Rafferty hosted parties just like this one almost weekly in high school at his grandparents' lake house. Adrian, his father, would have never allowed them to happen under his roof, so Raff had to get creative. I never thought I was a wallflower at those, but retrospect has me thinking otherwise. Those parties were only fun because I was with them. The boys hosting them were *my* boys. I enjoyed those parties because I was with the Blackwells, and when I was with them, I was at my most content.

Pax was my confidant and my best friend. Born just months apart, there weren't many milestones we didn't experience together, hand in hand. He was my rock when I needed one and the first person who could make me laugh. While he was my steady constant, Rafferty was my wildcard. His chaotic and unpredictable nature excited me in a way it probably shouldn't have. He always had me on edge, but it used to be in a different way than now. It's no longer exhilarating and addictive. It's unsettling and nerve-racking.

"You're a new transfer, right?" A deep voice has my mind returning to the present instead of the past. "I saw you earlier this week. We have the same history class. You were running late, and the professor was *not* happy. I'm spacing it right now, but I want to say your name is … *Penny*? Am I close?"

That was the class I went to after Rafferty cornered me in the empty classroom. I was so shaken up and disoriented that I didn't retain any of the information or the faces from that class. I wouldn't be able to tell you what the professor looked like, let alone what one of the many students looked like.

The guy standing before me is your traditionally handsome frat boy. His dark hair is longer on top but the waves have been perfectly placed. Styled with precision and *effort*. It's as if he wants the effortless "*I woke up like this*" hair. Unfortunately for him, it's obvious that he's missed the mark on that one by the amount of product I can see in the strands. His short-sleeved shirt is collared, and I can't tell in this lighting, but I would bet my next paycheck there's a polo pony embroidered on it.

In other words, I'm really confused what a guy like him is doing at *Rafferty's* party. He's the kind of guy Raff eats for breakfast. I guess things really have changed and he just lets anyone into his house now.

I wince at the memory of walking in late for that lecture. The look on the older professor's face had me wishing the floor would swallow me whole. "That wasn't my best moment, and you were close-*ish*. I'm Posie."

"Ahh, okay. *Posie*. That's different. Is that a nickname or something?"

There're people out there named *Abcde*, and yet, there are people who act like my name is the most interesting one they've ever heard.

"It started out as a nickname my dad gave me before I was born, but it inevitably made it onto my birth certificate." There's a whole story there but it's not one I feel like telling. "What was your name again?"

"Ethan."

That tracks.

Ethan reaches out to shake my hand but before I can offer mine, the music cuts off and a booming voice accompanied by a high-pitched whistle fills the room. While everyone turns eagerly toward the source, thinking this will be an exciting occurrence, trepidation pools in my stomach.

"Hey! Eyes up here, fuckers!" Rafferty shouts from his place halfway up the exposed staircase. Like sheep, people do exactly as he commands. He's always had that effect on people. It's more out of fear than respect, but it's a skill that's always served him well, and it's one that will be hugely beneficial when he takes over the family business. "I have something I need to say real quick, and then we can go back to our regularly scheduled bullshit."

Hearing the commotion, people come in from the backyard and an echo of low murmuring moves through the crowd as they wonder what's going on.

Once they've stopped trickling in from outside, Rafferty continues, "As many of you know, since we're graduating, this will be the last of these beginning of the year parties. After this, there will be no more of this *open house* bullshit. So, those of you who *know* you shouldn't be here right now, savor tonight, because if you show up at my house again without invitation, I will drag you out the front door by your tongue." Next to me, Ethan shifts uncomfortably. *Well, that explains the mystery of what he's doing here.* "Since this is the last of these parties, it's fitting that we would have a special guest." Like he's known where I was in the crowd the whole time, his eyes cut to me, and as they connect with mine, my blood freezes. I'm a deer frozen on a dark road with a semi-truck barreling toward me. All I can do is stand here and wait for impact. "I want to welcome her right, so I have shots of tequila coming around because that was always her favorite."

People cheer as a group of guys dressed like caterers walk out of the kitchen with trays of shot glasses. The partygoers take the offered drinks without hesitation because they are blissfully unaware of what is happening. They probably just think Raff is being a generous host and kicking the school year off right with tequila. What they don't know is Rafferty Blackwell—*Wilde,* or whatever the fuck his last name is now—is not inherently generous. His gifts come with strings and ulterior motives.

Rafferty's lips turn up in a smirk as I'm handed a plastic cup from a passing-by waiter. Like Snow White who was just offered a poisoned apple, I inspect the golden liquid for signs of danger. Like bugs or razor blades. I don't possibly see a way he would have been able to control what specific cup I took with everyone helping themselves to the trays. Unless he's willing to drug everyone at this party. Which, let's be honest, is undoubtedly something he'd do.

Rome, who stands a few stairsteps below him, whistles again, regaining everyone's attention.

Lifting a glass of his own, Rafferty continues to pierce my soul with his glacial gaze as he says, "You have no idea how long I've waited for her to be here, and now that she is … well, I'm just so excited for the fun we will have." To anyone else's ears, his toast

57

sounds like a warm welcome. There isn't a drop of malice or hate in his voice, and that's what I find scariest. Like a seasoned actor, his sincerity is perfectly executed, but still, all I can hear is the silent threat. His hand holding the shot gestures in my direction, and heads turns, trying to figure out who he's talking about. "I want everyone to lift their glass to the one and only Posie Davenport. Posie, wave or something so they all know who you are."

Before I can decide whether to out myself or not, Ethan takes that into his own hands. "Right here! This is her!" He motions wildly at me like he's found the golden prize.

Fifty or more sets of eyes land on me, and with each stare, my plan to fly under the radar this school year dwindles into dust. This act from Rafferty is so out of character, news of it will spread across campus like wildfire. Which was exactly his plan. He doesn't want me to be able to hide. He wants me front and center where he can see me. Where he can expose me.

Rafferty cheers, "To Posie! May this be the homecoming you deserve!" And as he does, it feels like someone is sitting on my chest.

Like a routine that's been rehearsed, everyone erupts around me, repeating his exact words. Completely unaware of the punch line of this sick joke, they applaud and smile at me. One by one, they down the offered alcohol until it's just me standing with a full glass.

"Come on, guest of honor!" Zadie encourages, her elbow giving me a little nudge. "I had *no* idea you knew him, by the way."

Staring up at the man who was once my everything but now wants me as his enemy, I lift the glass to my lips. "There was a time I knew him better than anyone." The dark fog of hate around him has made him unrecognizable.

"What changed?"

The answer is easy.

"I broke his heart." With that, I down the shot, the burn of alcohol combining with the surge of emotion in my throat. "I need a minute," I tell her over my shoulder before pushing through the people.

I'm not sure where I'm going, I just need a second to readjust the mask I'd originally walked in here with. If tonight is the night our battle begins, I need to keep my armor up the best I can.

Drunk partygoers chant my name as I weave between them toward the back sliding glass door that looks like it was part of the other modern updates that were made to this historic site. With the door closed behind me and the sounds of my name drowned out, I finally feel like I can hear my own thoughts, and the fall air allows me to breathe easier.

Walking to the less illuminated side of the patio, I lean against the redbrick exterior of the house and close my eyes. Bearing the weight of this was so much easier when I was living on the opposite coast, but being back here, face to face with *him*, the weight feels like it's crushing me.

"You shouldn't have come back, and you *really* shouldn't have come here tonight."

A voice to my right has my eyes snapping open and breath catching in my throat. Jumping away from the wall, I face the person concealed in the shadows. They sit on the cold concrete ground with their back against the brick wall. He rests his tattooed arm over the knee that's pulled up toward him while the other is out straight. The bottle of booze, the source of his slightly slurred speech, sits close by without a lid.

"Pax..." It's a name I've said thousands of times, but this time it comes out as a mournful sigh.

He interjects before I can say anything else.

"I'm serious, P." The nickname has my heart constricting. It's a name that makes me long for the times we'll never get back because I struck a match to them. "Why would you come back here?"

In uncoordinated and sluggish moves, he pulls himself off the cold ground. The glass bottle clanks against the concrete as he does, the liquid left inside sloshing against the sides. On instinct, I move closer, hands reaching out to help steady him if need be. Before I can touch so much as his black shirt, he's jerking out of my reach to avoid any contact.

His own hands fly up to keep me at bay. "Don't," he snaps with a sharpness in his voice I don't recognize. Pax was always the gentle one.

Instantly, I regret my move. Fighting the desire to wrap my arms around him and bury my face in his chest, I step back to give him his space. "I'm sorry. I'm just…" I trail off, at a loss for words even though there's a hundred things I want to say to him. So, I go with the simplest option. "I'm just sorry, Pax. I'm sorry I couldn't be here for you but know I wanted to. Fuck, did I want to be here."

He doesn't answer, and the shadows cover whatever expression he wears on his face, but I can feel his eyes on me. I don't know what he sees when he looks at me. Does my face bring up only bad memories like it does for Rafferty, or does Pax remember the good times too, like I do?

My nose burns and tears threaten to fall. "You can talk to me. You used to be able to talk to me about anything." There wasn't a single thing we couldn't talk about. Every dark detail, we shared with one another.

His laugh is dark, humorless. "That worked out really well for us, didn't it?" His words cut deep, opening old wounds and creating new ones too.

His head shakes, and without a word, he pushes past me.

"Pax…" I try, wanting him to stay a little longer.

He stops feet away from the door, but he doesn't turn back

toward me. "For what it's worth, I'm sorry too, Posie. I'm sorry about your dad."

My dad. Two words have the oxygen disappearing from my lungs. They used to be two words that filled me with comfort and safety, but now they just make me sad.

Paxton disappears through the glass door, cutting off any chance of me responding, but it's fine since I'm not sure I'm able to speak without crying right now. And I *don't* want to shed any more tears over it. I spent my allotted amount last year and it cost me a scholarship.

Feeling uneasy from everything that's happened in the last ten minutes, I move across the patio, intending to sit in the place Pax had just vacated, but halfway there, my body begins to feel funny. Like every nerve beneath my skin is humming. It starts in my toes and fingers, then trickles down from the top of my head. Like a cascade, it takes over my body, and my vision starts to grow dark at the edges.

My eyes blink rapidly, like that will fix it but it only gets worse, and as it does, my legs begin to tremble.

You're going to pass out, a little voice says in my head, *sit down before you bash your head in on this concrete.*

I try my best to gracefully lower myself to the ground, but I end up falling backward halfway down. Through the fuzzy haze overcoming me, I can feel the burn of broken skin on my elbows after they take the brunt of the impact.

Footsteps come from my left and my head feels like it's a hundred pounds when it lolls in the direction of the incoming sound. I can see nothing but blurred shapes at this point, but the blurred figure standing over top of me is unmistakable.

"Okay, Butterfly, let's play," is the last thing I hear before I succumb to the darkness.

NINE
POSIE

I'M AWAKE, but it feels like I'm still submerged in the deep dark abyss of oblivion. The rushing water floods my ears, hindering my hearing, and the waves of unconsciousness I'm still fighting off have my vision cloudy. It's as if I'm no longer connected to my body, that I'm just floating there, limbless.

Desperately, I force myself to focus, to find a way to reconnect my mind to my body. Blurry eyes closed, I visualize that my hands are balling into fists and my toes are wiggling.

There isn't a doubt in my mind Rafferty has found a way to drug me. My gut told me something was wrong with that shot of tequila, but I still allowed him to goad me into consuming it. I should have known he'd have a way to control what glass I took. He's always been able to think five steps ahead of everyone. He's manipulative, but more importantly, he's highly calculating. He can walk circles around people and play games with them without them even realizing they're participating.

I'm so far out of touch and out of sync with him. My ability to anticipate his moves is like a muscle I haven't flexed in five years. I'm out of shape. Rusty. I need to get into fighting shape, or I'm never going to survive this.

Like a switch being flipped, sensation in my extremities returns and my vision corrects to its normal state. My breath comes in fast pants, a sound I hadn't been able to hear seconds ago, as my fingers curl into the damp ground I lie on. The prickly, dew-covered blades of grass weave between my digits when I sluggishly push myself up into a sitting position.

It's dark out here—really dark—making it clear we're no longer at Rafferty's house. There aren't any sounds of life, no passing cars or the low chatter of other people. The only noise is the distant sound of a sprinkler system.

Looking to my right, I squint to make out any shapes to help get my bearings. In the distance is a structure nestled between tall trees, and in front of that are perfectly spaced … boulders? No, not boulders.

Gravestones.

I'm in a cemetery.

Why the fuck would he bring me out here?

The thought only lingers in my head for a second because as my eyes drift to my left, it all clicks. His perfectly executed—and *morbid*—plan becomes crystal clear. He hasn't brought me out here to kill me and bury me in an empty grave. No, that would be too easy. Too quick for his liking. He brought me here so I will once and for all come face to face with the casualty of my treachery.

My heart is in my throat as I stare at the white marble gravestone before me. It's elegant and pristine, just as it should be. The lettering engraved on the slab is just as delicate and intricate as the angel perched on top of it. But it's not the angel watching over the resting place or the dead flowers in the ground in front of the stone that has my chest tightening and tears forming. It's the little line between the two dates.

It's a line that should have been longer and would have been had I not done what I did. It's the simple symbol of a life that was cut short.

On my hands and knees with hot tears falling down my cheeks, I crawl closer so I can trace her name with my fingertip. The surge of guilt is suffocating, and when the sound of heavy footsteps comes from behind me, I can't bring myself to face him. I know what I'll see when I look at his face. Five years of grief and built-up hate.

"She treated you like a daughter." His tone is a forlorn mix of rage and pain.

My nose burns as more tears fall. "I know," I choke out, finger still tracing the delicate lines of her name.

He moves closer, but still, I can't turn toward him. I don't know how to. All the healing I thought I'd done in New York... I'm now starting to realize it was just well-executed denial and detachment. I'm no more recovered than Rafferty is. It was just easier to separate myself from the agony and fault when I didn't have to face it daily like he has. Now, staring at the permanent monument of my choices has the patch work I'd done unraveling and falling at his feet.

"She was there for you when you had nowhere else to go. She was there for you when you got sick, with a washcloth for your forehead in hand. Every ballet you were in, she was sitting in the front row with a bouquet of pink roses waiting for you. She took you dress shopping for every dance because your own mother wasn't there to do those things. Shit, in hindsight, maybe we should have all followed her lead and left you behind just like she fucking did." With each word, he speaks nothing but the truth, and with each syllable, my heart breaks a little bit more inside my chest.

Rafferty squats down beside me, and when his fingers grip my chin in a bruising grip, I don't fight him as he forces me to turn to him. The look on his face has me choking on a sob. Hurting him was the hardest thing I ever had to do, and I wish more than anything I never had to do it.

"Read the stone aloud. I want to hear you say it," he snarls, blue eyes like murderous flames. When I hesitate, the sob sitting in my throat still stopping me from making a sound, his fingers dig harder into my face. "Read it. I won't ask again, Posie."

I don't have to look at the stone again to know what it says. The engraving is now permanently etched in my brain. *My soul.* Never will I be able to forget it.

My tongue wets my lips, and I search deep for the strength to speak. "Mollie Elaine Wilde-Blackwell. Wife, daughter, and beloved mother. 1972 to 2017." The dates come out like a strangled whisper.

"She was the mother you never had, but she was the *only* mother I ever had." Each word drips with toxic venom. "And you took her from me. From *us.*"

My head shakes, but his hold on me limits the movement. "I never meant…"

"You never meant to?" The sour laugh that comes from him has my blood running cold. "I warned you many times what would happen, but you didn't keep your goddamn whore mouth shut. That's all you had to do. You just had to keep the promise you made me, and my mother would be alive, and my brother wouldn't be…" he trails off like he can't bring himself to admit what's happening with Pax.

I want to ask him how bad things are with his brother. Based on the mostly empty bottle of alcohol he was carting around like a safety blanket tonight, I expect things aren't well. That was my concern five years ago too.

Instead, I whimper the same thing I told Raff the night our world blew up. It's like a script I've memorized, and it's the one I will stick to till my dying breath. "I just wanted to help you. *Protect you.* I loved you and I couldn't bear to see you in pain." The Blackwell boys were my family, and I would gladly sacrifice myself to protect them if they needed me to. And that's exactly what I did.

His free hand pounds on his chest to emphasize his wrath.

"But *I* could bear the pain, and I told you this! Your protection wasn't something that I needed or *wanted*. You sit here telling me you loved me but that's bullshit. If you loved me, we wouldn't be standing above my mother's *grave* right now. If you loved me, you would have put that above your self-absorbed need to be my fucking *savior*."

And that's really what it comes down to. I saved someone who didn't want to be saved. In doing so, I also sacrificed our relationship and his mom. And yet, knowing all of this, I would make the same choices I did five years ago. My heart may never heal from the damage I caused, but I know in the broken pieces left of it that I did the right thing. I did the *only* thing I could to keep him safe.

That's why I swallow the emotion clogging my throat and look him in the eyes as I tell him, "I'm sorry you didn't think you were worth being saved, and I'm sorry that you felt you had to endure that pain alone and in secret."

"You're about to be even more sorry because tonight is the night you will start to pay for your crimes against my family. The law may not be on my side, but make no mistake, Posie, you're a cold-blooded killer. A murderer through and through, and I'm going to treat you as such." His fingers loosen on my jaw, but it's only so he can trail them down my throat and wrap them around my neck like a choking necklace. The air that had been in my lungs rushes out between my parted lips as he applies pressure. "Do you know how you're going to pay?"

"No."

The way his lips curl into a grin reminds me of the way he used to grin before he broke someone's nose or ribs. Never has that grin been directed at me, and now that I know what it feels like to be the recipient, I pity the ones before me.

"You're going to be mine again, Butterfly." His other hand brushes the loose hair out of my eyes and tucks it behind my ear with a gentleness that is terrifying. "You'll be my bitch, my entertainment, and if I'm in the mood, my whore. Everything I ask of you, you'll do with a smile on your face and with unwavering enthusiasm." *His whore.* He used to call me that, but before, it had my heart fluttering and stomach muscles clenching. The degrading term used to be a turn-on, but now it's nothing more than a threat and wicked promise. "If I tell you to suck my cock, you're going to tie your hair up and fall to your knees. Doesn't matter when, where, or who's watching, you'll do it."

Anger that he thinks I'd be willing to do this flares up inside me. "What's stopping me from just biting it off?"

The way his face lights up tells me this is precisely the question he wanted me to ask. "You'll be obedient because you care too much about your brain-damaged daddy to jeopardize his health or whatever remains of his happiness."

And there it is.

Game, set, *fucking* match.

I knew Rafferty would play dirty, but I didn't think he'd bring my father into this.

The dread that has been a constant pit in my stomach since I stepped foot back in Washington amplifies tenfold. So much so, I feel like I might puke. "Leave him out of this, Rafferty. He's been through enough."

"Yeah, from what I hear, the accident resulted in a pretty traumatic brain injury. *Bummer.* But at least he's still breathing. We can't say the same about my mother though, can we?" The taunt in his tone has me fighting against his hold. The second my hands slap against his chest and arms, his grip on my throat increases in warning. Reluctantly, I'm forced to cease my assault. "*Relax.* I'm not like you. I won't kill him, but I will evict him. From what I've been told by his old nurses, stress is *really* bad for him. Causes seizures, right?"

The original injury to his brain resulted in a hemorrhagic stroke. The lasting effects from it have been detrimental and have permanently altered him. Never again will Henry Davenport be the man who raised me. Mourning that new reality was an unimaginably painful process and I lost my place at Juilliard because of it. Along with the loss of motor skills, memory, and cognitive issues, he developed epilepsy after the stroke. Preventing those subsequent seizures is now the utmost priority for him. Stress or agitation have been the constant and primary reason for their occurrence. The calmer he is, the better.

Moving him out of the only home he remembers ever living in will cause him an indescribable amount of stress and anxiety. Displacing him when he's as unstable as he is now is the worst thing that we could possibly do to him. On top of that, his police department had a fundraiser for him to make the entire house wheelchair accessible. They made all the necessary modifications in the bathroom and bedroom so my aunt, Josephine, could properly care for him.

The money it would take to make another home accessible for him just isn't in the budget right now. Which is something we knew the last time we feared we'd need to relocate him.

We almost lost the house eight months ago when the medical bills started to pile up. Jo didn't see a way to keep it, and we made the heartbreaking decision to sell it to recoup as much money as we could. She was looking at small, bottom-floor apartments when our luck turned. Someone was looking to invest in property in Seattle and was willing to rent the house back to Jo and my dad.

At the time, I thought the deal was too good to be true, and now, staring at Rafferty's knowing smirk, I know it was.

"It was you? You bought the house," I grit out between clenched teeth.

He nods gleefully. "Technically, an LLC bought the house. Either way, I overpaid for the fucking thing, but it was worth every penny because now I've got you trapped." His finger catches the tear that falls, wiping it away. "Are your tears for your dad or for my mom? Perhaps, they're falling for *me*?"

"I can't cry for all of you?"

"No," he snaps. "Not when you're the one who burned everything to the fucking ground. You've mistakenly made yourself believe you're a victim in all this too. That you've also lost things. Even now, you look at me with pity and empathy in your eyes like we somehow share in this pain. I'm going to change that. By the time I'm done with you, you'll hate me as much as I hate you."

Hate him? I know the trouble I'm in, and I'm fully aware of how dangerous he's become, but still, hating Rafferty doesn't seem possible. How can you hate someone who used to be your other half? Hating him would be admitting the boy I once knew is really gone, and I'm not ready to grieve him too.

"Will making me hate you truly help you heal? Is that what you need, Raff?" Before I ever struck the match that blew everything up, I'd accepted there would be a day that Rafferty would take justice into his own hands. He even warned me that night in the rain that he would get his revenge. I told myself then I'd handle it with as much grace as I could when the time came, but now that he's standing before me with murder in his eyes, I can't help but want to run. To flee. Rafferty has gone ahead and done the one thing that could possibly make me stay. He's threatened my dad. "Okay, give it your best shot. As long as you stay the fuck away from my father, I'll play your sick game."

His brows furrow with skepticism. "Just like that? You'd give in that easily? You disappoint me."

"I won't let you jeopardize my dad's health."

"The hypocrisy of that statement is laughable." He falls quiet, like he's trying to figure out if I'm trying to trick him. I'm sure that's a move he expected from me, to act as if I'll participate in his game willingly, only to run away when his guard is down. Finally, with a sigh, his hand releases from my throat, and he stands to his full height in front of me. If I had to guess, he must be close to six-three now. "Okay, Posie, let's see just how compliant and obedient you can be."

Sitting on my heels, I look up at him. "What are you going to do? Put a collar on me and make me perform tricks like a show dog?"

"Interesting idea, but no. You're going to suck me off." He grips his cock through his faded jeans. "My hate for you keeps me hard, and you're going to do something about it."

Lips parting in horror, I gape at him and then at the white marble headstone next to me. His mom's name is visible in the sliver of moonlight. *"Here?* You can't be serious."

"Why? Would you be more comfortable in my car?"

My stomach turns and my palms become sweaty. What I *should* be arguing is the very notion that he wants me to do this and *not* the location of where it takes place. But there is something so macabre and vulgar about doing it over his mother's final resting place. "I mean ... *yeah.*"

He smirks, triumph clear in his expression. "And that is precisely why you're doing it right here. Now get to it, I don't have all night. Take me out and put me in your mouth." My momentary hesitation has him growling. "You either do this voluntarily, or I will do it myself, and if I have to do it myself, I'll break your jaw and make you suffocate on it. While you're passed out, I'll make all the necessary calls. Your dad will be sleeping in a bedbug-infested Motel 8 by tomorrow evening while your aunt scrambles to find him new accommodations."

Six feet below me, Mollie is probably rolling in her grave as I sigh and reach for the button of his well-worn jeans. Rafferty now has more money than God, but by the way he dresses, you'd never know. His boots are scuffed and the laces shredded. His jeans look like they're way past the point of being well-loved. He couldn't give a single shit though. His mom was the one who always worried about outward appearances, the opinions of others mattered more to her than anything.

As I pull his zipper down, my heart sinks with it. An act that I used to do for him freely and eagerly is now my punishment. Any sense of familiarity is tarnished by the fact I've been coerced into this position. To protect myself from the reality before me, my brain tries to take me back to those happier times. It's nothing more than a desperate dissociation tactic. Memories flash in my head like a nostalgic flip-book, but I can't find salvation in them no matter how much I wish I could.

The only way I'm making it through this is to face it head-on.

Tugging his jeans down his hips just enough that I can better access his boxer briefs, I reach beneath the elastic waistband and pull him out. He's hard and thick in my hand—far thicker than I remember him being. I start to wonder what else has changed about him but discover my answer when the silver metal glints in the moonlight. A barbell stud now goes through the tip of his dick.

"You did it. We used to talk about you getting it pierced," I muse, remembering how he would tell me if I got my nipples pierced, he'd go with me and get an apadravya piercing. The idea undoubtedly intrigued me, but a part of me always thought he was just joking. The barbell that's currently eye level with me tells me that I was very much wrong.

"Don't think for a second that I did it for you," he bites. "Now shut the fuck up, I'm tired of listening to you speak." Tilting his hips forward, he pushes the pierced tip against my closed mouth. The bead of precum drips on my bottom lip. "Be a good girl and open."

My breath hitches in my throat as my lips part. Rafferty wastes no time pushing forward. It's been years since I've done this, and I have to remind myself to breathe through my nose as he nudges the back of my throat. My hands ball into fists at my side and I resist the urge to gag. Showing him any kind of weakness or distress will only further stroke his ego, and I have no desire to do such a thing.

I'm trying to get my body to reacclimate to his size. You'd think it'd be like riding a bike, but it is, in fact, not.

I must be moving too slow for his liking because before I can back away and stop it from happening, Rafferty's fingers tangle in the strands of my already mussed hair and he holds me painfully in place as he surges deep down my throat.

"I told you to suck me off, not just sit there with my cock in your mouth," he snaps, his punishing tone louder than the strangled sounds coming from me. My fingers pull on the waistband of his jeans, trying to push him away but he doesn't move an inch. He continues to choke me with his dick.

The thought that he'll just kill me now and bury me somewhere out here crosses my mind as my vision dims and black stars form around the corners. Instead of having a beautiful headstone like Mollie, I'll be in an unmarked grave. The good news is my father won't agonize over my mysterious disappearance. He'd have to actually remember who I was for that to happen.

My frantic slaps to his hips and thighs I'd started to do become more sluggish as my vision darkens more. Before I can truly drown, Rafferty pulls me from the deep end. Like I'm surfacing from being submerged underwater, I gasp loudly when his grip on my hair relaxes, and I can finally pull away from him.

Doubled over in front of him, I pull in greedy gulps of precious oxygen. "Please..." is all I manage to get out.

Tightening his hold on my tangled strands, he stands me back up on my knees. "Begging me already? I swear you used to have a better gag reflex than that. Now, do what I told you. If you don't, I'll fuck your mouth while you're unconscious."

"*Fine!*" I cry out, my shaking hands held up between us in surrender. "I'll do what you ask. Just don't fucking do that again."

Wrapping my fingers around his shaft, I use the saliva left there to glide my hand up and down as I take the smooth head back into my mouth. Not wanting him to think I'm hesitating again, I waste no time finding a pace and rhythm that works for me. Raff used to like it best when I took my time and took him deep, but I don't want to prolong this any longer than I must.

The quicker we get this over with, the faster I can get out of this godforsaken cemetery.

Licking up his length, I swirl my tongue around the tip. The way his breath hisses when I graze the ball of the piercing has me curious. To see if I can get him to make that noise again, I repeat the motion, this time staring up at him so I can see the shadowed expression on his face.

Something flutters in my belly when his eyes squeeze shut and air rushes through his parted lips in a pant-like sound. My reaction to this has me torn. One part of me is disgusted he's making me do this, the other part of me is pleased I can still make him feel good. The fact he chose me as the person to make him feel that way used to make me feel like I won the lottery. It filled me with a sense of pride. The hallmark of Rafferty Black-well's personality has always been that he hates everyone, but he let me get close.

Now is a completely different scenario, and yet, those old feelings still emerge from the depths in which I stored them.

Curious to see if he'll shove himself down my throat again if given the opportunity, I breathe deeply through my nose and take him as far back as I can manage without panicking. When his dick nudges the back of my throat, I expect him to force me to keep taking more, but he doesn't.

Instead, he praises me. "That's it. Fuck, Butterfly. See what happens when you use your mouth for good? Maybe had I kept you silent with my cock back then, we could have avoided all this."

Nothing was going to silence me back then, but there's no

point in arguing with him now. My only response is to take him an inch deeper before pulling back so I can play with his piercing a little bit more. My jaw, which hasn't been worked like this since him, aches, but I power through it.

A groan comes from him and his hips tilt toward my face, forcing him to shove deeper into my mouth. It's a sound I know well and used to love. It would drive me absolutely mad but in the best way possible. My scalp prickles with sharp pain as he uses the strands of my hair to hold me perfectly in place. Hot salty cum drips down my throat and coats my tongue. He holds himself deep in my throat as he rides out his release. It's just bordering on too much and it triggers my gag reflex once more, making my eyes water.

Both of our chests are heaving when he pulls out, but for completely different reasons. A combination of spit and cum drips off my lip, and before it can fall to the grass below me, Rafferty's thumb catches it. His cold eyes lock with mine as he pushes it back into my mouth. On instinct, I suck the digit into my mouth and swirl my tongue around it.

"I knew you still had it in you," he praises. "My good little whore has always liked getting me off."

I hate that he's right, and that's why I don't respond. What is there for me to say, anyway?

Wordlessly, he tucks himself back into his pants and zips up. "Alright, let's get out of here. It's getting late and I'm going to need you to stay well rested."

TEN
RAFFERTY
SIXTEEN YEARS OLD

SHE WALKS into the school courtyard with a pitiful look on her face. Well, it may only be pitiful to me because I can see through the brave mask she's wearing. To everyone else, I'm sure they really do see a strong girl with a steadfast *I don't give a fuck* attitude. No matter how hard she tries, Posie Davenport will never be that person. Her biggest character flaw is that she cares too much—that she *feels* too much.

She probably gets it from her father. You can't tell me being a cop doesn't come with an impressive savior complex. They both want to help everyone and everything that crosses their path. She's selfless in a way that will one day bite her in the ass.

Posie's completely out of her depth here at Hemlock Hill. She may have been raised around Pax and me, but she doesn't know these people. She doesn't know how they think or behave. Right now, as she sits alone on a stone bench with a sad tray of school lunch in her lap, I'm sure she thinks someone will take pity on her and join her.

Of course, she's completely wrong.

They'll stare and whisper about her, but they won't go over there. Not after what happened this morning with Fitzgibbons.

Gossip spreads faster than wildfire here. Every student and staff member under this roof knows I all but peed an imaginary circle around her. I told one person to stay the fuck away from her, and by doing so, I made it clear everyone should keep their distance. It wasn't my original intention, but the second I saw that douchebag Bryce grinning at her like a perv eyeing his new victim, I couldn't stop myself.

It was a mistake. I should have just let the wolves have her, but the damage is done. I just haven't figured out what the consequences will be.

Hannah, who's been sitting across from me with a pinched scowl ever since she realized everyone's focus isn't on her, rolls her eyes in Posie's general direction. "I don't understand what's so special. We get scholarship kids like her every year. Why is everyone making such a fuss over *this* one?"

As if it wasn't obvious who she was directing that question at, her pointed stare does a fabulous job of clueing me in. Hannah has the male student population by the balls. They fawn over every step she makes in her Italian leather stilettos. She's hot with her curly red hair and curvy body, but she's got a way about her that's comparable to nails on a chalkboard. There's a constant whine in her voice that is grating. I can't begin to imagine the sounds she makes in bed. My hope for whatever poor soul she lures into her bedroom is that they've invested in a good ballgag.

"Are you worried you have some competition now or something?" I question, sitting back in my chair with my arms crossed.

I'm not completely sure why I'm bothering to have this conversation. Perhaps it's because I'm curious what everyone is thinking about the girl I've known my whole life. I know what I see when I look at her, but do they see something different?

Her jaw drops in horror. Her insulted expression is so exaggerated, you'd think I just offended every single member of her family. "Competition? You can't seriously think a *scholarship* girl is in the same league as me, Rafferty."

Everyone who sits at our table is watching this interaction like they're at a tennis match. They're just as quiet too, like any noise would completely disrupt the show at hand.

"You're absolutely right, I don't."

"Thank you. *Jesus*, I thought you were being serious there for a second." Hannah's look of relief is instant and palpable, but it's gone in a matter of seconds because I just can't seem to keep my mouth shut today.

"I think you're miles away from being in *her* league. In looks *and* personality, she's got you fucking beat. Not to mention general intelligence. Tell me, are you still blowing the math teacher after class to earn that passing grade of yours? Have you figured out what you need to do for an A yet?" I find joy in the way her face progressively turns a deeper shade of red the longer I talk.

Normal, well-adjusted people probably don't find entertainment in embarrassing the ever-loving shit out of people. Me, on the other hand? I'm finding more and more that it's one of my favorite pastimes. Then again, I've never claimed to be well-adjusted. No, I'm a therapist's wet dream and utter nightmare wrapped into one pretty package.

Her loyal friends that sit around her stare at me wide-eyed but remain silent. Meanwhile, the rest of the students sitting among us are absolutely losing their shit.

Flustered and furious, Hannah shoots up from her seat. The palms of her well-manicured hands slam against the stone table as she screeches, "You can't talk to me like that!"

"Yeah? And why is that? Are you going to stop me? I'd love to see you try. Come on, Hannah, let's see what you've got." I hold my arms out at my side, taunting her to give it her best shot. Her brown eyes simmer with rage and maybe a hint of tears but she remains frozen. "That's what I thought. Now do us all a favor and shut the fuck up. There are dogs howling two blocks away from here because of that voice of yours."

With that, I grab the paper bag that contains the remaining half of my sandwich and push away from the table. Whispers erupt because of my exit, but I don't give a shit. They can talk all they want. I have no problem being their topic of conversation.

Posie's honey eyes lift in my direction as I approach. The way she does a double-take when she realizes it's me has me smirking. Stopping directly in front of her, the toes of our shoes almost touching, she scowls up at me.

"What are you doing?" she questions, her tone more curious than annoyed.

Not knowing the answer to her question myself, I ignore it and ask one of my own. "Are you seriously eating that?"

She looks down at the food in her lap that she's been politely picking at. "I guess so." Her narrow shoulders shrug under her navy blazer.

I think it's adorable she's wearing each piece of the mandatory uniform. You could offer me a hundred grand right now to tell you where my blazer is, and I still wouldn't be able to tell you. I haven't worn that thing since my first week here freshman year. Meanwhile, Posie even has the plaid headband on that matches the skirt she wears and the black socks that go up to her knees. So sweet and law-abiding, but little does she know she's a pair of heels and skirt that's an inch shorter away from looking like she walked out of every man's schoolgirl fantasy.

Grimacing at the soggy salad and dry piece of chicken, I wordlessly steal the tray away from her and walk to the closest trash can. Plastic tray and all, I dump the entire thing in there. Her mouth is pulled in a frown when I return and sit down on the bench next to her.

"The food here is fucking foul. Either pack a lunch or eat a big breakfast beforehand."

You'd think they'd allocate some of the millions they make

in tuition each year toward the cafeteria kitchen, but the school board thinks the money is better spent on our already well-over-funded football team and a new yoga studio. What kind of school has yoga as an elective?

Lifting the bag containing the other half of my sandwich in front of her, I tell her, "Eat this. It at least won't give you food poisoning." When she continues to glower at me and not take the offered food, my eyes roll in my head. "Do you want it or not, Posie?"

With a defeated sigh, she reluctantly takes the bag from my hand. "Thank you." Taking the food out, she hesitates before taking a bite. "How did you get this? You don't have a car."

"Yet." My mom ordered my car six months ago. It's being brought over from Germany on a boat as we speak. "And I borrowed a car." The kid owed me one, so when I asked for his keys, he handed them over freely.

Where Posie's generous acts come from a selfless place, mine come from a more … *self-serving* place. I see it purely as a transactional act. If I scratch your back, you're going to scratch mine harder, and if I find dirt on you, you're going to give me whatever I want to keep me from using it against you. I could have gotten something out of Hannah's little math teacher secret, but the look on her face as I rubbed it in her face was payment enough this time.

"*When*? You don't have an off period."

"Jesus Christ, you ask a lot of questions," I groan, suddenly regretting coming over here. "I went during math." I can do the lesson we're working on in my sleep, and I don't need some dorky mathlete with a bowtie lecturing at me for an hour. There are more conducive ways to spend my time than being bored to death by algebraic equations.

Pensive eyes inspect me as she chews a bite of food. Swallowing, she finally says what's on her mind. "I doubt there're more than five people in this building who know how smart you are. You hide it from them. Always have. You'd rather them think you're nothing more than a broody asshole with a pretty face."

That's the problem with Posie. She's been a permanent spectator to my life since she was in diapers. Every time I came home from school with a note from my teacher and was lectured by my father for misbehaving in class, she was there to witness it. She was also there to watch as I was praised for my perfect grades by my mother. It's not hard to put the two together. Like a working dog with not enough stimulation, I get destructive when I'm bored.

It would be easy to get angry at her for her unfiltered comment, but instead, I decide to focus solely on the last part of her comments. "You think I have a pretty face?"

Her mouth parts and I watch the panic reflect in her eyes as she tries to come up with a way to take back what she said. In the end, she simply sighs and shakes her head. "You're impossible."

"So I've been told," I concede, standing from the hard bench. "The car will be waiting right at three. Don't be late or I'll have the driver leave you here." Not bothering to wait for her reply, I leave her there to eat the rest of her lunch alone.

HER FACE LIGHTS UP when we walk into the kitchen. Putting the gold-trimmed teacup down on the marble counter, my mom rounds the large island in the middle so she can properly greet all three of us. She's always made an effort to be here when we got home from school. Her parents left her home alone so often growing up that she's always said she doesn't want that for us.

The only time she's not here waiting is when she's forced to travel with my dad for business or when she doesn't feel well enough to get out of bed. The latter seems to be happening more frequently, but the way her blue eyes are bright and clear, tells me today is a good day. Or a better day I should say. I'm not sure my mother has ever experienced a *"good day"*. It's a horrible thing when your brain is your enemy. If you're constantly at war with yourself, can you ever really win?

She hides her silent battle behind a well-practiced *Crest Whitestrip* smile and a perfect appearance. Never is there a dark hair out of place or a wrinkle in her designer clothes. From the outside looking in, Mollie Wilde-Blackwell is the embodiment of perfection.

I know better.

She used to be better at hiding her flaws from me, but the older I get, the more obvious the cracks in her porcelain veneer are. Like with everything else, I try my best to shield Paxton from it.

"Did you all have a good day?" Mom asks, kissing my cheek before doing the same to Pax. Reaching Posie, she takes her face in her hands, and smiles at her. "What about you, P? How was the first day? Did you meet anyone?"

The way Posie's eyes flick in my direction before she answers the question has me fighting off an arrogant smirk. "No, not really. I'm not sure I made a great first impression."

"Well, that can't possibly be true. Just give it time. You'll find your place there before you know it." Mom gently pats Posie's cheeks once more and backs away. "The winter dance is coming up at the end of the month. Maybe you can volunteer to help and meet some people that way."

Reaching into the bag of grapes Pax had pulled out, I pop a few in my mouth as I scoff. "The winter dance? Are people actually going to that?"

Pax nods his head. "There's a big group of freshmen going together. Sadie's mom is reserving the back room of her restaurant for us to eat at beforehand."

Stepping around me, Posie bumps Pax with her shoulder and

gives him a knowing grin. "Sadie, huh? Are you going to ask her to the dance?"

"What? *No*." Pax's head shakes and he stares down at the fruit in his hand like he's suddenly finding it incredibly interesting.

However, he doesn't look away fast enough. I still catch the way his face turns a shade of pink, and that tells me more than his words ever could.

Apparently, it doesn't go unnoticed by Posie either because she pokes him in his flushed cheek. "You sure about that?"

Had I done that he would have become defensive and annoyed, but with Posie, he laughs it off, playfully pushing away her hand. "Yes, I'm sure. Plus, I didn't know if you'd want to go, and with you not knowing anyone, I don't want you to be alone while I'm stuck with my date."

And right there is a prime example of their friendship. One doesn't make a move without first considering the other. They're so close, my dad has always said that one day they'll end up together. He doesn't seem exactly *thrilled* by that prospect when he talks about it though.

"That was very sweet of you, honey," my mom remarks, digging for something in her leather purse.

Posie nods in agreement but her brows are pinched. "*Too* sweet. Pax, you should take Sadie. I'm not sure that I'm even going to go, and I want you to have a good time. Don't worry about me."

"I'll just wait to ask her until you figure it out. We have time."

"Nope! *Nuh-uh.* You're going to ask her this week because if you don't, somebody is going to ask her before you and then you'll be sad which will make *me* sad. So, for purely selfish reasons, I'm going to need you to get on this. I'll help you. What do we need? A poster board with some cheesy question on it? Flowers?"

With a new mission at hand, Posie marches out of the room with my brother following behind her.

My mom smiles at their backs like they just made her entire day before nodding her head at me. "What about you, Raff? Will you ask someone?"

She can't be serious. "I can't think of a single person I'd want to dance with under sparkly lights. It doesn't matter how much glitter they add, or how much snow covers the ground, you're still slow dancing in a high school gymnasium."

"Really? You can't think of a single person?"

"Nope."

"You sound like your father." She chuckles, but it's not a happy sound. It drips with the melancholy that's taken over her heart and head. "He was never much of a romantic."

The amount of willpower it takes to not roll my eyes at this should win me an award. "Really? Could have fooled me," I mumble sarcastically. "He's just so remarkably affectionate."

The light that had been in her eyes when we first got home is gone as she frowns at me. "Rafferty. Please don't."

Pulling her hand from the designer purse, she pops something into her mouth. The column of her throat moves as she swallows it dry.

This isn't the first time I've seen her do it, but this time I can't stop myself from opening my mouth. "What was that?"

She can't bring herself to look at me as she answers with a casual shrug of her shoulders. "Just a breath mint."

Yeah... sure.

ELEVEN
POSIE

NUMB.

That's how I felt sitting in the passenger seat of his Mercedes SUV as he drove me home in suffocating silence. That's how I felt when he barely slowed down the vehicle for me to climb out, and that's how I feel now opening the door to my apartment.

Rafferty had been thoughtful enough to bring my crossbody bag with us after he drugged me so I could have my keys and phone when he was done with me. Well, done with me for the night. He's made it clear he's nowhere near being done with me. He's just getting started.

All I want to do is take a scalding-hot shower and climb into bed so I can sleep off the events of tonight. Hopefully, I don't dream about the cemetery. Over the past years, I've found refuge in dreaming about Rafferty. The fact that he will now cause me nightmares is heartbreaking. All I can do is hope I can at least get some sleep.

Tomorrow will be too long of a day to be exhausted. I have a twelve-hour shift at the studio.

Until now, I've been supervised by the owner of the studio.

After over a week of training, they say I'm ready to teach my classes by myself. They know I know the material backward and forward as I've been dancing since I was younger than my students. The little girls' cute faces as they twirl around the mirrored room always make me smile, but they also have waves of crushing self-pity slamming into me.

I was their age when I decided I wanted to go to Juilliard. Of course, I was too young to understand what the prestigious school truly was. All I knew or cared about was that the people who went there became the dancers in the most reputable and famous ballet companies. They were who I wanted to be when I grew up. I wanted people to travel to see the productions I was in. I wanted my name to be listed on the program they passed out to the audience before each performance.

The little girls I teach remind me of the optimistic girl I was, and the fact that I let her down and probably broke her heart.

All hopes for a restful night's sleep go out the window when I open my bedroom door and something with wings darts into my face. Startled, my eyes squeeze shut out of instinct and my hands wave wildly in front of my nose to dispel what I'm thinking is just probably a moth.

When I squint one eye open to check if the coast is clear, I make the alarming discovery that I was very much wrong. It wasn't a moth, and it certainly wasn't just *one* of them.

It's impossible to count them, but there must be at least a hundred butterflies soaring about my room. The ones that aren't flying around are perched on every available surface they can find. From the shelf on my wall with pictures of my dad and me, to the pillow on my bed, orange and black butterflies take up residence.

Holy shit…

Completely dumbfounded with my jaw basically on the floor, I take it all in. How the hell has Rafferty managed to do this? When did he do this? Based on the current time, I wasn't passed out *that* long. There is no way he had time to come here, release butterflies in my room, and then drive across town to the cemetery.

The only possible answer is he's getting help. An uneasy feeling creeps up my spine knowing that a stranger had managed to not only get into my apartment but had also been in my room. Who knows what they did or touched while they had free access to my personal space and items.

I'm frozen in place until they start to fly in the direction of the door I hold open. Stepping fully into the room, I quickly shut the door behind me and thwart their escape.

"How the hell am I going to get you all out of here?" I question aloud with a pitiful whine. "All I wanted to do was go to bed." That's not going to happen until every last one of these things is gone.

The window is my only hope.

With my hands making constant movements in front of my face to stop the insects from dive-bombing me, I make my way across the room. The window isn't big by any means. It would probably be easier to let them into the main living area of the apartment because at least there's a larger door that leads to the quaint balcony. The only reason I don't attempt to do it is because I don't want Zadie to come home and find her apartment completely overtaken by *bugs*.

More importantly, I don't want her to ask why they're here. That's a conversation I can't fathom going well.

Why are there butterflies in here? Well, you see, when I was sixteen, I broke a promise, and it resulted in Rafferty's mom dying. It was horrible and tragic, and now five—almost six— years later he's getting his revenge.

Attempting to have that dialogue would result in so many questions that I can't ever answer. It's best I just get rid of the evidence while she's still at the party.

Whatever ones I don't get through the window, I'm going to

need to trap in a cup or something and release myself. By the looks of things, I won't be taking that shower I desperately want anytime soon.

Goddammit, Rafferty.

TWELVE
POSIE
FIFTEEN YEARS OLD

SADIE SMILES and wraps her arms around Paxton's middle. The students that surround them still applaud and cheer him on, which only makes me happier for him. Everyone in this town might know who he is, but that doesn't do anything to help with his shyness.

Asking the girl he's had a secret crush on since seventh grade to the dance wasn't easy for him, *especially* with a crowd of students watching him. But still, my best friend stood there with the dorky sign we made and a bouquet of daisies with pride.

I cheered just as loud as everyone else while I took pictures for Mollie. She'd secretly pulled me to the side last night and asked that I snag a couple for her since she obviously couldn't be here.

Paxton catches my eye across the courtyard and gives me a small wave. A gesture that I return instantly. We'll catch up and talk about it later, but for now, I want him to have his moment with the pretty blonde at his side.

"Well shit. Now you definitely can't go to the dance," Rafferty's voice comes from behind me. "You went and told the one person who was willing to go with you to go with someone else. Not exactly a smart move on your part."

To others, it probably seems out of character that Raff would show up to watch something like this. The indifferent and "*above it all*" attitude he's perfected over the years has an air of superiority clinging to him, and he finds joy in making them choke on it. For the most part, he truly doesn't give a shit about most things or other people, but Pax is an exception to the rule.

He has and always will look after his baby brother. His protectiveness for his family is the most endearing thing about him.

My eyes roll at his remark, knowing he's trying to get a reaction out of me. "Like I said the other day, I don't have any plans to go to the dance. These people hardly want anything to do with me during the school day, what's going to be different at a dance?" I glance at him over my shoulder but don't bother turning my body toward him.

Rafferty leans against one of the building's stone columns with his arms crossed. "Not a damn thing, Butterfly." He's completely unapologetic about what he's done to my possible social life.

Even the teachers are acting weird toward me. A sixteen-year-old shouldn't have this much power over people. His name carries a lot of weight like he told Bryce, but that alone isn't what has people falling over themselves to stay on his good side.

The Wilde Corporation is the only USA-based defense contractor that rivals Lockheed Martin. They get billions of dollars in contracts just from the government every year, and that money only makes up about seventy percent of their revenue. Meanwhile, Adrian Blackwell is a world-renowned engineer who is known for revolutionizing the computer chips that go in the Department of Defense's equipment. He sold off his patented ideas decades ago for a pretty penny, and has been working alongside Raff's grandfather at The Wilde Corp.

While Rafferty has never particularly gotten along with his father and he takes more after his mother in appearance, Raff inherited his intellect from his father. Which is good because one day when Adrian and Grandpa Wilde retire, the family's company will fall onto Rafferty's shoulders.

It's not just his last name that influences people, it's his own reputation. Rafferty has found a way to make a name for himself. He's been doing it since grade school with small tidbits of innocent information and gossip shared on the playground. He simply takes what he's learned and finds a way to make it benefit him. The older he gets, the grander his ploys get. The fact that he does this isn't a secret to me. I've just been lucky enough to not be a rival player in his games.

With one last smirk at me, Raff disappears into the crowd of students heading back inside.

"You must have done something really bad or really good to have Rafferty Blackwell talking to you like that." A voice I don't recognize comes from my side.

Turning, I look at a face that is somewhat familiar. We share a couple of classes I think, but I haven't yet heard what his name is. His short hair is dark blond, and his green eyes are kind, which is a rare occurrence here at Hemlock Hill. He also lacks the ever-present cocky grin that everyone in this goddamn place wears. It might as well be part of the preppy uniform.

He's different. *Approachable.*

That's why I find myself responding. "I haven't done anything." *At least, I don't think I have.* I can't think of anything specific off the top of my head. "I've just had the astounding pleasure of knowing him for a *very* long time."

Shoving his hands in his blue and white letterman jacket, he asks, "Is that why he calls you Butterfly?"

Jesus, how long had he been standing there listening to our conversation?

There's a second where I almost consider telling him the

origin of Rafferty's nickname, but something about doing so feels as if I'd be betraying him. It's a name that's been shared between us since I was no older than six, and he only uses the moniker because he knows the story about my mom. In general, I try not to talk about my mom, but Rafferty has always been privy to all the dark stories in my life, just as I have his. When he calls me Butterfly, it lessens the hurt my mom left in my heart all those years ago. The name may have started with the woman who abandoned me, but it now belongs to Raff. And that's why telling this random guy about it feels like I'm revealing a sacred secret that is shared between us.

I keep my answer as vague as possible. "It's just a spin on something a family member used to call me. Rafferty just made it his own and has been calling me that since we were young." The nickname stuck and I'd be lying if I said I hated when he used it.

The guy could ask more questions or make a snarky comment like everyone else here would probably do, but he just smiles at me. "Man, I wish I had a cool story behind my name. My parents named me Chance after one of their grandpas."

Chance. I repeat his name in my head to not forget it. "I like those kinds of family traditions, though. My family is *very* small so there aren't many people to pass names down to." With no contact with my mother's side of the family, all that is left is my dad's. His parents were both only children, and when they passed, the only Davenports who remained were Dad and Aunt Jo.

"Again, I'm jealous of you. My family is gigantic. Both of my parents have five siblings, and let's not even talk about how many cousins there are." Chance's handsome face contorts into a pretend grimace. "They're all coming in for the holidays, and I'm trying to get myself prepared. Half of them are Italian and the other half are Irish, so you know they're loud as fuck."

I can't stop myself from looking around to see if anyone is

watching him talk to me. Did someone put him up to this? Is this a test from Rafferty to see if I'll follow his silly orders? If it's neither of those things, why is Chance talking to me while everyone else is still scared of Rafferty's wrath?

It's a question I find myself asking him point blank. "I'm sorry, but why are you talking to me?"

Confused and probably a little bit offended I'd ask him something like that, Chance's face falls. "Umm... do you not want me to talk to you?"

"No, no! That's not it. I just mean the people here either avoid making eye contact with me or they turn their noses up at me." There's a redhead I share a class with who looks at me like she's imagining what I'd look like if I were on fire. I'm not sure what I did to piss her off.

Rubbing the back of his neck like he's suddenly anxious, Chance shifts on his feet. "I'll admit I was initially curious because of Rafferty's behavior toward you. I mean everyone's been talking about what he said." Is he talking about the Bryce incident or did something else happen that I missed? "But then I started to talk to you and finally got a good look at you, and fuck, if I were Rafferty, I'd be a territorial piece of shit too if you were mine."

You could give me an hour to describe the emotions I'm feeling hearing this, but I still wouldn't be able to describe them aloud. They're a chaotic mixture of annoyance and exhilaration. I'm annoyed he's made people believe he owns me even though there are times he goes out of his way to prove the opposite to me. Then there's the excited fluttering in my stomach and a dull longing in my heart at the prospect of being his. Both of those mean nothing but trouble for me, and I need to bury them as I always have. Rafferty's never done anything to prove he's capable of feeling those emotions which, by default, puts me in a position to be hurt.

Trying to shake off whatever I'm feeling right now, I clear

my throat. "Is that what people really think? That I'm *Rafferty's*?"

Chance's dark-blond brows rise. "Are you not?"

"No, I'm not." Why does saying that kind of hurt?

Like I've just told him the best thing he's heard all year, a big smile breaks across his face. "So does that mean you don't have a date for the dance?"

Eyes the color of moss stare at me with unadulterated interest. It's the attention I want, but it's not being given by the person I crave it from most. I wish when Chance looked at me like this that my skin would grow warm and my stomach would get that funny feeling like it does when Rafferty is near. If he could make me feel that way, it would give me hope that one day I'll be able to stop pining for something Rafferty has no intention of giving me.

"I haven't really decided yet, but I don't think I'm going." Just because the gym has been converted into a winter wonderland doesn't mean the other students are suddenly going to welcome me with open arms.

"That's too bad. I've been told I make an excellent dance partner." The bell sounds through the school's speaker system. Turning his head, he watches the crowd of students make their way toward the doors. With one last easy smile, Chance starts to back away from me. "Just let me know if you change your mind."

"I will," I promise, not entirely sure if I mean it or not.

"I'll see you in class later." With a quick wave of his hand and a flirty wink, he turns away.

THIRTEEN
RAFFERTY

"WILLIAMSON SAYS he can't afford the entry fee for next weekend's game and is wondering if you'll consider allowing him to pay for it with one of your more … *alternative* … payment options." Kason's voice comes through the phone in my hand while I take a long drag from my cigarette.

"Tell Mayor Williamson if he can't afford the charge to walk through my doors, he sure as shit shouldn't be sitting down at one of my poker tables." The only time I accept any alternative forms of payment is when they can't reimburse me for the *"favor"* I've done them, or they lose against the house. They show up to these poker nights reeking of unchecked masculinity and ego, but when they inevitably lose, they come crawling to me for a fucking loan or payment plan. It's embarrassing. "He's been playing at my table for almost two years now, he's not new to this game. My rules haven't changed. It's not my problem he spends his extra cash on whores and fucking cocaine."

I didn't always host these poker games, but two years ago I had a game at my house with a couple guys I knew. While it seemed like a casual gathering, the money was anything but. There were enough bills on the table to buy a luxury vehicle.

One of the guys invited was the son of a British ambassador, and unfortunately for him, he wasn't wise enough to stop playing when he should have. He lost miserably, and when it was time to pay up, he didn't have all the cash he needed.

Normally, when something like this would happen, I'd just have Rome hold him still while I made him choke on his teeth. This time, on a random whim, I decided to give him an out.

He either needed to find the money in the next hour, or he needed to give me information that was so valuable it exceeded the cost of his debt. He thought for about two minutes before he told me something that would have the British tabloids falling all over themselves.

Since I was young, I've been collecting secrets and trading them as if they were currency. People come to me when they need a favor or a loan. As long as they give me information that makes it worth my time and benefits me, I'll assist them. In return, I use what they tell me to get what I want and need.

The only reason Posie is on this campus right now is because I cashed in a secret I knew about the university president. He was more than willing to ensure Posie's transfer application was accepted as long as I kept the dirty details of how his mew relationship developed to myself. Unlike Posie, I'm more than capable of keeping my word. If I went around going back on my dealings, my operation would have crumbled in high school, and if that had happened, I wouldn't have as many powerful people by the balls as I do now.

I don't need to continue with the poker games. They're just a fun additional way to grow my 'client' base, and as the years have passed, word has spread about them. I have affluent people fly in monthly to attend. At one table, I can have a governor and a Mob boss playing together. The ensured privacy and high bet limit lures people like them to come play. The free booze and *entertainment* I provide also keep them coming back each month.

"I'll relay your message to the mayor," Kason answers, his English accent thick.

His father is the president of some company that controls most of the UK's petroleum. Kason came to Olympic Sound University like many children of wealthy parents do, but after six years he still doesn't have a degree. Much like Pax, school isn't really Kason's thing. He'd much prefer to work and make his own money. When he's not managing my poker games and doing other various tasks for me, he's making money in underground fights. He's a beast in the ring and has made a name for himself here in Seattle. I appreciate that he's trying to make something of himself outside of his family.

There was never any question of my taking over my family's business. I didn't get a choice like Kason did, and that's why I've put so much effort into my own side-dealings. I want to build something of my own that my family can't take credit for.

In my peripheral vision, Rome appears with the black hood of his sweatshirt over his head. Just like it has been a lot lately, his attention is glued to the cell phone in his hand. I don't have the slightest clue who he's been talking to so much, and even if I felt inclined to ask, he wouldn't tell me. All I know is whoever it is must be entertaining as hell because my friend has the attention span of a fucking squirrel. I've seen him get bored with a girl thirty minutes after meeting her and she'd even sucked his dick in that amount of time.

"Let me know if he causes any problems." My command to Kason serves as my farewell, and I end the call.

Dropping the cigarette I barely touched to the ground, I put it out with the heel of my well-worn leather boot and turn to Rome.

"Hey. How did the rest of that night go?" he asks, finally looking up from the screen.

Rome knew my plan was to take her to the cemetery three nights ago, but he didn't know what I'd do once I got her there.

I went into it thinking I was just going to finally have her face what she'd done to me and what she'd *taken* from me. Posie wasn't here for the funeral because she was already three thousand miles away, moving on at her new prestigious boarding school. She didn't have to watch them lower my mother into the ground or watch the way Pax's entire body shook as people said their empty condolences. She got to skip all of it, but I wanted her—*needed* her—to experience a *sliver* of what we went through.

I did everything I'd planned on doing. She sobbed over my mother's grave while she learned what the consequences of her actions were going to be. Her big honey eyes were full of sorrow as she stared at the headstone I had custom made while she discovered what her new role in my life would be. Now, she's nothing more than something for me to use in any way I see fit.

Everything I set out to do that night, I accomplished. The blow job, however, was unplanned but not entirely senseless. Having her on her knees with my cock down her throat cemented her new reality in her head. She now knows with certainty that I'm not bluffing.

Posie Davenport is once again mine, and I'll play with her until she breaks.

I don't bother giving Rome any details. "It went exactly how I needed it to go. What about you? Did you have any trouble getting into the apartment?"

Fishing in the pocket of his black jeans, he returns the key I'd procured for him. "*Please.* Give me some credit. I can set up one fucking camera in my sleep." Compared to the shit he's usually doing for his dad, the tasks I had Rome do last night were mundane. "It should be set up and attached to the app on your phone."

Opening my phone screen, I pull up the app I downloaded last week. Right away, live footage of Posie's empty bedroom shows up. Her bed is unmade and clothes are thrown across the rust-colored bedding like she'd gotten ready in a hurry this morning. I'm sure she did as I doubt she was sleeping well over the weekend.

Over my shoulder, Rome watches the feed. "It's in the light switch. She'll have no idea it's there unless she decides to look too closely at the fake screw in it."

That's exactly how I want it. Just as I was able to keep tabs on her while she was in New York, I want to do the same here. Only here, I won't have people relaying information to me secondhand along with grainy pictures, I'll be able to get it all myself in real time.

"Does it have audio?" I want to be able to hear every sound she makes while she's alone, whether it's her cries of despair or self-induced moans, I want to be privy to all of it.

"Yep."

"Good." I shove the device in my pocket and step away from the campus building I'd been loitering around. "Let's go."

FOURTEEN
RAFFERTY

THE DARK CIRCLES and redness in her eyes tell me I was right about her lack of sleep. Whether it was from the infestation of viceroy butterflies in her room or nightmares of me, is unclear. I can only hope that it was a healthy combination of both. I want to dominate her thoughts while she's awake, but also while she sleeps. At any part of the day, I want to consume her.

"Hello boys," Lark greets from her place next to Posie at the outdoor table. We're nearing the months in Washington where we don't see any sun and it's nothing but gray clouds. Everyone is sitting outside soaking up as much of the good weather as they can before it's gone. "Sorry I missed you at the party the other night. Everyone disappeared before I could say hi." Deep-blue eyes narrow at me in suspicion. "That was a super weird speech, though. What was that about?"

Posie, who's been looking anywhere other than directly at me since we walked up, stares at the barely touched cup of fruit in front of her.

That doesn't stop me from staring at her while I answer Lark's question. "I just wanted to welcome Posie home. She's been gone for a long time and I'm just happy to have her back."

The blonde frowns at this. "Posie, I thought you said you didn't know Rafferty?"

Finally looking up from her food, her mouth opens and closes like she's trying to come up with an excuse or answer.

Stepping around the table so I'm standing directly at her side, I respond to Lark for her. "It wasn't a complete lie. It's been a really long time since we've been around each other. We're basically strangers now. Isn't that right?"

When she hesitates to answer, I put my finger under her chin and tip her face up to look at me. The slender column of her throat moves as she swallows hard. "That's right," she mumbles, a noise just barely audible to my ears.

"Oh, okay. I just don't understand why you didn't say so the other day when I asked." The look on Lark's face remains skeptical. She's been raised by politicians and has an excellent bullshit detector.

Eyes narrowing at Posie, I silently instruct her to add in on this conversation. I want to hear what she'll say. How will she spin our sordid tale so she doesn't look like the villain in it?

She clears her throat before explaining vaguely. "We... we just have a really complicated history. I grew up with Paxton and Rafferty, but I moved away a few years back and we lost contact."

"I would have loved to reunite with her sooner, but I'm sure it'll be worth the wait." I love she's the only one who understands the unspoken message in my words. "Speaking of which, I have a homecoming present for you, Posie."

Dropping my hand from her jaw, I reach into the back pocket of my jeans. My fingers wrap around the leather of the object as her head shakes in refusal.

"You really didn't have to get me anything." She's trying to keep her voice even and pleasant to not alert Lark to what's happening, but she's doing a terrible job. Posie excels at a lot of things, like ballet and destroying lives, but acting is a skill she sorely lacks. "Don't you think you've surprised me with enough gifts lately, Raff?"

This has me smirking. The butterflies weren't meant as a gift, but she knows this. They were to prove to her there's nowhere she can go that is safe from my reach. Her bedroom is supposed to be her sanctuary away from everyone and everything, and I easily infiltrated it.

"I thought you could use one more." Pulling it from its hiding place, I reveal the leather choker.

She made the sarcastic comment about me putting a collar on her in the cemetery, but little did she know, that was exactly what I planned on doing. The black leather is about an inch thick, and where there's traditionally a silver ring in the middle, there's a butterfly instead. The leather attaches to both hollow wings and, in the middle where the body of the butterfly is, is a tiny keyhole. Once this is on her, the only way she's getting it off is if I allow it.

Her lips part in a silent gasp. "Is that a…" Not able or *willing* to say the words aloud, her soft whisper trails off.

Submissive collar? Why yes, yes, it is, Posie. "It's a butterfly for my Butterfly," I tell her in place of the truth. "Stand up."

Pale brown eyes dance between me, Lark, Rome, and whoever else might be watching her humiliation. Every thought and conflicted emotion she's experiencing are reflected in her face. I know she's thinking about telling me to go fuck myself. It's what she *wants* to do most, but I also know that she won't. Not with her father's well-being at stake.

The moment she concedes and gives up any semblance of a fight goes straight to my dick. Her pathetic look of defeat and acceptance is an intoxicating sight. Breaking her is going to be my greatest joy.

Pushing back from the table, Posie rises to her feet and stands before me. I'll give her some credit; she doesn't look away this time. Her perfect white teeth dig into her bottom lip as

I push her long strands of hair behind her shoulders. The only time she flinches is when my thumb grazes the purple bruise I'd left on her throat the other night. As I place the leather around her slender throat, she searches for something in my eyes. For what? I'm not sure. Perhaps she's searching for any remnants of the boy I used to be.

The sound of both sides locking together has her shifting on her feet, but she doesn't try to pull away or stop me.

"There," I say, tracing the metal butterfly positioned in the middle of her throat. Her jaw twitches in silent revulsion as I admire the new accessory. Wanting to see if I can make her snap, I tilt my head with a smirk. "I got you a present. What do you say?"

The flash of fury across her face is a stunning sight, but it's even more beautiful when she's able to completely rein it in and tell me what I want to hear. Doing this in front of our friends and anyone else in the quad was the right move. It verified to me just how willing she is to play my game.

"Thank you for my present, Rafferty."

Running my thumb along her pink bottom lip, I praise her. "Good girl." She's anything but good, and we both know it. "Now, I have something next Saturday that I'm going to need you at. If you're not already, make yourself available."

Brows pulling together, she frowns at this. "I have a shift until eight that night, and then I have to be back at the studio at seven the next morning."

"What part of that is my problem? Drink a coffee or do a line of coke, I don't care what you have to do as long as you're ready at nine Saturday night."

"Fine. I'll figure it out."

"Of course, you will. We wouldn't want you disappointing me so soon, would we?"

Her only answer is a single shake of her head.

FIFTEEN
POSIE

I'M ready for this day to be over, and it's nowhere near being done.

For three nights now, I've been trying to catch up on my sleep. Friday night when I returned exhausted to a roomful of butterflies was the start of my demise. It took almost two and a half hours to remove each insect from my room, and once I'd showered and finally climbed into bed, the sun was just starting to light the sky. With back-to-back twelve-hour shifts at the studio, I should be able to come home and crash without a struggle.

But that's not the case. I find myself lying there in my dark room with my mind racing a million miles an hour. Between reliving the depressing events of this week, I play the "*what if*" game. It's a special way to torture yourself, and a surefire way to hurt your own feelings. It's also something I find myself doing a lot. *What if I'd kept Rafferty's secret? What if I hadn't given my dad the evidence he needed to build a case? If I'd just kept my mouth shut, would everyone be safe and healthy?*

It's always when I get to that last question that I'm once again reminded of *why* I betrayed Rafferty, and with it, my resolve for my actions strengthens. Knowing you did the right thing doesn't make it hurt any less.

And Rafferty wants me to hurt.

The leather choker around my throat feels like a chain connecting me to him. With a simple tug, Rafferty can have me falling to my knees without any objection. Nobody warns you when you accept the burden of a secret that you must bear all degrees of degradation to keep it. I made a promise that I would never tell, and while I hate everything about Rafferty's collar, I'll wear it because the bigger picture is more important.

I'm trying to do my best to ignore Lark's inquisitive and concerned stare as we walk across campus toward our next classes.

It's the blonde I'm quickly becoming close to who finally breaks the awkward tension. "I'm not Zadie, so I'm not going to come right out and ask you what the fuck that was about. All I will tell you is I'm here if you want to talk about it."

There's nothing more I want to do than to talk to someone about what's happening. The only other people who lived through that time with me are my father and Pax, and neither one of them is talking to me right now. Granted, it's for different reasons, but the silence hurts all the same.

"Rafferty blames me for something that happened a few years back. He hates me and wants revenge." My mouth is forming words before my brain has fully comprehended I'm speaking aloud. Apparently, the need to confide in someone is taking over and I've lost all control. My only saving grace is I kept it vague enough to avoid any real trouble.

Lark's hand wraps around my upper arm, stopping me from continuing down the pathway we're on. She's about three inches taller than me, and she has to look down at me when she talks. If she wasn't trapped in the world of politics, I'm sure she'd make an amazing model.

"And you're just going to let him treat you like this?"

"It doesn't matter how good my reasoning was almost six years ago, Raff will always have every right to be mad at me." My shoulders shrug nonchalantly even though I'm feeling anything but.

I don't realize my crucial mistake until Lark's perfectly symmetrical face falls. "Six years? You mean this happened before he transferred out of Hemlock Hill?"

A stress headache instantly wraps around my skull like a vise. Eyes squeezed tight, I rub my temple as I sigh her name in an unspoken plea for her to not take this any further. "Lark..."

She doesn't hear my silent begging, or she chooses to ignore it. So much for her not being like Zadie...

"So, when you said the other day that you don't know Rafferty Wilde, you were telling the truth. You haven't seen him since he dropped his father's name after his mom—"

That's enough! Eyes snapping open, I frantically grip the hand that still holds my arm. "*Please.* Just... just don't, Lark."

For the first time, I get a small taste of what it must have been like for Rafferty and Pax during the aftermath. There wasn't a soul in town who didn't know who they were or what had happened to their family. No matter where they went, I'm positive they couldn't escape the stares or whispering. Their tragedy became another's entertainment. I doubt their grand-mother switching them to the other private school in town did much to help them.

I'm met with nothing but unwavering sympathy when I lift my chin. She has no idea what part I played in the brothers' story, and yet, she doesn't look at me like she believes for a second I am the bad guy. Meanwhile, that's the only thing Rafferty sees me as. To him, I was the monster sleeping in his bed that took his mom's life.

"So, when you say you knew them, you *really* knew them. You were there when it all went down?" I'm not sure if it's her intuition or my visceral reaction to her prodding that makes her draw that conclusion. Maybe it's both.

"*Yes*," I whisper hoarsely.

"I'm so sorry, Posie."

Rafferty's been telling me that he's the only one who lost something, that I have no right to grieve. Lark's earnest apology goes right to my heart, making the fragile pieces of it crack a little bit more, because for the first time in a long time, it allows me to acknowledge that I too lost things. I lost my best friend, my surrogate mom, and my first and only love.

"Thank you." Exhaling a shaky breath, I try to regain my composure. "I don't want… I can't talk about it. It's not my story to tell." Rafferty would explode with fury if he heard me say that. He'd be calling me out for my hypocrisy seeing as I had no trouble telling his story back then.

"I understand." Her free hand reaches for the leather collar, and her finger runs over the silver wings. "Can you tell me just one thing, though? Why the butterfly?"

I've lost track of how many times people have asked me about my name. As if it were an oath I'd made to him, I guarded the nickname he'd given me like it was hallowed. When he put this butterfly on my throat, he took the thing that was once sacred to us and made it into the symbol of his control over me.

Keeping the origin of the moniker a secret is no longer something I owe him. So, I tell her. "My mother was from Spain. When she was pregnant with me, she said when I kicked her, it felt like little butterfly wings fluttering in her belly. She started to call me her mariposa. It's Spanish for butterfly. My dad eventually joined in, and shortly after, the name was shortened to Posie. It stuck, and they decided that's what I should be named. Not that it really mattered what my mother wanted to call me since she was gone by the time I was two. Rafferty knows this story and started calling me Butterfly when we were younger because of it."

My mother came from an affluent family in Spain. She moved to the States for college and while she was here, she met Mollie and my dad. He was a couple a years older, and I think she was enthralled by the idea of being with someone who was the opposite of the boys she'd dated before. Dad was simple, hardworking, and down to earth. The charm of being a stay-at-home mom in a middle-class family wore off quickly. Before I had a chance to develop real memories of her, she was signing divorce papers and giving all parental rights to my dad. We haven't heard a word from her since, but I can't help but think we're better off for it.

Lark falls quiet for a moment. "So, he took a story that could have made you sad and twisted it into something that would make you happy?"

The first time he called me that, the smile that broke across my face was so big, it hurt. "I guess that's one way of looking at it."

"I don't know the full story between you guys and I'm not asking you to tell me, but I find it interesting that he still uses the nickname. If I hated someone, I sure as hell wouldn't be calling them any cute secret nicknames anymore."

"I'm pretty sure that's his point. He's trying to tarnish the sentimental name he called me, just like he's trying to ruin everything else."

Lark doesn't look convinced. "Hate's a funny emotion. It blinds us from feeling anything else."

"I don't hate Rafferty."

"I know you don't. If you did, you'd be a *lot* more pissed about that thing around your neck. I'm just wondering if he hates you as much as you think he does." Lark's more optimistic outlook on this is charming and appreciated, but as the person who was choking on his dick in a graveyard, I think I'm the authority on this matter.

And I still think he hates me.

SIXTEEN
POSIE

AS A GENERAL RULE—ESPECIALLY as a female—it's never wise to get into random cars with random men. The black Escalade with heavily tinted windows pulled up in front of my apartment complex right when Rafferty said it would, and the only reason I got into the back of the vehicle after hesitating several moments was because of the text I received from an unknown phone number.

It simply read *"Get in"* with a butterfly emoji following it.

If my father knew I was currently letting a mysterious man drive me God knows where at this time of night, he would be calling every available squad car to come find my stupid ass. Of course, this would have only happened prior to his accident back when he was still captain of the police department. Now, he doesn't remember I exist. The letters I write to him each week are nothing more than tales from a random pen pal that Aunt Jo reads to him.

After we saw how agitated my dad got when I was around, Jo and I decided it was best I kept my distance for the time being. While he's lost the ability to speak, his frustration over the fact he can't remember who I am is clear. Jo also admitted a few months back that she has a theory he thinks I'm my mother. I've seen pictures of her when she was young, and our resemblance is undeniable. If Jo is right, his agitation at my presence makes that much more sense. Why would he want the woman who abandoned him and their child around?

Understanding why I can't be around my dad doesn't make it any easier. I miss him every day.

The depressing thought has my eyes and nose burning as the SUV comes to a stop behind a building I recognize. The entire campus is laid out around the brick structure, and I just studied here two nights ago.

Why would he have me come to the university's library?

Last week, when Rafferty told me to make myself available tonight, a million different theories came to mind. Not once did it occur to me that he'd want to meet *here.*

The driver, a man with a graying mustache and bald head, turns in his seat. "Go through that metal door. You'll get further instructions inside."

The alarm system that is wired into me sounds off, telling me I should stay right where I am, and when I do just that, the middle-aged man grunts at me.

"I don't have all fucking night, girl. Now get out."

This might be where I die. Though, if it's between this and the graveyard from before, I'm picking the library every time. The unwanted thought floats through my head as I reluctantly climb out of the car. The soles of my shoes barely touch the pavement before the driver is peeling out of the parking lot like he's fleeing a crime scene.

Well, it might be too early to call it a crime scene seeing as I'm still breathing.

Checking for any signs of life lurking in the surrounding bushes or shadows as I go, I walk the few yards to the door he'd pointed to. The reddish paint is chipped, and the door handle is rusted. What lies behind it is completely beyond me. Every horror movie I've ever seen comes to mind as I contemplate the possibilities.

Turning my head, I lean close, hoping I can get a clue about what I'm walking into, but the only sound I can hear is my pounding heart and the wind blowing between the buildings. About to give up, I start to pull my face away from the metal surface when the door flies open.

I jump back just in time to avoid a broken nose.

"*Jesus!*" My body preparing to flee from any possible danger has adrenaline shooting through my veins and into my limbs.

"Afraid not," Rafferty's voice fills the night air. "Although, I do have a knack for getting you on your knees, so maybe I do have something in common with the Almighty." For a second, I'm taken aback by the joke. It's precisely the kind of thing he would have said back in high school. The only difference now is the humor is lacking in his tone. The nostalgia is a fleeting sensation because he wastes no time reverting to his regularly scheduled programming. "You're late," he snaps.

"You're lucky that I'm here at all." I stifle the yawn that appears on cue with my hand. Chasing after little kids in leotards for multiple hours with little to no breaks is *exhausting*. I almost cried when I got home from work tonight and saw my comfy bed. The fact that I had to come do whatever the fuck this is for Rafferty instead of snuggling down in my sheets broke my fatigued little soul. "I'm so tired."

I can't cut back on hours at the studio because I need every penny I make. My schedule was already going to be tight when it was just work and school, but now having to add in Raff's extracurricular activities, I'm burning it at both ends.

"I'm failing to see how that's my problem." He doesn't bother waiting for me to step inside on my own accord. Taking a handful of my simple black long-sleeved T-shirt, he drags me inside behind him. His legs are several inches longer than mine, and I have to take twice as many steps to keep up with him. "We need to get you changed."

"*Changed?*" I repeat like a dumb parrot as I finally take in his attire. Gone are the faded jeans and scuffed boots he's worn forever. In their place is a pair of black slacks and a black button-down shirt with the sleeves rolled up his forearms. I haven't seen him wear something like this since the night of the winter dance. "Why are you dressed like that at the *library?*"

"Because we're not in the library, we're in the library's basement."

I'm more confused than I originally was, but all questions go out the window when he walks through another dingy metal door. It's one big room, and at some point or another, I'm sure it was filled with things that belong to the university, but now it's been turned into an underground poker room.

It feels kind of like walking into a secret speakeasy. Once you're on the other side of the door, you completely forget that you're in a basement.

The lighting is dim, creating a moody and mysterious ambience. The brightest source of light comes from the red pendants hanging above each of the four green velvet-covered tables. At each table sit men and women dressed like they are spending their evening at the opera and not some random campus basement. Along the perimeter of the room, through the haze of cigarette and cigar smoke, I can see various sitting areas set up. Each area is illuminated by a cluster of candles that sit on the tables in front of each of the leather couches. Some people sit alone, enjoying their drink in peace, while others sit huddled together, sharing a bottle of champagne.

The source of their alcohol sits on the far wall. The bar is a large dark wood structure that looks completely out of place. Then again, everything down here is out of place. Two men in white shirts and red velvet sport coats make drinks behind the bar. One of them passes a drink off to the woman sitting at the bar top, but the other passes a couple glasses off to a girl wearing nothing but scraps of black fabric. Her outfit looks as if it's being held together by a single string and sheer will. It crisscrosses and wraps around the curves of her body. The only parts of her that are covered are her nipples and crotch, and even then, one wrong move could have the miniscule pieces of fabric shifting. Since her entire ass is displayed in the thong, it really is a wonder why they bothered concealing her anatomy at all.

The dark-haired girl puts the drinks on her tray and teeters off in her six-inch heels to deliver them to players sitting at the closest table. She looks nothing but confident as she smiles flirtatiously and places her hand on one of the men's shoulders. Even with the gold ring around his finger, he doesn't shy away from her attention.

Scanning the room, I find two more girls dressed in similar attire.

It suddenly dawns on me what I'll be doing here tonight. A complex mixture of repulsion, embarrassment, and annoyance mixes in my stomach. Arms crossing over my chest, my eyes slide to the mastermind behind all of this. "You can't be serious. That's what you want me to do?" My chin nods in the direction of the girl flirting with the married man. "You want me to pass out drinks and flirt with your patrons?"

He ignores me and asks a question of his own. "What makes you think they're mine?"

I roll my eyes at this. "You're the only person I know who could create something like this on a *college* campus and get away with it. Something as big as this can't go unnoticed forever, so campus officials *must* know about it. If they could have done something to stop it, they would have by now, which means they *can't*. My guess is you've made a deal with someone powerful to remain in business." In many ways, Rafferty has become a stranger, but I would wager that I still know him better than most. Being apart for as long as we have doesn't mean we

117

forget our past. "It's the same old games you used to play. You've just upped the price and scale of them."

He doesn't confirm that I'm right, but he doesn't have to. We both know I am.

"I don't want you to wait on and flirt with the players," he says, going back to my earlier sentiment like we hadn't been talking about something else entirely.

"You don't?"

"No, I want you to wait on *me*. Remember how I told you that you'd be my bitch, entertainment, and whore?" The smirk on his face used to make my heart skip a beat, but now it only fills me with dread. "Welcome to the bitch part of your punishment."

SEVENTEEN
POSIE

THE OUTFIT he holds up on a hanger looks like nothing but scraps of random leather. It doesn't look like something that can be—or *should be*—worn. For most of my life, I've danced in a leotard in front of hundreds. On stage with spotlights shining on my every movement, I thought *that* was the most exposed I could possibly be. Rafferty has just proved me wrong.

"That's what you want me to wear?" I gape, pointing at the... I don't even know what I should call it. Saying it's an outfit feels too generous.

"I picked it myself."

"*Of course*, you did." It's the kind of thing someone would wear when they're suspended from the ceiling of a BDSM dungeon. There're even silver rings connecting pieces of the leather which I would bet are meant for exactly that. "I never thought for a single second that you didn't."

"You always knew what I liked." While his statement sounds void of emotion when it comes out of his mouth, to my ears it's the equivalent of someone poking at a healing bruise.

I'm proud of myself when I'm able to keep my face from reacting to his words. I don't want to be sad anymore, but more importantly, I don't want him to know he's succeeding at doing so.

Lifting my chin, I boldly meet his cold gaze. To think, once upon a time, I found warmth in those icy depths. "Just give me a minute to catch up again, Raff. You know I'm a quick learner."

"That was a skill I once admired about you." I wonder if the same memories that are circulating in my head are also in his. All my firsts, Rafferty claimed as his own, and as he did, he became my teacher. He taught me everything I'd need to please him. He was happy to do so, and I was an overeager student. "But I'm not interested in your ability to learn right now, Posie. I'm interested in seeing how well you can follow an order."

Walking to the door of the small dressing room we're in, he reaches for the handle and locks us in together. There's not much in here. A vanity with various kinds of makeup thrown across it takes up the majority of the far wall, and there is a silver rolling rack of outfits similar to the one in Rafferty's hand on the other side. In other words, there's no escape and there's nothing in here to defend myself with if I need to. I have no clue what he's planning on doing, but I don't think a tube of mascara is going to help me much if push came to shove.

Swallowing, I find the courage to ask, "What is it that you want me to do?"

Returning to stand before me, he widens his stance and crosses his arms over his chest. The fabric of his button-down pulls at his shoulders as he does this, reconfirming my theory about his dedication to the gym. The daunting outfit is still draped over the hanger dangling off his finger, mocking me because we both know I'll be wearing it soon enough.

"Get undressed."

Taking a deep cleansing breath, I nod my head. There's no point in arguing with him over it. I might as well just get it over with. "Okay, give it to me. I'll be out in a minute."

Glancing between my outreached hand and my body, the

corner of his mouth lifts arrogantly. "We're already having a communication problem. I told you to get undressed. At no point in time did I allude that I would be leaving while you did so." *Oh ... shit.* "I'll give you one more chance to do what I ask voluntarily."

Knowing Raff, if I don't start stripping down right now, he'll take the knife he always keeps in his pants pocket and cut my clothes from my body himself. He'll leave me with nothing to get home in, and I *refuse* to sit in the back of that driver's SUV again while wearing only that leather thing.

"Fine." Teeth clenched so hard, I'm worried I'll crack a molar, my fingers grip the hem of my black cotton shirt. The first time I got naked for Rafferty, I was shaking like a leaf. Any before-show jitters I got paled in comparison to that first time. To my surprise, I'm not anywhere near as nervous now as I was then.

Maybe it's because this time around, I already know he'll like what he sees. He can hate me all he wants for what I did, but my body never betrayed him. Fuck, my body has been more loyal to him than I'd like. Any attempts to move past my first love were met with resistance.

Never once breaking the intense eye contact between us, I pull the shirt over my head and toss it at his feet. It lands on the tip of his leather dress-shoe, but he doesn't bother looking at it or kicking it away. His attention remains firmly on me.

There's nothing sexy about the bra I'm wearing. It's simple and made of black cotton. Had I known he'd be making me take it off, I wouldn't have bothered strapping it on my chest in the first place.

Leaving it in place for now, I toe off my white Vans so I can get my pants off without obstruction, and while I do, I reach for the elastic waistband of my Lululemon leggings. They cost me a fortune but they're worth every penny. If he doesn't give them back to me, I'll lose it.

Just as I'd done with my shirt, I toss them at his feet. Standing before him in nothing but my black thong and bra, I try not to shift on my feet with restless energy as his piercing eyes scrutinize the pieces of my bare skin. He looks at me now like he can't decide if he wants to devour me or kill me. Or both.

As far as deaths go, being devoured to death by Rafferty Wilde wouldn't suck.

My fingers have just brushed against the clasp of my bra when he gives a terse shake of his head. "Stop."

I do what he asks, my hands returning to my side.

"Turn around."

"Why?"

The harsh look contorting his features silences any other questions I might have. Doing what he wants of me, I turn in place and give him my back. They've always told us when faced with a dangerous predator, we should never turn our backs on them. Yet here I am doing exactly that.

I'll just add it to the list of reckless things I've done tonight.

Hands opening and closing at my sides, I wait for his next move with trepidation. My body is bracing for the possibility of some sort of pain when he pushes the long strands of my hair over my shoulder. It's a tender move, and I hate that I enjoy every second of it. I shouldn't like *anything* he does, and yet, I find myself exhilarated when his fingertips travel from the collar at my neck and down to the clasp of my bra.

My cheeks heat when a rush of air escapes through my parted lips involuntarily. I expect for some shitty comment to come from him, but he doesn't acknowledge it. Which is a more alarming move than when he unhooks my bra from my body.

Rafferty pushes it from my shoulders and continues to trace a trail down my spine with a touch that's causing goose bumps to erupt across my skin. I'm glad I can't see his face right now because I can pretend he's looking at me with the same ache I've always had for him and not his permanent mask of hatred.

I hate that mask and I hate even more I'm the reason he wears it.

His touch reaches the edge of my thong, and instead of stopping there, he drags his fingers along the entire waistband. My heart skips in my chest when his light touch skims past my hip bone and continues to move toward the front of my body. His arm circles my torso in a move that could almost be considered an embrace, but I'm not naive enough to believe it. It takes everything in me to remain perfectly still and not lean into his strong frame.

Heart pounding and blood rushing in my ears, Rafferty's path comes to a stop on my thong's waistline directly below my belly button. If he moved two inches lower, he'd be touching me. I would have lost a lot of money if someone had asked me all those years ago if Rafferty and I would ever be in this position again. But he's so close now, and it's making me second-guess every thought I've ever had.

I'm just close enough that I can feel his chest expand with each breath he takes. It's coming in a ragged and fast rhythm now. Knowing that I'm affecting him as much as he is me fills me with a sense of victory.

Unfortunately for me, the sensation only lasts another second or two because Rafferty catches on to his mistake. His hand leaving my thong to wrap around the leather collar is like ice water being thrown on the heated situation. Like a switch being flipped, the euphoric energy returns to the hostile one I'm quickly growing used to.

"It's pathetic how much you enjoyed that," he growls in my ear. His fingers curl around the collar, making it pinch the sensitive skin of my throat.

I can stand here and let him hurt my feelings, or I can throw his words back in his face. The hurricane of varying emotions storming in my veins has me choosing the latter. "*I'm pathetic?*

That's a bit hypocritical coming from a guy whose dick is currently poking me in the fucking back."

I didn't notice until he took hold of the choker and pulled me closer to him. Now it's all I can feel.

"I'm allowed to get turned on. What's the point of having a good little whore if you don't give her jobs to take care of?"

Using his grip on the collar, he violently pushes me away from him. While I'm trying to soothe the ache now on my neck, he throws the outfit at me. I bite back a wince when the leather slaps against my skin and the metal hanger scratches my chest.

I manage to catch it before it can fall into a tangled mess on the floor.

"You have ten minutes to get ready."

EIGHTEEN
RAFFERTY

THE ORIGINAL THOUGHT behind this plan was if I had her dress like the whore she is, then everyone in attendance would also see her as such. Had I known how spectacularly it would backfire on me, I would have let her stay the fuck home.

Posie emerged from the dressing room looking like a piece of fucking art. Instead of my patrons staring at her like she's nothing but a cheap piece of meat for them to use, they're staring at her like she's something displayed at the goddamn Louvre. The point of having the women working here is they're meant to fawn over the players and make them feel important. It's never supposed to be the other way around.

But I can't blame them.

The top resembles something like a harness. It interweaves across her chest and shoulders in one-inch leather straps. Two pieces create an X over her nipples, but other than that, her perfectly-sized round breasts are on display for everyone's enjoyment. Over the black thong I'd been toying with earlier is a leather garter belt. It wraps around her waist and thighs, and leaves her ass completely exposed.

While those two things were enough to draw attention, she

didn't stop there. In the dressing room, she'd found fishnet stockings and knee-high black boots. Her long hair has also been pulled back into a sleek ponytail and she helped herself to the makeup sitting on the vanity. The dark shadow around her eyes only makes them more alluring.

We keep the dressing room fully stocked with various items as we provide the attire for the girls that work here. I have absolutely no idea what's kept in there since Kason oversees things like that, but had I known she would come out dressed in those additions, I would have removed them from the building before she stepped foot in there.

There's a part of me that is silently raging they're admiring her so much. I was under the false impression I wouldn't care if others paid attention to Posie, that their stares wouldn't anger me. I believed the overly jealous part of me died when my mom did, and that is the *only* reason I went through with this plan. Again, I was sorely misguided. It's taking everything in me to not throw a coat over her bare shoulders and drag her away from their approving looks.

While everyone else stares shamelessly in her direction, I've been doing my best to ignore her. Her current appearance isn't doing any favors for the *unfavorable* state she left me in before I exited the dressing room. I don't have an issue being turned on by Posie when *I* control the scenario in which it happens. Like the cemetery. Tonight, I forgot the very *meaning* of control.

I wasn't supposed to touch her, only observe. That rule was blown into oblivion when she stood before me mostly naked and stared at me like she did when I was seventeen years old. I let myself get pulled back into those memories and feelings, and I forgot momentarily who she is and what she's done.

I may have been able to stop, but for the past hour, as she's stood behind me like a silent shadow, I've struggled to regain control. My cock, still throbbing for her, has been distracting me this entire game. If I don't find a way to pull myself together,

I'm going to be the one who owes money at the end of the night. And that's not how this works. The house always wins and *I'm* the fucking house.

Lifting my empty rocks glass off the table, I wave it at Posie. "Another." Perhaps with a little bit more alcohol, it'll help me ignore her.

Reaching over my shoulder, she takes it from me. My jaw clenches when her slender fingers brush against mine in the process.

"Do you want the same thing?"

"Make it a double," I grit between my teeth.

She makes it no more than a foot away from the table when the ruddy oil tycoon from Texas calls out to her. "Hey, darlin', would you mind grabbin' me a refill too? Only if it's no trouble, of course."

From his spot across the table, he lifts his empty glass with a friendly smile. He seems harmless with his Southern charm and friendly appearance, but he's a bigger piece of shit than most of the criminals that grace my tables.

When I turn my head in her direction, she's already looking at me. As if waiting for me to grant her permission, she quirks a brow. For a moment there, I believe she's starting to understand her new role, that, for the foreseeable future, she can't make a move without my say-so. The belief is fleeting because with a bright smile, an expression I don't think I'll ever be the recipient of again, she abandons her post at my side.

Strutting around the table, she heads toward the Texan. "It's no trouble at all, honey! What are we drinking tonight?" Her voice is sweet like sugar, but I know it's laced with venom. She's as much of a snake as the corrupt politicians sitting around us.

He grins at her like a lovesick puppy, relishing the fact her attention is exclusively on him. It strokes his ego in just the way he likes. "Whiskey. Jim Beam. One ice cube." He passes Posie the glass once she's close enough.

"You got it."

The flirty wink she throws him over her shoulder has my chest burning and blood boiling. She knew doing this would piss me off, and that's why her mouth pulls in a knowing smirk as she passes me on her way to the bar.

Muscles tense, I sit rigidly in my chair and attempt to return my focus to the cards in my hand. But the Southern cocksucker doesn't allow that to happen because he opens his dumb fucking mouth again.

"Wilde, I like the new girl. Can we expect to have her here in the future? I sure do enjoy havin' a new piece of eye candy struttin' around while I gamble. It lessens the sting of losin' my money to you." He chuckles loudly, it's a hoarse sound that results in a ghastly coughing fit.

Tilting my head, I examine the man sitting across the table who looks like he's eaten about one too many *cows* in his lifetime. "You've never met a twenty-one-year-old girl you didn't like, Martin."

"You're absolutely right about that!" He tips his cowboy hat at me. His entire appearance looks so out of place here. The only reason I keep inviting him back is because he never knows when to stop playing. That ego I talked about always keeps him in the game longer than he should. Each time he sits at my table, I make a minimum of five figures.

Martin's trying to get me to smile or laugh like he is, but I'm entirely unimpressed with him and my face conveys that. "She's not the '*new girl*'. Posie is not employed here."

"Oh, well, how was I supposed to know any better? You've got her dressed like those other sluts you've got walkin' around."

Putting my cards down, I shift forward in my seat and clasp my hands together on the green velvet table. "You've falsely assumed Posie is here for *your* entertainment. Let me set the record straight for you. The only person in this fucking building she is meant to entertain and please is *me*. The next time you tell her to get you a drink or call her *darlin'*, you'll be walking out of here without your money *and* your tongue." Everyone around the table has fallen silent as they listen in. Good. I want them to hear this too. "Now do us both a favor and stop looking at what's *mine*."

Out of my peripheral vision, I see Posie return to the table with two drinks in her hand. I'm not sure how much she heard, but I know she heard something because she hesitates a second before walking toward Martin.

She's two feet away from the cowboy when I stop her.

"Butterfly." The use of her nickname has her coming to an abrupt stop and her head snapping in my direction. Her brows are furrowed in suspicion, but she still does as she's told when I beckon her with my two fingers. "Come here."

She's fully aware of everyone's eyes on her as she comes around the table. The fluidity and gracefulness with which she moves are evidence of her years spent dancing. It's truly a shame she fucked up at Juilliard. She was going places. If she still wants to be picked up by a ballet company, it's going to be much harder for her.

Stopping before me, she asks softly, "Yes?"

"Give me his drink."

Posie hands me the glass with the single ice cube floating in it. Martin's already red swollen face deepens multiple shades as I swirl the cheap alcohol around the glass a few times. "Jim Beam? *Really?*"

With that, I hold it out at my side and let go. The thin glass shatters into pieces on the polished concrete floor beneath me and the whiskey splashes against our shoes. The crashing sound echoes across the vast room and has heads turning in our direction. Everyone at my table is taken aback by this move, their eyes darting around to each other as if they're having an unspoken conversation.

The only person who doesn't flinch or make a sound stands

at my side. Completely unfazed by my antics, she simply nudges the broken glass around her feet with the toe of her shoe.

"You know where the bar is, Martin." The Texan looks like he wants to reach across the table and strangle me. "I suggest you retrieve your own drink," I tell him, dismissing him.

He's breathing hard when he pushes away from the table, whether it's from anger or his bad heart is unknown to me, and I don't care either way.

Posie leans over my shoulder and places my replenished glass of scotch in front of me. She's just about to pull back when I see the pink lipstick print on the rim. It's the same shade she came out of the dressing room wearing. My hand locks around her wrist before she can move away from me.

Her face is right over my shoulder in this position, so I turn my head slightly to speak to her. "Did you enjoy my scotch? It's from a forty-year-old bottle that's worth more than you ever will be."

If my words affect her, she doesn't show it. In fact, she hardly skips a beat. Her narrow shoulders lift as she whispers in my ear, "That's an unfortunate price tag because it's *disgusting*."

"Maybe you just haven't had a proper taste of it yet." I push my chair back from the table to ensure there's enough room and pull on the wrist I still hold captive. "Sit down," I order, motioning toward my lap.

I don't give two shits that there are four other players and a dealer watching us, or that I'm holding up the game. This is far more entertaining and important.

Expecting her to hesitate and fight me, I'm surprised when her long leg swings over my lap and she straddles me without complaint. Her hands hold on to my shoulders to keep herself balanced. I want to despise her touch more than I do. It enrages me that I still enjoy the feeling of her body pressed against mine.

"Hand me my glass."

Reaching behind her, she picks it up off the table and hands it to me. The liquid inside is only a couple shades darker than her inquisitive eyes scanning me. She's confused but being such a good girl by doing what I say.

Lifting the cup, I take a drink and savor the burn as it goes down my throat. "Your turn."

Posie frowns at this. "*My* turn?"

With my free hand, I clasp her jaw. Applying just enough pressure to make it clear she shouldn't try to pull away, I tell her what to do next. "Open your mouth."

Her lips are just barely parted when I take in another mouthful of scotch. This time I don't swallow it. Yanking her face closer to mine, her eyes widen as my plan dawns on her. To my delight, she doesn't try to stop me when I bridge the remaining gap between us. Her entire body tremors in my lap when my lips just barely brush across hers. The contact is almost nonexistent, but it still goes straight to my dick.

Her chest heaves beneath the leather straps crisscrossing over her skin when I repeat the same move, this time applying just a little bit more pressure. I'm not sure if it'd classify as a kiss, but either way, it causes her to release a shuddering breath. As she does so, my grip tightens on her face to keep her perfectly still and I spit the contents in my mouth between her parted lips.

Posie's body stiffens when the spicy scotch hits her tongue. Shifting my hand on her face, I drag my thumb across her bottom lip, smearing the lipstick that resides there. "Swallow." My command is a dark murmur only she can hear. "We both know how good you are at that."

The column of her throat shifts under her butterfly collar as she swallows the scotch. To further prove she did as told, she wraps her lips around my thumb and sucks. Her eyes with pupils the size of saucers flick downward as her hips rock ever so slightly forward against my cock. She knows what she's doing to me. Posie said in the dressing room that she's a quick learner, and with each passing day, she's relearning how to get through my defenses.

After releasing my thumb, she presses a kiss to the pad and says, "Maybe I can learn to like scotch after all." Then a wicked grin splits her face as she grinds against me once more. "Too bad I'm just your bitch tonight, because it feels like you could really use a whore."

She's referring to earlier when I told her tonight would be the bitch part of her punishment. "You're whatever I need you to be, whenever I need you to be it," I correct.

Fingers digging into the fabric on my shoulders, Posie tilts her head. "Tell me, Rafferty, what do you hate more? Me or the fact your body still craves me?"

Reaching between us, she cups me through my slacks. My hands hold onto her hips in a punishing grasp as I hiss out a breath between clenched teeth. I hate that she can still guess what I'm feeling and what internal struggles I'm having.

She doesn't wait for an answer because she doesn't need to. She knows I hate her more. I hate what she did, I hate she felt I was the one who needed to be protected, and most importantly, I hate that she made me hate her. Holding on to me to stay balanced, she climbs gracefully off my lap. Not bothering to wait for permission, she turns and heads toward the dressing room.

NINETEEN
RAFFERTY

I SAID two words tonight I have never once said since I started these poker games.

I'm out.

Tossing what would have been a winning hand on the velvet table, I stood up from my seat and left. It's a move that cost me more money than most Americans make in a year, but the look on Posie's face when I stop the door she's attempting to slam makes it worth every lost penny.

She had no idea I'd been that close on her heels the whole time. Why would she? I did something so wildly out of character by forfeiting the game that I even surprised myself. The last thing she would have expected me to do is follow her back into the dressing room when I have an image to uphold in front of my patrons.

I've never spent so much time in this room as I have tonight. Hell, now that I think of it, I'm not sure I've ever stepped foot in here before, and now I'm shoving the door Posie's holding on to for dear life open so I can force my way in.

Wrestling the door easily out of her control, I step inside the room, and she backs away from me. By the look on her face, she seems to be more exasperated than scared that I'm trapping her in this room with me. Perhaps it's because she hasn't quite figured out that's exactly what I plan on doing to her. I'm trapping her here until I've had my fill.

"Why'd you run off?" I ask her, shutting and locking the door behind me. "I wasn't done with you."

Her chin lifts and her arms cross in front of her, as if to create a barrier between us. "I was done with you."

"Is that so?"

Her response is an immediate "*Yes.*"

Like we're dancing, I match every move she makes. For every one of her steps back, I take a step forward. Any space she creates between us, I take back. Like well-rehearsed choreography, we do this until her back touches the plaster of the far wall.

Nowhere to go now, I press my palms on either side of her head and cage her in. Looking for a way to escape, her honey eyes dart around me, but we both know that there's no getting around me in such a tight space. I would be pulling her back by her hair before she could make it two feet.

Posie's tongue wets her bottom lip and her chest heaves with rapid breaths as she lifts her head so she can look at me and not my chest. "What do you want, Rafferty?'

"I want you to finish what you started out there."

Her eyes flick down to where my cock is straining against my slacks. "Take care of it yourself, or better yet, I'm sure there's someone out there who would be more than willing to finish you off. I would even wager they'll fight over who gets to fall to their knees. It'll be the highlight of the year getting to suck off the great and powerful Rafferty Blackwell—sorry, it's Wilde now, right?"

My body has a visceral reaction to hearing my old last name. My father's face flashes in my head along with the unapologetic look he'd given me that night. There wasn't a sliver of remorse in his eyes when he got in the back of that car.

"It's Wilde," I bite. "And I don't want anyone else. I want you." Leaning close, I trail my nose down the side of her face and breathe in the sweet citrus smell that clings to her skin. Her breath skips as I do so.

Shifting restlessly against the wall, her head shakes. "Rational people don't want to fuck the people they claim to hate the most."

"When have I ever claimed to be rational?" I murmur in her ear before scraping my teeth on her earlobe. Startled by this, Posie jolts and her hands instinctively fly up to push me away. Even after she discovers I can't be swayed, her palms remain pressed to my abdomen. My muscles tighten under her warm touch. "You're wrong, by the way. People who hate each other definitely want to fuck. Ever heard of hate-fucking? It's popular for a reason."

"I don't hate you."

I wish you did. It'd be so much easier. "Pretend you do." Taking a hand off the wall, I trail the pads of my fingers across the metal butterfly on her throat before dragging them down and over the swell of her breast. There's a sharp, barely audible inhale when I graze over her scarcely covered nipple. "I've drugged you, blackmailed you, and made you my bitch. That should be plenty for you to draw anger from. Pretend you hate me as much as I hate you, and even though it's a pathetic lie, pretend you hate when I touch you."

"Who says it's a lie?" she sniffs indignantly.

Finger trailing lower, I make slow circles around her belly button. Her skin is growing warmer by the second and her muscles are quaking under my touch. She turns into stone when I travel inches lower and tease the edge of her thong just as I did earlier.

"I bet your pussy would. Can you honestly tell me that you haven't been wet since we first left this room?" Her hand wraps around my wrist like a vise and panic reflects in her eyes when I slip my fingers beneath her thong's waistband. Her actions speak louder than words, but I still want to hear her say it. "One way or another, I'm going to find out. I'm giving you a chance to be honest with me for once."

Glaring at me, she snarls, "Fuck you."

"Oh, don't you worry. You will be soon."

Delving deeper beneath the fabric, her teeth sink into her pink bottom lip and as if she's too embarrassed to witness me discover her not-so-secret arousal. The soft, almost pitiful sounding, whimper that comes from her is music to my ears when I graze her clit. Her body jerks against mine, but she still doesn't try to escape my touch.

When my fingers sink inside her without resistance, I chuckle in her ear. "And you said you were done with me. You're such a fucking liar."

Her hips jerk as I slowly pump in and out of her. She doesn't want to like it, but she does. The hand that holds onto my wrist shifts in a way that causes her nails to dig into my flesh. No doubt I'll have scratches there tomorrow.

I finger fuck her until she's panting hard and grinding against my hand. Just as she's reaching the brink, I pull out of her and retract my hand from her thong.

With a frustrated cry, Posie throws her head against the wall behind her. "God, you're such an asshole."

"What? Did you really think I'd let you come that easily?" I sink the fingers coated in her arousal into my mouth and groan in approval. "Who knew traitorous pussy would taste so good?"

She glares at me, but it doesn't have the desired effect she was aiming for. I *want* to see her get fiery and mad. This arrangement won't be any fun for me if she remains as docile as she's been. I want her to do what I say, but I also want her to fight me on it.

"Either keep touching my *traitorous* pussy or leave so I can get myself off," she snaps, shoving at my chest again to emphasize her words.

I shake my head with a disapproving *tsk*. "You'll do no such thing. The only person who's making you come for the foreseeable future is *me*, and if I find out you've used your fingers or a fucking vibrator to get yourself off, I will put you over my knee and spank you until your ass blisters. And trust me, I *will* know if you do." The camera I put in her bedroom ensures it. "When you're horny, you will have to come to me and ask me to take care of it."

Rage takes over her features and her jaw tics as her teeth grind.

Lowering my head, I brush my lips over her bare shoulder. When her body relaxes from the touch, I then scrape my teeth over the same spot just so she doesn't get too comfortable.

"Ask me, Posie," I instruct against her soft skin. "Ask me for what you want."

She hesitates, her whole body shaking as it fights to not tell me what I want to hear.

With a dejected sigh, she gives in. "Please make me come, Rafferty."

Her reluctant acceptance is the sweetest sound, and it has the reins of my control snapping. "That's my good girl," I praise darkly as my fingers wrap around the leather garter belt circling her hips. Not being gentle in the slightest, I whirl her smaller body around. The air rushes out of her lungs when her chest collides with the wall she'd just been leaning on.

The outfit I'd made her wear was intended to embarrass her. It hadn't crossed my mind I would be appreciating it for the easy access it gives me as I hadn't planned on touching her. Yet here I am, delighted as fuck that I only have to shift her black thong to get to what I want.

Pulling her hips back, I tell her, "Put your hands flat on the wall and bow your back as much as you can. I don't care if it hurts. If you move from this position even an inch, I will stop. Do you understand?"

Her head nods, but that's not enough. My hand coming down on her bare ass cheek has a yelp escaping her lips. "Words, Posie. I want to hear you tell me you understand."

She swallows hard before answering. "I understand."

With her legs slightly spread, Posie moves her hips back as far as she can while keeping her palms on the white wall. Loving the way her spine is perfectly curved, I trace my fingers along it. Responsive as ever to my touch, goose bumps dance across her skin in my wake.

She tries to turn her head to look at me when I kneel behind her. *"Uh-uh.* What did I just say about moving? Keep looking straight ahead."

Moving her thong as far to the side as I can, I bury my face in her hot core. At the first swipe of my tongue through her slit, her entire body shudders and I groan against her sensitive flesh. Fuck, how I've *missed* this. We were only teenagers, but I knew then that I was going to spend the rest of my life between her thighs. She was it for me. There would never be anyone I wanted more than Posie Davenport, but she destroyed that dream along with everything else.

"Oh god..." she moans.

Licking, sucking, biting. I devour her like a man starved. Her hips grind against my face just the way I like it as I spear my tongue in and out of her over and over again. She always preferred my tongue over my fingers, it's good to see that hasn't changed.

Reaching around her waist with my free hand, I slip my fingers under the fabric of her thong and begin to strum her clit. The intensity of having both my mouth and fingers on her has her hand flying off the wall and wrapping around my wrist. I'm not sure if it's meant to slow me down or encourage me to speed up, but either way I come to a complete stop. I pull away from her cunt with an agitated growl.

The sound that comes out of her is a hoarse sob. She knows what she did wrong. Her hand releases me and returns to the wall. "No, please. I didn't mean to. I'll be good."

I lick my wet lips and smirk hearing this. "I fucking love it when you beg, Butterfly."

"Please. Don't stop, Raff. I was so close."

Sinking my teeth into the curve of her ass, she cries out in pain. "That was your one chance. You fuck up again, I'm going to make you leave here needy and desperate for me."

I admire the bite mark I'd left on her smooth skin. Something primal in me loves seeing my mark on her. Every time I look at the collar she wears, the possessive part of me purrs with satisfaction.

"I won't move. I promise."

I pick up where I left off, and quickly bring her closer to the edge. With every stroke of my tongue her body writhes and moves as if she's unable to control her movements. The soft cries and moans that keep coming from her incite me. Relentlessly, I assault her with pleasure from both my mouth and fingers until she's screaming my name.

She comes on my face, and while she does, I never let up. I greedily lick up every drop with my tongue, and as she comes down, my fingers continue to create small circles around her clit. With each pass, her body twitches with aftershocks and I don't stop until she's completely come back down from her high.

Standing to my feet, I undo the buttons of my black dress shirt and throw it off to the side. Posie, whose head hangs to her chest between her raised arms, perks up when the unmistakable sound of my zipper going down fills the small room. I know she's fighting the urge to look back at me, but she does as commanded, and stares at the blank wall before her.

I almost tell her to look back so she can see how hard she's made me but decide I'd rather her just *feel* it instead. "Let's see how well your body remembers how to take my cock."

Dipping my hand back between her soaked thighs, I gather some of the wetness left there and use it to lubricate my dick. Admiring the way her ass is a pretty shade of pink from my rough touches, I stroke myself, paying extra attention to the piercing. Once, twice, three times.

"Did your pussy miss me?"

Not yet thrusting inside her, I line myself up behind her and slide through her wet center. She gasps when the head of my cock bumps against her clit.

"Tell me, Posie. Am I still the only man that's fucked your cunt?" I feel confident asking such a devious question because I already know the answer. I know each of the names of the men she spent time with on the East Coast. Their phone numbers, social security numbers, home addresses, and work addresses were also delivered to me. If a man so much as breathed the same air as Posie for too long, his information was sent to me.

"That's none of your business."

"False," I growl, nudging the entrance of her pussy. I push forward, just barely stretching her before pulling back and continuing on with what I was doing before. With each stroke through her pussy lips, my cock is further coated in her arousal. "Everything about you is my business. Now, answer the fucking question."

With a frustrated sigh, she does something she historically hasn't been good at. She tells the truth. "I dated a couple guys while I was gone. It was never serious, and it never got very far. None of them ever..." she trails off, fighting off the moan I pull from her when I bump her clit again. "I never fucked them. So, for whatever it's still worth to you, Raff, you're the only one I've been with."

With triumph spreading in my veins, I smirk. "It's still worth everything."

Holding on to her hip, my fingers digging into her skin in a bruising touch, I push inside of her. Posie's mouth opens in a silent gasp, and as I ease deeper, she stops breathing altogether. The world around us fails to exist and I'm momentarily brought back to the world where there's only her and me. Every thought and cell in my body is consumed by her.

Fully seated inside her, I come out of the haze I find myself in. It's been almost six years since I fucked her, and like a junky relapsing on their favorite drug, I begin to chase the high that's waiting for me.

I pull back and drive into her. Ruthlessly and without any restraint, I take everything I want from her. Her muscles squeeze around me eagerly, like a welcoming hug, every time I bury myself to the hilt inside her.

Despite all the time that's passed since she was properly fucked, she doesn't shy away from the brutality of my movements. She meets each of them with her own vigor and unyielding need. Knowing she's going to be sore as fuck tomorrow from this—from me—pleases me.

"Such a whore for my cock," I bite, my fingers wrapping around her long ponytail.

She grunts when I force her head back. I suck and bite at her neck, right over the leather choker she wears. She'll have marks there tomorrow and I hope she wears them with the same kind of dignity she wears my collar. I'm going to have to keep coming up with ways to brand her as mine. I wouldn't be surprised if I woke up one morning wanting to tattoo my name across her perfect ass.

I would love to see my name peeking out the side of her leotard while she danced.

At this new angle, her head is slightly turned. Her dazed and heavy eyes lock with mine. Her face is close enough that I can feel each of the rapid pants that escape her parted lips against mine. In the past, this is when I would have kissed her. I loved when I got to swallow her moans as she came.

Instead, I decide to make her choke on them. Releasing my hold on her hair, I shove my fingers that still taste of her into her mouth. She gags when they go just a little too far. Posie tries to move her head to free herself, but I push down harder on her tongue, keeping her in place.

A mixture of moans and choking sounds fill the room as we both barrel toward our own climaxes. The walls of her cunt begin to quiver around my dick, and my spine begins to tingle. Everything feels like it's too hot—the room, the air we breathe, our skin.

Posie falls over the edge first. Her teeth sink into my fingers, and for a moment, I worry she might actually bite them off, but all care leaves me as white-hot pleasure blasts through my system.

I thrust deeply once more inside Posie. We groan in unison as my hot cum fills her pussy.

Both of us panting hard, I remove my fingers from her mouth and wipe the drool I'd caused from her chin with the back of my hand. Her arms are shaking as she struggles to keep herself in my desired position against the wall.

Her breath catches in her throat when my still semi-hard cock slips from her center. As I watch my cum drip out of her, I can't help but wonder if fucking her was the best or worst thing I could have done.

Gathering what's already escaped her pussy, I push it back inside her with my thumb. "I want you to feel me dripping out of you on your ride home so you remember what a good whore you were for me."

TWENTY
POSIE
FIFTEEN YEARS OLD

IT'S ALWAYS weird when Adrian joins us for dinner.

The banter that is usually had throughout the meal between the three of us is nonexistent. Paxton hardly looks up from his plate and Rafferty's spine is so rigid, you'd think it was made of a metal rod.

Mollie, who is never hungry in general, just pushes her food around her plate and cuts it into smaller and smaller pieces. At least when he's gone, she'll take a few bites of whatever the chef prepared. She seems more relaxed when her husband is away at work. When he's here, she becomes a doting housewife. She's never cooked a meal in her life, but she makes him his plate as if she'd been the one standing over the stove for hours, and she gets up multiple times from the table to refill his glass. When he tells her thank you, her eyes, which are usually kind of dull, light up with joy.

The whole dynamic is off when he's home. Thankfully, he only eats with us a couple times a month. The rest of the time, he's either out of town or wining and dining business clients.

Taking a bite of green beans, I try to make eye contact with Rafferty. He sits directly across from me at the big grand table.

That's another thing. We only eat in the formal dining room when Adrian is home. The rest of the time, we're at the smaller breakfast nook in the actual kitchen. It's a lot more casual, and I'd prefer it if we were there now.

Rafferty is looking anywhere but directly at anyone sitting at the table. It's as if he's doing his best to block out his current surroundings. I wish I knew why he gets so tense when his dad is home.

Adrian uses a cloth napkin to wipe his face before saying, "Paxton, your mother tells me that you asked a young lady to the upcoming dance the other day."

Pax's eyes snap up from his plate and he sits up straighter in his chair. "Uh... Yes, sir. Her name is Sadie. She's in my class."

Mollie's face splits into a big smile at this. She's so proud of her son. "You know who her mom is, Adrian. She's the chef at that French restaurant you like downtown. The one with the soup you really like? You know, the onion one..."

"*Yes*," he interjects, harsher than I think warranted. His shift in tone has Mollie flinching in her chair. "I knew what you meant. There's no need to elaborate further."

Sitting here with all of them, it's easy to compare their features and know which parent they inherited it from. The only thing they got from their dad is their height and broad shoulders, and they both have inches to go before they're done growing. I would bet they'll both end up being taller than Adrian. The rest of their features they got from Mollie. I've always thought she resembled Snow White with her dark hair and pale skin. Her eyes are the lightest shade of blue I've ever seen. She's slight and slender and looks amazing in her designer clothes.

She's a stunning woman, but she's always seemed sad. If my mom were still around, I could ask her if Mollie was the same way when they met in college.

"What about you, Rafferty?" Adrian turns his attention to his older, broodier son. "Are you going to this little dance thing too?" He doesn't even attempt to hide that he believes the whole thing to be a ridiculous waste of time. Pax, who also catches on to his dad's blasé attitude physically deflates in his seat. It's not often I see Pax get excited about something, and I hate that his dad is shitting on it.

"Nope." Rafferty shrugs, flicking a piece of meat across his plate. "Not interested."

"What about you, P?" Mollie jumps in. "Have you given any more thought to going?"

Adrian looks at me with the same look he always has. Indifferent. He doesn't care if I'm going to the dance or not. He's never loved that Mollie stepped in when my mom decided being a wife and mother wasn't her thing and headed back to Spain and her affluent family. He's simply tolerated my presence. While Mollie feels guilty her best friend left me behind, Adrian doesn't owe me anything. I'm thankful to him nonetheless for allowing me to be here as often as I am because it means my dad can excel at his job.

Putting down my fork, I shake my head. "No, I don't think I'm going to."

Mollie frowns. "That's too bad. It would be a good way to meet kids outside of a stuffy classroom."

"Maybe," I offer, not wanting to completely disappoint her.

Then Pax says something I really wish he hadn't. "Well, if you don't go with Chance, you can still come with my group."

At the same time, Mollie and Rafferty speak.

"Who's Chance?"

"*Chance?*"

I wince at Rafferty's bitter tone and glare coming from across the table. Anxiety pools in my tummy, and I wring my hands nervously around my cloth napkin.

Delaying looking directly at Raff for a minute, I turn to my best friend first. "How do you know about Chance?" I haven't told him about my brief interaction yet. Hell, I hadn't even decided if it was a story worth repeating.

Pax, seemingly unaware of Rafferty's shift in mood, happily relays the story, as if he's sharing a juicy bit of gossip. "He told a couple people at lunch that he asked you to the dance, but you hadn't given him an answer yet."

I think back on my conversation with Chance. Had he really *officially* asked me to the dance, or was it just a casual comment he made in passing? Looking back, I'm not totally sure of the answer. "That's not... that's not what happened," I stammer. "He asked if I was going, and I told him I didn't think so. He made some joke about being a good dance partner and if I changed my mind, I should let him know. Either way, I told him no." Finally looking at Rafferty, I repeat, "I told him *no.*"

Rafferty doesn't have to say anything. One look in his cold blue eyes tells me the damage has already been done. He's pissed and he's probably going to take it out on me.

I don't really understand why he's mad though, if I'm being honest. The mixed signals coming from him lately are giving me whiplash. Is he mad because I'm going against his so-called rules about making friends with the fellow students at Hemlock Hill, or for some *other* reason? I wish he would just use his damn words and stop with the mind games.

My heart sinks in my chest when he leans back in his chair and shrugs nonchalantly. "I think you should go with him."

There's an ache behind my sternum as I frown at him. "You do?" Him saying this is a complete one-eighty from what he had said the other day.

"Yep."

It's one word, but it hurts more than it should.

Tossing his napkin on top of his half-eaten plate of food, he stands up from the table. He steps two feet away when his father calls him back.

"I haven't excused you from the table, son," Adrian snaps over his glass of bourbon.

He looks completely calm when he turns around, but I've known Rafferty long enough to notice the little things, like the way his fingers tap his thigh in rhythmic moves or the way his muscles flex. He may look it, but he's anything but calm staring at his father.

"May I be excused, *sir*?"

Adrian's nostrils flare and his eyes narrow at Rafferty's question. The tension between them is suffocating everyone else at the table.

"You may," Adrian finally relents.

Without a word or glance back at me, Rafferty leaves the dining room.

IT'S BEEN two days since the awkward dinner, and I haven't seen Rafferty since. My dad was able to pick me up himself yesterday and spend the evening at home with me. Which is a rarity these days since he was promoted to captain.

I'm sitting under an awning in the school courtyard, eating the packed lunch my dad made for me himself after I told him about what Rafferty said about the food here, when a willowy figure appears in front of me. Looking up from the book I'm reading, I met with the bitchy redhead I've seen glaring at me since I first stepped foot on campus. Her two friends, equally as pretty, stand behind her with equally judgmental expressions on their faces.

"Uh..." I start, really confused about what they could possibly want from me. "Can I help you with something?"

Her perfectly-filled lips pull in an arrogant smirk. "With the way Rafferty's been acting since you got here, I really thought you two had a thing going on and that he'd ask *you* to the dance."

My mouth opens and closes a few times as I try to process what she's saying. It's so random and out of left field that I'm struggling to keep up. "Rafferty and I aren't a thing…" I say slowly, while closing the book on my lap.

"Well, I know that *now*." Her voice is kind of shrill. It reminds me of that old sitcom *The Nanny*. I have to bite my tongue to keep from laughing aloud at the realization. "I'm not sure what crawled up his ass the other day when he was being a douchebag to me, but since he asked *me* to the dance, I know now it wasn't because he has a thing for you."

A pit grows in my stomach and my heart aches. "Rafferty asked *you* to the winter dance?"

Why would he ask *her*? More importantly, why the fuck is he even going to the dance in the first place? He said from the beginning that he wouldn't be caught dead attending something like that.

"Yep! Just this morning." Her head tilts and the long curls of her red hair falling over her shoulder. The biggest, fakest smile splits her face. It's the most condescending look I've received since being on this campus, and that says a *lot*. "I just wanted to clear the air, you know? Just so there isn't any confusion on either side. Do you have a date yet or are you not going? I'm sure you don't feel super comfortable going since you're … the *new* kid." When she says *new* she really means '*scholarship*'.

The way her friends giggle behind her confirms my theory.

Deciding to not answer her question about attending the dance, I wave my hand, dismissing her. "Well, thanks for stopping by and letting me know about Rafferty. I'm so glad to hear he's taking a nice girl like you with him." I match her patronizing tone with one of my own.

Her fake smile falls instantly. "*Mmmhmm … yeah.* You're so welcome." With a flip of her hair, she turns her back on me and struts away. Her friends are on her heels like they're her obedient terriers.

My legs start to bounce restlessly as I ponder over this information. What is his play here? Is he making a point or just trying to make me jealous?

I don't care what his plan is. I'm not going to let him think he's won whatever weird fucking game we're playing.

Across the courtyard, I spot Chance standing at the end of one of the stone tables eating an apple. I'm contemplating waiting to talk to him when it's more private since he's currently talking with his friends, but then I spot Rafferty leaning against a wall on the other side, watching me.

Fuck it.

Leaving my belongings on the bench, I stalk across the courtyard toward the lanky blond. He smiles brightly at me when he spots me approaching, which helps settle the nerves swirling inside me.

"Hey!" he greets, swallowing his bite of apple.

Subtly, my eyes flick to where Rafferty is to make sure he's still watching me before smiling back at Chance. "So, is it too late to accept your offer about the dance?"

I won't lie, guilt bubbles in my stomach as I ask him this. I know I shouldn't be using him to … what? Get back at Rafferty? Fuck, I don't really know what I'm doing right now. What I do know is Chance is the only person who's been nice to me since I got here. It was very kind of him to offer to take me to the dance, and maybe once we get there, it'll be the best night of my life. *That's it, Posie. Twist this narrative so you feel better about your actions,* I silently chide myself.

He looks completely shocked and elated by my question. "What? I mean, you want to go to the dance now?"

Tucking my hands anxiously behind my back, I shift on my feet. "If you've already asked someone else—"

"No!" he cuts me off. "I haven't asked anyone. I was still

kinda hoping you'd change your mind. *Wow*! Okay, this is great. We're going to have so much fun together."

I can feel Rafferty's eyes on me as Chance and I exchange phone numbers. The way my skin is heating because of it is already making me regret my decision.

What have I done?

TWENTY-ONE
POSIE

I GOT a text from him as I was locking up the studio and about to start walking home.

There's a mountain of assignments waiting for me there. I've worked back-to-back shifts for the past week and have fallen behind on my schoolwork. I can't complain about the extra hours at work because I'm the one who asked for them. I had to buy new textbooks and needed to make up the money I lost on them so I can pay rent at the end of the month. And afford food.

My dad's pension is mostly going to his expensive therapies, doctors, and all the medical equipment he now needs. There really isn't much Aunt Jo can spare for me, and I understand. I'd much rather the money go toward Dad anyway. I can take care of myself. I just have to hustle and spend my time wisely to do it.

It's been over a week since the night at Rafferty's poker game and I've been picking up as many shifts as I can while Rafferty's been radio silent. I take advantage of his absence to make some money since I never know when he might be calling me away to service him.

I haven't heard a word from him since that night.

He got quiet after we were done and had rushed me out of

the building. He hadn't let me get properly dressed either. Just had me slip on his button-down and made me carry my own clothes and shoes out in my arms.

He loaded me into the same SUV that dropped me off and wordlessly closed the door once I was inside. I attempted to roll down the window to say something to him. What was I going to say, you ask? I have no freaking idea, but it felt weird leaving without saying anything after doing what we did in the dressing room. But, of course, the grouchy driver with the mustache had the windows child-locked. Rafferty stood outside the dark building as I was driven away. The look on his face was completely unreadable to me.

Which was fair because I also couldn't decide how I was feeling after our encounter. The whole ride home, while his cum dripped out of me onto the leather seat beneath me, I tried to process what I'd done. In so many ways, sleeping with Rafferty felt as familiar to me as my own touch, but in the same breath, it was like fucking a guy I'd only just met. The opposing emotions made it confusing and only left me feeling shameful that I'd allowed it to happen in the first place.

And I say "*allowed*" loosely seeing as telling Rafferty no has ceased to be a real option for me. It's a meaningless word that doesn't hold any weight with him. He's made sure of that by holding the roof over my dad's head hostage.

That's why I couldn't refuse his text ordering me to come to his house tonight. It was either I went voluntarily, or he would show up with more drugs and force me. Tired, I chose the path of least resistance.

I thought about calling Lark for a ride, but I didn't want to bring her into whatever mess I might be walking into. Instead, I tapped into the money I'd only just recouped to call an Uber. Rafferty's firehouse is over two miles from here, and I didn't feel comfortable walking that far in the dark.

The driver is still three buildings away from his house but I can already hear the music. The heavy bass line and loud voices come through the windows. When we come to a stop in front of the brick building, I spot the partygoers milling about with red SOLO cups in their hands. From the way they're all swaying and stumbling on their feet, I would bet this party has been going on for hours.

I thought he said he wasn't going to have any more parties?

With a heavy sigh, I thank the driver and climb out of the back seat of his Honda Accord. I can't decide if I'm happy that there are other people here tonight or if I wish it were just going to be us. At least with other people around, there will be witnesses if Rafferty is in an exceptionally bad mood tonight.

One thing I know for sure is I'm not dressed for a party.

If he hadn't ordered me to come right away, I would have changed out of my work clothes. I have an oversized black loose-knit sweater over the black leotard and pale pink tights I'd worn today. Before leaving the studio, I'd changed out of my flats for a pair of black combat boots to walk home in. The only makeup I have on is some mascara and blush. My hair has been up in a claw clip all day, so I'm sure it's full of kinks. In other words, I'm *not* party ready.

Arms crossed tightly to my chest, I keep my head down and make my way into the loud and overcrowded house. It was easier walking in here last time with Zadie at my side, but ever since that night, I haven't seen much of her. I was paranoid for a couple days, thinking I'd done something to make her want to avoid me, but I concluded the other day it's probably just our conflicting schedules. Or I guess, I really hope that's the case.

I've managed to still catch up with Lark on the days we both have class. It's nice being around her. She doesn't know the gritty details of my story, but at least with her, I don't have to hide it. She knows just enough for me to feel comfortable around her. Plus, having someone to confide in has been beyond nice.

Shoulders and drunken bodies bump into me as I make my

way farther into the house. Over their heads, I search for his familiar face. I don't know the reason I'm here tonight, but I'd rather just get whatever it is over with.

I spot Rome before Rafferty. The look in his brown eyes instantly has me on edge. Every other time I've been around him he's had this carefree energy about him. Tonight, he looks *concerned*. When he sees me approaching, his lips form a silent curse.

This isn't good.

Boots feeling like they're suddenly made of lead, I approach Raff's friend. "What's going on?" I search around us for signs of the man who's wreaking havoc on my head and heart, but he's nowhere to be seen.

Rome scrubs a tan hand over his face. "You probably shouldn't have shown up here tonight, baby girl. He's *on* one." Dropping his hand, he sighs. "Not that I can really blame him. Today's always a rough day for him."

"Why is it a rough day?" I question, going through all the dates of our shared bad days in my head. We're still a couple months away from it being the anniversary of the night the cops showed up at his house, and the anniversary of Mollie's death isn't till the second week of January.

Rome stares at me for a second. I can't tell if he's offended on behalf of his best friend that I don't remember what today is, or if he's surprised I've forgotten. Maybe both.

"Today is his mom's birthday."

My heart turns to ice in my chest and my stomach rolls. *How could I have forgotten this?* Every year on her birthday, all Mollie wanted was to decorate sugar cookies and watch a movie with us. The older her boys got, the less interested they were in decorating dessert, so by the time I was twelve, it would just be me and her. She never took a single bite of the cookies, but she would always lick the frosting off the spoon. The boys would show up again when we put on the movie, and they always ate all the popcorn.

I celebrated Mollie's birthday with her more than I ever did my dad's. He was always working and never made a fuss about his birthday, and that fact only makes it hurt more that I forgot.

My throat burns when I attempt to swallow the emotion building there. "Where is he?" I question. "And what about Pax? Have you seen him today?"

Rome nods. "Raff's got him in his room sleeping off the damage that he did last night. Pax was a mess when he got home this morning, which only further set off Rafferty."

"Pax has been sleeping all day?" My heart breaks for the little boy I once knew. We all tried so hard to protect him.

"More like passed out. You can't wash down your opiates with a bottle of whiskey without there being some repercussions." At my panicked expression, Rome keeps talking before I can suggest anything. "Don't worry too much. He's done it before. He'll probably sleep for another four or five hours and then be okay."

"*Okay?*" I repeat, not convinced. I didn't know Pax had turned to pills. When I saw the bottle in his hand at the last party, it was easy for me to deduce he may be drinking too much, but I never would have guessed drugs. Especially with his family's history with pills.

Rome's wide shoulders shrug under his white hoodie. "Well, whatever Pax's version of okay is. The boy's been a mess since I met him."

Feeling an immense surge of protectiveness for Pax, I snap, "You would too if you went through what he did." People think they know what happened, but they don't. No one knows the full story, and I will die making sure they never do. "Watch your fucking mouth."

Instead of Rome being angered by my outburst, he seems

impressed. His eyes flick up and down my body and the corner of his mouth curls into a smirk.

Feeling a little self-conscious, I cross my arms tighter to my chest. "*What?*

"I think I'm starting to figure out why Rafferty's been hung up on you all this time. You're kinda the whole package. Hot, but smart. Strong, but submissive. Hell, if Rafferty wouldn't chop my balls off with a rusty axe, I might even make a play for you."

I scowl at him and choose to ignore the flirty bits of his comment, focusing only on the first part. "Rafferty isn't hung up on me. He *hates* me."

"I'm a firm believer you have to first care about someone to truly hate them."

"You sound like Lark."

This has him grinning. "She's a very smart woman. Maybe you should listen to her."

Interesting.

Someone screams joyfully in the living room, bringing me back to the real issue at hand. Pressing my fingers to my temple to alleviate the headache growing there, I sigh. "Do you know what I'm doing here? Or why he's even having a party?"

"I don't know," Rome answers truthfully, the worried look from before returning to his angled features. "Maybe he thinks if it's loud enough, he won't be able to hear his own thoughts. If that doesn't work for him, the amount of alcohol he's had might do the trick."

"So, what you're telling me is not only do I have to deal with an angry and grieving Rafferty, but also a *drunk* Rafferty."

"That is correct."

My headache intensifies. "*Fuck.*"

"I told you that you shouldn't have come here."

I throw my hands up and point at the collar around my throat. "It's not like I had much of a choice."

"You're absolutely right about that." Completely unsympathetic to my current situation, Rome snags a beer out of the bucket behind him on the kitchen counter and pops the tab. He takes a long swig before handing the can off to me. "To take the edge off."

I look between him and the offered drink with a frown. "No, thank you. The last time I drank something here I was drugged, and I'd like to avoid waking up on top of a grave again if I can." *I'm just going to add that to the list of things I never thought would come out of my mouth.*

"That's fair," Rome offers as a loud voice comes from behind me.

"Well, if it isn't my favorite liar."

Turning, I find Raff leaning against the kitchen doorway with a bottle of scotch in his hand. It gives me déjà vu of Pax from a few weekends ago. His blue eyes are glassy and a little red. He sways on his feet when he pushes away from the door hinge. The laces of his well-loved boots are undone, and I worry for a moment that he'll trip over them.

But those things aren't what have my hands sweating and dread snaking down my spine. It's the length of chain currently hanging over his shoulders like a scarf. On either end of the four-foot-long chain are leather cuffs. I don't have to waste my breath wondering who will be wearing those.

"What took you so long to get here?" he questions.

Dragging my attention away from the small padlocks on each of the cuffs, I scowl at his question. "I got here as soon as I could. I had to wait for an Uber since I don't have a car."

His fingers snap. "That's right! And you can't very well borrow your dad's either since his is now nothing but scrap metal. That's what happens to a car when it's hit by a semitruck, right?"

My muscles turn into rigid pieces of stone beneath my skin and fury bubbles in my chest. "Don't talk about my father," I snap, loud enough that the people lingering around us turn their heads. The last thing I want is to draw attention to this conversation, but Rafferty isn't giving me a choice.

Taking another long drink from the bottle in his hand, he prowls closer to me. "I'd ask if he's planning on purchasing a new one, but if he can't even remember who the fuck you are, he probably shouldn't be behind the wheel." Once he's close enough, he reaches out to skim his fingers down my face. It takes everything in me to not slap his hand away. "That's what he gets for trying to be a hero."

This has me jerking out of his reach. How *dare* he say that? "My dad *is* a hero."

His entire career was dedicated to helping people, and he got hurt trying to do just that. He was on his way home from a statewide law enforcement conference when he passed a car that was flipped on the side of the road. It had only happened minutes before he got there, and he was the first on the scene. There were small children in the back and a young mother pinned in the front seat. The doors were too bent for Dad to open them, and he'd run back to his vehicle to call in the accident. The driver of the semitruck going twenty miles over the speed limit didn't see my dad's car before it was too late. It slammed into it with my dad sitting in the driver's seat. Dad's car became an unrecognizable ball of metal.

"You Davenports are always fucking trying to *save* people. Look how well that's worked out for the both of you. For his efforts, Daddy Davenport ended up with brain damage, and you... Well, you don't help people, do you? Not really. You just kill them." His rage and hatred drip from each of his words like poison. "Just ask my mom. Oh wait, we can't because she was one of your casualties."

The silence that falls over the party is deafening. My skin runs cold as thirty pairs of eyes stare at me in horror. One sentence is all it's taken for me to become the campus pariah. After tonight, I won't be able to walk to class without the looks

I'm getting now. I'll be followed by a chorus of whispers everywhere I go. *There she is! She's the one who killed Rafferty and Paxton Wilde's mother.* And I'll have to grit my teeth and take the gossip because I can never set the record straight. Rafferty has once again fucked me, but this time it's in a completely different way.

Out of the corner of my eye, Rome slips out of the room through the other kitchen entrance. I wonder if he didn't want to watch this train wreck?

"Rafferty…" There are a hundred things I want to tell him, but a thousand things I can't. The saddest part in all of this is if he'd just look past his rage, he could discover the truth himself.

"Give me your wrist," he orders, cutting me off. Not that I really have anything else to say to him. An apology is the last thing he'd ever want to hear from me because there's only so much damage the words *"I'm sorry"* can fix. We're so far beyond that, it's not even in our rearview mirror anymore.

I hold my breath and clench my teeth to keep from releasing the sob building in my chest. The physical things he demands from me are tolerable. He wants me to be his whore and wear his goddamn collar? Fine, I can do that, but the emotional warfare might just kill me.

Holding my arm out for him, he wraps the brown leather around my wrist and locks it in place. Not bothering with the other side, he turns, and as if I'm a dog on a leash, he drags me out of the kitchen and into the living room. People wisely jump out of his warpath. Rafferty's current state isn't one they should fuck with.

He reaches the brass fireman's pole and stops. Roughly yanking me closer to it, he wraps the chain around it and reaches for my free wrist.

Panic builds as realization hits. My attempts to pull away from him are futile, and with little effort on his part, he's got the other cuff on my wrist, and I'm officially shackled to the pole.

The leather is tight on my arm and no matter how hard I pull against it, I can't slip through it. I will be stuck here until Rafferty decides otherwise.

Moving away, he leans on the back of the leather couch directly in front of me. "You used to take pole dancing class from your friend Ophelia in New York, didn't you?"

It shouldn't surprise me Raff had been keeping an eye on me while I was away. The fact he knows about the classes Ophelia taught tells me he was keeping *very* close tabs. I met Lia at a coffee shop totally randomly and we got to talking about what we did. She was a student at NYU but taught these classes on the side for extra cash. We bonded over our respective dances and the fact we were both from Washington. We hung out occasionally and she let me join the classes for free. I liked what a good workout they were, and it was a nice break from the stricter dance I was accustomed to.

"Yes, I did," I answer.

His strong arms cross. "Dance for me." Turning his head back and forth, he takes in the rest of the people watching me with curiosity. "For us. Dance for us."

"I can't."

"You can. The chain is long enough for you to move."

He's right, I could probably do a few moves before running out of slack or getting caught up. "Yeah, I know. That's not the problem. I can't do it while wearing *tights* and a *sweater*," I correct through gritted teeth. "I wouldn't be able to get a good grip on the pole."

Grinning, he reaches into his jeans and retrieves his pocketknife. It looks like the same one he had all those years ago. "I can fix that."

Returning to stand in front of me, he takes the neck of my beloved sweater in his fist and cuts down the front of it. Once he's made a big enough cut, he's able to tear the rest off my body. He tosses the ripped fabric on the floor before squatting in front of me.

My breath hitches when he pulls on the pink fabric at the apex of my thigh. Doing my best to not flinch or move to avoid being cut, he runs the blade down the front of both of my legs.

"Take off your boots."

Once I've toed them off, he cuts the tights down to my ankles. He rips and slashes the thin fabric until he's able to pull them completely off.

I stand before him and a roomful of strangers in nothing but my spaghetti-strap leotard. Seeing as the last time I was with him, Rafferty had me dressed in that leather outfit, I shouldn't be embarrassed now since this is far less revealing. The difference is, at poker night I wasn't half naked in front of my fellow class-mates. I will have to spend the next year and a half with these people doing group projects and presentations.

"No more excuses. Dance."

I glare at him, my pulse pounding in my ears and my skin growing hot with anger. His nostrils flare when I remain in place. Then he does something I never would have expected him to do. He pulls a gun from the waistband of his jeans. With no hesita-tion, he marches forward and presses the barrel of it to my forehead.

Why the hell does he have a gun?

My heart seizes in my chest, and for a moment, I forget how to breathe. On their own accord, like they can't bear to see him like this, my eyes squeeze shut. Adrenaline shoots violently through my veins, making my limbs shake.

The people who had become our pseudo-audience scream and shout, the sounds of their feet against the floors as they run for the doors fill my ears. A smart move on their part, because I always knew Rafferty was a wildcard, but I never would have considered him to be unhinged. Right now, that's exactly what he is. He's blinded by his sadness and anger and not thinking this through. The booze in his system also isn't helping matters.

I yearn to be the girl that could once calm him down, but now I'm the very reason for his violence.

"Do you really want to kill me, Rafferty?" I question. Opening my eyes, I discover we're completely alone. All witnesses have left me to face this by myself. I don't know what his plan is, but I don't intend on giving him the satisfaction of seeing me scared if that's what he's craving. "Will me being gone finally bring you peace?"

"I want you to feel every agonizing moment my mom felt those few weeks. She always felt everything more deeply than us. She couldn't handle the scrutinization and shame. I want you to feel as defeated and hopeless as she did before getting into that fucking bathtub."

The awful image of Mollie submerged underwater comes to me. I never saw it myself because I was already at the school in Massachusetts when it happened, but the picture I've created in my head feels as if I had been. Even if I had been brave enough to face Rafferty, my father told me it wasn't smart for me to come back for the funeral. I knew he was right, but it hurt all the same.

"I never wanted that to happen," I choke out, my voice more even than it probably should be. "I wanted to protect you."

"I'm so fucking tired of hearing you say that." The gun presses harder to my face and my whole body flinches. "I didn't need you to protect me. I was fine."

Swallowing hard, I lift my chin and meet his eyes. "Show me the scars on your back and tell me you didn't need help." The first time I saw them, my heart shattered for him. He tried to brush the matter under the rug like it wasn't happening, but it was all I could think about. I was blinded with rage. That emotion hasn't lessened any over the years. I'm as angry for

Rafferty now as I was then. "Show me the scars that he left on your skin for no reason at all and tell me you were fine."

"As long as my mom and Pax were safe, I could take it." He stumbles back a step, still unstable on his feet. The pressure of the gun lessens. "I had to protect them from him."

The tears that have been building in my eyes fall down my face in hot streams. "And I had to protect you."

For the first time since we reunited, the walls wrapped with barbed wire he'd built around himself drop, and I'm staring at the boy I fell in love with. He looks at me like he's finally seeing me and not the enemy I'd been forced to become. The only way I can describe the sensation that overtakes me is it's like returning home after being away for too long.

I'm not sure how long we stand there staring at each other. It could have been just seconds or it could have been minutes; I've lost all sense of time.

It's Rafferty that breaks the silence. Shifting the gun, he repositions it on the center of my forehead and asks a question that physically hurts my heart. "Do you hate me yet, Butterfly?"

"No." My answer is a barely audible hoarse whisper.

"Why not?"

"Because when I still look at you, I still see the boy who stole my first kiss and danced with me in the rain."

That's what finally has him dropping the weapon. As if I shoved him in the chest, he staggers back a step with the gun at his side. The distressed look on his face has me wanting to wrap my arms around his middle. His hand shoves through his slightly wavy hair, forcing the strands off his forehead. He turns away from me, still holding his head in his hand.

"Rafferty... Please look at me." My soft plea doesn't work, but the loud, fast-moving footsteps coming down the stairs does.

We both turn and look at Rome who stands at the base of the staircase with a troubled expression.

"What?" Rafferty manages to ask.

"Pax isn't here. I've checked the whole house."

Like a switch being flipped, the walls fall back into place around him, and the rigidity returns to Rafferty's muscles. Whatever breakthrough I'd just had with him is gone in a blink of an eye.

"*Fuck!*" he roars, already storming toward the front door. Whatever drunken state he had seemed to be in just moments before now vanishes with the knowledge Pax might be in trouble.

I attempt to follow, momentarily forgetting about the chains around my wrists. "Let me go with you. I can help look for him." It's been too long since I was properly there for Pax. "I need to do this. I *need* to help him, Raff."

Rafferty glares at me over his shoulder as he shoves the gun back into his waistband. "You've done enough to him."

Rome goes out the door first and Rafferty slams it behind him. Not knowing what else I can do, I slump to the floor in defeat.

RAFFERTY WAS RIGHT. They turned the school gym into a winter wonderland. There is fake snow covering the edges of the room and the tables are set up with drinks and snacks. Snowflakes of different shapes and sizes hang from the ceiling with about a million strands of string lights. If you didn't know any better, you would never know this is where the basketball team practices. I have to hand it to the dance committee. They did an amazing job.

"I can't get over how amazing you look," Chance says, looping his arm through mine as we walk farther into the room.

My palm smooths down the front of the velvet emerald-colored dress Mollie had helped me pick out. It has a high halter neck with a slit up the leg. I fell in love with it the second Mollie found it. She was so excited to go shopping with me for a dress. She'd made a whole day of it. We went into every store at the mall that sold formal dresses, and then went to three more stores to search for the perfect pair of heels. When I told her I didn't feel right about her spending so much money on a dress for me, she waved me off.

"You deserve to be spoiled, P," she told me with a soft smile.

It'd been a really long time since I'd seen her that energized. It was nice.

"Thank you," I tell Chance.

He's been wonderful tonight. When he told me we wouldn't be going to dinner with one of the big groups of people, I was relieved. He's a year older than me and has his license. He picked me up in his father's fancy Lexus and drove us to a restaurant overlooking the sound. Even though I'd been anxious about this night for the many weeks leading up to it, I found myself really enjoying Chance's company.

He's funny in a dorky kind of way and he hasn't once made me feel bad about being at Hemlock on a scholarship. He asks me questions like he genuinely wants to get to know me and seems interested in what I have to say.

In theory, it should be the perfect night, but still, there's a twinge in my stomach.

Rafferty has barely talked to me since he asked Hannah to the dance, and I hate how much bigger the rift between us has grown. His blacked-out G-Wagen was delivered two weeks ago, and on the days I go home with them from school, I can see his icy glare in the rearview mirror. He's never given any indication he wanted to go with me to the dance, but standing under these sparkly lights, I can't help but wish it were Rafferty at my side and not Chance. Which is *so stupid.*

Chance has made every effort to be here with me and is clearly interested in me. I shouldn't be pining over a moody, egotistical *douchebag* who's done nothing but play games with my head. And heart.

I need to get over this stupid crush before it causes some real psychiatric damage.

Spotting Paxton across the room, I tug on Chance's arm. "I'll be right back. I want to go say hi to Pax."

"Okay, I'll get us some punch."

"Great!" With a quick smile at my date, I weave across the gym toward my best friend.

On top of Rafferty being a righteous prick the past three or four weeks, Pax has also been off. He's been a little withdrawn and more quiet than normal. I thought it was just me who picked up on it, but I've seen Mollie looking at him with concern multiple times. I've tried to talk to him about it, and all he tells me is he hasn't been sleeping well. Which is something I know to be true. On a handful of occasions, he's shown up in my room when I've spent the night and asked if he could sleep with me. He hasn't said it, but I think he's having nightmares. He curls up next to me and I hold his hand until he falls asleep.

I just wish he'd talk to me about it. He knows I'm always there to help him.

Pax smiles at me when he sees me approaching, but it doesn't really reach his eyes. He lets go of Sadie's hand and wraps his arms around me once I'm close enough. "You look very pretty, P," he tells me in my ear, making me smile so hard it hurts.

Pulling back a little so I can see him, I hold his cheeks between my hands. I examine his face, hoping I can see the reason for his personality change hidden somewhere. "You do too," I tell him. "How was dinner?"

He looks at Sadie, who still stands close by in her pretty cream-colored dress. "So good. Sadie's mom is so talented."

Like a typical kid unimpressed with their parents, Sadie rolls her eyes. "She has an entire kitchen full of staff. It's not *just* her."

"Well, either way, I hope I get to try it one day." The only way I'm ever eating there is if the Blackwells want to go. Dad has the palate of a seven-year-old and wouldn't be caught dead going to a fancy French restaurant in the city. He'd gladly take me to get a burger and fries, which is always a good time. We always eat in his car with the music playing. He gives me a hard time for picking the tomatoes off my burger and I tease him for dipping his fries in his strawberry shake. It's been that way since I can remember. It's almost like a tradition. "Okay, I better get back to Chance." Leaning up on my tiptoes, I kiss Pax's cheek. "Save me a dance?"

"Always."

Smiling at the pair, I give them a quick wave before heading back to my date. He's waiting right where I left him with two cups of dark pink punch in his hands. He looks good in his tux with his matching dark green tie. I had no idea he planned on color-coordinating with my dress. It's something he did completely on his own.

"Here you go," he tells me, handing off one of the cups. "No one has spiked the punch bowl yet, but it's only a matter of time."

"Okay, great." I'm not that into drinking. The only time I've gotten drunk was at a party Rafferty threw last summer when his parents were out of town. He'd laughed at me the next morning when I was green around the gills.

He clinks his glass against mine and I take a sip. Restlessly, I shift on my heels. Not wanting to stand awkwardly on the outskirts of the room all night, I turn to Chance. "Want to dance? I remember you saying something about being an excellent dance partner."

For the first time tonight, he looks nervous. "I think I may have oversold my dancing ability," he says as he sheepishly rubs the back of his neck. "I said that to you before I learned you were on track to becoming a prima ballerina."

The best chance of that happening is if I get into the boarding school in Massachusetts. I still haven't heard anything from them regarding my application status. Once I'm there, the dream of Juilliard becomes more of a reality.

Taking his drink from him, I place it on a nearby table before taking his hand in mine. "Come on, this isn't really dancing. You just have to kind of sway in a circle and try not to step on my toes. You can do that, right?"

"Okay…" he relents, allowing me to pull him with me. "But I make no promises about not stepping on your toes."

There are lights above us that are shining a blueish color onto the dance floor and another light that casts spinning snowflakes on the ground. They both help to conceal the basketball court beneath our feet.

Showing Chance where to put his hands on my waist, I place mine on his shoulders and slowly set the tempo. He catches on quickly and begins to move in slow graceful circles. It's nice but being this close to him doesn't make me feel … anything. My skin doesn't grow warm from his touch, and there are no butter-flies in my stomach.

Closing my eyes, I try to force myself to enjoy it more, to *feel* something for him. I've never kissed a boy, but I wonder if I let him kiss me if I'd feel a spark then. Do I really want to waste my first kiss to test a theory, though? Not really. I guess I'm more of a romantic and want my first kiss to mean something.

Chance is a good guy, but I don't see how this could go past a friendship. I'm trying to figure out how I'll have that conversa-tion with him when my eyes crack open and immediately land on a pair of icy blue ones.

Leaning against a wall partially hidden by the long hanging pieces of white and blue tulle, Rafferty stands alone, his redheaded date nowhere to be found. While the rest of the guys are wearing suits and tuxedos, Rafferty wears a white button-down shirt with the top buttons undone and the sleeves rolled up his forearms and a pair of black pants. He hardly put any effort into his wardrobe or his wavy hair, but he still looks better than all of them. He stares at me with his stony mask firmly in place while he brings a silver flask to his lips.

One look at him has my heart rate picking up. The muscle pounds against my rib cage, demanding I feel what Raff does to me. My lips pull in a shadow of a smile in greeting, but it's only met with a deepening scowl.

Chance, feeling me shifting restlessly against him, moves his hands down to my hips. His fingers are basically touching my butt. It's a move that doesn't go unnoticed by Rafferty. If looks could kill, both Chance and I would be dead on this dance floor. There's murder in those cold blue orbs.

I don't realize I'm moving until I've stepped completely out of Chance's embrace, and I stand several feet away from him. The blond frowns at me, confused by my sudden retreat. I wish I had an answer for him, but I'm just as lost as he is.

"Are you okay?"

Over his shoulder, I watch as Rafferty ducks through the tulle and weaves through the impressive dessert tables. He doesn't slow down or look back as he walks through the double doors of the gym.

"Yeah…" I answer, nibbling on my bottom lip. "Yeah, I'm good. I think I just need some air."

Chance looks around for the exit and reaches out to me to guide me toward it. "I'll take you outside."

I step back farther to avoid his outreached hand. "No, it's okay. I'll only be a minute." Turning around, I leave him before he can offer to come with me again. When I get back, I'm going to need to apologize profusely for ditching him like that.

Pushing through the same doors Rafferty had disappeared through, I take off in a run after him. *Why are you doing this?* I ask myself as the sound of my heels echoes through the empty hallway. It's a silly and pointless question since I already know the answer.

It would just be better for me if I didn't.

TWENTY-THREE
RAFFERTY
SIXTEEN YEARS OLD

THE SCHOOL'S doors I'd just come through fly open again with so much force the metal handle slams into the stone building. The sound of my name being called quickly follows, but I don't turn around to look at her.

"Rafferty."

Her voice carries over the sound of the rain hitting the metal awning above us and cement ground in the parking lot. The gym has a separate entrance connected to the back parking lot I'd parked in. I'd hoped for a clean exit, but apparently that won't be happening for me since she followed me out here.

Her heels click on the walkway as she moves closer to where I stand. Sighing deeply, I throw my head back in frustration. My breath makes a plume of smoke in front of my face when I exhale. I wish it was real smoke, but I ran out of the cigarettes I stole from my dad. He hasn't figured out I've been helping myself to the stash he keeps in his home office desk. I could get them elsewhere, but there's something fun about stealing from him.

"Rafferty," Posie repeats like an incessant broken record.

Turning in a slow and lazy manner, I finally face her.

I'm irrationally angry about how good she looks. It was never a question of Posie Davenport being pretty, but tonight she's downright stunning. Her hair, which has a few new blonde highlights thanks to my mom's salon day idea, is tied up with tendrils framing her face. The combination of her green dress and her makeup has her soft brown eyes appearing lighter. The high-necked dress accentuates every curve I didn't know she had. There's a slit up the side and, well, that's just the cherry on top.

"What are you doing out here?" I question tersely. "Where's your *date*? I'm sure he misses you."

Her bare arms fold tightly in front of her, and she scowls at me. "Where's your date? I haven't heard her voice all night. Did you put a muzzle on her?" Posie dramatically looks around me as if Hannah is going to magically appear at my side.

"There was no need to go that far. I just left her at the restaurant." We didn't make it through the appetizers before I was standing from the table and walking out the door without her. Asking Hannah to the dance was an impulse decision fueled by anger and a whole lot of jealousy. The ironic part about the latter emotion is I didn't realize that's what I had been feeling until tonight when I saw Chance slow dancing with Posie.

The personal discovery was so unsettling I decided I needed to leave. Had I not lingered in the shadows as long as I had, I could have slipped away before she knew I was there. Instead, I watched long enough for her to spot me. She's always had an uncanny ability to find me in a crowd.

"You just *left* her there?"

"She makes terrible company." Entirely apathetic to the whole situation, I shrug my shoulders. "Unlike your date, it seems. You guys looked like you were having a great time. He just can't seem to keep his hands off you."

"We were just dancing."

"Is that why he was touching your ass then?"

Her mouth opens and closes multiple times like she's trying to find her words. Giving up, she throws her hands in the air in frustration. "I don't understand you, and every time I try to, I'm left more confused. For as long as I can remember, you've kept me at arm's length, but the second I step foot in this school, you pee a circle around me. You tell me I should go to the dance with Chance, and when I accept his offer, you look at me like you hate me for doing so. You kept saying that you had no interest in coming tonight, but then you go and ask *Hannah*, and then you *leave* her at the restaurant."

All the years we spent with Posie were mostly at our house. We never went to the same schools and or had the same extracurricular activities. No matter what she might think, I always did like when her attention was on me even if I didn't show it. Growing up, the only person I ever had to share her with was Pax. When she walked in the front doors of Hemlock Hill and everyone's eyes turned on her, I didn't *like* it. Then, the dumb cocksucker Fitzgibbons started to flirt with her, and I fucking *hated* it. It became clear I was going to need to do something to stop it. My plan was working until Chance got ballsy and asked her to the dance.

I have no idea how to admit this to her, so I continue with my impassive facade. "Was there a question in there somewhere?"

Her eyes light up with anger and irritation. "Yes, *multiple!*"

"Would you mind narrowing it down?"

"Why must you always be such an asshole?"

I cock my head at her. "Was that the question you wanted answered?"

Her lips are pressed into a straight line, and she stares at me through narrowed eyes.

Wanting this interaction to be over before we both say things we might regret, I step back. "Okay, if we're just going to have a fucking staring contest..."

She cuts me off. "Why did you ask Hannah to the dance?"

173

"Why did I ask her? Did you really just ask me that?" My voice starts to raise as my anger bubbles closer to the surface. "Why did you agree to go with *Chance*?"

She doesn't hesitate even a second before answering. "Because you asked Hannah!" Her blunt honesty has me jerking back. "And you fucking told me to, *remember*?"

Of course, I remember. That was the same night my dad laid into me for being *'disrespectful'* to him. Later, when I couldn't sleep, I thought more about Posie and Chance than about what my dad had done. The stuff with my dad has been going on since I was old enough to realize what an absolute piece of garbage he is. He likes when people fear him. That's probably why he latched on to my mom. The second I stopped finding him scary and started talking back to him is when it all started. As long as he doesn't take his rage out on my brother or Mom, I can handle the belt. The situation with Posie and Chance was new, and I didn't know how to handle it. That's why I stayed up thinking about it.

"I didn't think you'd actually go through with it!" I bite back.

This has her brows drawing together. "Why not? Because of your little rule about staying away from everyone?"

"No, because I didn't think you liked him enough to go with him."

"I don't!" she yells at me, the frustration she's feeling getting the better of her. "And it's so fucking stupid because he's actually a great guy but I don't feel *anything* for him! I *can't* because I'm still hung up on *you*; a guy who has given me nothing but mixed signals and emotional whiplash!"

I freeze in place and the world around us seems to grow quiet.

"You don't mean that," I tell her, not fully believing what I'm hearing. While I've been so busy being confused and frustrated by my own ... *feelings*... has Posie been secretly hiding her own? Or have I just been blind to them the whole time?

She assumes I'm talking about the wrong thing. "Yes, I absolutely do. If you keep this hot and cold bullshit up, I'm going to end up in therapy, and I *will* be sending you my bills."

"No, not that part," I correct, shaking my head at her. "You said you're hung up on me."

Her arms cross in front of her again like she's trying to put a boundary between us as the tips of her cheekbones grow pink. "You probably think I'm sad and pathetic, don't you? I mean, it's ridiculous how long I've liked you, but you started calling me butterfly and I just haven't been able to shake it since."

She was barely seven years old when I started calling her that. That means for almost a decade, while I was struggling to understand how I felt about her, she was feeling a similar way? How could I have missed it?

At my silence, Posie shrinks back a step or two and rubs her temple like our conversation has given her a headache. "I'm sorry, I didn't mean to unload all this. It was not my plan. You were just standing there watching me dance, and the look on your face... it looked like you hated me, but a little piece of me hoped that it may have been because you were jealous. I guess I just finally needed to know which it was..." she trails off awkwardly, eyes looking between me and her shoes.

At my lack of response, she sighs in exhausted defeat. With her head down, she pushes past me and moves in the opposite direction of the building. Stepping out from under the awning we've been standing under, she walks into the rain.

"Posie!" I call, running after her. The rain is freezing and instantly soaks through my white button-down shirt. I can't imagine how cold it feels on her bare arms. "Posie, wait."

She whirls around. With the water running down her face, I can't tell if she's crying or not, but something in my gut tells me she is. "Why are you even here, Raff? You abandoned your date, so it's not like you're here to rub her in my face," she asks.

I've been lying about how I feel about her for so long, that being honest doesn't come easily. But I find a sense of freedom when I finally tell her the truth. "I'm here for you."

"*Why?*"

I stalk toward her, and once she's in reach, I grab the sides of her small face and thread my fingers through her hair. "Because I don't hate you."

Her entire body stiffens as my mouth collides with hers. She gasps against my lips and, out of instinct, tries to pull away. It's as if it takes both her mind and body a moment to figure out what's happening, and when they finally do, Posie melts into me. Her movements are timid and unsure, but I gently coax her with my own and she soon catches on. Knowing I've just stolen her first kiss pleases something inside me.

The cold rain falls on us, soaking our clothes, but I can't feel it. I'm lost in the feeling of her lips on mine and her tentative hands exploring my chest and arms. You don't know just how hard you're fighting something until you finally give in. There is peace in surrender. The weight I'd unknowingly been carrying around for years lifted the second she started to kiss me back, and a calm I've never known wrapped around me like a blanket.

I kiss her deeply once more before pulling back so I can look down at her. The smile that is on her face could break hearts and knowing that I'm the reason for it… Well, I don't know how to describe how that makes me feel. The makeup that had been perfectly done around her eyes is running down her cheeks from the rain, and the loose pieces of hair around her face are sticking to her forehead and cheeks. She's never looked more beautiful.

Lips skimming against her temple, I breathe her in before pressing my forehead to hers. Her hands hold my sides, her fingers curling into the wet fabric.

"I'm not good at this, Butterfly. Emotions and feelings… They're not where I excel." This feels like an understatement since it took me years to figure out what it was I was feeling toward her. "I'm going to mess up. Just promise you'll be patient with me."

Reaching up, her thumb swipes across my bottom lip, wiping away the raindrops that have collected on my skin before kissing me softly. "I promise," Posie whispers when she pulls back.

In the distance, I can hear faint music coming from inside the gym. "Can I have this dance?"

In the freezing rain in a dark parking lot with only our combined heartbeats as music, Posie dances with me.

TWENTY-FOUR
RAFFERTY

THE ALCOHOL I'd been drinking all day like my very being depended on it has long turned sour in my stomach. The headache that's building feels like someone is stepping on my skull. All I want to do is sleep off how terrible the last sixteen hours have been, but I can't focus on my needs right now. I have to prioritize my brother.

It took five hours for us to find him. We searched all the usual places and hit up all the people that we could think of. It was when we were about to do our twentieth lap around the city that Rome's cousin, Vinny, finally woke up from his oxy-induced nap and saw our missed calls. He's a dealer and way worse off than Pax is. My brother is in the throes of addiction, but I have to believe he's not too far gone. I can still pull him back from the edge before he drowns in the pills.

It is my fucking *job* to make sure what happened to my mom never happens to Pax. I will die for my brother before I let his dependence on pills pull him under like it did her. It's a slippery slope and we both saw how one too many can cause irreversible damages.

"Pax, you have to help me out," I grunt as I lug my brother

through the front door of my house. This would be easier with another person, but Rome had to stay behind at his cousin's and wait for his uncle to show up. I wasn't going to wait around with him to see how an Italian mobster deals with his druggie son. I had my own addict to deal with and I needed to get him home.

Pax's legs give out from under him, and I almost lose my grip on him. Repositioning my shoulder underneath his arm, I manage to get him into the living room.

At the sound of our approach, Posie, who had fallen asleep leaning against the pole I chained her to, opens her eyes. It takes her a second to figure out what she's staring at, but when she does, her face loses color and she springs to her feet.

"Oh my god, is he okay?" She tries to get closer, but the leather cuffs on her wrists stop her from getting more than three feet.

"Does he fucking look okay?" I snap cruelly at her. How dare she ask that? She is the reason his mom accidentally overdosed on pills and is now dependent on them himself. This is *all* her fault.

At the sound of Posie's voice, Pax's head rolls toward it as if he's seeking her out. Even in this condition, his connection to her still stands. Posie sees this and pulls on her restraints again. "Let me go so I can help you get him upstairs."

"How many times do I have to say—"

She cuts me off, her voice rising overtop of mine. "*Fuck*, Rafferty! *I get it.* You don't want my help, but right now you *need* it. You barely got him through the front door, how do you plan on getting him up those stairs without him falling and cracking his head?"

I hate that she's right.

Choosing my brother's safety over my revenge, I reach into my jeans pocket and retrieve the small key. It makes a *tinging* sound when it hits the floor in front of her. Not waiting for her to free herself, I use the time to move Pax closer to the base of the stairs. While this house has been renovated and modernized, the stairs are original and steep as shit. Pax is smaller than me, but we're both tall fuckers. Carrying him up them is going to be a bitch.

Posie, free of her chains, appears at my brother's other side. His glassy eyes crack open when she touches his face and whispers, "*Pax.*"

I can only describe the sound that comes from him when he realizes who's standing there as a choked sob.

"*P...*" he slurs, his jaw wobbling.

Something deep inside me aches watching this. I haven't seen him cry since our mom's funeral, but one look at his long-lost best friend has him breaking.

She rubs her thumb over his cheekbone where a bruise is starting to form. I don't have the slightest clue how he got hurt tonight, and I doubt he'll be able to remember himself.

"It's okay," she tells him softly. "We've got you. You're safe."

His head rolls farther toward her and he presses his forehead to hers. I'm not sure if it was his goal as he has little to no control over his body right now. Nonetheless, that's where he ends up and Posie leans into it. She holds his face in her hand, her thumb wiping away each of the tears that fall from his hooded eyes.

"*P...*" he chokes again.

"Shh... I'm here," she soothes gently. "Come on, let's get you upstairs."

She looks at me and nods her head once, signaling that she's ready.

It's slow, strenuous work but we manage to get him up to the first landing of the curved staircase before his bones turn to Jell-O again. He slips from both of our grasps and collapses on the small landing. He slumps awkwardly in the corner where the walls meet. His legs are bent at odd angles beneath him. His short dark hair is greasy and standing straight up on his head and there's dried blood around one of the black hoops in his bottom lip, like he'd accidentally pulled on it.

Dropping to her knees beside him, Posie tries to pull him away from the wall so we can get him up again, but he's dead weight right now.

"Pax, focus. You have to help us get you up so we can get you into bed," she tries.

He manages to fully open his eyes and look at her, but I don't know if he's really *seeing* Posie. "I'm sorry," he hoarsely tells her.

"You have nothing to apologize for," she reassures him and grabs his tattooed hand in hers. "Absolutely *nothing*."

His head moves in jerky moves. "That's not true. This is my fault. *I* did this. I'm sorry."

"None of this is your fault. I promise," she insists. Her honey gaze flicks to me, but she can't retain eye contact for long. "Raff, help me get him up."

"Yeah, because your promises are worth so much," I comment under my breath.

She doesn't look at me as she snaps, "*Honestly*, Rafferty. Can you shut the fuck up for once? If you haven't noticed, now is not the time. I promise you can continue to take it out on me at a later date."

Teeth grinding to keep from arguing, I bend down and haul my brother off the ground. He sways on his unsteady legs out of my hold, and Posie jumps in front of him before he can topple down the stairs we'd just gotten him up. My heart lodges in my throat when his heavy weight has her smaller frame stumbling back. Her hands are on his chest, trying to keep him from falling forward, but in doing so she jeopardizes her own safety.

Pulling my brother back by the collar of his shirt, and without thinking about it, I'm reaching for her with my free hand. She reaches out for me at the same time. Her fingers intertwine with mine and I pull her upright. My whole body breaks out in a cold sweat as fear grips me at the thought of her falling. I don't breathe again until she regains her balance once more.

A little pale, Posie stares at me and then at our joined hands. The swarm of conflicting emotions I'm experiencing are reflected in her eyes. I used to dream of Posie's demise, my fury at her making me believe that it would be a joyous event to witness. Now, as the icy fear eases its grip on my chest, I'm wondering if I may have been wrong.

It's Posie who lets go first. She returns all her attention to my brother. I shake my head, trying to clear it of these unwanted thoughts and do the same.

I wrap my arm around my brother again and Posie mirrors this move on his other side. Aside from incoherent mumbling from Pax, we work in complete silence until we reach his room. The brick walls are covered in various pictures he's sketched over the years. He always used to excel in the elective art classes at Hemlock Hill. His artistic side was always something my mom loved and my dad merely tolerated. After everything happened and Pax grew quiet, he began to draw more.

We get him to the king-sized platform bed that's been pushed into the middle of the spacious room for some reason, and as gracefully as we can, drop him onto the mattress. He lands halfway onto his stomach and side, his knees bent up toward his chest.

Posie kneels beside the bed and continues to lightly trace her fingers over his face while he comes in and out consciousness.

"Will you stay with me?" he mumbles partially into his black pillowcase. "Like you used to?"

She pulls in a breath, preparing to answer, but whatever is on the tip of her tongue ceases when she looks at me.

My arms cross in front of me and I stare down at her through narrowed eyes. "She can't, Pax." I can't let him get close to her again. He won't survive it if something else happens with her, and I don't trust her to not betray us again. "She has to leave."

Posie stares at me with an expression I can't quite decipher before leaning forward to press a kiss to Pax's temple. "He's right, I can't stay here."

Pax repeats the same thing he told her on the stairs multiple times, "I'm so sorry, P."

Her breath catches like she's trying not to cry as her chin bows to her chest. When she lifts her head again after a quiet moment, her light brown eyes are shiny with unshed tears. "You never have to apologize to me, Pax. I'm okay, and you've done *nothing* wrong."

"You're right, he hasn't. This is all on you. You're the reason he's like this," I tell her coldly.

She doesn't try to argue this, but *Pax* does. "*No*, that's not true. Don't say that to—"

Posie cups his face and stiffly shakes her head, cutting off whatever else he was going to say.. "It's okay. He can blame me." She reaches over him and grabs the balled-up blanket. Silently, she puts it over him before kissing his forehead one more time and standing up. "Just get some sleep. You always feel better in the morning."

She wipes her face and leaves the room without another word. Pax is asleep before she closes the door behind her.

Something about their whole interaction tonight isn't sitting right. There's a nagging feeling in the back of my head I can't shake. Just the fact that my brother cried tonight seeing her speaks volumes to me, and that's why I storm out the door after her.

TWENTY-FIVE
RAFFERTY

POSIE'S already at the bottom of the stairs before I reach the staircase. She's moving like the building is on fire and she's trying to get out before she gets trapped in the rubble.

She's shoving her bare feet into her discarded boots when I enter the living room.

Not turning to look at me, she asks, "Is there a jacket or shirt I can borrow for the ride home? Or maybe a pair of sweats? I don't really feel great about getting into the back of a stranger's car with basically nothing on. I promise I'll give it back and I'll even wash it so you don't feel like you need to *burn* it after I wear it."

I ignore her and ask a question of my own. "Why is Pax telling you that he's sorry?"

Her hands, which had been busy tying the laces of her boots, momentarily freeze in place. She recovers quickly and her back remains to me when she answers, "I'm not sure. He's probably upset that I saw him like that."

"No." I immediately disagree with her. "It was something else. It was like you guys were having a secret conversation, and the way he looked at you…" There's been pain in his eyes since

185

the day our father was taken away in the back of Captain Davenport's car, but when he looked at her with his glassy gaze, it amplified.

With a heavy sigh, she finally turns around. Her eyes are red, and she looks emotionally exhausted, but I don't care. I need her to answer the question.

"I don't know what you're talking about, Raff. The only conversation we were having was the one you heard. Pax is high and clearly feeling vulnerable. Honestly, me being here probably only made matters worse." What she's saying makes sense, but every cell in my body is telling me she's lying.

"He hasn't cried in almost six fucking years, and one look at you has tears falling out of his eyes. I want to know what it is about you that has him breaking like that!" My voice is starting to raise and there's a pain in my palms from my hands clenching so hard.

She throws her hands up. "I was his best friend! He lost me and I lost him! We've simply *missed* each other. If you're too angry to see that or *understand* it, then I don't know what to tell you."

"He's hardly mentioned your name in all these years."

This has her rolling her eyes and releasing a frustrated breath. "I'm sure he didn't. How could he when he lived with you?"

I take a step toward her. "What the fuck does that mean?"

"Did you make him feel like he could talk about me, or did you try to push the hatred and blame you feel onto him? Did you try to force him to see me the same way you do?"

"Of course, I tried. I had to protect him from all forms of danger, even if he couldn't see them himself." He was never receptive to it. Pax remained quietly loyal to his best friend despite my best efforts. "But none of that has anything to do with why he's apologizing to *you*!"

She lifts her chin and crosses her arms defiantly. "I already told you I don't know. Your guess is as good as mine."

"Tell me the fucking truth!" I demand, not buying her act. Just as she can still see through me and get in my head, I can do the same. Something is off about her right now, and she's not leaving until she admits it.

"I am!"

I've had enough of this. Something uncontrollable snaps inside of me and I'm halfway across the room, charging toward her, before I realize I'd taken a step. Her eyes are wide, and her lips are parted in a silent gasp. All the air she'd managed to suck into her lungs is forced out of her when her back collides with the wall behind her.

Her delicate hands claw at my bare forearm while I press it to her throat and use it to hold her in place. The choking sounds she makes barely register to my ears as I glower down at her.

"You're lying to me!" My roar reverberates through the high ceilings of the room and against the large arched windows on the walls. "*Again!*"

Posie, with utter terror on her pale face, shakes her head. "I'm not," she manages to get out through her restricted airways. "I promise."

I laugh cruelly at this sentiment. "You've proven to me already that your promises are nothing but hollow words." I don't feel in control of my body. It's like I'm sitting back watching a rageful monster take over and I don't know how to stop it. Every fiber of my being is aflame with anger and grief, and they're burning away the pieces that remain of my soul. "Why does my brother think he owes you an apology?"

Her throat moves against my arm as she swallows. Tears are running down her pretty face and dripping on my too-warm skin. "I don't know!"

My free hand wraps around the pocketknife in my jeans and she whimpers when she sees the glint of metal.

I press the end of the knife into her flawless skin, but not yet hard enough to break the skin. "I'm going to give you one last chance to be honest. If you don't, I'm going to carve *liar* into your fucking chest. That way everyone will know with one look at you what you fucking are."

Her panicked fighting has both of us shifting. When she pushes against my arm, the knife slips and slices her skin. As if someone has pressed pause on the situation, we both freeze in place, and I watch the crimson blood trickle down her chest from the cut.

The visual of her blood forces whatever is controlling me to let go, or like a spell being broken, I emerge from under its red mist. All the fight evaporates from my bones when I look at her face. The way she's looking up at me causes a sharp pain to spear my chest. I truly thought I'd never see her look at me like that, but it appears I was wrong.

Posie's body shakes against mine in silent sobs. Giant tears form in her eyes and fall down her face in a steady stream.

I don't even know what to say to her, but I manage to say her name. My voice cracks when I do. "Posie…"

She sucks in a shuddering breath, and she wipes at her face the best she can with my forearm still holding her hostage. "The way you're looking at me right now is the same way your father looked at you that night in his study." Her raspy words are like a hot poker to my soul. "He was a horrible and *cruel* man who took his anger out on others, and I *never* thought you'd remind me of him." Posie glances down at the cut I gave her. "If you're going to give me scars, make them match the ones he left on you. Fuck the pocketknife. Go light up one of your cigarettes and put it out on my back just like he did to you."

The dozen or so circular scars across my back and shoulders are long healed but now burn and ache as if my dad is standing behind me with his lit cigarette again. I always preferred his belt over that. The leather would leave welts and my skin would be tight for a few days, but at least there wasn't a reminder of what I'd let him do to me permanently etched into my flesh after. Welts heal, burns leave ugly scars.

My knees, suddenly feeling weak, begin to give out and I stumble back away from her. The second she's free of my grasp, she crumples to the floor against the wall. Seeing the pocketknife still in my hand, I drop it and it skids across the hardwood and out of sight.

Her words are like bullets, and they cause a pain I haven't felt since I heard Paxton's cry when he found our mom in the bathtub. Just like the sound he made will forever be engraved in my head, so will her words. And it's because they're the god-awful ugly truth.

I'm starting to become the man I hate most.

Losing my balance, I fall back another step but manage to catch myself on the edge of the leather couch. Leaning against it, I hold my hands on my knees and try to slow my ragged breathing.

For so long, I didn't let myself feel anything but my anger at Posie and grief for my mom. While I was busy focusing on those, I was becoming the one person I never wanted to be. The person I swore I would never be. I've completely lost control, and in doing so, I've lost myself.

I thought Posie's deceit and betrayal were the reason I changed, but I changed because I *let* myself be corrupted.

My head is a hundred pounds when I lift it. She's curled in a ball with her knees pulled up to her chest. She looks up at me through her tear-soaked lashes and her body continues to visibly shake.

"Posie…" I have no idea what I'm going to say next, but she doesn't give me the chance to figure it out.

She wipes her face with the back of her hand, sniffing as she does. "You finally did it, Raff. You win. I hope your trophy is worth it and will finally make you happy." Looking down at her chest, she wipes the blood that's dripping from the cut. It ends up just smearing across her chest in a bright red line. "In this moment, I hate you. I hate you almost as much as I love you," she pauses with a heartbreakingly sad smile, "and my god, is that a deadly combination."

I hate you. Those are the three words I've been craving to hear come from her lips since she's been back, but right now, they aren't the ones I'm fixating on. No, it's the three words I haven't heard since I was seventeen years old that are echoing in my ears like distant screams. Hearing them again feels like someone's poured rubbing alcohol in an open wound. *I love you.*

I'm numb, frozen in place when she starts to pull herself off the ground. Moving stiffly, as if she's in a daze, she goes to the pile of clothes I'd shredded many hours ago. This has been the longest night of my life. It feels like it was days ago that I'd chained her to the fireman's pole.

Shifting through the pieces of her ruined sweater, she finds the pocket and retrieves her cell phone. She opens it, the bright light illuminating her sullen face. I don't have to ask to know she's ordering a car to come pick her up.

She flinches when I manage to stand up on my feet and step toward her. Reaching into my jeans, I retrieve my car keys. "You can take my car. It's parked out front," I tell her. My voice is hardly recognizable to my ears. "I don't want you to have to wait for someone to pick you up. You need to get away from here—away from *me*—right now."

I'm not telling her this because I'm angry at her and want her out of my sight. I'm saying it because I scared even myself tonight, and if it were possible, I'd try to run away from me too. I thought I wanted her to fear me, but right now, I can't physically bear the sad look in her eyes for another second.

When she stands there like a statue, I shake the key fob at her. "I mean it. You need to leave. There's a jacket in the back seat you can wear."

Finally, she gives in and steps forward to take the keys. Her fingers wrap around them, and she pauses, looking up at me.

"How did we get here, Raff?"

For the first time in years, I don't immediately want to blame her for everything bad that's happened.

"I don't know."

TWENTY-SIX
POSIE
SIXTEEN YEARS OLD

IT'S BEEN six months since the school dance and six months since I started dating Rafferty.

I never did make it back into the gym or back to Chance that night. Rafferty and I, soaked and freezing from dancing in the rain, ran to his car and left without letting anyone know.

That following Monday morning was awkward when I had to face the nice boy I had abandoned. He asked me a million questions while I tried to apologize to him for bailing. I hadn't gotten a chance to admit the reasoning for my quick departure when Rafferty walked up behind me. All of Chance's questions were answered when Rafferty wrapped his arm around my waist and kissed my neck. As realization hit, Chance's face fell. In the end, he wasn't super happy about it, but he had been gracious and that's all I could have asked for in a situation like that. Two weeks later, I saw him making out with Hannah in the stairwell, so I think it's safe to say that everything worked out okay for everyone involved.

People stared and whispered when news spread that Rafferty and I were together, but neither one of us could be bothered to give a shit what they thought about us. We were happy.

We *are* happy.

Something that we both needed fell perfectly into place that night and we've been side by side ever since. We didn't come right out and announce we were dating to our parents, but when Mollie found out after about a month, she seemed genuinely happy. Paxton seemed okay with it too, saying he'd always suspected we both had feelings for each other, but like with everything else lately, he was fairly quiet on the matter. Adrian… well, Adrian wasn't and still isn't thrilled. He hasn't said anything, but I can tell by the way he looks at me when he's home that given the chance, he'd choose someone else for his son.

My dad told me I was old enough to decide who I wanted to date and that he didn't really have any say in who I picked. He also made some comment about how he wasn't surprised since I spend more time with the Blackwell boys than anyone else. He shrugged and added, *"I just always thought it would be Paxton"* before changing the topic to something completely unrelated. I've always appreciated how my dad trusted me to make my own decisions and supported me in any way he could. This was no different.

With a robe over my sleep tank and shorts, I step out of the guest bathroom that had become mine a very long time ago and into my bedroom. Using a towel to wring the excess water out of my hair, I'm surprised I don't find Rafferty lying across my bed waiting for me like he said he would be when I got out of the shower. He doesn't spend the night with me every night, but it's becoming more frequent.

I never sleep alone when I'm here because the nights he's not in bed with me, Paxton is. His nightmares are getting worse, and he says sleeping next to me helps keep them at bay. I've asked him if he should talk to his mom about maybe going to see someone for help, but he shoots down the idea every time. Since he won't talk to me about what's going on, letting him sleep with me feels like the only way I can help him right now. I'll keep doing it until he decides otherwise.

Dropping my towel on the floor, I head out the bedroom door to look for Raff. His room is in the other wing on the opposite side of the house, but he's nowhere to be found when I get there. Every light is off, and it doesn't look like he's been in there all day. Deciding to check downstairs, thinking he might be getting a late-night snack or watching TV, I tiptoe down the grand staircase.

The lights were turned off when Mollie went upstairs to go to bed, but now there's soft light streaming out of the kitchen. I hope to find Rafferty at the end of the illuminated path, but the only thing I find in the kitchen is a full bowl of microwave popcorn that's long gone cold. My theory about him getting a snack was right, the only difference is he's not here eating it.

Leaving the kitchen, I wander the large house for signs of him. I even look out the big windows and down at the backyard to see if he decided to take a dip in the heated pool, but there are no signs of him out there either. My next guess is he may be working out in the home gym. The stairs leading to the finished basement are on the other side of the house, so I move quietly in that direction. I don't want to accidentally wake up Adrian. He got home late tonight and immediately went upstairs to his bedroom. I haven't seen him since and I'm assuming he's been sleeping.

My theory is proved wrong when I reach the top of the stairs but see the light on in Adrian's office down the arched hallway. Rafferty is never in there so I'm not even remotely considering that to be the location of his hiding spot until I hear his voice.

I know I shouldn't, but I find myself stepping in that direction before I can stop myself. Something in my gut tells me I need to see what's happening in there so late at night. Pulling my gray fluffy robe tighter around my body, I move as quietly as I possibly can toward the cracked wooden door.

When I discover what's happening behind it, my blood turns to ice.

For as long as I can remember, I've asked my dad what it felt like to see horrific crime scenes and the cruel things humans do to each other. He's always said it's hard to describe unless you've witnessed it yourself. Standing here watching as Adrian brings his brown leather belt down on Rafferty's back, I finally understand what my father meant.

It's hard to describe the emotions because it's impossible to pinpoint exactly what you're experiencing. You feel everything at once but you're also numb. Your skin grows warm but you're freezing. Things are moving fast but painfully slow at the same time. You want to help but your fear and shock are keeping you firmly in place.

How can this be happening? How long has this been going on? Why isn't Rafferty fighting back? The questions circulate around in my head like a broken record but come to an abrupt stop when the sound of the belt on Rafferty's skin hits my ears again.

He's kneeling in front of his father's big wooden desk with his discarded shirt in front of him. His head is bowed, and his hands are braced on the rug on either side of his legs. When the leather whips him, he remains perfectly still and silent. The only evidence that it hurts him at all is the way his eyes squeeze shut and his lips pull in the slightest grimace. I have no idea how he's sitting there taking it, but like with everything else, he faces it with unwavering stoicism.

I know Rafferty and that's why I know, while he might not be showing external pain, his mind is in anguish. His body will heal from this brutality, but can his head ever properly recover from experiencing something like this?

For longer than I should, I stand there doing nothing, unsure how I could possibly help him right now. Can I tell my dad, and can he then do something to put an end to this? He'll need more than just my testimony to go against a man like Adrian Black-well. Adrian's six-figure attorneys will have the case dismissed before it even reaches a jury. No, my dad will need tangible evidence.

Holding my breath, my hand slips into the pocket of my thigh-length robe and my fingers wrap around my cell phone. If I get caught doing this, it will not go well for Rafferty or me, and that's why my heart thunders almost painfully against my chest wall as I begin recording.

"One day, you'll learn to fucking respect me and we won't have to do this," Adrian snarls, his fingers running over the smooth leather he's using to hurt his child. "One day, you'll do as you are told and not fucking *embarrass* me."

"I missed two classes. That's it," Rafferty grits out between his teeth.

Oh crap, he skipped his first two classes today because he already understands the units. A teacher must have grown tired of his absences and called his father. Usually, they don't even attempt to punish Rafferty, but I'm thinking Mr. Cornwell has finally had enough of Rafferty's shit. Last week, Raff pissed off the calculus teacher when he asked in front of the whole class how he'd managed to hold on to his job for so long seeing as he barely seemed to understand the material herself. He found it wildly entertaining at the time to embarrass him in front of everyone, but it looks like it might be biting him in the ass now.

My hand is shaking holding my phone and my lungs are burning because I'm too afraid if I breathe they'll hear me. When Adrian brings the belt down on Rafferty's back again, I flinch at the horrific cracking sound it makes. The way Adrian appears so comfortable doing such a horrible thing tells me that this isn't the first or the last time he plans on doing this to his son. And Rafferty, the way he sits, just *accepting* his tarnished reality, also confirms this isn't new for him.

How have I never seen welts or marks on his back? I think

back to all the times I've been around him shirtless, but for the life of me, I can't remember ever seeing any evidence on his skin. When he's lain naked with me in bed, my fingers trailing over his pale skin, I've never felt welts. Somehow, he's managed to find a way to hide this from me. Does he keep his shirt on and me at arm's length after it happens to ensure I don't find out?

I just don't understand how I could have missed that this was happening. It makes so much sense now why Rafferty is always so tense when his father is home. He knew what was coming.

Adrian lifts the cigarette that's been burning in the ashtray on his desk and brings it to his lips. He draws a lungful of the nicotine and his eyes close in satisfaction. I can't help but wonder if he gets more pleasure out of the cigarette or leaving red marks on his son's back. My gut tells me it's the latter.

"What you do reflects on *me*," Adrian explains, blowing out a plume of smoke. "When you look like a lazy degenerate, people assume that's what *I've* raised you to be, and that is simply not the case. We both know what kind of man I'm raising you to be."

Rafferty lifts his head, and he stares at the wall next to the door I'm behind. His eyes look as dull and lifeless as Mollie's can be.

"You're raising me to be just like you."

Adrian pauses at this, a murderous glare forming on his face. "You say that like it's a bad thing."

Raff stiffly shrugs his shoulders. "I'm not convinced it's not."

Dropping the belt on the rug at his feet, Adrian marches forward. My stomach rolls as he flips the lit cigarette in his hand, and he presses it to his son's back. This finally has Rafferty making a noise. He groans, his perfect teeth digging into his lip, stopping it from being too loud, and tries to pull forward to escape the pain, but Adrian holds him in place.

"You're such a little shit," Adrian seethes. "I'm going to burn those smart-ass remarks right out of you."

Finally letting go of him, Adrian steps back and Rafferty sags forward. His entire body moves as he takes big deep breaths through his nose. Behind him, his dad is weaving his belt through the loops in his pants, preparing to leave.

Adrenaline shoots through me. I have to be out of sight when he leaves his office. With my tear-filled eyes, I look at Rafferty one more time. I stop recording and stash the phone back in my robe.

As gracefully and quiet as I can, I tiptoe back away from the door and down the hallway. When I'm far enough away, I pick up my pace and race toward my bedroom. With each step I take, my heart breaks a little bit more for the boy I've fallen in love with.

TEN MINUTES LATER, I'm sitting in the middle of my bed with my knees pulled to my chest when Rafferty slips into my room.

If I wasn't looking for signs of what had just occurred, I probably wouldn't notice that his skin is slightly paler than usual and his movements are a little rigid. He either has an amazing pain tolerance or needs to take up a career in acting because had that happened to me, I would still be lying on the ground unable to move. The strength that this boy has is awe-inspiring to me, and so, so fucking sad.

No one should have to be that strong.

I almost choke on a sob when he looks at me and asks, "Are you okay?"

Even if I wanted to, I couldn't stop the tears from falling when I blink. "You're asking *me* that?"

Moving to the bed, he rests his knees on the mattress and leans over so he can wipe the tears off my face. "You're the one who's sitting alone in their room crying, so *yes*, I want to know if you're okay." Frowning at my current state, he gently cups my cheek in his hand. "What's got you so upset, baby?"

I turn my head and kiss his palm, my hand holding on to his wrist for dear life. Once I tell him what I saw, we can never go back to how things were, but that's a risk I have to take. I have to know how I can help him because I can't sit back and allow his father to hurt him like that for a second longer.

"I saw, Raff," I whisper, looking up at him.

"What did you see?"

"I went looking for you when you didn't show up here like you said you would," I start, the anxiety is like a boulder sitting on my chest. "I saw the light on in your dad's office and I heard voices, so I checked to see if you were in there…"

When Rafferty rips his hand away from me like I'd been the one to burn him, it's like a hot blade to my heart. He stumbles back a step from my bed, his face now ghastly pale and his eyes have this wild look in them.

"Raff…" I try, shifting so I'm sitting on my knees. "You have to tell someone what he did. He *can't* do that to you anymore."

His head shakes. "He didn't do anything to me, Posie. I don't know what you saw."

There's a twinge of anger flaring in my chest that he'd try to gaslight me into thinking I mistook what was happening in that office. "I know exactly what I saw." I stand my ground. "He used his belt on you and then he"—I choke on my words as emotion builds in my throat again. "He put his cigarette out on your skin."

"*No*, he didn't."

"Lift up your shirt then and prove me wrong, Raff. Prove to me that you don't need help."

He stares at me for what must be longer than a minute before

I watch his strong facade crumple. Like a perfectly constructed wall, it falls apart brick by brick until it's nothing but dust. His fingers shove through his hair as he falls back another step.

Walking on my knees closer to the edge of the bed and him, I say, "We have to go to my dad. He can help you and keep you *safe*." If I could, I'd be dragging us both to my dad's police station right now. Every cell in my body is screaming at me to get him to safety.

Panic takes over his distraught expression. His hands drop to his sides, and he rushes toward me. "No!" he hisses, trying to keep his voice down so his parents don't hear us. "No cops. No one can know."

I disagree instantly, my head shaking. "No, we have to tell someone. He can't get away with this, Rafferty."

"We can't," he argues sharply, making me jerk back from him out of instinct. Catching his mistake, he drops to the floor in front of me and gathers my hands in his. He kisses my fingers before continuing, this time in a much softer voice. "We can't let anyone know. My mom..." he pauses, swallowing hard. "My mom won't survive it. Our names will be plastered on every news outlet, and everyone will know she was married to a man who did ... *this*. The scrutinization and the gossip will destroy her. She's been so sick for so long. She used to be on better medication that helped her, but she's self-medicating now. I'm afraid of what she'll do if I tear apart her life like that."

I'd be lying if I said I hadn't seen Mollie taking pills. I've never known what they are, but I knew she was taking too many of them throughout the day. There are nights she takes so many, that she's not even awake before we get home from school. The vacant, glassy look in her sad eyes is caused by the pills.

"We can get her the help she needs," I argue, desperate to find a solution. "She can go to rehab."

"She's not mentally strong enough to do that and she'd never risk her reputation by checking into rehab. She'd rather slowly fall apart in her picture-perfect home and in her designer clothes than let the world know she needs help. My dad's used the last twenty years to brainwash her into thinking their image is the priority." He looks away, like he can't stand to look at me as he adds, "My dad may not leave marks on her skin, but make no mistake, Posie, he's abused her in other ways. He saw her as an easy target when they started dating, and over the years, he's torn her down until she's a shell of a human."

"There has to be something we can do. You can't endure his pain and wrath forever."

He looks back at me. "I can," he insists vehemently, leaving no room for argument. "I can because as long as he's taking his anger out on me, he stays away from Pax, and as long as I keep it a secret, my mom is okay. For them, I can bear anything. They are my priority."

"While you're protecting them, who is protecting you? How can I sit back and know this is happening and not tell my dad? He would help you. *All* of you—"

I'm cut off when Rafferty's hand wraps painfully around my chin. His fingers dig into my skin, and I worry he's leaving marks. "If you go to your father, I will deny everything you tell him. Without evidence, it's your word against mine, and you won't win that fight, Posie."

It's on the tip of my tongue to admit I have video evidence, but he speaks again before I get the chance to tell him.

"And if for some reason this gets out to the press and it affects my mom in *any* way, I will *never* forgive you." He releases my face and drops his forehead against mine. "It will ruin us. You will lose me if you betray me, and I'm not ready to lose you. So, I beg you, Butterfly, please don't say anything."

My eyes flutter closed. There are so many conflicting feelings coursing through me. The pain that his father causes will pale in comparison to the pain of something happening to his mom or little brother. It's a fact set in stone, but it doesn't make it any easier to swallow.

"I promise I won't tell anyone but know all I want to do is protect you. I don't like seeing someone I love in pain." Everything comes to a screeching standstill as I realize what I just said.

Rafferty's thumb, which had been creating small circles on the back of my hand, freezes, and he lifts his head so he can look at me. I don't immediately do the same, instead choosing to stare at the gray and blue comforter a moment longer so I can conceal my embarrassment. Nothing I said wasn't true, I just hadn't planned on letting it slip like that.

Tipping my chin up with his finger, he forces me to make eye contact. I'm afraid of what I'll see on his face until I spot the corners of his mouth pulling up in a small smile.

"What did you just say?"

My cheeks feel like they're on fire. "Come on, Raff, you heard me. Please don't try to embarrass me by making me repeat it," I groan, wishing I could bury my face in my pillow.

"I don't want to embarrass you," he insists, not a hint of humor or mockery in his voice. In fact, he looks very serious. "I just want to hear those words come from your lips one more time."

Breath catching, I stare at the boy I am somehow lucky enough to call mine. "I love you, Raff." My voice may only be a whisper, but I feel what I say with so much intensity it's an all-consuming sensation. My heart beats for Rafferty Blackwell.

His face retains that serious look, and for a second, I start to worry I've ruined everything by opening my big dumb mouth, but when he leans forward and captures my lips with his, my fear evaporates.

I will never get tired of the way my heart skips a beat when he kisses me. It's like no matter how much time passes or how many times we've kissed, I still get that delicious mixture of nervousness and excitement in my belly like I did the first time he kissed me. I hope it's a feeling that never fades.

My lips part for him and he groans as my tongue licks against his teasingly. His hands release mine and travel down my arms in a ghostlike touch before reaching my hips. Never breaking our kiss, he slowly stands to his feet and his hold on me tightens. As he deepens the kiss, he lifts me off the bed with surprising ease. My legs circle his waist and my arms loop around his neck in a desperate attempt to somehow bring myself closer to him. The only thing separating us is our clothes, but he still feels too far away.

With one hand, I reach between our bodies and untie the robe. I manage to shimmy it off my shoulders. It falls to our feet, and Rafferty steps over it as he lays me down on the bed. He's trying hard to not crush me, but I love his weight on me. While some might find it claustrophobic being trapped like that, I feel safe. Protected.

Abandoning my mouth, he kisses along my jaw and then down my throat. My back arches into him when his lips softly suck at the sensitive skin there.

"Say it again," he pleads against my neck, his warm breath causing goose bumps to dance down my spine.

I smile at this and my hands thread softly through the wavy strands of his hair. "I love you," I tell him in his ear.

Pulling back, he looks down at me with a look in his eyes I've never seen before. It's so soft. Warm. I could drown in that look and die happily. "I've been in love with you longer than I've probably known." He pushes the still-damp strands of hair off my face, tucking them behind my ear. "I think I always knew you were going to be mine, but I just didn't understand what I was feeling when I looked at you. I do now."

I can't think of another time I've ever been happier. Lifting my head, I seal my lips to his once more and gently wrap my arms over his shoulders, careful to not touch the skin on his back.

Between my legs and through the thin cotton of my pajama shorts, I can feel him growing hard. When I first got together with Rafferty, I thought he would be in a race to take my virginity, but to my surprise, he's been patient with me. He's been taking his time and making sure I'm comfortable with him.

We've fooled around before, and the first time he put his mouth on me, I thought he was pulling my very soul from my body. I was nervous about doing the same for him, but he talked me through it and was happy to teach me how he liked it. After discovering the sounds I could force out of him, falling to my knees became one of my favorite things to do.

We've done everything but actually have sex. I know he's been waiting for me to tell him that I'm ready, and I've never felt surer about anything than I do right now.

"Raff," I whisper against his mouth, my pelvis starting to grind against him. "I'm ready."

His body freezes. "Are you sure?"

"I'm positive." I nip his bottom lip with my teeth before licking away the bite of pain with my tongue. "I want you."

He groans. "Fuck, Posie, those are my second favorite three words you've told me tonight."

"I meant everything I said."

Rafferty bows his head and kisses me deeply, and with each stroke of his tongue, I forget about the video sitting on my phone. Instead, I fall into oblivion as he finally claims the last piece of me as his.

TWENTY-SEVEN
POSIE

"ARE you sure you don't want to talk about it?" Lark asks from where she sits under a blue knit blanket across from me on my balcony.

When I didn't attend the English class we share for the second time this week, she showed up at my door with a bottle of white wine and a family-sized bag of potato chips. I didn't have to say a word for her to know what happened. One look at my face had her placing her things on the floor in front of her and her arms wrapping around my shoulders. I didn't realize how badly I needed that hug until I buried my head in her shoulder.

"What did he do?" she asked, rubbing my back, but I couldn't answer her.

How can I put into words what that night was like? It was an assault on my body and emotions, and it's taken me the last five days to recover. It physically hurts my soul that he made me hate him. He's always been the one person I couldn't hate, but when he stood there with his arm on my throat and his knife on my chest, he was a monster I didn't recognize.

This whole time, I've been trying to remember that somewhere buried beneath his rage and grief is the boy I gave my heart to. That somewhere inside him, the boy who told me to be patient with him because he is bad with emotions still exists. As he screamed in my face, I started to lose faith that I would ever see that boy again.

It was my tipping point, and it not only broke my heart, but it made me say the one thing I promised myself I never would. *I hate you.*

Three words have never been harder to say. They tasted like poison on my tongue and felt like nails in my throat but saying them did something to him. The dark fog that had been clinging to him like a lethal shadow parted. Like clouds allowing the sun to break through, I saw a glimmer of the boy I once knew.

And that's when I knew I couldn't give up on him. Not yet. It would be the safest and easiest thing for me to do, but no one else is around anymore to fight for him. I'm the last one standing. I'm not sure if this makes me reckless or delusional.

Rafferty is broken, but I'm just as damaged and sick as he is because I still love him with every fiber of my being. That tiny glimpse I got when his anger lifted only further confirmed those feelings.

I sigh, leaning my head back against the cushioned chair. "Loving someone you know is bad for you is a special kind of hell."

The rain that's been falling is our soundtrack for the afternoon. The distant thunder brings me a sense of comfort. I love when the weather matches my mood, makes me feel like the universe understands what I'm going through.

Lark takes a big drink of wine and nods her head. "Yes. Yes, it is."

I raise a brow, silently asking her to elaborate but she waves me off with her hand.

"It's not something I'm ready to talk about."

Not one to push for information, I let her keep her secrets. "It seems we both have a lot we can't talk about."

"Well, I'm not talking about mine to protect myself. Who are you protecting by keeping your secrets?"

"The same people I always have," I answer over my wineglass. "It's not easy. It's getting harder to lie." And Rafferty is finally starting to see through them. I almost broke the other night, but, by the grace of God, I was able to remain in control. "Being the villain is a lot easier when you don't have to look your victims in the eye."

Seeing Pax like that was horrific. When he asked me to stay with him, all I wanted to do was crawl into bed beside him and hold his hand like I used to, but Raff never would have allowed it. The despondent look in his glossy eyes when I told him no was one of my hardest moments. And his apologies... If Rafferty hadn't been there, I think I would have fallen to the ground and bawled my eyes out, but I couldn't let him see how they affected me. He can't know the meaning behind them.

The whole long night was hard and draining. My soul ached more than my muscles. The ride home in Rafferty's Mercedes SUV, I could barely see the lines in the road through my tears. I walked into the apartment and into my room. Where I landed on my bed is where I stayed for the next sixteen hours. I didn't bother changing out of my leotard or his jacket I'd found in the car. Surrounded by his scent, I tried to dream of our happier times.

I wish I could say I was successful.

"Have you figured out if you're doing more harm than good by keeping up these lies?" Lark asks. "Maybe it's time for you to tell Rafferty the truth. Whatever that truth may be."

I wish I could. "My lies are protecting secrets that aren't mine to tell."

She stares at me with a sad smile. "What you're doing... I hope you know how selfless you are, Posie. If I ever have a secret, I know it'll be safe with you."

I laugh at this, but it sounds sad even to my ears. "I appreciate the faith you have in me, but if I have to keep another person's secret, it might put me in an early grave. I'm hanging on by a fucking thread over here."

Reaching across the small side table between our chairs, Lark takes my hand in hers. "I wish I could do more to help you."

I squeeze her hand and hold up the wineglass. "This is helping me. I know I can only tell you so much but being able to talk to you has made me feel a lot less alone."

"You're not alone. I'm here for you. If you ever decide you want to get it all off your chest, I'm here to listen, and if Rafferty continues to be a supermassive *dick*, I'll kick him in the balls and slash the tires of all his dumb expensive cars."

I can't help it, I completely lose it hearing her say this. It's just so out of character for her. Lark has a quiet and almost demure elegance about her. It's a persona that's been instilled in her since birth by her stiff politician parents. Her father, who is very likely to be the next leader of the free world, would be appalled to hear that his daughter is willing to be a vandal on my behalf. Her mom would stand behind him clutching her ever-present string of pearls.

"You're not as prim and proper as you want the world to believe, are you?" I joke, still laughing.

She shrugs at me before taking another sip of her wine. "We all have roles to play, don't we?" Lark says it with a nonchalance that would sound believable if I weren't looking at her. The sad look in her deep blue eyes tells a different story.

I don't get the chance to ask her anything about it because the sliding glass door behind us is slowly pulled open and Zadie's head pops out. Her wavy dark hair is pulled up into a knot on top of her head with tendrils framing her face. There isn't a stitch of makeup on her face and she's only wearing a hoodie and leggings. This appearance is entirely not like her. She doesn't leave the apartment without at least mascara and blush on.

"Are you okay?" I ask, turning in my chair so I can look at her better. "I haven't seen you in a while."

As if she's nervous, another behavior that is unlike her, she crosses her arms tightly in front of her and shifts on her feet. "Yeah, I went to see my mom." Her green eyes flick to Lark and then back to me. "Can I talk to you? Alone?"

Stomach pulling into a knot as my nerves are kicked up, I nod at her warily. "Sure…"

Lark gives a subtle shrug when I glance at her, silently indicating she has no idea what's going on. Leaving her on the balcony, I follow Zadie into the apartment.

Zadie, who's usually one of the most confident people I know, rocks back and forth on her feet in front of the velvet sofa. "I have to tell you something," she blurts when I close the glass door behind me.

"Okay…" I drawl, slowly approaching the sitting area. "Is this like a 'I need to sit down' moment, or can I stand?"

"Sit," she instructs, but right when I'm about to reach the sofa, she changes her mind. "No wait, you can stand. Actually, you can do whatever you're comfy with. I really don't know if there's a right or wrong choice here."

Deciding I'd rather stand, I raise my brows at her. "You're starting to freak me out. What's going on?"

She releases a big sigh as she scrubs a hand down her face.

"*Zadie,*" I press when she continues to hesitate.

"A little less than a year ago, my dad got in trouble. He was drinking and driving on his way home from the hospital. He was pulled over and got a DUI. The medical board almost took his license but ultimately decided against it. It didn't really matter though because the hospital he's worked at for almost two decades fired him as their chief of general surgery and he lost his place on their board."

I knew Zadie's father was a surgeon at the big hospital in Seattle, but I didn't know this. That being said, I don't know why she feels I need to know this. "That's really unfortunate, Zadie. I'm sorry that happened, but I don't understand what that has to do with me…"

"I promise I'm getting to that part, just let me finish," she pleads. "Dad had made some bad investments and lost a *lot* of money. When he was fired, he couldn't get hired at any of the other hospitals because of the DUI being on his record. He was starting to lose hope and was considering filing for bankruptcy when Rafferty showed up…"

Oh shit. Now I can see where this is going.

"Rafferty pulled his strings and got your dad a job," I guess.

She nods, the curly bun on her head bouncing. "Yeah, but not at a hospital. At the prison upstate. It's the one where…"

My stomach drops. "Where his father is."

"Yes," she confirms. "But you know Rafferty. You know how he works. His favors aren't free. In exchange for getting my dad a job, he wanted something in return. From *me.*"

I know I'm not going to like the answer, but I still ask as dread moves like a mist through me. "What did you do, Zadie?"

Her jaw wobbles and her voice cracks when she starts to speak again. "When my dad couldn't find a job, he started to give up and drink a lot. I know what he did was wrong, and he could have really hurt someone, but he's still my dad, you know? I wanted to help him, so when Rafferty told me he'd get my dad the job if I did favors for him, I agreed. It all seemed like easy stuff at first. He paid off my old roommate to move out, and then had me post a listing on all the school message boards so you'd see it. He dropped the rent price and is paying the difference so you could afford to live here. All I had to do was accept your application, and once you got here, he told me to befriend you. That was the easiest part out of all of it because you were instantly likable. Which made it even harder to pressure you into going to that party. I started to catch on that things really weren't good between you two when I saw how jumpy you were and how angry he seemed once you got on campus. I knew he had something planned for the party, but he demanded I get you there. I know it sounds like a lie to stand here and tell you that I didn't have a choice, but it's the truth."

It all makes so much sense now and I'm honestly embarrassed I hadn't put two and two together until now. The way everything fell into place with ease should have raised red flags. I think I was just grateful that things seemed to be going my way for the first time in a while and couldn't see anything else.

Exhaling a long breath, I look at my roommate. "I know it's the truth because I know how Rafferty operates. If you didn't do what he asked, he would have made things ten times worse for you and your dad."

"I thought I would be okay doing his favors, but then I saw him carrying your unconscious body out to his car at the party and I knew I was wrong. I didn't know how to lie to you or face you after that." Her arms cross and uncross anxiously, like she's full of restless energy.

"Well, that at least explains why you've been avoiding me for weeks," I remark jokingly, but my lightheartedness does little to make her calm down. The look on her face still looks like she's bracing for me to yell at her for her deceit. "Zadie, I'm not mad at you. If you didn't do what he wanted, he would have found someone else that would. As weird as it sounds, I'm glad it was you because he could have set me up with an *actual* psycho and that would have sucked. Instead, he gave me you, and you, at least, were honest about what happened."

"How can you not be mad at me?" Her mouth gapes in shock. "You don't even seem like you're mad at *him*. He *drugged* you!"

"Funnily enough, that's not even the worst thing he did that night." I laugh at my own inside joke but stop when her eyes look like they're going to fall out of her head. "Sorry, I guess that might only be funny to me." Have I completely fucking lost it that I'm laughing at this shit now?

"I don't understand you guys."

"That makes two of us," I sigh. "Rafferty and I ... share a complicated and ugly past. There's a lot of turbulent water under that bridge, but…"

"*But?*"

"But I don't know how to let him go," I admit. "He's vicious and callous, but it's because he's in *pain*. I have to keep reminding myself of that when he lashes out and loses control."

She shakes her head in disbelief. "I don't know how you can deal with it."

"He once told me that he was going to mess up, and he made me promise I would be patient with him when he did. He *really* messed up this week and I *should* walk away because of it, but I've broken one too many of my promises to him already. I don't want to do the same with this one."

Even if it's really fucking hard.

STARTLED AND STILL HALF ASLEEP, I fly up in bed when someone shakes my arm. Dazed, it takes me a second to comprehend they're also whispering my name.

"*Posie.*"

Blinking hard, trying to get myself to focus on what's happening, I turn toward the person standing next to my bed.

"*Zadie?*" I ask groggily. "What's going on?" My hand blindly reaches for my cell phone on my nightstand, and when I see the ungodly time, I'm even more confused. "It's two in the morning."

"Yeah, I'm aware." She sounds as tired as I feel. "It's a *really* shitty time for guests, but it appears we have one. Or you have one, I guess. Their knocking woke me up."

"Guests?" I repeat, my sluggish brain struggling to keep up with what's happening. Lark and I finished the bottle of wine she brought, and when Zadie joined us on the balcony, we opened another one. I think I might still be a little drunk and it's not helping me comprehend any of this. "Who's here?" I pause, my chest seizing. "Is Rafferty here?"

I'm not sure I'm ready to be in the same room with him yet. While I'm not giving up on him, he did scare the absolute *shit* out of me last week. I'm still recovering and need time to get my head and heart straight again.

"Nope, it's not him. It's Baby Wilde and he looks *rough*," she shocks me by saying. "Like, he looks like he should be in the ER and not standing in my kitchen. I say *standing* loosely since he's kinda *leaning…*"

Paxton.

Suddenly very awake and on alert, I spring from the bed and push past Zadie. I fly out of my room, and the door Zadie had left cracked hits the wall with a thud when I throw it open. The only light out here comes from the salt lamp Zadie keeps plugged in on the kitchen counter. Through the dim lighting and shadows, I can see his lanky figure leaning against the front door.

Hearing me approaching, Pax lifts his head. His hair, which is longer on top, falls onto his forehead and in his eyes. He's wearing dark clothes, but in this lighting, I can't tell what color they are. My guess is black. Both brothers have always had an aversion to color.

"Pax?" I whisper, reaching for his face. His skin is clammy against my fingers.

"I shouldn't have come here." His voice is clearer than it was the other night, but it's still slurred. This close, I can smell the alcohol on his breath. "I just didn't want to be alone."

215

Heart breaking, I wrap my arms around him and hold on for dear life. He hesitates a second, as if he's not sure he's still allowed to do the same, but after a moment, his tense muscles relax and he hugs me back. He presses his head to my shoulder, and I feel his breath hitch as he does.

"It's okay. You're not alone," I assure him, speaking into his chest. "I'm right here. I've got you."

"Can I stay here tonight?" he asks. "I'm so tired, and the nightmares... They've been bad lately."

Telling him no isn't an option. I've already done that once this past week and I refuse to hurt him like that again. If Rafferty is going to take issue with it, then that will be his problem to figure out and not mine.

Taking his bigger hand in mine, I pull away from him and turn to leave the kitchen. Standing in front of her bedroom door is Zadie. Her eyes are full of concern and skepticism. I don't have to ask to know she's worried about how Raff will react. It's not only my dad's comfort that's on the line, but also hers. I'm not as worried about word getting back to Rafferty as I am about word spreading about Pax's vulnerable state. We are the only ones who need to know how he's struggling. It's no one else's business.

Pax follows behind me, silently letting me lead him toward my room. As I pass Zadie, I tell her, "Don't tell anyone about this."

She nods in understanding. "Yell if you need help with anything."

She was right about Pax being in rough shape, but while I know the alcohol and pills are playing a factor, so is his lack of sleep. If he's still like he used to be, he'll crash after a few minutes and be dead to the world for hours. Not even a tornado could wake him back then and I'm hoping it's the same now.

TWENTY-EIGHT
RAFFERTY

THERE ARE eight pieces of cutlery sitting in front of me on the table, and I can't decide which one I'd prefer to stab myself with. I would figure out how to use the teaspoon as a weapon if it meant I could leave.

I don't usually mind these dinners with my grandma, but I'm not in the mood to talk about my future at The Wilde Corporation. Or any future for that matter. How can I discuss what I'll be doing in seven months when I graduate when I barely have a handle on what I'm doing now?

When my grandfather passed two years ago, his majority shares of the company were passed down to me. While on paper, I'm the president of the company, I'm not allowed to officially take the reins until I've received my degree. It was a stipulation in his will that has been strictly enforced despite my arguments. One of my grandfather's most trusted men has been handling things while I'm being lulled to sleep by my econ professor.

Pax will receive our parents' shares of the company when he turns twenty-five, but he has shown zero interest in working for the family business. Which isn't a huge shock. His mind is more artistic and imaginative. He would die a slow death if he had to sit in on board meetings and schmooze politicians in DC to ensure we get the defense contracts we want.

That's the reality I'm looking at for the next fifty or so years. The only thing that's keeping me from leaving it all behind is knowing there are priceless secrets coming my way. My poker games and business here are lucrative as hell, but my income now will look like pennies once I get to the big dogs in the capital. Those connections will then branch overseas, and I'll have enough debts and dirt on our world leaders to do whatever the fuck I want.

That is what excites me.

"It's a shame that Paxton could not join us," my grandmother, Claire, comments from across the grand dining room table. "Was he not feeling well again?"

When Mom died and Dad was sentenced to fifteen years in prison, we were forced to move in with our grandparents. They were kind and generous, and best of all, they didn't hover. As long as our grades remained steady and we gave them a courtesy heads-up so they wouldn't worry, they didn't care if we stayed out late or didn't come home at all. Grandma Claire, who had long stopped working as a lawyer for the company, stepped up in all the ways we needed her. While she took on our mother's role, she never tried to replace her.

I can't very well tell her that her grandson was too drunk to come with me, so I simply nod my head. "Yeah. I think it's a virus or something."

Claire, who looks so much like my mom, furrows her graying eyebrows at this. I know she doesn't believe me, but she doesn't push the subject any further. "Very well. Perhaps next time." She takes a bite of the small starter salad the chef made that just tastes like raw kale. "Is there anything new in your world, Rafferty? How is your last year of college going?"

I should lie and tell her nothing new and exciting is happening. Instead, I stupidly open Pandora's box and tell her, "Posie is back."

I'm not entirely sure why I'm opening the door for us to talk about her. Perhaps it's because I haven't gone a second in the past week without thinking about that night and the way she left bleeding.

Her head cocks to the side. There's so much hairspray in her coiffed hair that it doesn't shift on her head when she moves. "Posie? You mean the young girl who turned your father in?"

"Yes."

She doesn't react to this with any malice or contempt, as if Posie turning my dad in had zero consequences in her eyes. "How is she doing? She was always a very sweet girl when she was young. If I recall correctly, she was quite smitten with you. My goodness, she looked at you like you hung the moon." She smiles over her wineglass. "Have you two reconciled?"

I stare at my grandmother through narrowed eyes. "How can I reconcile with her when she's the reason Mom is dead?"

To my dismay, she scoffs dramatically at me. "Don't be *ridiculous*, Rafferty. Your mother's death was *not* Posie's fault."

"How can you say that?" My hand tightens around my fork. "Had she kept her mouth shut like she promised me she would, Mom never would have been as depressed as she was. The fallout of Dad being sent to prison put her in that bathtub."

Claire sits up straighter in her chair and calmly folds her arms over each other on the table. "Do not blame that young girl for the tragic decision your mother felt she needed to make," she pauses, eyes falling to her hands. "And do not be angry at Posie for doing something your mother should have done herself."

"What should Mom have done?" I ask.

"Protected you."

"You say it like it was that simple."

Her head shakes once, and she frowns. "You're right, the situation was anything but simple. It was complex and a very difficult place for you all to be in. That doesn't change the fundamental fact that a parent protects their child. It should never be the other way around. You were unfairly put in a place where you felt you needed to do that for her, and because of it, you feel like you have failed her."

I swallow hard, hand flexing on my fork again. "I *did* fail. She died."

Standing from her chair, she comes around the table to stand next to me. "Look at me, Rafferty." Doing as she says, she holds my face between her wrinkled hands. "You need to hear me when I say this; Mollie's death was no more your fault than it was Posie's. It was devastating and heartbreaking, but it was *no one's* fault. She was my daughter and I miss her greatly, but it isn't doing anyone any good pointing fingers and placing blame. She wouldn't want that for you."

"What do you think she'd want me to do?"

"She'd want you to let go of it all. The anger, the guilt, the blame. It's only hurting you now, my boy." Bending down, she kisses my forehead, no doubt leaving a mauve kiss print. "Now, I'm going to go ask the chef if the next course is ready. I don't know about you, but I can't eat any more of that kale."

I'M DRIVING down the highway with my windshield wipers going at full speed and weaving between cars in my Jaguar F-Type when Rome's name comes across the car's Bluetooth system.

Pressing a button on the steering wheel, I accept the call. "Hey."

"Did Pax end up going with you to see Granny W?" Only Rome can call her that. If anyone else tried it, she'd probably whack them with one of her books. She pretends to just tolerate him, but everyone knows that she has a soft spot for him.

"No, he was staying home tonight. He didn't look like he'd make it through the car ride there without passing out." Something is wrong if he's calling to ask me that. "What's going on?"

"I'm over at the house because I'm avoiding my father as per usual, and I just checked everywhere. Pax is gone again."

"Goddammit!" I shout, slamming my palm against the steering wheel. "Did you call your cousin?"

"Vinny knows if he sells to Pax again, I'll make him wear his balls as a necklace," Rome assures me.

I don't want to be angry at my brother because I know this isn't his fault, I just wish he'd stay in the fucking house so I didn't have to keep hunting his ass down.

"Who else would he go to?"

"Hold tight, I'm going to make some calls." Rome ends the call, leaving me with only the sound of the engine roaring and my thoughts.

I thought I could handle Pax on my own and that he didn't need to go to some rehab where they have sharing circles and shit, but I'm starting to worry that it's spiraling further and further out of my control and capabilities. I just don't know how to have that conversation with my brother. How do I tell him that I can't help him anymore and we need to send him somewhere? It feels like yet another way I've let down my family.

My grandmother's words echo in my head. *Let go of it all. The anger, the guilt, the blame.*

It's the last part I'm struggling with the most.

Blame.

For the longest time, I could only blame *her*. In the red mist of rage that consumed and blinded me, Posie was the only viable culprit I could see. It wasn't until recently, when the fire that has been burning below my skin started to dim, that I started to wonder if I've misplaced some of my own blame onto her.

I know I've been alone in blaming her. Everyone else around me seems to not hold her accountable in any way. My grandmother sat across from me with a hopeful look in her eye while she asked if we'd gotten back together. If she believed Posie was to blame, she wouldn't want her grandson anywhere near her. The way she sees it, Posie's actions were a kindness.

And then there's Pax, who *apologized* to her as if he'd been the one to do something wrong. His emotions have been numbed for years and yet, when he looked at her, he *cried*. He cried and begged her to stay with him.

Stay with him…

Keeping my eyes on the road the best I can, I dig into my pocket and pull out my phone. The app Rome had put on my phone sits right there on my home page, and when I open it, I find myself relieved at what I find on the live footage of Posie's room.

Weeks ago, I would have been livid to see my brother with her but knowing he's there—*safe*—is all that matters to me now.

They lie together on her bed with a blanket thrown over them. It looks like Pax is already asleep, but Posie is awake, gently stroking his hair. She brings him a level of comfort and peace I haven't been able to give him, and for that I'm thankful for her.

I redial Rome as I shift gears and speed faster down the highway.

"Did you find him?" he asks as a greeting.

"Yes, he's with her."

There's a long pause before he asks, "What are you going to do?"

"I'm headed there now."

ZADIE, who looks like she's been fighting a bear in her sleep based on her wild hair, swings the door open. Her tired eyes widen when she sees it's me standing in her doorway, and her shoulders tense.

"He just showed up on his own," she blurts. "So don't be mad at Posie."

"I'm not mad."

Her head cocks. "*You're not?*"

"No, I'm not." Not bothering to wait for an invitation, I push past her and into the apartment that smells of the sugary citrus scent that clings to Posie. Zadie follows close on my heels as I walk farther inside and toward the closed bedroom door on the left.

"Just so you know, there's nothing romantic going on between them. You don't need to be jealous or mad she let him stay. It's clear she loves him, but it's not the same way she loves you," Zadie may talk in hushed tones, but her comment has my back straightening like she'd screamed it at me.

I don't look back at her when I ask, "How could *you* possibly know that?"

"I don't know all the shit you've pulled with her, but I know enough, and despite all of it, she's *still* not ready to give up on you. She said so herself just earlier tonight. The only reason a person would hold on to someone like *you* so tightly is if they loved you. *Unconditionally.*"

In this moment, I hate you almost as much as I love you. That's what she'd told me after I cut her with the knife. This whole past week, I haven't been able to get the look on her face out of my head. It's haunted me when I close my eyes at night and there's been a crushing weight on my chest. I saw myself reflected in her honey gaze, and I didn't like what I saw. Or more so, I didn't like *who* I saw. How can she not be ready to give up on me after that?

Not knowing how to respond to Zadie, I turn the door handle and step inside the dark room. Careful to not make too much noise, I close the door behind me with a soft click. The only light comes from the small window on the far side of the room. The moonlight streams in, casting shadows on the space.

There's just enough light for me to make out their curled-up shapes on her queen-size bed. Sometime during my twenty-five-minute drive here, Posie had fallen asleep too. In the middle of the bed, her back is pressed to Pax's, and her head rests on her hands. Pax's tattooed arm is flung off the side, and his chest rises and falls with each of his steady deep breaths. His sleep is peaceful, but my guess is he's actually passed out cold from the alcohol. I doubt he'll remember how he got here tomorrow.

The only person I ever tolerated sharing Posie with was Pax. Their friendship and connection have been solid—*unbreakable*—since they were toddlers. Zadie's warning about there being nothing romantic between them wasn't necessary. That's never been something I questioned, but none of that can stop the twinge of jealousy that flares in my veins at the sight of them sharing a bed.

Walking to the side of the bed Posie is facing, I crouch down and reach for her. My knuckles trail down her face, and when my thumb swipes across her bottom lip, she jerks awake. She's tense for a moment before she relaxes with a soft exhale across my fingers. In so many ways, this moment reminds me of those mornings I woke up next to her in bed. It was in those first few moments of the day when my only focus was on the gentle look in her eyes and the peace that surrounded us. I knew what would be waiting for me outside my bedroom door, and I savored every second of those quiet minutes I had with her.

"Don't make him leave," she whispers her plea. "He needed this."

"I'm not making him leave." Pulling my hand away from her, I stand to my full height and toe off my boots.

She lifts up on her arm, and I can feel her eyes on me in the dark. "What are you doing?"

I take off the charcoal sport coat I'd worn to appease Claire and fold it in half, placing it on top of the leather shoes. "I'm not leaving either."

"What do you mean you're not—"

Her question is cut off because I answer it when I lie down next to her on the bed. It's a tight fit, and there's barely an inch between us, but unless she demands I leave, I have no intentions of moving from this very spot until morning.

"What are you doing?" she questions, lying back down on her side with her hands tucked to her chest.

Even though I know it's not the full truth, I tell her, "He must have been in a really bad state to show up here. I'm not letting him out of my sight." I turn on my side, so we're basically nose to nose.

She's facing the window and the dim light illuminates the soft angles of her face.

"Do you want me to go?"

She hesitates, brows furrowing. "Are you going to yell at me again?"

"No." I tuck her straight hair behind her ear, and she leans into my touch. "Not tonight."

I don't know how or *if* I can promise her I never will again. Letting go and moving past the anger that's satiated me for all these years isn't an easy task. Forgiveness also isn't something that comes naturally to me. It's foreign, and it still feels in many ways like it's a betrayal to my mother's memory, but I can't ignore the piece of me that wants to try. If I don't want to become my father, I need to figure out how to do what Claire said and let go.

"Then you can stay." Between us, her fingers absentmindedly play with the thin cotton of my black shirt. "I *want* you to stay." Her words are so quiet, they're barely audible to my ears, but they make my heart pound in my chest.

"I don't understand how you can still want that."

"Me neither, but it's the truth."

She shifts closer and her nose brushes against mine. Posie's movements are soft—*gentle*—but they're like a wrecking ball to my defenses. Each soft breath of hers across my lips breaks down another one of the bricks I'd built around myself. We've been physically close since she's been back, but this is *different*.

We've been at war. We're bloodied and scarred, but tonight we're waving white flags. I'm not sure if the battle will restart when the sun rises, and I'm not sure if I want it to anymore. All I do know is that surrender doesn't sound all that bad.

Eyes closing, my forehead drops against hers. Between us, her fingers tangle with mine. We stay like this—still and calm like those mornings when we were teenagers—and I allow myself to remember what it's like to feel something other than anger toward her.

I remember that it feels *good*.

"For just a moment, can you be honest with me?" she asks, nose running along mine again.

"Maybe."

There's a long pause, like she's trying to talk herself into speaking. "Did you ever miss me?"

It would be easy to lie—I find it's usually the simplest path for me—but something about the innocence and sincerity of her question has me wanting to be honest. "Every day, Butterfly. Every. *Fucking*. Day. And it only made me hate you more."

Eyes still closed, I feel her lips ghost against mine. A calming heat travels through my veins from the brief contact. She's always found a way to be a sedative to my chaos.

"I don't want you to hate me anymore. It *hurts* me that you do."

My hand, on its own accord, reaches for the place on her chest I'd cut. She only wears a camisole and my fingertips brush across the exposed bandage. The heavy weight returns to my chest as I relive that moment in my head. Instead of allowing my rage to fuel me, I'd allowed it to control me. The precision planning I'd put into her return went out the window and I became a passenger in my own body that night. Posie had handled me with as much grace and bravery as she could until I drew blood. That was both of our breaking points.

Freeing one of my hands from her grasp, I cradle her face in my palm and thread my fingers through her soft hair.

"I know," I tell her in a barely detectable whisper before pressing my lips to hers.

My overall plan for showing up here wasn't fully thought out, but I know I didn't come here with the intention of kissing her. After what happened last week, the possibility Posie would *want* that seemed wildly unlikely. It appears I was wrong, because at the first brush of my lips against hers, she sighs as if in relief and her body relaxes into mine. The sliver of space that has been between us vanishes as she melts against me.

It turns out this is exactly what she wanted and exactly what I didn't know I needed.

I've never been good at putting my thoughts or emotions into words, and all week I've been trying to figure out how to tell her I haven't completely turned into my father. That I haven't been fully corrupted and that I'm still here *somewhere* under the veil of darkness. I could be given six months to come up with the appropriate words to tell her but they'd never come to me.

What I can do—what I've always been able to do—is *show* her.

They say actions speak louder than words, and I can only hope she can still hear me in my silence.

Running my tongue along the seam of her lips, I coax her to open for me. Posie, who's always enjoyed following my lead, does as she's told. The kiss deepens, our tongues sliding against each other as our hands begin to wander. Her lean muscles are strong beneath my fingertips from hours of dedication to her art form and her soft skin is warm against mine. Her hand dips beneath the hem of my black shirt and my abs tighten under her delicate touch.

I thought I remembered what it felt like to kiss her, but as she gives in to me and her soft moans fill my ears, I realize I'd forgotten. More importantly, I'd forgotten how much I *liked* it. I didn't enjoy making out with girls before Posie, and I liked it even less after her. The act itself became a sloppy stale tequila tasting event that I simply went through the motions of doing to get to what I really wanted. Mindless fucking with faceless women.

With *her* it's different. I'm certain I could kiss Posie all night and not get bored of it, and I don't think I would give a shit if we didn't go any further than this even though my dick is already straining against my zipper.

The second she started to trace the defined muscles under my shirt, I was done for, and with each stroke of her tongue against mine as she ventures lower to my waistband, I only grow harder for her.

Tonight, I have my control in a death grip and I'm not letting go until she tells me to. But that doesn't mean she's making it easy for me.

When she hooks her leg over my hip and grinds herself against me, every muscle in my body stiffens as my restraint is tested.

Breaking our kiss, she breathlessly pants against my lips. "Touch me."

Eyes opening for the first time in minutes, I look at her and then at the back of my brother's head. If I was selfless, I would be more worried about waking Pax, but because I'm selfish, I'm more concerned about the possibility he will hear the noises she makes. I may be willing to share her attention with my brother, but I will not share the sounds she makes as I bring her to the brink with him. Those belong to me and *only* me.

At my hesitation, she shifts her hips again, urging me. "You told me before I had to come to you when I was horny and ask you to take care of me. I'm asking now."

Wanting to give her what she craves, I nip her bottom lip and lick the burn away. "If you make too much noise, I will stop. Do you understand?"

She nods before crushing her mouth to mine once more and sighs happily when my fingers dip below the waistband of her thin cotton pajama shorts.

When I find she's not wearing panties, I can't stop the rush of possessiveness that washes over me. "I'm going to look past it this *one* time that you're pantyless with another man in your bed." I don't give a fuck if the man is my own brother.

Whatever her reply was going to be is silenced when my fingers delve between her thighs and find her already wet for me. She sucks in a breath, hips rolling against my palm as I begin to make circles around her clit.

For the first time in a long time, I'm prioritizing someone else's needs. My dick is painfully hard and eager for her touch, but it's the last thing on my mind. My only thought is making sure Posie feels good. The desire to do this is a foreign sensation and contradictory to the way I've been operating for these years, I know it's what I need to do for her. It's what I *want* to do for her.

Her hand threads through the strands of my hair, pulling ever so slightly, and I swallow the needy sounds that are starting to form in the back of her throat. I kiss her deep when I sink two fingers inside of her and she grinds against my palm in whatever rhythm pleases her best.

Posie's movements become more erratic as she closes in on her high.

"Easy, baby," I warn, skimming her delicate jaw with light kisses. The term of endearment falls from my mouth effortlessly, like I'd never stopped calling her that. I don't allow myself to dwell on it too much because I know what will happen if I do. I'm enjoying this—enjoying *her*—and I don't want to ruin it.

As she begins to shake, ecstasy cascading over her, she throws her face into my shoulder and bites down in a desperate attempt to muffle the sounds I force out of her with my fingers. It's not enough to break the skin, but I know I'll be wearing her mark tomorrow. A month ago, the idea of being marked —*claimed*—by Posie Davenport would have filled me with disgust. And now... Now I find myself liking it.

Panting, she pulls back and looks at me. In the darkness, I can't pinpoint what emotion is reflected in her eyes and I wish I could. I want to know what she's thinking. Is she as conflicted over the whole thing as I am? Does she regret letting me in her bedroom tonight?

Smoothing her hair off her face, I press my lips to her temple. She clings to me as I do, her hands holding me like she's afraid of what will happen if she lets go.

The storm from earlier continues outside her small bedroom window, and as lightning flashes across the sky, it momentarily lights up her face. Eyes hooded and lips pulled in a sly smirk, she swings her leg completely over me and gracefully climbs off the bed. Confused, I turn onto my back and watch her walk toward the door. Over her shoulder, she looks at me briefly before reaching for the hem of her camisole and pulling it over her head. Once the cotton fabric is on the floor, she bends at her waist and pulls her shorts off.

"We both know you're not done with me." With nothing but her leather butterfly collar on, she opens her bedroom door and turns her head again. "Coming?"

She walks out the door before I can say anything. Posie knows she doesn't have to wait for my answer. We both already know what I'm going to do.

I'm off the bed and pulling my clothes off, leaving them in a pile next to hers, before leaving the room after her. The small living space connected to the open-floor plan kitchen is empty when I close the door softly behind me, but the slider leading to their balcony is open. The sound of the pouring rain gets louder the closer I get to the glass door and thunder rumbles in the distance.

She lives on the seventh floor of the building, and luckily the surrounding buildings are half the height. If they were any taller, they would have an unobstructed view of Posie's naked ass leaning against the metal railing. Knowing they can't easily see her, and the fact it's dark as hell out here are the only reasons I'm not pulling her inside by her throat.

I'm not shy and I don't give a fuck if they're looking at my body, but I care a shit-ton if they're looking at her.

"Do you remember the first time you kissed me?"

I don't have to think hard about her question. The memory of that night with her dressed in green velvet comes to mind instantly. I step outside and leave the sliding door cracked. "I was pissed because that fucker had his hands all over you. You stopped me in the parking lot when I was leaving." Lightning flashes over her head as I move closer to her. "It was raining then too."

Many of our big moments happened in the rain. It was raining the night I finally stopped fighting my feelings for her and accepted them for what they were. The night the cops showed up at my house to arrest my father, it was pouring. Water soaked through our clothes when I screamed at Posie in the middle of the street surrounded by flashing cop cars. She was crying, but I couldn't tell the difference between the raindrops and the tears running down her face.

Right now, it feels a lot more like our first encounter.

Her head tilts and she looks at me like she's seeing past all the walls we've put between us. "This is kinda like a full circle moment, isn't it?" Her hand reaches for me, her fingers dragging down my chest and then over the hard ridges of my abs. My cock jerks at the contact, still craving attention. She knows it too. Lips pulled up in that smirk of hers, she nods toward the cushioned chair behind us. "Sit down. You took care of me. Let me return the favor."

"Are you telling me what to do?" I run my knuckles down her face, pushing her loose hair back.

"I wouldn't dream of it."

She pushes on my chest, urging me to do what she asks. I fall into the chair, and the second my arms rest on the wicker armrests, she's climbing on and straddling my thighs. Her lips crash into mine in a quick and deep kiss, her tongue licking against mine. One of her hands rests on my shoulder to keep her steady and the other reaches between us.

My entire body jolts when her deft fingers wrap around my cock and her thumb spreads the drop of precum over the head and my piercing. When I hiss out a breath, I feel her smile against my lips. After everything, pleasing me *still* makes her happy. I'm not sure at this point which one of us is more fucked in the head. We might be in a tie, and I'm okay with it.

She holds my dick in her fist as she lowers herself slowly down. Inch by inch, her body stretches to accommodate me, and as it does, she throws her head back. Her moans mingle with the sound of the thunder miles away and her bare flesh heats against mine despite the cold wind.

Hands moving to grip her hips, my fingers dig into her delicate skin. "Fuck me," I order, desperate for her to move. My hold on my control is hanging on by a damn thread.

Lifting onto her knees, she rises almost completely off my dick before slamming her hips back down. The move has both of us moaning. She does this twice more before she falls into a steady, fast-paced rhythm. With each of her downward thrusts, I match her with one of my own. We collide violently into one another, but we can both take it. We both want it.

No, we both *need* it.

Her temple rests against mine and her arms snake around my neck. With each breath of air I force out of her lungs, I feel it whoosh against my ear. I kiss along her neck and shoulder, licking, sucking, and biting at her smooth skin. The anticipation of seeing what kind of marks I'm leaving behind runs through me.

Her breathing turns into harsh ragged pants and her thrusts pick up speed. She's close and the way my balls are starting to tighten, I know I am too.

"That's it," I encourage through clenched teeth. "It's like you never stopped riding my fucking cock. Your body remembers exactly what to do and what it likes." Hand fisting in her hair, I pull her head back, exposing her delicate throat. "Did you think about this—think about *me*—when you let those other men touch what's mine? Did it help you get off?"

Her nails scrape over my shoulders and down my chest. "*Yes*," she all but purrs. "Did you imagine it was me on my knees for you when you let other whores suck you off?"

I tried to stop myself, but I was never successful. When I looked down at those faceless women, I saw Posie's honey eyes staring up at me. "Every time. I never could scrub the memory of you."

"Good," she groans before crushing her mouth to mine. When her thighs start to shake and her pussy clamps down on me, I greedily swallow her moan like a shot of alcohol as she comes for me.

I pump into her twice more before I'm overtaken by white-hot pleasure, and I spill deep inside of her. She milks me of every drop and damn near steals my ability to breathe in the process.

THIRTY
POSIE

I DON'T KNOW how long I've been lying here, my head on his shoulder, while he traces circles down my spine, but it's been long enough for the wind to change direction and my skin to grow cold from the constant rainy breeze.

Rafferty must feel me shiver against him because his hand smooths down my back. "You're freezing. Let's go back inside." He tries to sit up, but I don't move with him. If anything, I tighten my hold. "Baby, seriously, you have goose bumps."

The return of him calling me such an endearing name has heat flashing through me and a twinge of fear echoing in my bones. Tonight feels like a turning point, but I'm terrified the change is only temporary, and he'll wake up in the morning and remember he thinks I betrayed him. That he still hates me. And that's why I cling to him and am reluctant to move. I don't want this moment to end.

He didn't have to say the words aloud. I heard him in the gentleness of his touch and look in his cold eyes. Those actions are the closest thing to an apology that Rafferty is capable of right now. He knows he went too far last week with the gun in my face and then the knife. I also know why he was behaving the way he was, but that doesn't mean it still didn't scare the absolute shit out of me.

I know him well enough to know the tenderness he's shown tonight won't last. This isn't him. He's rough and demanding, and I *enjoy* that about him. I just don't want the hostility that's clung to him like a toxic cloud to return. I don't want the barbed wire walls to erect between us again. It's wishful thinking, but I'm going to hold on to this sliver of light like it's my lifeline back to him.

"Just a minute longer."

He doesn't listen to my request. Taking matters into his own hands, he holds me under my thighs and stands from the chair with surprising ease. My arms snake around his neck instinctually to keep myself from falling even though I know he won't drop me.

Biting back a smile, I tease, "Now you're just showing off."

He hardly makes a sound, but I know he's chuckling by the way his bare chest slightly shakes against mine. It's a small victory that has my heart soaring. I used to be able to make him laugh with hardly any effort, and it's now my goal to do so again. That is, if he'll let me.

He doesn't put me down until we quietly enter my bedroom again. With a look over his shoulder, I check on Pax. I feel a little guilty for leaving him, but it doesn't look like he's moved an inch since we left the room. If it weren't for the fact I can hear his heavy breathing from across the room, I would be going over there to check on him. Whatever combination of alcohol and pills that are in his system makes me nervous. All it would take is one too many pills to do something irreversible like Mollie did.

Feet back on the carpet, I hold on to Rafferty's sides and nod toward my bathroom door. "I need to shower and get back to him."

He stares at his brother's sleeping form, brows pulled in

worry. "I know he gets nightmares. I've heard him screaming in the middle of the night, but he's never told me what he dreams about. Has he told you?"

"No, he hasn't." And that's the truth. I have a fairly good idea, but Pax has never gone into detail about what monsters occupy his dreams. "All I know is it helps him when he doesn't have to sleep alone." Looking at the ground, hands flexing nervously on his warm skin, I quietly add, "He needs help, Raff. More help than either of us can give him."

I'd hoped that one day Pax would open up to his brother, and they'd be able to get him the help he needed together. It's clear he's still carrying the weight of it all alone and it's slowly killing him in the process. I tried to talk to him about getting the proper help when we were sixteen, but he wasn't open to it, and I didn't push him. *Couldn't* push him. I fully understood and respected it was something he would have to deal with at his own pace. He made me promise I'd never tell a soul and it's a secret I will take to my grave no matter what.

"I know," Rafferty solemnly responds a tense moment later.

I don't want to push Pax, but I can't sit back and let him self-medicate. There has to be a way to help him without forcing him to admit something he's not ready to.

Raising onto my tippy-toes, I press my lips to his stubbly jaw. "We'll figure it out."

I'm not sure if Rafferty wants my help, but I'm still letting him know I'm here.

Letting him go, I head to the bathroom to take a quick shower. I don't know if he plans on joining me, so I leave the door unlocked just in case.

It's not until I've stepped under the hot spray of water minutes later that I hear him enter. My heart pounds wildly in my chest when he steps into the shower behind me and pushes my wet hair aside so he can kiss my neck.

His dick poking me in my back has me giggling. "Again?"

"I'm making up for lost fucking time." He sucks my skin, no doubt adding to the collection of hickeys I'll have in the morning.

Rafferty repositions us so his back is to the spray and my hands are on the white-tiled wall. The only reason I don't cry out as he pushes inside of me is because he wisely shoves his fingers in my mouth. The only sound I can manage to make is a gurgling, gagging sound. He growls in my ear when I sink my teeth into his flesh, but I know he likes it. He picks up speed and pounds violently into me, ensuring I'm going to feel him every time I move a muscle tomorrow.

THIRTY-ONE
POSIE

"*HOLY* HICKEYS." Lark's blue eyes are huge as she sits down across from me and passes a black coffee my way. "No wonder you need this. *Jesus*, did he even let you sleep?"

Adjusting the hood of my cropped white sweatshirt around my neck, I nod in agreement. "He may have overdone it."

Not only was Pax gone when I woke up, so was Rafferty. He may have been missing from my bed, but he left me with ample proof that he'd been there. Even if I was inclined to try to hide the marks covering my neck, shoulders, and *boobs*, I don't have enough concealer in my makeup bag to do the trick. Plus, I know him. He wouldn't want me to cover them. The hoodie will have to be our happy medium.

Lark sits back in her chair, the straw of her green juice in front of her smirking lips. "You like it, don't you? You like that he's basically put a neon sign on your ass that reads *'she's mine'*."

Sighing, I put my elbows on the table and hold my face with my hands. "Does it make me totally pathetic that I do?" I ask through my fingers.

Peeking across the table, Lark shrugs her narrow shoulders and takes a long sip of her drink. "I'm not in a position to judge."

"Mystery Guy?"

"Mystery Guy." Her nails painted in a pristine white polish tap against the side of her cup. "Does it make us batshit crazy for wanting guys that are without a doubt toxic for us?"

I don't even hesitate before answering. "Oh, yeah, it for-*fucking*-sure does."

Dropping my hands, I cross my arms over my chest. My leg bounces anxiously under the table. Last night was good—*really good*—but when I woke up this morning and he was gone, familiar dread filled my tummy. There's a voice whispering in the back of my head telling me Rafferty thinks last night was a mistake and he's brooding somewhere, rebuilding the walls that had dropped between us while he sharpens new knives.

I don't know if I can survive any more emotional—*or physical*—cuts from him. My eyes close and I press my fingers into my temple as a stress headache starts to form.

Lark has just asked, "Are you okay?" when someone sits down beside me and an arm snakes around my waist. Eyes snapping open, I'm dragged from my seat and pulled into his lap. My back rests against his chest and all the tension melts from my body when I feel his lips against my temple.

He's here.

Rafferty's large hand spreads over my exposed tummy and I cover it with mine. Intertwining our fingers, I rest my head back on his broad shoulder. It's scary how a simple touch can instantly put my mind at ease. If any of my fears were even remotely true, he wouldn't be here right now, and he definitely wouldn't want to be anywhere near me.

"Hey, Raff." Rome, who had appeared in the chair next to Lark, points at my neck. "I think you missed a spot."

With his free hand, Raff pulls at the collar of my hoodie. "Really? Where?" I shiver when his fingers trail over the marks he's left. "I think I covered my bases enough to get my point across. Or maybe not since you're still fucking looking at her."

Instead of being deterred by Rafferty's change in tone, Rome's dark eyes light up in amusement. "Oh, come on, don't be like that. You've never cared about sharing before."

Everyone at the table knows Rome's just trying to push his buttons—even Raff knows—but that doesn't stop him from tensing beneath me. It also doesn't stop Lark from giving Rome a look I can't quite put my finger on before her big eyes roll in annoyance.

"You say that like *I* have any interest in being shared, Rome," I pipe up before Rafferty can issue some kind of violent threat to his friend. It does exactly what I wanted it to. He relaxes in the chair again and his thumb starts to casually rub back and forth above my navel.

"Fair enough." Rome winks at me before throwing his hands up in surrender. "All I'm saying is you better hope that shit is gone before the gala next week. Otherwise, you're going to be the center of some *real* unwanted attention. Or you're going to have to wear some ugly ass turtleneck."

Totally lost on what he's talking about, I look between Rafferty and the pair across from us. "What gala?"

Lark groans, lowering her head to the table and bangs her forehead against the hard surface. She doesn't answer my question, all she does is mumble, "*Ugh*, don't remind me."

"Daddy Holloway is having a big fundraising gala for his presidential campaign next week at the Seattle Art Museum. Attendance is unfortunately mandatory." Rome pauses, head cocking at me. "Well, *ours* is at least. I don't actually know about yours."

Rafferty finally speaks up, his chest rumbling against my back. "She'll be there."

I turn in his lap so I can look at him. "*I will?*"

This is brand-new information to me, and something I

probably should have known about seeing as I need time to prepare for such a grand event. I can't exactly show up there in the sundress I bought from *H&M* this summer and my ballet flats. The only pair of heels I own are the ones Mollie picked out for me for the dance when I was fifteen, and the platform stripper heels Ophelia gifted to me in New York for her pole dancing class. I have a *small* hunch the latter option might be a little inappropriate given the elite guest list that will be at this *gala*.

Rafferty nods once. "You're my date."

He's not asking me a question or giving me an option. He's informing me of what I'll be doing, and I could be annoyed at him for not telling me sooner, but I'm not. I'm actually a little bit excited. It feels like a somewhat *normal* way for us to spend time together again.

"What the hell am I going to wear to something like this?"

The corner of his mouth twitches in a ghost of a smile. "I've got it covered."

"My only advice is to wear something with pockets." Lark speaks into the table she's still resting her face on. "It's easier to hide your flask that way."

HE'S WAITING for me outside my class's building hours after we parted ways at the campus dining hall. His attention is glued to his cell phone and there's a lit cigarette between his fingers.

Before he knows I've spotted him, I take a minute to take him in. It's not very often he takes off his well-loved leather boots, but today he's traded them for a pristine pair of white Nike sneakers. He wears black jeans and a charcoal denim jacket over his black hoodie. His wavy dark hair is falling over his forehead and curling around his ears.

The teenage version of Rafferty was hot, but the grown-up version of him has many knees weak and panties wet.

He looks *good* and the girls who are passing with their greedy eyes glued to him know it too. Within the small group heading his way, I spot a girl nudging her friend and gesturing not so subtly at Rafferty. Their heads dip close to each other while they whisper and stare.

Leaning against the railing of the short staircase that leads to the building's door, I wait to see how this plays out with jealousy swirling in my gut. It's an ugly and bitter feeling, and I don't quite know if I have any right to feel this way, but I can't control it. It's like it has a mind of its own.

The girl who'd spotted him first waves her hand coyly at him as they approach, and her painted lips move as she greets him. From here, I can't hear what she says. Not that it matters. I don't need to hear it to know I don't fucking like it.

Rafferty barely lifts his head to acknowledge her. His cold icy eyes blandly stare at her. The girl tries to say something else to him, but he's not listening to a word she's saying because he's finally found me staring.

Arms across my chest and my ankle crossing casually over the other one, I cock my head at him. Lips pulling up in a knowing smirk, he wordlessly flicks his cigarette at the girl's feet. She screeches and high-steps away to avoid being burned. The flirty look disappears from her face in an instant. Glaring, she snaps something I can only assume isn't very nice as he pushes past her and heads in my direction.

Her pissed-off look only deepens when he hooks his fingers under the leather around my throat and yanks my face to his. The last thing I see before my eyes close and I succumb to his toe-curling kiss is her storming away with her friend following close behind.

The whole thing reminds me of our time at Hemlock Hill. I don't know how he got away with it, but he was always waiting for me outside my classroom before the bell dismissed us. He'd kiss me in front of everyone like he is now, as if he needed to remind himself and anyone watching that I was his. I can't help but wonder if it's his motive now as his tongue runs along the seam of my lips and I open for him.

Wrapping my arms around his neck, he kisses me until my skin feels too warm and my breath is coming in short, needy pants. I have to pull back before we reach the point of no return and I'm dragging him inside to an empty classroom. If I had time for it, I wouldn't think twice about doing so, but I have to get to work in twenty minutes and I still have to stop at my apartment to change.

"I don't think she'll ever flirt with you again," I tease, teeth sinking into my bottom lip. Just to see what he'll say, I sarcastically add, "*Bummer.*"

His eyes narrow and I don't miss the glint of humor that flashes in them. "I'm devastated by the loss." Thumb swiping over one of the many love-bites he left behind on my throat, he says, "You should get jealous more often. I like it."

I shouldn't say anything because I don't want to ruin the good mood he seems to be in, but I can't stop myself. "I wasn't aware I had any right to be jealous."

He stands there, staring at me. While he's not saying anything aloud, I can see a hundred different thoughts reflected in his blank expression. He's doing what he's always done. Working through his thoughts and emotions and trying to find a way to put them into words.

Knowing I shouldn't have pushed him, I wince and nervously take a step back. "Sorry, I shouldn't have said—"

He surprises the hell out of me by cutting me off and saying, "You have the same right as I do." He pulls me to him by the cropped hem of my sweatshirt. "I meant what I said. I like when you're jealous. It's really fucking hot."

I'm trying not to get too content with the change that's

happening between us, because I know he hasn't fully forgiven me. Almost six years of anger doesn't just disappear in one night. I think he's trying to let go of it, but I know all it would take is one wrong move for it to all come rushing back.

"Okay," I nod, fighting a small smile. "When I woke up this morning and saw you'd left without saying goodbye, I thought maybe you regretted everything."

He takes my hand, and we walk down the few steps side by side. People are staring at us—well, at *him*—as we pass. Everyone on campus knows who he is, and they also know Rafferty Wilde doesn't *hold hands* with girls. If he's aware of the attention, he doesn't acknowledge it.

"Pax woke up and almost puked on your carpet. He made it to the bathroom in time, but I knew there'd be more of it, so I got him out of there as fast as I could. You were out cold, and since I'd already kept you up most of the night, I didn't want to wake you."

"*Oh...*" I mumble, feeling a little embarrassed by how much anxiety I felt all morning over the whole thing.

He's quiet until we reach the parking lot and I spot his flashy black sports car.

"Shit, I keep forgetting." Letting go of his hand, I dig through my canvas bag until I find what I'm looking for. "Here are your car keys back."

The key fob with the Mercedes logo dangles from my finger-tip, but he doesn't reach for them. His head shakes instead. "Keep them. I don't want you walking home in the dark anymore."

I gape at him. "I'm *not* keeping your *G-Wagen*."

His eyes roll at me. "I'm not giving it to you, I'm letting you borrow it." Brows pulling, his face turns serious when I open my mouth again. "Don't fucking argue with me. You'll lose and you know it. Driving home will be safer."

He's right. I'll lose this argument, and I don't have time for it anyway. Reluctantly, I drop the key back in my bag.

Stepping close, he kisses the top of my head. "Pack a bag when you get home and head to my place after work. You're staying with me."

"I am?"

"Pax is sleeping in his own bed tonight, and I need to be there to make sure he doesn't leave again. If I'm doing that, I can't be in your bed fucking you. So you'll need to come to me, because if you think I'm going a night without your pussy, you're mistaken."

"Is that an order?" I question, ignoring the way my stomach flutters and core muscles tighten.

"You're damn right it is."

Laughing at him, I shove at his chest. "Okay, I have to go find an outfit that will hide your artwork. I don't want to explain what a hickey is to a roomful of seven-year-olds." *Or their parents.*

THIRTY-TWO
RAFFERTY

I COULDN'T HAVE DEVIATED FURTHER from my original plan if I had tried.

The goal was to break her and make her hate me. When I was done with her, she wasn't supposed to want to be anywhere near me. I wanted her to run from me with fear and terror, but since that night in her bed, the drastic and *effortless* shift has only further progressed. I mean, for fuck's sake, I told her to pack a bag last week to spend one night with me, and we're going on day ten of her being at my house.

And it's not because she's decided to shack up with me and never leave again like a stage-five-clinger. Posie has attempted to go back to her apartment every single night, but *I'm* the one stopping her from doing so. *I* don't want her to leave, and the chaotic thoughts that come with that are confusing as hell.

What I felt for her when I was younger is reemerging from the depths where I buried it, and it's starting to overshadow the anger and blame I'd placed on her for so long. The things I'd planned on doing to her have become distant thoughts, and every morning I wake up next to her, it feels less and less like I'm being disloyal to my mother's memory.

And that's what I've been struggling with when I've been alone during this past week. Can letting go of it all be this easy? And more importantly, *should* it be this easy?

The conflict happening in my head dissipates during the small moments. Like when she gets cold at night and moves closer to me, or when she smiles softly at me when I enter the room. My concerns are *completely* silenced when I see her with Paxton. Since she started spending the night, I've seen a change in him. His eyes, while still glassy, are clearer than they've been in years and he's spending less time holed up in his room. He smiled this week. It was quick, and if you blinked, you may have missed it, but it was there.

It's these small moments that keep me from succumbing back into the dark angry mist.

Standing in front of my big bedroom window, I'm completely lost in these thoughts again while I fix my sterling silver cuff links, but the second her reflection appears in the glass, they go quiet.

"Okay, so hair and makeup have never been where I shine, but I did the best I could." She's been stressed all day about going to Mr. Holloway's fundraiser tonight, and it's clear in her tone she's still not at ease about the whole thing. "Also, are you aware there's basically *no* back on this dress? One wrong move and the future president might see my ass crack."

Posie nervously rambles as she flounces around my room, collecting various things to put in her small clutch. Stumbling over the open box of leather heels I'd purchased for her, she bends at the waist and swipes them up.

"I don't know why I'm asking you this. That's probably *exactly* why you picked it out in the first place." In the glass reflection, she bounces on one foot while she shoves the four-inch-tall stiletto on the other one.

"It was definitely a strong deciding factor."

Turning from the window, I finally take her all in. The black silk gown has a slit reaching all the way up to the top of her thigh, and the spaghetti straps that crisscross over her exposed back are basically thick pieces of dental floss. Her hair, which she wears loose and straight, falls over her shoulders. The end pieces that have been lightened are a nice contrast to the dark dress. Her light brown eyes are surrounded by smoky eyeshadow and her full lips have been painted in a shade that reminds me of red wine.

"And it appears I decided correctly." Maybe I chose *too* well. With the way she looks, I already know I'm going to be knocking teeth out tonight. They already stare at her when she's not dressed to the nines, and now I've basically wrapped her in a pretty package to be served to them.

Her eyes rake over me, and I don't miss the heated glint that flashes in them. "I'm never going to see you in an actual tux, am I?" Walking closer, she trails her fingers over the collar of my black dress shirt. The top buttons are undone because I flat-out refuse to a wear fucking bow tie. "You always have to go against the grain. I guess I should just be glad you're not wearing those boots of yours."

The best they're going to get from me is a black sport coat and matching slacks. My dress shoes that have the same red bottoms as Posie's heels are almost pushing my generosity. "It's bad enough I've become a frequent flyer at these kinds of fucking events. I just barely tolerate being there, and I'm not about to let myself look like a penguin or a *server* while I grit my teeth through endless small talk."

It's not that I don't understand the importance of my presence at things like this. In one night, I'll be able to grease the elbows of many of the people who'll ensure my contracts in the capital. While I do that, I just might get lucky and collect a few debts and secrets for my own growing business.

Without having to ask for help, she takes the cuff link that is still in my grasp and deftly pins my sleeve for me. "I can say with almost one-hundred-percent certainty that *no one* will ever mistake you for waitstaff. You don't exactly give off *'how can I serve you'* vibes."

Hand dipping between the high seam of her dress, my fingertips trail toward the inside of her exposed thigh. "I'm pretty sure I *radiated* those vibes last night when I had my face buried in your pussy." My eyes snap to hers when I feel her bare flesh. "No panties?"

The tops of her cheekbones flush. "In *this* dress? Not a chance. Silk doesn't exactly hide panty lines."

"Let me get this straight. You're completely naked under there? No bra or underwear?" I'm this close to saying *"fuck it"* and telling her we're staying home when she smiles wickedly and pats my chest with false sympathy.

"Bet you're regretting your outfit selection now." Turning, she snags her clutch from my unmade bed and heads for the door. Looking at me over her shoulder, she quirks an arched brow. "Come on. We don't want to be late, now do we?"

THIRTY-THREE
RAFFERTY

THE SEATTLE ART MUSEUM has been covered in tacky red, white, and blue balloons and banners. If the wall doesn't have a priceless art installation occupying its space, there's a sign with Senator Holloway's campaign slogan written across it in bold lettering.

Guests, both those of influential status and those who were simply invited to ensure a vote, mingle about, happily sipping their room-temperature champagne. They smile and laugh as they indulge themselves with mediocre surface-level conversations. They're just *tickled pink* to have been included, meanwhile, I feel uncomfortable in my own skin being here.

"If one more person approaches me to discuss the *'wonderful legacy'* my grandfather left behind, or how proud he and my mother would be of me, I'm going to end up in jail." I growl to Rome under my breath before taking a long sip of my old-fashioned.

There are a lot of reasons Holloway is a human piece of shit, but I have to commend him for the open bar. It's the only reason I'm somewhat making it through this tedious night. That, and the woman across the room who keeps eyeing me over her champagne flute. Posie was at my side for the first hour, but Lark whisked her away half an hour ago and has yet to return her to me.

Lark, like a true politician's daughter, walks her around the room introducing her to people with a gracious and pleasant smile on her face. Rome, Posie, and I are probably the only ones in this whole building who know how miserable she is. If her parents did know, they wouldn't give a damn. Their children's happiness has always come secondary to their father's career.

Wherever Lark takes Posie, I keep my eyes on her. Like I'm a bodyguard or some shit, I survey the people around her to make sure they're not looking at what's mine for too long. I don't care if this is a fancy political fundraiser. I won't think twice about drawing blood if they move in too close.

Rome turns to me with a shit-eating grin. "Well, look at the bright side. If that happens, you might get a chance to bond with your dad."

I stare at him through narrowed eyes.

"What? Too soon?"

"Why the fuck am I friends with you again?" I ask.

He snaps his fingers and then points at me. "You know what? I ask myself that same question about *you* all the goddamn time."

Head shaking, I look away from him and search the crowd for familiar faces.

This is the last place you would expect to find the son of an Italian Mob boss, but Rome has been forced to attend these events for as long as I have. Maybe longer. The Valentinos and Holloways have a long-standing partnership. The senator pulls strings and proposes bills that will benefit the Italian's business all while helping to make sure the Valentinos continue to look like a family of real-estate moguls in the eyes of the law. In exchange, the Valentinos handle the dirty work that's often hidden in politics and donate large sums of money to the senator's past and future campaigns. Rome's family's hands get bloody while the Holloways remain clean.

From the outside, you'd never think Rome and Lark's worlds would ever intersect, but they're more enmeshed than anyone really realizes.

"What's Banes doing talking to Posie?" Rome asks, nudging me with his shoulder.

Head snapping back in the direction I'd last seen her, I find the university president and his new bride chatting up my girl. Annoyance flaring in my veins, I down the rest of my whiskey and head toward them.

Astor Banes played a big role in making sure that Posie's application to Olympic Sound was accepted. If it weren't for him making concessions and offering Posie a scholarship she'd be insane to turn down, she probably wouldn't have come home. Which wasn't an option for me. One way or another, she was coming back to me. He, and his dirty secrets, just made the process that much easier for me.

It's not very often I get the chance to blackmail men like Astor. The Banes name carries a lot of weight in a lot of social circles. They have their powerful fingers in a lot of different businesses, and not much happens without their knowledge. He gave up the opportunity to run his family's empire and passed the mantle to his utterly *unhinged* brother Emeric. I've had dealings with him once or twice, but I know next year when I become CEO of The Wilde Corp, we'll be in contact more.

"Banes," I greet stiffly, snaking my arm around Posie's bare back.

Turning her head, she smiles up at me quickly before turning her attention to the couple. "Astor was just reminding me that his son, Callan, went to Hemlock Hill. He was older than both of us, so I don't think we shared any classes."

"I remember Callan. He used to party with us before he graduated early last year. Indie knew him pretty well too, didn't you?"

Indie, Banes's new, much younger wife, gives me a tight smile. "Yep. I guess you can say I met Astor through him."

Astor looks like he wants to put his fist through my face when he catches me smirking. Posie is the only one unaware of how funny this whole interaction is. She has no idea that last year Astor decided he wanted his son's girlfriend and made it happen in his own devious way.

"That sure is *one* way to look at it," I manage to say without laughing.

"Watch yourself, Wilde," he warns darkly.

I don't know if she's not sensing the tension or if she's just electing to ignore it, but Posie cuts in. "I think it's great, and based on that rock on your finger, Indie, it looks like things have worked out really well for you guys."

Indie lifts her hand and shows off a diamond I'm fairly certain sank the Titanic. *You never do anything halfway do you, Banes?* His wife, who's a little bit more reserved than he is, tucks her hand quickly down at her side like she's self-conscious about showing off the ring.

With her other hand, she tucks her short dark hair behind her ear. "Yeah, it took us a while, but we finally figured our crap out." She smiles up at her brooding husband.

As if she's the antidote to his constant "*I have a stick up my ass*" attitude, the harsh lines of his face soften when he looks at her. Never thought I'd see the day the great Astor Banes was pussy-whipped but here we are.

Indie points at Posie's almost empty glass. "You're almost out too. Want to go up to the bar with me?"

I refrain from making a remark about her not yet being of legal drinking age. I mean really, who am I to judge?

"Sure!" Posie squeezes my hand once before leaving me alone with Astor.

Banes is prone to giving me unsolicited advice, so before he has the chance to jump into some lecture I'm in no mood to hear, I start to turn away from him. I've barely moved two inches when he's opening his goddamn mouth.

Fuck.

"From the looks of it, she's not the shell of a human you swore to me she'd be when you got your hands on her. I think it's safe to say your grand plan isn't exactly going as you'd hoped." He doesn't ever have to raise his voice. Astor has a way of speaking that instantly holds your attention regardless of volume. It's *super* fucking annoying. "Or maybe once you touched her again, you realized you didn't hate her as much as you thought."

Instantly on edge, I step into his space. I have at least an inch on him, but I have no doubt it'd be an equal fight if he decided to try and kick my ass. "You have no idea what you're talking about."

He's unmoved by my shift in demeanor. "That may be true, but I do know the Rafferty who broke into my office last year with hatred in his eyes would have torn that girl to pieces with his fucking teeth. I'm just wondering what's changed that she's here with you tonight and looks *happy*." His eyes, the color of a stormy sky, inspect my face. "Or better yet, what's changed in you, Wilde? Where's that darkness that's been following you around since you were a teenager?"

What changed is exactly what he guessed. I touched her and held her in my arms while she slept. While I did, I started to second-guess ever blaming her in the first place. For so long, I thought everyone around me was in the wrong for not being as mad as I was at Posie, but now I'm starting to painfully learn I may have been in the wrong the whole time.

I have barely admitted this to myself, let alone to Posie. Astor doesn't need to be the first to hear me say it, so I simply stare blandly back at him.

At my unwavering silence, he shakes his head with a chuckle. "Alright. That's fine. You don't have to answer." Stepping around me, he pauses before leaving and claps my shoulder with his hand. It's a move that reminds me of something a dad would do to his son. Not that I'm the authority on the matter. "You can choose who you hate, but you can't choose who you love. Take it from me and stop fighting it. You're allowed to be happy, Rafferty."

You can't choose who you love.

Do I still love Posie? Did I ever stop? I can't remember what it's like to be in love. That emotion evaporated from my soul when the police showed up at my house. I was content never gaining it back. Or, at least, I thought I was. Now I'm questioning that along with everything else. She told me she loved me still but was that the truth? Everything was so fucked that night. We both could have been saying things we wish we could take back.

At the same time Astor steps away, Indie reappears in front of him.

"Hi, pretty girl."

"Hi," she greets back, smiling at him like he's the only reason she wakes up in the morning.

Turning, I look all around her for Posie but find that she's alone.

"Where's Posie?" I ask, scouring the room for signs of my butterfly. I ignore the way Astor's face pulls into a knowing look at the sound of my concern. *This arrogant old man is about to taste my fist if he keeps it up.*

Indie gestures behind her with her thumb, and I immediately look in the direction she's pointing to. "Some guy who said he knew her when she was in high school showed up. He was really freaking chatty, so I excused myself. She said she was good."

Pushing past the annoyingly in-love couple, I search over the top of heads trying to lock down her location. I'm halfway across the room when I lock eyes with Rome. His dark eyes look worried as he lifts his chin toward the hallway leading toward the other exhibits.

Turning that way, my blood boils when I discover who's holding her attention captive. He looks the exact same as he did when he was sixteen years old. That same misguided cocky look sits on his face as it did back then, and I can't wait to tear it off him like a bad Halloween mask.

Bryce Fitzgibbons.

Posie says something to him and attempts to step around him so she can leave, but the asshole blocks her path. He laughs at this, finding it entertaining he's forcing her to keep him company.

Rome is already heading my way without me having to ask him for backup when I look back at him. He knows what's about to happen, and the smirk on his face tells me he's just as excited as I am about it.

I reach them in time to watch as Bryce not so subtly reaches out for Posie's arm and grins at her with fucking stars in his eyes.

"Davenport, I never thought I'd see you again. I figured for sure Blackwell chased you out of town for good when all that ugly business went down with his dad."

Posie scowls up at him, dark-red lips pulled in a small frown, and steps back out of his reach.

"It's Wilde now," she corrects him tightly just as she spots me approaching. She knows with one look at me that I'm pissed, but with the way her face pales, I think she's falsely assuming I'm angry at *her*.

She moves toward me, eyes wide. "Raff…" Whatever else she's about to say dies on her tongue when I reach for her. Arm circling around her waist, I smooth my hand down her bare back and pull her to me. I press my lips to her temple, and while I do, I stare down Fitzgibbons over the top of her head.

"Hey, man," he greets like we're *buddies*. It's an unfortunate assumption on his part but it won't last long. I'll be correcting his mistake shortly. "I was just catching up with Posie here since it's been so long. I was actually shocked to see her here since this was never really her crowd, but uh…" He gestures toward my hand resting on her back. "Her attendance is now starting to make more sense. You two back together?"

The more words that fall from his idiotic mouth, the deeper the hole he's digging for himself gets.

I don't bother acknowledging his question. It doesn't matter if we're *"together"* or not. She's mine. Always has been, and I'm going to remind him of just that.

"Funny you should say that." From the corner of my eye, I watch as Rome appears. "I was just wondering myself how you scored an invite here. Last I heard, you were selling *Subarus* at your dad's dealership."

Posie turns around, but I don't let her get far. Standing at my side, I keep my arm hooked around her waist. While she knows now that I'm not angry with her, she's still tense because she knows what's about to happen. This isn't the first time she's been in this position, and I'd bet my trust fund it won't be the last.

Bryce shifts and stands up taller as his ego further inflates. "Didn't you hear? I'm engaged to Mayor Williamson's daughter. Her entire family was invited."

The very mayor who couldn't afford to get into my poker game will be his future father-in-law? Shit, this interaction keeps getting better.

Under her breath, Posie mumbles, "Poor girl."

Biting back a grin, I shake my head like I'm truly upset I didn't know this information. "I must have missed that Facebook status update. Congrats." He thinks I'm being serious and grins proudly. It's not until my head cocks and my eyes narrow does his dumb fucking smile vanish. "But wait a second, if you have a fiancée mingling about somewhere in this shithole, why are you talking up *my* girl?"

At the same time he holds his hands up in a surrender-like fashion, I nod at Rome.

"Wait a second—"

Bryce doesn't get the rest of his sentence out. In one fluid motion, we move in on him. Rome stands behind him, holding him in place, while my fist slams into his stomach. The air is knocked from his lungs, and he doubles over gasping. The whole action was fast. Discreet. No one around us is aware of what's happened.

Hands threading through his perfectly styled hair, I yank his head up and lean close. "I fucking warned you, didn't I? I told you what would happen if I caught you sniffing around her, and you didn't listen to me."

Like an ant under my shoe, you'll remember where you stand on the food chain.

"We were sixteen," he chokes out, face ashen.

I let go of his hair and pat his shoulder patronizingly. "That doesn't fucking matter. My warning didn't come with an expiration date, and you're an idiot for thinking it did."

Rome yanks him up into a full standing position but doesn't release him. He knows I'm not done with him.

Bryce's eyes are wide as his head shakes. "I didn't think you were still into her or that you *cared*. Not after she ratted on your dad like she did. Hell, I thought you'd be happy if someone took her off your hands for the night and treated her like the cheap whore she is."

My vision starts to turn red, and I begin to vibrate with rage. Over the sound of blood rushing in my ears, I hear Posie whisper, "*Shit*."

"*That* was a *big* mistake," Rome cackles. "You better buckle up because you're in for it now, fucker."

At my slight nod, my friend drags Bryce down the hallway. The fact the preppy douchebag thinks he stands a chance at escaping Rome's hold is pathetic. He fights tooth and nail to free himself as Posie and I follow closely behind, but it's no use. He's not getting free until I'm positive he's learned his crucial lesson.

Rome pulls him into the first empty room that has doors. The narrow space has art hanging on every wall, and while I can't personally appreciate the aesthetic, I would wager majority of it costs more than most people will earn in their lifetime. There's a long-padded bench running down the middle of the room for people to sit on while they admire the artwork.

"Close the doors," I order Posie. When she hesitates, staring up at me with unsure eyes, I repeat myself, this time with more force. "I said close the fucking doors!"

She does what I ask, and when she's just barely turned the lock, my fist slams into Bryce's face. His nose makes a crunching sound that is music to my ears. Rome lets go of him at the right time, and he stumbles back onto the polished concrete floors. He lands unceremoniously on his ass, which throws Rome into a fit of hysterics.

"What the hell is your problem?" Bryce chokes, wiping his face with the back of his hand. Blood smears on the piece of his white sleeve that is poking out from under his tailored coat. "You've always been fucking unhinged!"

"The fact you thought you could *touch* her and *live* is my problem," I seethe. A familiar controlling anger comes over my shoulders and wraps itself around me in a choke hold. It's suffocating me, but I don't care. "The fact you thought she could be your *whore* is my problem."

Grabbing him by the lapel of his coat, I drag him off the floor and slam his back into a wall. The ceramic—*something*—that'd been hanging there falls to the ground and breaks into a hundred pieces. Somewhere behind me, Posie gasps at the loud crash.

"You've wanted to get your hands on her since you were a teenager, and you thought tonight was your opportunity, didn't you? You thought you were going to *finally* live out your adolescent fantasy." When he doesn't answer me, I press my forearm into his throat. "Answer me."

The best I get out of him is a jerky nod.

To reward his weak reply, I ease up and he sucks in a greedy breath when I do.

"Haven't you figured out by now the only one who gets to touch her is me?" Backing away from him, he slumps forward with his hands on his knees. Scared eyes watch me as I step behind Posie, and my hand grasps her hip. "Did you really think she'd have any interest in *you*?"

Posie's head turns and she stares at me like she's trying to figure it out. Figure *me* out. I keep eye contact, thumb moving languidly over the silk covering her skin. It's as if we're having another one of our silent conversations and she's hearing every single word. Once she understands what I want, she leans back into my chest and her body relaxes into mine.

Hand venturing lower, I dip my fingers under the edge of the slit in her dress. "You should have realized by now, Bryce, I'm the only one she wants."

Posie's breath shudders when my fingertips brush over her pussy. As a rule, I generally refuse to put a moment like this on display for someone to watch. My possessive need to not share her has never allowed it, but right now, my overbearing sense of jealousy is muted by my need to prove to this fucker he'll never have Posie. And more importantly, I want to prove to him she'll never want anyone the way she wants me.

Rome being here to witness this isn't ideal, but it's necessary. I need him to keep Bryce in place while my hands are occupied.

As Posie's sharp inhale echoes off the white walls, Bryce's face turns an ungodly shade of red. Thinking he has a choice in whether or not he's going to watch me finger her, he pushes off the wall and attempts to leave. Rome is on him before he makes it two feet.

Rome's foot slams into the back of Bryce's leg and his knees give out. He crashes to the ground with a sharp curse.

"*Shit!*"

"What is it, Bryce? Do you not like watching someone else live out your fantasy?" I growl, kissing the side of Posie's neck. The hickeys I'd left there had finally faded and I'm feeling the need to leave more in their place. Fingers pumping in and out of her at a leisurely pace, her head falls back on my chest and her eyes flutter closed.

I could easily get her off right here, but even in my current state, I know to draw the line somewhere. I'll gladly reward her for her participation when we're alone. She whimpers when I pull my hand away from between her thighs and bring my fingers to my mouth.

"How does it feel knowing you'll never get to taste her?" His eyes flare with anger and jealousy when I suck my digits clean.

Fighting against Rome's hold, he shouts, "You've made your point! Let me go!"

"I don't think I have. My point won't be made till you fully grasp she'll only ever be a whore for one person. *Me.*" Gathering her long strands of hair, I pull her head back so I can growl in her ear. "Get on your knees, Butterfly."

Brows pulling, she pulls out of my grasp and turns to me. It wouldn't be unwarranted for me to find disgust or uneasiness on her face after receiving that order, but I don't. She doesn't recoil. Hell, she hardly blinks. The only thing reflected in her eyes as she looks at me is understanding, and that's because she *does* understand. There have been times I swear Posie comprehends what I'm feeling better than I do. It makes sense she'd have that ability. She's the only one in my life who's truly ever bothered to learn what goes on in my head.

Posie *knows* me and accepts me. That's what I love about her most.

Love?

Fuck. There's that word again.

In a soft voice, she simply asks, "Is this what you need?"

Yes. I need him to know he can't touch you. That you're mine.
"Get on your knees."

"Okay."

Crouching, she pushes the pieces of ceramic that scatter the floor below her away to ensure she doesn't cut herself. Once she deems it safe, she nimbly transitions onto her knees. Big eyes flick between the men ten feet away and then back up to me.

"Don't look at them. Eyes on me, baby."

Nodding, she doesn't wait for any instruction or further orders. She knows what I need and how I need it. In the next breath, she has my belt undone and my zipper down. My teeth grind as she pulls my hard cock out of my pants and strokes it. Her thumb glides over one of the silver ends of the barbell going through the head, making me jerk in her hand.

My fingers tangle in the strands of hair she spent so much time perfecting before we left. I'll make it up to her later for screwing it up. "I'm going to fuck your mouth, and you're going to show him what a good girl you are for me." *And only me.* "Open."

I watch the tip of my dick slide between her painted lips. It's a sight I will never get tired of seeing. It's one I've dreamed about for damn near a fucking decade. She may have been gone for all these years, but she was never far from my mind. Every time I jerked off, it was her mouth and her pussy I was envisioning.

Her tongue swirls around the tip, flicking against my piercing before taking more of me into her mouth. My grip on her hair tightens and I groan as I bump the back of her throat. I don't push her to take me deeper. She didn't find that entirely enjoyable when I did that to her in the cemetery and right now isn't about causing her pain.

My teeth sink into my bottom lip when she takes it upon

herself to swallow me deeper. She gags, and tears begin to fall from her pretty eyes but she doesn't pull back. I feel a sense of pride watching her do this. My girl is showing off for me, and I fucking love it.

Her hands, which grip my ass like it's her lifeline, flex, and her eyes squeeze shut, causing more tears to fall down her face. She's going to look like a wreck after this. It doesn't really matter because when we're done here with Bryce, I'm taking her home to properly fuck her.

Desperately needing oxygen, she pulls back and sucks in a breath, filling her lungs. Her tongue licks up and down my shaft, tracing the thick vein underneath, before burying me back in her throat. She sucks me deep until I'm close. Normally, I'd love to spill down her throat, but right now is different.

Pulling completely out, I tip her chin up with my fingers. "Open your mouth."

She does as she's told, pink tongue peeking out from her dark-red smeared lips. I stroke my cock until I'm coming all over her mouth and chest. I catch her before she can swallow the cum that landed on her tongue.

"Don't swallow," I order breathlessly. "Poor Bryce has been left out this whole time. Go kiss him."

"*What?*" Bryce squawks like a displeased parrot.

Posie's eyes flare, and for the first time tonight, there's a glimmer of doubt. She's just revealed the line she's not sure about crossing, but I'm going to force her hand this one time.

Wiping the combination of cum and drool from her chin with my thumb, I repeat my request so she knows I'm not changing my mind on this. "Kiss him, Posie. It's the least we can do for forcing him to watch our little show."

Holding her hand, I help her off the floor. Her tall heels click loudly against the concrete floors as she makes her way to him. Rome is already holding his head between both of his hands to make sure he doesn't try to pull away from receiving my gift.

"Fuck!" he shouts as Posie's lips cover his.

He struggles against it and his eyes remain wide open with terror the entire time her mouth is sealed over his.

"That's enough," I tell them, shoving my semihard dick back into my slacks. Posie backs away from him like she can't put distance between them quick enough and Rome finally lets the douchebag go. "Did you enjoy your taste? It's the only one you're ever going to get."

Bryce scrambles off the floor, almost falling over in the clumsy process. He spits on the floor and wipes his mouth with his hand. "You're sick! Something is wrong with you."

"You're probably right," I concede with a casual shrug. Belt back in place, I stuff my hands in my pockets and shift toward him. He instinctively backs away from me. Smart. "The next time you think about her being your whore or you wonder what she tastes like, remember she tastes like me."

"I'm pressing charges."

His weak threat makes both Rome and I laugh.

"Try it," I warn. "You think this was bad? This was child's play compared to what I can do to your life, your family's life, and your poor little fiancée's life. Three phone calls and maybe a single text is all it would take for me to set your world and future on fire. Although, I do love a challenge. Perhaps I'll try to do it in two phone calls."

It's moments like these I'm glad I've been collecting secrets and debts for as long as I have. Getting money in return for them is great, but the look on Bryce's face right now is priceless.

"What's it going to be?"

He glares at me like he's trying to kill me with his stare. The moment he gives up, I grin triumphantly at him.

"Fuck you, Blackwell."

I don't bother correcting the name. There's no point, I've already won.

"I'm going to tail him to make sure he doesn't make a

fucking scene." Rome tells me before slipping out of the room after Bryce.

The all-consuming darkness that had been controlling me since I first saw Bryce touch her melts into nothing. Something I can only describe as peace settles in my chest.

Sighing contentedly, I turn on my heel to look at Posie. Just like what Bryce was doing, she's now wiping her lips with her hand.

Her honey eyes narrow as she points at me. "Don't *ever* make me do that again, Rafferty."

"I'll take public blow jobs off the list," I relent. It's a reasonable request after all.

"No, not *that*." She wipes her hand on her expensive silk dress. She can dirty it all she wants. I'm never letting her wear that in public again. I already had a half-baked plan circulating in my head to cut it off her once we were home. "Don't make me kiss *Fitzgibbons* ever fucking again."

I can't help the laugh that escapes my chest. That is the last thing I expected her to take issue with, but once again, her reaction to a complicated situation surprises me.

She gestures to the pieces of ruined art around our feet as I approach her. "I don't even want to know how expensive that piece of crap was. You better have your checkbook because you're making one hell of a donation tonight."

"I don't care," I tell her, wiping the smeared makeup under her eyes. "It was worth every penny." Before I can stop myself, I'm murmuring the words, "Thank you."

I don't know what exactly I'm thanking her for, but something tells me we both know it's not just for tonight.

She doesn't press me for further explanation. She simply turns her head and presses a kiss to my palm. "Always."

THIRTY-FOUR
RAFFERTY

"THE WAREHOUSE IS JUST the right size for what you're wanting to do, and it's fairly close to that penthouse you've been looking at in Bellevue." Kason flips the iPad around and shows me the pictures he'd taken of the available building. "If you're serious about running the underground fights now too, there's space for them on the other side. You'll be able to keep the poker games and bar separate."

I'm graduating in a handful of months, and when I do, I'll be forced to change the location of my current games. It doesn't make sense to keep them on campus anymore since I'll no longer be here daily to keep an eye on things.

The Wilde Corporation is going to become mine, but I'm not willing to give up my own side business. I want it to grow as I do, and that's why when Kason started to talk about how much money is in these fights of his, I started to wonder if I should be investing in them. It'll be easy money for me, and I already have someone on staff who knows the ins and outs of it all. Sounds like a no-brainer to me. This warehouse Kason found might just be the perfect solution to it all.

"That is if you're still planning on leaving Seattle next spring," Kason adds, shoving his hands into his jacket when the rainy wind picks up around us. His hood is already pulled over his head, concealing his buzzed hair. I'm not usually one for meetings in dark parking lots, but he mentioned he was going to be passing by Posie's dance studio around the same time I planned on being here.

I flip through the pictures and pause when I get to the mock-up of the floor plan. He's right. It's exactly the right size for what we'll be doing.

"Why would my plans be changing?" I ask, still looking at the screen.

"Rumor is you have a girl, and she still has some time before she graduates. I didn't know if you'd be leaving her here." The Englishman takes the device back from me when I pass it over to him.

"The penthouse is twenty minutes away from here without traffic." It's basically just on the other side of Lake Washington. "It's not like I'm moving across the country."

"I know this." Kason's wide shoulders shrug. "I just thought, knowing you, you wouldn't be willing to have her live somewhere you don't. Thought you were more of a *I need her naked and waiting for me in our bed every night* kind of guy."

"We don't live together," I tell him, even though it feels like a lie.

Posie's slept at her apartment twice in the past three weeks, and that's only because she needed to study for early exams the following morning. As it turns out, I don't make the most conducive study partner. I tend to selfishly monopolize her time. School has always come easy for me, and studying isn't something I've had to do much of. Posie, on the other hand, has to put more effort into her studies. It's something I've been trying to remind myself of when she has her face in a textbook instead of my lap.

"Alright, mate." His big hand claps my shoulder before reaching for the door handle of his dark gray jeep. "Figured I'd just ask the question before I start getting things together for you to purchase this location. If you do change your mind and want me to look for locations in Seattle instead, just say the word."

"I will."

He gets in the car and, with a quick wave, leaves the parking lot. There are only two cars remaining in the poorly lit parking lot, and they both belong to me. Posie had parked under the sole streetlight, and I'd parked beside her when I got here.

She has no idea that I planned on stopping by tonight, but when she mentioned this morning that she was closing the studio by herself tonight, I decided to use that information to my advantage.

Opening the passenger side door, I grab the hand-sized dark purple box from the seat and head inside the building. Along with the open sign, most of the overhead lights have been turned off. There's only one fluorescent light that remains lighting up the reception area and the long hallway. On either side of the hall, there are identical rooms. There are big glass windows that allow you to see inside each of the mirrored rooms. I'm sure they're there so the parents can watch their kids dance during their classes.

I peek into the first two rooms, looking for signs of Posie, but it's not until I'm halfway down the hall that I hear the soft music. "Never Let Me Go" by Florence + The Machine is a song I'd recognize anywhere because it's one she used to listen to over and over. I used to tease her about it, but she'd simply just tell me it was her favorite, and it appears it still is.

Coming to the last room on the left, I find her dancing. She's alone and in the dark, but she's completely in her element. Dressed in her long-sleeved black leotard and pale-pink pointe shoes, she gracefully twists and leaps across the space with her long legs spread wide.

I was in the audience for many of her ballet recitals in our youth, which I was forced to attend by my mother, and I don't remember her dancing like this. The choreography always seemed highly technical and *strict*. They'd rehearsed for months to achieve absolute perfection. The dedication that Posie and her fellow dancers put into those performances was impressive, but I think I like the way she's dancing now more.

She's using the same techniques that have been instilled in her since she was young, but there's a carefree element to her actions now that I enjoy. Posie isn't following the steps provided by a demanding choreographer, she's letting the music and her body dictate how she moves.

Completely lost in the dance, she doesn't notice when I slip through the cracked door and lean against the far wall. I'll need to have a conversation with her about making sure to lock the front door from now on if she's going to continue to be here by herself. She's lucky a monster she knows has snuck in on her.

It's not until she's spinning repeatedly in place that she finally spots my reflection in the mirror covering the entire wall.

With a screech, she comes to an uncoordinated stop. Hand flying to her mouth, she stares at me with big eyes. "*Jesus Christ*, Rafferty!" she shouts from behind her fingers while her chest heaves for breath. "What the hell are you doing here? Why are you sneaking up on me like that?"

"I knocked."

She doesn't believe me for a second. "No, you didn't."

Moving across the room, she picks up her phone that's connected to the speakers mounted on the wall and turns off the music. The silence that falls over the space is almost deafening.

"You're right. I didn't." I push off the wall and make my way toward her. "What are you doing?"

Like she's embarrassed for being caught, her arms cross in front of her and she stares down at her shoes. "I don't know where my future stands with ballet, but I … I just don't want to get rusty while I figure it out."

We've never talked about it, and I guess I've never really bothered thinking that hard about what it was like for her to lose her place at Juilliard. The only things I cared about when it happened was that she was miserable and heartbroken, which, not too long ago, were my hopes for her. I haven't considered what her plans would be moving forward.

"Is this still what you want to do after you graduate?"

Her narrow shoulders shrug. "I honestly don't know anymore. After messing up in New York, I feel a little bit like a failure."

"After what happened to your dad, it doesn't make you a failure that you let your grades slip. It makes you fucking human. Bad things like that can't happen without there being some kind of fallout or collateral damage."

Her head lifts and her eyes lock with mine. I don't have to be a mind reader to know what she's thinking about right now. Each of her thoughts are written across her face.

Frowning, she murmurs, "Yeah… I guess you know that better than anyone."

I brace myself for the flood of ugly emotion that normally slams into me when the subject of my mom comes up, but to my disbelief, it doesn't drown me like it usually does. It's still there, just below the skin like a dull ache. For the first time ever, it's bearable.

Is this what it's like to heal?

Wait? Is that what I've been doing these past few weeks with Posie? Have I been healing?

The startling realization hits me. That's exactly what's been happening. I started to let go of my anger and blame like my grandmother told me to do, and while I did, the gaping wounds that were left in my heart and soul started to mend. Posie—the girl I thought I wanted broken and destroyed—took the broken pieces she left behind and stitched them back together without me noticing.

Posie did what she's always done. She saved me.

"Raff?" Her hand wraps around my forearm, pulling me from the sudden jarring self-realization. "Where'd you go?"

"Nowhere." I clear my throat. Even if I did want to talk about it, I don't quite know how yet. Before she can ask me anything, I bring the conversation back to her future. "If you were offered a place in a ballet company tomorrow, would you take it?"

Her head cocks, the messy bun she has on her head sways with the movement, and her eyes narrow with suspicion. "Did I rightfully earn my place, or is this one of those scenarios where you call in a favor or use a secret for blackmail to get me in?"

I don't bother lying, she'd see through me anyway. "Probably the latter."

"If I can't earn my position in a dance company, then I don't want to be part of it. It wouldn't feel right."

I can't help but groan at her. This shows how different we are. Where I wouldn't have thought twice about cheating the system, Posie would never consider it. "You may have grown up around us, but you're your father's daughter through and through with those strong morals."

Eyes rolling in her head, she shoves at my chest, backing away a step or two. "My morals aren't *that* strong."

"Oh yeah?" I ask, reclaiming the space she'd just put between us. *Where do you think you're going, baby, I'm not done with you yet.* Her chin tips up when I cage her in my arms. "What makes you say that?"

"I'm with you, aren't I? If I had strong morals, I wouldn't let you do half the shit you do to me, and I sure as hell wouldn't enjoy them as much as I do."

She's with me. Is there any point in denying that truth any longer? It's a waste of my time and it's not doing me any good.

It's been *nice* not feeling miserable every second of every day, and with Posie back in my life, that hollow spot that's been in my chest all this time has started to fill. I know it will never be whole. The piece my mom took with her when she left us is something I'll never get back.

"That's probably a fair deduction," I tell her before skimming my lips across hers. The small contact instantly has her hands reaching out for me. Her fingers grab hold of the edge of my jacket. "Speaking of shit I make you do, how do you feel about dancing for me?"

"The last time you asked me to do that, you held a gun to my head."

That was not my finest moment, I'll admit. "If I remember correctly, I never did get my dance though. I have something better in mind this time if you're willing to play with me."

Her white teeth nibble on her bottom lip while she makes up her mind. After a minute, she smirks. "I'm always willing."

She moans into my mouth when I kiss her again. This time, deeply and borderline too rough. My fingers wrap around her throat, applying just enough pressure to let her know I'm in control, and she doesn't flinch or try to pull away. Anyone else might be turned off by the harshness of my touch, but not her. Never her. She takes everything I give her, and in return, she does the same. Her arms wrap around my neck, pulling me down to her as I back her toward the mirrored wall.

A wooden barre runs along the entire length. Usually, it's where Posie's students would stand and follow her instructions, but tonight, we'll be using it for a more *alternative* reason.

Once her back hits the glass, I rip my mouth away from hers and turn her away from me by her hips. "Hands on the barre," I order, digging in my jacket pocket for the box I'd brought with me. With it in hand, I tear my jacket off and toss it to the floor.

"What is that?" Posie asks, meeting my gaze in the reflection.

I'm smirking as I take the purple U-shaped vibrator out. One end will be directly on her clit, while the other is working its magic inside her. The elastic of her leotard will keep it in place while she spins around the room. The best part is I'll be able to adjust the intensity and settings with the small remote control it came with.

"I want to see how well you can dance for me while this is inside you. Let's see how long you can last before you come."

"Um…" Her hands flex on the barre with either nerves or excitement. Maybe both.

Dipping my head, I kiss and suck on her neck above where the collar still sits. Every time I see it around her throat, it pleases me, but I'm starting to think it's time to give her the key. If she still wants to wear it after that, it's up to her. My reasons for wanting her to wear it have shifted from my original sinister intentions. The collar isn't the only thing I'm going to need to reevaluate. Her father's home is a bigger issue that needs my attention.

"*Shit*," she sighs, head falling to the side to give me better access to her sensitive skin. "Okay, play with me."

Music. To. My. Fucking. Ears.

The box falls to the ground, joining my jacket after I've put the remote in the back pocket of my jeans.

"Open your mouth," I instruct, running the soft silicone across her bottom lip. She parts for me, and I push the rounded end in. "Suck. Get it wet for me."

She keeps eye contact with me through the mirror as her cheeks hollow and her tongue swirls around vibrator. When I've deemed she's done enough, I nod my head and she releases it from her mouth.

"Use one hand to pull your leotard to the side so I can see your cunt."

She reaches down and pulls the stretchy material as far as she can to the right. It exposes just enough of her that I'll be able to access what I need to.

Pressing the button on the device, it comes to life, vibrating in my hand. My arm wraps around her trim waist. Her chest rises and falls quicker, anticipation shooting through her as I bring the buzzing silicone closer to her sensitive flesh.

Her sharp intake of breath echoes off the walls of the otherwise silent room at the first brush of contact. Her pelvis jerks forward and then back, like she can't decide if the sensation is too much or if she wants more of it. I don't give her the option to decide. Holding her hips in place with my free hand, I force her to remain still when I press it to her clit.

Her teeth sink into her bottom lip as she tries to fight back moans, and for over a minute, she remains still for me. When she begins to grind against the vibrator, I know she's exactly where I need her to be. Just on the brink of ecstasy.

Posie whimpers in despair when I lift the vibrator away. "Sorry, baby, but you don't get to come yet." My teeth scrape across her neck. Her skin tastes salty from sweat. "Not until I get my dance."

"Oh, god," she groans as the realization of how hard this is going to be sets in.

Putting the device on the lowest setting, I turn it around in my hand and position it at her opening. She groans, throwing her head back into my chest when I push it easily inside of her. She's already so wet, and she's not going to last long, but that's alright with me. The sooner she's overcome and can no longer dance, the sooner I can watch her in all these mirrors as I fuck her.

With it in place, I nudge her hand away and right the crotch of her skintight outfit. The only thing giving away what's happening between her legs right now is the faint buzzing sound. She stands facing the mirror with a dazed look in her light brown eyes.

Hands skimming down her arms, I back away from her. Across the room, there's a stack of plastic chairs. Taking the top one off the stack, I position it in the middle of the room and straddle it. Once settled, I take the remote control out of my pocket.

Thumb hovering over the button that increases the vibration, I smirk at her. "Alright, Butterfly, show me how you fly."

THIRTY-FIVE
POSIE

THE UNRELENTING VIBRATIONS are washing away my every basic thought and with them go all the memorized choreography I've stored over the years. He had me turn the music back on, and I can barely hear it. If Rafferty would give me a second to think and recoup, I'm sure I'd be able to remember one of the many dances I know, but the bastard hasn't let up since he started this whole thing.

My only choice is to let my body take the reins and let it lead me across the room in various leaps and turns. I'm on my toes with my other leg extended far behind me and my arms raised at my sides when he ups the intensity. Instantly, both feet are flat on the ground and my knees are squeezed tight.

"Oh my god," I hiss through my teeth, head bowed to my heaving chest. I was fairly close before he told me to start dancing, and if I stand still for just a moment longer, I'll fall over the edge.

"I know that's not all you've got," Rafferty chastises from the chair he's casually straddling. His bulky arms are crossed over the back of the chair and his icy eyes haven't left me once.

With each move, I feel them raking over my body with approval. "You can last longer than that."

He thinks by taunting me that he'll be able to bring out the competitiveness in me, and he's annoyingly right. I want to come —*need to*—but I also don't want to give in too fast.

Shaking my head, I try to clear some of the pleasure-induced fog and refocus as the song changes to the next one on my playlist. The low, steady beat of "Edge Of The Dark" by Emmit Fenn speaks to me, summoning the performer in me. The lyrics are also perfect for our current situation.

Taking a steadying breath, I rise back onto my toes in my pointe shoes and restart my dance with a little bit more concentration. I twirl over to him as elegantly as I can manage. He probably didn't expect I'd use him as a prop, but he was wrong.

Standing behind him, his eyes lock with mine in the mirror when I hold my hands on his shoulders and bring my leg straight up over my head. The shape of the vibrator and the snugness of my outfit keep it in place, but my inner muscles are like a vise around it too.

The corners of Raff's lips pull up when I bring my leg down and hook it around his chest. I yank his body back with it and hold him there while I rake my fingers through his wavy hair. A breath hisses out between his lips when I pull on the strands. Dropping my leg, I turn his head toward me and bend down like I'm going to kiss him. His chin tilts up to meet me, but before my lips can ghost his, I turn away from him.

He fights dirty and changes the setting. The low constant vibration turns into a rapid pulsing that has me stumbling out of position. Hands, which had been arched above my head, fall to my sides as my steps falter.

"Teasing me is never wise, baby," he warns darkly, like he's a wicked mastermind. Though, in many ways, I guess that's exactly what he is.

Eyes almost rolling back in my head, I try to stop my knees

from giving out. My muscles are shaking, making it a very real possibility that I'm going to collapse to the Marley floor. Sucking in air, I look over my shoulder at him.

"I don't know, it feels like teasing you might give me exactly what I want."

"Oh yeah? And what is it you want?" His dark brow quirks. "Tell me with your words, and I might feel inclined to give it to you."

The answer is easy, or, at the very least, it should be. *I want you to make me come.* I know that's what he's expecting me to say, and I know that's what I should say but tell me why that's not what I say.

My breath stutters and my skin begins to prickle as warmth grows in my core before I allow the words to fall from my mouth. "I want you to tell me that this is real and you're not going to push me away tomorrow when you suddenly remember you hate me."

I knew I was craving reassurance from him, but I didn't realize how much until he hesitates to respond to me. He sits there with a blank face and his spine rigid. I'm this close to wishing the floor would swallow me whole and help me escape the embarrassment I just waltzed into when I see the shift.

It's a small change, and I highly doubt it would be noticeable to anyone but me. I grew up searching his stony expressions for changes like this because I always wanted to know what was going on in his head. It wasn't until he let me behind his walls that I became fluent in his silent language. I found it's the small changes in his body language and expressions that scream the loudest.

They're also often the most important ones that he *needs* to be heard, but they are almost always missed by the people closest to him.

My heart lodges in my throat when the ice melts in his eyes and he stands from the low plastic chair. The combination of my building pleasure and turbulent emotions as he walks to me wreaks havoc on my body. It's like I'm being pulled in two different directions from the inside.

He tilts my head up by my chin with two fingers. The way Rafferty is looking at me almost makes me forget how to breathe. It's the one thing I've known how to do since birth, but he can make me forget the basic function with a single stare.

"It's real," he murmurs so softly it almost gets lost in the music. "Fuck, Posie, it's always been real. That's why it feels good even when it fucking hurts."

I willingly gave him up to protect Paxton and it was the hardest thing I ever had to do. I never thought I would get him back, and for years I struggled to come to terms with the loss. It was like a death that needed to be mourned. This very moment is one I would dream of at night to soothe the shredded pieces left of my heart. It felt like such a wild impossibility that I would wake up sad that I'd let myself imagine it. It was akin to torture. Now that I've been faced with the real thing, I'm struggling to believe it's actually happening until Rafferty's lips crash into mine.

It's a toe-curling kiss, but I can hear the silent promise in it. This is his way of promising me he meant everything he said. That we are real.

I hold on to him like I'm still afraid to let go and kiss him back fervently. His hand moves from my chin to cup my cheek. The tender way his thumb swipes over my cheekbone has me fighting a smile. I love his harsh abrasiveness, but these small moments pull at my heart just the same.

While his tongue slides against mine, he ups the vibration between my legs to a level that steals my ability to function. His arms wrap around me when my knees give out, holding me as I convulse, and he swallows every one of the sounds that escape my throat.

I've just barely come down from the flash of white-hot pleasure when I'm grappling at the button and zipper of his jeans. "Take off your pants," I say breathlessly against his lips. "I need you right fucking now."

As if we're in a race against time, we tear at our clothes, and when we're done, they're scattered around us on the floor. Rafferty's just barely positioned himself on his back on the ground when I'm straddling him.

Reaching between my thighs, he pulls the purple vibrator from me, making me gasp. He doesn't bother turning the thing off and it buzzes against the floor when he tosses it aside.

His hands hold my hips as I position the tip of his dick at my opening.

"Look in the mirror," he orders gruffly. "Watch yourself as you ride my cock and see for yourself how fucking beautiful you are while you do it."

The only answer I can give him is a jerky nod.

We collectively groan as I sink onto him. He stretches me in that borderline painful but delectable way that has me seeing stars. It's an intoxicating feeling being filled by him. It makes me question how I went so long without it.

Fully seated on his dick, I open my eyes and look into the glass like he'd ordered. I find him already staring at me through it, his cold eyes are on fire and they make my skin warm.

We hold each other's stares and never look away as I ride him. His fingers are holding me in a way that will no doubt add to the bruises that have been scattered across my skin since I started staying at his house. I don't look at them as battle wounds but badges of honor. *"Rafferty Wilde fucked me so hard he left bruises"* is definitely something I think is worth bragging about.

Needing more control, he wraps an arm around me, and before I know it, my world is spinning. I barely feel it when my spine collides with the hard floor because the only sensation I can focus on is him driving relentlessly into me. Head turning, I watch the perfectly sculpted and corded muscles of his body tighten and move under his skin. When I say it's a downright beautiful sight, I mean it.

Reaching over his shoulders, I dig my nails into his back. It's only fair I get to leave my own marks on him. The sound of him growling in my ear goes straight to my core and makes my pussy flutter. So, I do it again.

"That's it. Make me fucking bleed, Butterfly." His teeth nip at my neck before his tongue wipes away the burn. "I'll wear your marks with *pride*."

He hooks my leg over his hip. The new angle has my back arching off the floor and my mouth gaping in a silent gasp. He takes advantage of the new position. Dipping his head, he takes one of my nipples into his mouth. While he licks and bites, I scrape my nails up the back of his neck and into his hairline. There will be no hiding those marks with a shirt tomorrow. Everyone will be able to see them, and I'm excited about it.

Lifting his head, he takes hold of my jaw in a punishing grasp. "Do you like marking your territory, baby?"

My lips are parted as my breathing turns into labored pants, and his hold on my face forces me to keep my mouth open. I'm close again and he knows it.

"Yes," I choke.

"Me too." He spits in my mouth, and I groan.

I should find the action degrading and maybe a little gross, but I love it. It wasn't until he spit his drink into my mouth at the poker game that I realized I enjoyed it. He has a way of forcing me to discover my hidden kinks, and I'm curious what else we'll uncover together. As of right now, I'm just convinced I'll like anything he does to my body.

His thumb wipes the saliva that landed on my bottom lip off before he crushes his mouth to mine. Our tongues tangle and our teeth clash in a messy kiss until we're both so close to the edge, we're panting and sharing oxygen.

I succumb to the euphoria first, and this time he doesn't try to quiet the sounds that erupt from my throat. He lets them join the melody of the music coming out of the speakers. I'm so blinded by the sensations taking over my body, I can barely hear the song that's playing. It's a distant sound, like I'm submerged underwater.

Rafferty follows suit. He grunts, missing his next thrust and messing up the rhythm he'd set for himself. Hand back on my hip, his cock drives deeply into me and that's where he stays as he comes. His cum coating my walls in hot surges, making us both moan.

The second his body allows his muscles to relax, his forehead falls against my chest. He keeps most of his body weight off me by keeping his elbow under him so he doesn't crush me against the unforgiving floor. A smile grows on my face when I feel him press a kiss under my collarbone.

Peace and contentment settle over me, and for the first time, I don't question it. I allow myself to freely sink into it.

This is real.

THIRTY-SIX
RAFFERTY

"OKAY, THAT'S ENOUGH," Rome suddenly announces at my side. "You have to stop. You're starting to freak me the fuck out."

Turning my head, I raise a brow at my friend who stands with me at the wooden bar. The varnish is starting to fade on it and every inch of it is covered in something slightly sticky. I'm electing to believe it's from spilled drinks because if I let myself think about any of the other possibilities for too long, I'm going to end up throwing Posie over my shoulder and leaving this decrepit hole-in-the-wall dive bar.

Seriously, of all the bars in Seattle, why the hell would Rome pick this one? I'd rather get drunk in my own living room over this. At least I know it's *clean* there.

"What?" I ask, confused at what he's yapping about now.

Grimacing, he waves a hand in my face, and I promptly smack it away. "*This*," he repeats. "You're *smiling* and it's weirding me out."

"Shut the fuck up," I bite, taking a sip of the bottled beer in my hand. "I'm not."

"False." His hand points out at the dance floor and then back at me. "You've smiled *three* times since she started dancing with Lark. Which, for anyone else, wouldn't be a lot, but for *you*, it's a fuckton. It's making you look … *happy*."

In the middle of the busy makeshift dance floor, Posie and Lark dance to the country music blasting through the speakers. They've both had enough to drink that they're a little slap-happy and having the time of their lives pretending they know how to line dance. No one else here is trying to line dance, they're just in their own world enjoying the night. It does something to my chest to see Posie smiling freely like that. There hasn't been much for either of us to smile about for a long time, but we've finally reached a point where that's changing, and it feels good.

Astor Banes' words come back to me. *You're allowed to be happy, Rafferty.*

Shoulders shrugging, I lean against the bar and the wood digs into my back. "I wasn't aware that it had become a bad thing."

The annoying dumbfounded look remains on Rome's face as he continues to examine me like I'm an alien anomaly. "It's not a bad thing, it's just a little jarring to see you like this. It's like watching a goldfish suddenly learn how to ride a bike. I'm not going to lie. I didn't know you knew how to smile. Just kinda figured you were born without the necessary muscles or something."

"I've smiled before," I scoff, trying to casually brush him off because I know he's right. He's never seen me like … *this*. Rome's only ever known the *"after"* version of me, and that version was pissed at the world for a very long time.

"*Yeah*, but it was never a *happy* smile. It was a *I'm going to put my fist down your throat and make you eat your teeth* smile. Surprisingly enough, I find that one less unsettling than whatever this new shit is."

"Rome. Just stop." I pinch the bridge of my nose between my fingers and sigh. "I'm not talking about this with you." There's only one person I'm willing to have conversations like this with, and even then, I'd still stumble through it and struggle to find the right words.

Lifting my head, I find him staring at me. All the humor that's been on his face has disappeared. It's a rare sight to find Rome taking something seriously, so when it happens, you take notice immediately and pay attention.

"So, you didn't hate her as much as you originally thought, did you?"

Eyes locked on where she spins around Lark with an elegance out of place for an establishment like this, I shake my head. "No."

I love her.

I think I always knew I never stopped loving her. It was always in the back of my mind, whispering incessantly at me. I refused to acknowledge it because the very notion that I could still feel that way for the girl I held responsible for ruining everything was an unbearable thought. I tried my best to bury the unwanted emotion by piling every ounce of rage I carried with me onto her memory. For the longest time, I naively thought it was working but I figured out I'd simply been lying to myself that night in her bedroom.

"For what it's worth, I think this is a good thing. You can only head down the path you were on for so long before you let it permanently change you. I'm glad she pulled you back." The fact that Rome Valentino, the heir to the Italian syndicate, thinks I was going too far into the darkness proves it was time for me to let go.

"Me too."

The corner of his mouth lifts in a faint smile. "What are you going to do now? What's the plan for you two?"

I don't know where we're going or what our future holds, but I do know one thing. "I'm never fucking letting go of her again. I'll attach a goddamn chain to her collar if I have to." Almost six years was long enough for us to be apart, and I have no desire to let it happen again. Fuck, one night away from her makes my chest ache in a place I can't reach. Maybe Kason is right, and I should be trying to find a new place in Seattle instead.

"It makes me so warm and tingly inside when you're all possessive and shit." And just like that, the humor returns to my best friend's face as he slaps me on the shoulder. "Pussy-whipped looks good on you, dude. And don't worry, if I can get used to my mom's wack-ass facelift, I can get used to your smile."

He grunts, doubling over when my fist connects with his ribs.

"I fucking hate you," I growl, taking another drink of my beer.

I didn't hurt him *that* bad. If I did, the fucker wouldn't be laughing like he is. Eyes rolling, I turn my attention back to the dance floor and stand up straighter when I don't find her dancing where I'd last seen her.

Whatever concern that was shooting through my system fades when she, hand in hand with Lark, pushes through the edge of the crowd and heads directly for me. She's talking to Lark about something that has her laughing. The ponytail she'd thrown her hair into before we left has pieces falling out around her face and there's a light sheen of sweat on her forehead from dancing. She's completely at ease.

I'd be lying if I said I didn't pick up on the notable change in her after that night in the ballet studio. She needed to hear those words from me more than I could have guessed. At night, she sleeps soundly at my side. The restless shifting that I hadn't paid much attention to before has all but stopped and the dark circles under her eyes have faded.

She releases Lark's grasp when they're close enough and takes the hand I hadn't realized I'd offered her. It's an action I did absentmindedly like it's just second nature for me to reach out for her. She allows me to pull her in close and she settles in at my side.

"Damn, princess, you look like you were rode hard and put away wet," Rome teases Lark.

The blonde pushes the hair that is sticking to her forehead back and huffs out a breath. Her cheeks are red and her makeup, which is usually perfect, is smeared around her eyes. "You just say the sweetest things, Valentino. You sure do know how to flatter a lady."

"*A lady?*" He repeats incredulously with a quirked brow. "You're anything but a lady and you know it."

Lark's dark blue eyes flare as she glares at him with her lips pressed into a flat line. "Do you ever shut the fuck up?"

Rome holds his chest like he's offended by her question. Everyone here knows that couldn't be further from the truth. "That is the *second* time someone has told me that tonight. Keep it up and you guys are going to seriously bruise my ego."

"Yeah *right*. Like that's possible," she scoffs as she pushes around him to get the bartender's attention. Rome grins at her like a fool as he turns to stand next to her.

Posie tilts her chin and gives me a look that tells me she's also starting to pick up on the weirdness between those two.

Shrugging her shoulders slightly, she turns her full attention onto me. Without thinking about it, I dip my head and press my lips to hers in a brief kiss. She smiles against my mouth, and when I try to pull back, her fingers thread through my hair and keep me in place.

"Do you want another drink or are you ready to go?" I ask her when she lets me go. After that kiss, I'm ready to get the hell out of here. Or at the very least take a brief trip out to my car. It'd be a tight fit, but it'd be better than fucking her in the scummy bathroom here.

I'm never letting Rome pick the bar again. His aunt owns a nice one not far off campus. I don't understand why we didn't just go there instead of this place.

Eyes lighting with mischief, she runs her fingers down my

chest and over the ridges of my abs before skimming them ever so slightly over the zipper of my jeans. My dick jerks in my pants at the light touch.

"Seems to me you're the one who needs us to leave." Her teeth sink into her bottom lip as she fights a knowing smile while she palms me through the black denim of my pants.

The amused look vanishes from her face when I lock my hand around her wrist and yank her with me toward the exit door.

Over my shoulder, I yell out to Rome and Lark. "We're fucking out of here."

They can figure out their own ride home. I have more pressing matters than being their goddamn Uber driver.

The cold night air hits us when we shove through the glass door of the bar. Posie laughs behind me, finding it funny that she's all but having to run to keep up with my fast pace. I'm staring at the back of my Jaguar wondering if she'll be able to fit on my lap if I put the seat back as far as I can when my phone buzzes in my back pocket.

I've been waiting for a call from Kason all day about a client who owes money, or I wouldn't bother checking it right now. Growling, I yank the device out of my pocket and look at the screen. It's an unknown number. Usually, I'd ignore it or send it right to voice mail, but something in my gut tells me I need to answer the call.

Coming to a stop at the driver's side door, I accept the call and bring the phone to my ear.

"Hello?"

Posie steps in front of me, a wicked smile still on her face as her hands slip under my shirt and her nails rake down my abs.

"Is this Rafferty Wilde?" an unknown woman asks me. There's something about her voice that puts me on edge instantly, and everything fades around me. Even the girl who stands before me ceases to exist for a moment.

"It is." I gruffly answer, dread already making my chest tight. It's not until she starts talking that my world completely turns on its axis and my body loses all sense of feeling. I can no longer feel the chill of the wind or the heat of Posie's hands on my skin.

Posie, sensing the change in my demeanor, stills in front of me, her hands freeze in their exploration of my abdomen and big brown eyes stare up at me with concern.

"I'm calling from Seattle Medical Center. Your brother Paxton was brought into our emergency room an hour ago. It appears to have been an overdose…" She says more about how he was found in his parked car with the engine running some-where on campus, and the cops and an ambulance were then called, but I'm not really listening. I'm waiting for her to say the one and only thing I care about.

When she doesn't, I manage to get the words out to ask myself. "Is. He. Alive?"

It's the longest seconds of my life while I wait for the answer. I can physically feel each second that passes.

"He's stable. The medicine the paramedics administered put him into immediate opioid withdrawal. We're trying to regulate his heart rate and blood pressure by letting him sleep through the worst of it." She tells me what floor he's on and what nurse to ask for at the reception desk when I get there before the line goes dead.

Backing a step away from me, Posie drops her hands to her side. "Raff?" she says softly, immense concern dripping off the single syllable.

I'm numb. I think it's my body's way of protecting me as I'm flooded with the memories of my mom and the night she took those pills. I don't want to feel that pain again.

"Pax overdosed." Those words feel like razor blades in my throat and on my tongue as I say them. "I have to go to the hospital."

Her hand flies to her mouth and her skin pales. "Oh my god." Her head shakes like she's in denial. "Is he okay?"

"He almost fucking died. He's not *okay*," I snap, a familiar rage flaring in my chest toward her. It's the very emotion I thought I'd finally put to rest, but that phone call was like kindling on the dying fires of anger, and I can feel it burning under my skin again.

When I move robotically toward the driver's door, she scrambles around the car. "I'm coming with you."

It's on the tip of my tongue to tell her no, but I stop myself. Debating with her will waste time I don't have. My priority is getting to my brother.

THIRTY-SEVEN

POSIE

SIXTEEN YEARS OLD

IT'S ALMOST one in the morning and someone is knocking on our front door. My dad's heavy footsteps come from the hallway as I fly ungracefully out of bed. People don't just show up at your house at this time for a social call. They show up because something is *wrong*.

In the dark, I blindly search the chair in my room where my clean clothes go to die and grab the first sweatshirt my fingers touch. I've barely yanked it over my head before I'm leaving my room and heading toward the front door where my dad already is.

Dressed in a pair of plaid boxers and a gray T-shirt, his stocky frame blocks whoever stands at our doorway. My arms fold in front of me as I approach from behind. The sound of a late summer rainstorm outside fills my ears the closer I get.

"Dad?" I ask, moving forward another small step. "What's going on?"

He stares a moment longer at whoever is at our door before he turns to me. "It's for you."

I can only make out a head of dark hair, and at first, I think it's Rafferty standing there, but when Dad shifts out of the way and the light illuminates his face, I find it's not my boyfriend.

"*Pax?*"

There's something more alarming about Pax being here than Raff. If he's here, he went through a lot of trouble to do so. He still only has his driver's permit and doesn't have a car. Not only did he break the law to show up here, but he also stole one of his parents' cars too.

I dash toward him, and the closer I get, the clearer the look on his face is. It's that same despondent look he's had for the past year that I've asked him about a hundred times, but tonight it's different. Tonight, it's a heartbreaking sight. My best friend, with tears running out of his blue eyes, looks broken.

I reach for him, but he backs away from me before I can touch him. "Pax... what's wrong?" I question, heart in my throat.

He looks between me and where my dad stands. "I'm sorry..." He swallows hard, fighting a sob. "I know it's late, but I didn't know where else to go. I'm sorry I woke you up, Mr. Davenport."

Dad shakes his head. "Don't worry about it, kiddo. Why don't you come on inside and out of the rain." He gestures Pax inside with his hand, and after a moment of reluctance, Pax steps inside.

Turning away, Dad walks away from us toward the living room. He snags the beige woven blanket off the back of the leather armchair and hands it to me.

Pax stands like a statue as I wrap it around his damp shoulders. He reaches up to hold both sides, pulling it tighter around him. I can't figure out if his hands are trembling from being cold or with fear. Something in my gut tells me it's the latter.

"Pax, do you need a glass of water or anything?" Dad asks. There's a worried look on his face as he examines my friend. We both know something is really wrong, but neither one of us is going to rush Pax into speaking. I'll sit with him all night in silence if that's what he needs me to do.

"No, sir."

Dad shifts back a step, hesitating to leave us alone. "I'm going to go to the kitchen and make some coffee. Holler if you need anything." He's not actually going to drink coffee—not at this hour. This is his way of telling us that he'll be awake if we need his help.

He's never liked Pax being in my room even though he knows there's nothing romantic between us, but tonight, as I lead Pax down the hallway, Dad doesn't question it.

Once inside, I close the door behind us and go across the room to turn on the little lamp I have on my dresser. It's not the brightest lamp, but it casts enough light that we'll be able to see each other.

"Do you want to sit?" I ask, shifting toward my full-size bed.

Pax just silently nods and follows my lead, stiffly climbing onto the bed next to me. We both sit with our backs against the simple white-wood headboard in complete silence. After a minute or so, he pulls his knees up to his chest, and rests his head there. I've lost count of how many times we've shared a bed over the many months since his nightmares started. The only time I sleep alone anymore is when I'm sleeping in my own bed at my house.

Sleeping alone is something I'm going to need to get used to and fast. Three months ago, I got my acceptance letter into the performing arts boarding school in Boston.

During the last few weeks of summer break, I will be packing all my stuff and moving across the country on my own. Transferring into two new schools this close together isn't ideal, and I was *this* close to turning down my spot, but Rafferty convinced me I needed to go. He knew how important my dream was to me, and he also knew the biggest reason I'd want to stay in Washington was for him. Leaving my dad and the only home

I've ever known will be hard, but leaving Raff behind is border-line painful.

Rafferty's reassurance and grand plan are the only reasons I'm going through with it. He has one year left at Hemlock Hill before he graduates. With his grades and his last name, he can get into any school he wants. His plan right now is to move to New York first and get a place for us. He'll start school at NYU, and the following school year, I'll join him in New York when I'm at Juilliard. It'll only be a four-hour train ride or one-hour flight to get to each other in the meantime. While I'm skeptical, he has full faith that I'll get a scholarship to my dream college.

His plan has always been to attend the top private college here in Seattle. That way he'll be close to the headquarters of his family's business, and he can learn the ropes there while getting his degree. There's a very small piece of me that feels guilty that he'd change his plans for me, but the bigger part of me is ecstatic to get him away from his father's reach.

Now, we've just got to find a way to convince Pax to come with us. It wouldn't feel right leaving him here alone. What would happen to him when Raff is no longer here to be Adrian's punching bag?

There's an inch of space between Pax and me, and I'm careful not to cross it. The way he pulled away from me at the door tells me he doesn't want to be touched right now and I want to respect that.

"We can sit here for as long as you need," I whisper my promise to him. "Just know I'm here to listen when you're ready."

He turns his head on his knee so he can look at me. "I... I don't know how to say it."

"That's okay." I snuggle down farther on the bed, getting comfortable. "I'll wait here until you figure it out, and if you don't figure it out tonight, that's okay too. There's no rush. I'm not going anywhere."

He reaches for my hand and intertwines our fingers, but my chest aches when he turns away from me.

We stay like this, the only sound in the room coming from the rain hitting my window, until the clock changes from one, to two, and finally to three a.m. In those silent hours, he stops shaking and some of the tension eases from his body. Outside my door, my dad is still moving around, waiting for us to tell him if we need him to step in.

There's this knowing *feeling* in my bones that we will. It's the same kind of gut feeling I've had all this time telling me something has been going on with Pax. Even when he's repeatedly denied it, I knew. I just wish he felt he could have told me sooner.

My air locks in my chest when he finally turns back to me and speaks. "My dad is hurting Rafferty."

"I know," I choke out, throat burning.

Every time a new round scar appears on Rafferty's back, I want to march into my dad's station, hand him the video I took, and report Adrian. The only thing stopping me is Rafferty's fear about Mollie. I don't know if I could live with myself if I got Adrian sent to jail and Mollie did something to herself because of it. That's a weight I'm certain my shoulders couldn't bear.

Paxton sits up straighter in bed. "You do?"

"He made me promise not to tell anyone. He thinks he's protecting you and your mom by allowing it to keep happening. I've begged him to let me help, but he's adamant that he can take it." But I don't know how much longer he can. Every time he comes out of his dad's office with new marks on his back, I can see the shift of darkness in his eyes. It's starting to change him.

The next three words that fall from his mouth will haunt me the rest of my life. I'm not sure if there will be a night that I don't fall asleep hearing them echo in my head.

"But I can't," he says so quietly I barely hear him. "I can't take it anymore."

My blood is like ice in my veins and my heart shatters for my best friend. *"Pax..."* I hoarsely say his name and trail off, unsure of what else I can say. *I'm sorry* doesn't seem like enough.

Pax's legs stretch in front of him and his head hangs to his chest. He pulls his hand away from mine and rests it in his lap. "I know Rafferty lets our dad hurt him because he thinks if he does, Dad will stay away from me. For a long time that worked, until one night it didn't."

"Does he—" I swallow the emotion clogging my throat. I don't want to cry. Not now when Paxton needs me to be strong for him. When I'm alone, I'll cry for my best friend, until then, Pax is my concern. "Does he use his belt on you too?"

My stomach turns to stone when he shakes his head. "No. Not anymore."

"What..."

The rest of my question is silenced when Pax turns on the bed and lifts his shirt, exposing his back. Across the top of his shoulders and scattered across his shoulder blades are bite marks. All but one of them is healed. A new one on his shoulder still has fresh blood around it. This happened *recently*, and now I'm thinking it's the catalyst for why he showed up at our door tonight.

"Oh my god."

Without thinking, I reach out to touch one of the pale scars but stop myself when I realize what I'm doing. Dropping my hands to my lap, I ball them so tightly my nails dig into my palms.

Pulling his shirt down, he turns back around, putting his back to the headboard once more. He can't look at me when he talks. "I've tried so hard, Posie, to bear it like Rafferty does. I want to be strong for Mom too, but I can't do it anymore. I don't want to hurt her. I swear I don't." The entire bed shakes when he chokes on a sob. "I need help. I can't... I can't have him trap me in his office or come into my room anymore."

"He comes into your room?"

It clicks. The source of his nightmares comes from a literal monster under his bed. Only, this monster wears his father's face. The pain that's resided in his eyes has been telling me that this whole time. How could I have missed it?

He wipes his face as more tears fall. "He didn't at first, but then he started to show up there a lot. I tried to tell him to leave, but he didn't like that. He'd make it hurt worse if I said anything, so I just stayed quiet and let him..." The sob that escapes his lips is like a thousand painful paper cuts to my soul.

I have to take several steadying breaths before I can speak. "Pax, did he..." I trail off, unable to say the actual words.

At Pax's solemn nod, I let the tears forming in my eyes fall and my stomach rolls with nausea. How could a *father* do this to their *child*?

Holding his head in his hands, his shoulders shake as he cries. "I never wanted him to be there, but he *never* listened to me. He'd *laugh* at me."

"I know, Pax." Reaching for him, I lay my hand on his shoulder. If he pushes me away, I'll let him, but I need to let him know I'm here for him. The second I touch him, he turns into me and wraps his arms around me. He buries his head in my shoulder and cries. "He never should have been there, and it is not your fault that he was."

I don't know if he understands what I'm saying yet, but nonetheless, I need to say it to him. I'll say it over and over again until I run out of air if I need to just so he will know none of this is his fault. It's that heinous monster Adrian's.

"I need help," he repeats into my shoulder. "But how do I make it stop without telling everyone what he's done to me? I don't want anyone to know. You can't tell anyone, P. You have to fucking promise me you won't tell anyone." He pulls back so I can look in his face as he grabs hold of my hands in a death grip.

"I can't… I just can't do it, but I don't know how else to make him go away."

I do. My stomach rolls and the nausea intensifies to the point that I'm starting to sweat. Since that night when I watched Adrian's belt come down on Rafferty's back, I told myself I wouldn't be able to betray him or put Mollie's declining mental health at further risk. I told myself I couldn't live with the consequences, but now that I know what is happening to Paxton under that roof, I'd rather face those consequences than allow Adrian to continue to *abuse* his child. Allowing this to go on any longer when I have a video sitting in an unmarked file on my computer that can send Adrian away for years isn't a fucking option.

I know without a doubt that this will always be the hardest decision I'll ever have to make, and I know what I'll be losing by doing it, but I also know who I'll be *saving*.

My heart will be broken, and Rafferty will hate me, but Paxton will be safe and that's all that matters in the end.

"No one will ever know because I know how to help you."

"You do?"

"Yeah, I do." *I just have to betray the promise I made to Rafferty so I can keep yours.* I wrap my arms around his neck and pull him close before whispering, "I promise, Pax. I'll always protect your secret." *No matter the cost.*

THIRTY-EIGHT
POSIE

WHEN I WAS SIXTEEN, I made a promise that I would protect Paxton from Adrian no matter what. I did it knowing all the collateral damage and blood would be on my hands, and I would be losing the only boy I ever loved in the process. It broke my heart into a thousand shards of glass doing it, and with every beat, those pieces sliced me a little deeper, but it's something I'd do again. Whatever pain I felt didn't matter, not really, because easing Paxton's pain was always my priority. I could bear anything as long as he was safe.

Safe.

That doesn't feel like the appropriate word to use right now. Not when I'm currently trying to keep up with Rafferty's hurried steps as we follow a nurse to Pax's room.

I may have saved Pax from Adrian, but I couldn't save him from the residual trauma that haunts him. Being the whistle-blower meant I couldn't be there to help him heal, no matter how much I wanted to be. The weight of that guilt on my chest is suffocating. I can't stop the voice in my head telling me that had I been there, this could have possibly been avoided.

The rational side of my brain keeps reminding me of two

crucial things, and those are the only reasons I'm not succumbing to the voice in my head.

The first thing I know without a doubt is, even if I had fought like hell to stay for Pax, Rafferty never would have let me near him. Which would have been a fair reaction given he only knew the part of the story where I betrayed his trust and set the spark for his mother's demise. If I were him, I wouldn't have wanted me to be around either. The second is, had I been there for Pax like I wanted to be, whatever help I could have offered him wouldn't have been the kind of help he really needs. The trauma he's experienced requires the kind of help that is outside of my capabilities. He needs a professional.

I don't know if he's reached a point where he's realized that for himself yet, but until he does, I'll continue to support him in any way I can. And if he does ask for more help, I'll hold his hand through that as well. We're on his time frame until then. He has to decide when he's reached his limit.

The nurse dressed in dark maroon scrubs stops at a wooden door with a long narrow window in it and turns to us. "He was given a mild sedative when he first got here to calm him down. It should be wearing off shortly."

She waits for Rafferty to bow his head in dismissal before walking to the nurses' station close by. Her rubber shoes squeak against the polished tiled floor as she leaves.

I glance at Raff, hoping to catch his eye, but like on the tense ride here, he refuses to look at me. The entire car ride here, he kept his head straight, and since we've been at the hospital, he's acting like I'm not even here.

This is bringing up memories and emotions I'm sure he'd rather keep buried, but I can feel him pulling away from me. The vicious energy that rolls off him like a thick fog reminds me of how he was when we first reunited.

Wordlessly, he turns the handle and slips inside. Following a few steps behind him, I close the door softly behind me and move slowly into the cold room that smells of antiseptic.

The aroma reminds me of when I flew home for that week following my dad's accident. Other than to eat and shower, I didn't leave my dad's side. He was in a coma, and we didn't yet know the extent of his brain damage, but I needed him to know that I was there for him. I was eventually forced to go back to New York, and that's when Aunt Jo stepped in for me.

Unlike my dad, who was connected to more tubes and wires than I could count, the only thing attached to Paxton's sleeping form is a single saline drip. I won't say it out loud because it will only piss off Rafferty, but all things considered, Pax got lucky. His overdose could have been exponentially worse than it was. Every day there are people who aren't as fortunate.

His skin is a little gray and the circles under his eyes are intense, but other than that, he looks physically okay. Mentally is a whole other conversation to be had.

I don't know how long that will last, though. Sooner or later, he's going to start to feel the painful effects of withdrawal, and that's when he's going to need to decide what he wants to do. Either get help or continue down his current path.

Staying close to the far wall to give him space, I watch Rafferty approach the side of the hospital bed. His face is cold and stony, lacking all signs of emotion until his hand wraps around Pax's tattooed forearm. He cracks, the crushing reality that he almost lost his brother tonight slamming into him. Chest heaving with deep breaths, his eyes close and he hangs his head.

He stands there holding on to his baby brother while no doubt feeling a series of undeniably painful things.

The sight has my eyes burning and tears forming.

"Raff..." His name hoarsely falls from my lips before I can stop it.

My voice pulls him from whatever he's just lost himself to. His head snaps in my direction and his eyes burn with a familiar hatred. It instantly has my stomach rolling and nausea bubbling in my throat. With a single look, I can feel all the things I've recently gotten back being torn from me.

I'm going to lose him again.

"I can't believe it took my brother almost dying for me to realize how fucking blind I've been." He drops Pax's arm and turns away from the bed. For the first time since he got the phone call, all his attention is on me, and I don't like it. Not now. Not this kind of attention. "I did what they said. I tried to let go. I started to fucking *forgive* you." He spits the words at me like they're laced with poison. "I allowed myself to feel *happy*. For a second there, I really thought I was too, but now I know they were more lies. I fell for your lies. *Again.*"

Tears falling down my face, I shake my head. "You don't mean that." He's reeling and letting the hurt and anger seep back in.

"Yes, I do," he snaps, rounding the bed and heading toward me. I take a step back on reflex, but my back immediately presses to the wall. "I let myself get distracted by you and how good it felt to be with you again. You made me lose focus, but I'm seeing you for what you are again."

"Rafferty." As a last-ditch effort to keep some distance between us, I hold my arm out in front of me. "*Stop.* You have to stop and listen to me—"

He slaps my hand away, cutting me off and making me flinch from the sharp pain.

"I don't have to listen to a fucking word that comes out of your mouth." Just like he did that night with the pocketknife, his forearm crushes into my jugular as he holds me captive against the wall. His breathtakingly handsome face has a haunting mixture of fury and anguish on it as he leans in close to sneer at me. "You took my mother away from me, and now? You almost took my brother away too. It's your fault that he's here. It's your fault that he's using. He has to numb the pain that *you* caused our family!"

Each word he throws at me is like a knife piercing into my chest. What hurts more is I can't correct him. I can't tell him the truth. I have to silently absorb every painful word because that's the promise I made to Pax, and I'm not going to break it now just because it's hurting me.

"*Enough.* It's not her fault..."

Every ounce of air is trapped in my lungs when Pax's voice comes from behind us. Rafferty freezes in place when he hears his brother, and the pressure on my throat eases. Icy fear snakes through my veins when he turns his head and Pax speaks again.

"It's not her fault. None of it is," Pax repeats, this time a little stronger as the sedation further leaves his system.

Rafferty's moved just enough that I'm able to look into Pax's sad eyes over his shoulder.

My head shakes at him stiffly. "Pax. *Don't.*" *You don't have to say anything you're not ready to so you can help me. I'm fine. I can take it.*

With slow, rigid movements, he pulls himself into a sitting position on the bed. "It's time, P. You've lied for me long enough. You have to tell him the truth."

My stomach drops and my skin grows cold.

"What the fuck are you talking about?" Rafferty snaps, his head whipping back to me. "What the fuck is he talking about?"

I ignore him, keeping my focus on his brother. "*Paxton,*" I urge him harder this time.

But he doesn't listen to me. "You have to tell him the truth." A somber look appears on his exhausted face. "You've protected me long enough. I can't let you keep doing it. It's not fucking fair to you anymore. Look what it's doing to you guys... These secrets are going to end up killing all of us if we don't tell him."

Rafferty's nostrils flare and the pressure returns to my throat. "Start fucking talking. What does he mean you *protected* him?"

It's right there on the tip of my tongue, but I can't bring myself to say it. It's still Pax's story to tell, and not mine. Tilting my chin, I stare blankly up at him with my lips pressed flatly together. My strong, unwavering facade doesn't last long because every ounce of my resolve melts from my bones when Pax speaks again.

"She turned the video of Dad beating you over to the police because I asked her to."

"*What?*" Rafferty asks, head shaking in disbelief. "No, you didn't. Why would you lie about something like that?"

My eyes squeeze closed and hot tears run down my face. I slump against the wall and don't bother straining against Rafferty's hold any longer. The only thing I can do is accept what is about to happen.

"I'm not lying to you. I begged her to help me, and she gave Mr. Davenport the video. It was the only way to get Dad to stop."

Dad had been confused why I'd held on to the evidence of Adrian's actions for so long when I brought it to him. He understood a little better when I explained that Rafferty made me promise not to tell a soul. The story I'd spun for him was that Pax had shown up that night upset over what was happening to his older brother. I told Dad that we had both decided it was time to put a stop to it. The next morning, Dad was in the judge's office getting an arrest warrant for Adrian Blackwell. Twelve hours after that, I was standing in the rain watching him getting escorted out of his house in handcuffs. It happened so fast, I barely had time to breathe.

Rafferty, dumbfounded, drops his hold on me and spins to face his brother. "How did you know…" He trails off, shaking his head. He really thought that whole time that no one in his house knew what was happening in his dad's office. Pax knew for a long time, and I have to assume that on some level, Mollie did too. "I had it handled. *I was fine.* I didn't need help."

The column of Pax's tattooed neck shifts as he swallows hard. "But I did, Raff. I needed help making him go away." His eyes that look so much like Raff's fill with immense sadness and guilt. "I know you were trying to protect me all those years, and I wish I could tell you that it worked and Dad never … touched me." He all but chokes on those words. "But I can't. I can't tell you that because when he was done with you, he would show up in my room."

Not giving his brother a chance to ask any further questions, Pax turns awkwardly in the bed and pulls the shoulder of his green hospital gown down. He's covered many of the bite marks with tattoos in the years since I left, but the ridges of Adrian's teeth marks are still visible through the ink. I honestly don't know how Pax has managed to keep the scars a secret from Raff all this time. It had to have been difficult for him.

It's not my pain or my trauma that I had to live through, but my soul hurts like it is at the sight of his scars. It hurts just as much as it did when he first showed me, if not more. The fact he went through it alone as long as he did never should have happened.

None of this should have fucking happened.

The fight physically deflates from Rafferty's tall frame as he staggers back a step. All of the color has faded from his face, and he looks like he's going to be sick.

"When did this happen? Wh—why didn't you tell me? I could have helped you, Pax." The brokenness in Raff's voice is something I've never heard. There's no rough edge or anger in it. This time, there's only agony.

He's in agony.

"I was too ashamed," he admits, staring at the wall he's still facing. "I didn't know how to."

Raff's hand covers his mouth, and his eyes shut like he can't bring himself to look at the scars left by his father any longer. After a long pause, his hand falls limply back to his side. "You don't have anything to be ashamed of. It wasn't your fault. It wasn't either of our faults that he left these marks on our skin."

Pax stiffly turns to face his brother again. I watch as he fights to keep eye contact with him, but ultimately, he has to look at his tattooed hands when he speaks. "I wasn't ashamed of the bite marks, Raff. I was ashamed of what he was doing to me while he left them."

THIRTY-NINE
RAFFERTY

I HAVE FELT my world fall apart around me on two separate occasions. The first was when I screamed at Posie in the street while they put my father in the back of a squad car. The second happened when Pax found our fully-clothed mother submerged in her bathtub. Now, listening to my brother reveal the truth after all these years, I feel it crumbling for a third time.

It's not her fault. None of it is.

He would show up in my room.

I wasn't ashamed of the bite marks. I was ashamed of what he was doing to me while he left them.

I took the pain my dad dealt me with gritted teeth and with as much dignity as I could muster because I thought by doing so, I was protecting Paxton. If our father's wrath was directed at me, I thought it would stop him from doing the same to my little brother.

And now I'm learning all this time later that I was wrong and that I've *failed* my brother.

I failed Pax.

And the bite marks marring his back are proof of that.

The *anguish* in his eyes as he discloses the other unspeakable and sinister pain he'd endured at the hands of our father is proof of that.

Nothing I endured will ever compare to what Pax had to silently go through. The physical scars I carry with me pale in comparison to the emotional scars and trauma he's coped with all this time.

The beer I drank earlier is starting to turn violently in my stomach as I envision my father sneaking into his youngest son's bedroom.

There were so many chances that I could have dealt with my father—eliminated the problem altogether. I was bigger. Stronger. I could have had him on the floor bleeding before he had a chance to bring his belt down, but I never did it. I never did it because I was afraid of what the repercussions would be on my family. If I killed him, it would have destroyed my mother, and if I didn't, I feared he'd put his hands on Pax. I couldn't see a way to stop it without it hurting either of them.

All I ever wanted to do was keep my mother and brother safe, and I couldn't do that. I couldn't protect them from my father.

And now I know, I was never the one protecting him. It was Posie.

She selflessly took on the crushing weight of the blame and the ruthlessness of my hatred to keep my brother safe. When in reality, she'd done *nothing* to deserve either.

The vomit is coming up before I can make it to the small trash can in the corner. Half of my stomach's contents hit the side of the plastic bin, and the other half thankfully makes it into the plastic trash bag. I stand in the corner until there's nothing left in my system and I'm dry heaving.

My body is shaking when I wipe my mouth with my sleeve. On unsteady feet, I turn around to face both of them. While I'd been otherwise occupied, Posie had shifted from her place against the wall to stand at my brother's bedside. Her eyes are full of tears as she helps him retie the back of his hospital gown.

The unyielding loyalty he's shown her during my years of vengeance and wrath makes perfect sense to me. So does his substance dependency.

The lies that have been shrouding the truth for so long have lifted, and I'm finally seeing the full picture. It's gut-wrenching and heartbreaking, and I don't know how I never figured it out before now. It was all *right* there in front of me.

"This whole time … you knew?" I choke out, stumbling back to lean against the sterile white wall.

Her face crumples. Her brows furrow, and she presses her lips tightly together to keep back a sob. All she can manage is a jerky nod.

My brother lifts his head and finally looks at me. "She let you believe she'd done everything on her own to protect you because I made her promise to never tell anyone what Dad did to me. I couldn't—*can't*—handle anyone knowing. It was never Posie's fault, Raff." His arms wrap around himself like they're a protective blanket. "It wasn't her fault that Mom took those pills and died. It also isn't her fault I'm here right now. Both are mine."

Posie lays her hand on his shoulder. "*Neither* is your fault." When he wraps her hand in his, she gives him a ghost of a smile. "I know it's impossibly hard, but don't for a second let yourself believe that."

"I'm really sorry for what I put you through, P." Pax looks back at me. "What I put both of you through. I wish I could go back and handle it differently. The pain it caused you guys…"

My throat is so tight, I don't know if I can talk.

"Don't." Posie shakes her head. "Don't go there, because in the end, I'd still do what I did to protect you. *Both* of you. That's all that's ever mattered to me."

She's let me hate her—*hurt her*—just to keep my brother's

secret. She broke my heart and hers in the process because Pax asked for help, and she didn't think twice about it. She willingly sacrificed everything we had and the future we'd been planning to save him from the monster that is my father.

She saved him but I lost her.

My knees, which are shaking as badly as the rest of me, finally give out and I slump down against the wall. The laminate flooring is cold through my jeans and feels good against my too warm skin. Legs pulled to my chest, my head falls into my hands.

How could I have missed what was happening to Pax. We lived under the same roof, and yet I was completely oblivious to the pain he was being subjected to. The signs were there. The nightmares and the change in his personality halfway through his freshman year should have been like glowing neon signs alerting me.

Fuck. He was too goddamn young to have to deal with that.

Hand scrubbing my face, I wipe the tears away that I hadn't realized had fallen from my closed eyes. "I'm... *fuck.* I'm sorry, Paxton," I manage to rasp out. "I'm sorry I didn't know you needed help."

"How were you supposed to know? I tried really hard to hide that it was happening. From *everyone*."

"I should have paid better attention." Those nights when I snuck into Posie's bed and slept soundly next to her, I had no idea what heinous things were happening a few doors down. Had I not been so distracted and caught up in my relationship with Posie, would I have figured out what was happening?

Unable to sit still any longer, I manage to pull myself off the ground. I can feel two sets of concerned eyes on me when I begin to pace the length of the room.

"I'm sorry you were put in a position where you felt like you had to protect me from him. That wasn't fair to put on you. You were just a kid."

"So were you…" I mumble so quietly I'm not sure either of them hears me. "So. Were. *You!*" I repeat, but this time with a broken roar.

The sudden surge of rage that fires through me is uncontrollable and my fist is going through the nearby wall before I can comprehend what I'm doing. I don't feel it when the drywall shatters around my fingers. I'm sure I'll feel it tomorrow, but that's a problem for then.

Posie's foot lifts off the ground like she's going to come to my aid, but something on my face has her halting by the side of the bed. I want her to come to me, but I don't know how to let her be close to me right now. Not after what I've done to punish her for something she didn't do.

"My mother's death…" I trail off, not able to choke out the rest of the words.

"Wasn't her fault," Pax fills in. "I knew it would wreck Mom if Posie turned him in, but I told her to do it anyway. I was the one who put Mom in that bathtub. Everything you've blamed P for, you need to put on me."

My head shakes instantly. "No. I can't."

"You can. I'm the one—"

"You didn't do anything wrong!" I yell over top of him, storming to the other side of his bed. My hand grips his shoulder in a tight squeeze as I bend down so we're at eye level. "You didn't do *anything* wrong," I repeat to make sure he's hearing me. "I don't blame either one of you for what happened with Mom. I *can't* blame you because had I known back then what I do now, I wouldn't have thought twice about dealing with Adrian myself." How can I call him Dad after knowing what he's done? "I don't know if I could have saved Mom back then, but I *know* I would have done whatever it took to save you because you are fucking worth it, little brother."

My priority would have shifted to my brother's well-being over my mom's, just like Posie's did. My mom, while dealing

313

with her own struggles, was an adult. Paxton was a helpless and abused child. There is no question in my mind I would have done whatever it took to help him.

Pax's face falls before he drops it to my shoulder and his arm wraps around me. I hug him back just as tightly as his body shakes in silent sobs. Over his head, I meet Posie's tear filled eyes.

This girl.

She was my first love and then my enemy, but through it all she remained our guardian angel.

She never wavered in her promise to Pax. With everything I threw at her, she remained strong. The night Paxton kept apologizing to her has become so much clearer to me. Even when I held her at knifepoint, she kept all the blame on her. She bled to keep his secret.

I want to tell her something profound and all-encompassing for everything she's secretly been doing, but right now, all I can manage to say is, "Thank you."

It's only two small words, but the way the tension melts from her frame tells me she's needed to hear them for a very long time. I would also wager she never thought she'd hear them because she was committed to taking everything to the grave with her.

Wiping the tears falling down her cheeks, she nods at me. "I'm always going to protect you two."

I squeeze Pax with my arms once more before letting him go. "You don't have to anymore, because I'm going to take care of it," I announce, backing away to the door. "I should have done it when I was seventeen, and I will regret not doing it sooner for the rest of my life, but I'm going to make it right."

Posie's face pales and her eyes widen with worry. I'm turning away from her and stalking out the door as she calls my name.

"Rafferty! Stop! What are you going to do?"

I don't turn around. If there was anyone on this planet that could stop me, it would be her, but tonight, it won't work. Nothing is going to change my mind.

I ignore the nurses' worried faces when I charge past their station and down the short hallway. I'm too wired to wait for the elevator, so I opt for the stairs. My mind is consumed by a swarm of buzzing thoughts while I take the stairs two at a time. I'm going to be calling in a lot of debts to make it all happen, but it will be worth it. For Paxton. For Posie. For my *family*. The blood on my hands will be worth it.

I'm almost at the exit doors in the hospital lobby when I hear her behind me again.

"*Rafferty!*" My name sounds breathless from her running to catch up to me.

The automatic glass doors have just slid open when her hand wraps around mine and she pulls me to a stop. Body tense as stone, I don't turn to face her. Not willing to talk to my back, she shifts in front of me and blocks my path.

"Where are you going?" she repeats, the worry dripping off her every syllable. "You can't just leave him after that. He needs you right now."

"He's safe with you. I know that now." He felt so safe with her, he trusted her and her alone with his deepest secret. "I'll be back soon."

She doesn't accept this. "You're not thinking straight right now. I can see it on your face that you're planning on doing something reckless. You have to take a minute and be smart about this."

"No, you're wrong. I am thinking straight. For the first time in a long time, everything is clear, and I know what I need to do." I take my hand from hers so I can hold her face between my hands. She chokes on a small sob and her eyes flutter closed for a second before red-rimmed, honey eyes lock with mine. "You've carried the weight of this by yourself for too long. It's my turn."

"Raff…"

"I understand now why you did what you did," I murmur. "I don't know how I'm ever going to make up for what I put you through because of it, but this is a start."

"I don't need you to make up for it," she insists, hands covering mine. "I just need you to stay here with him. *With me.* We'll figure out what to do next together."

The years we've lost because of everything is time together we'll never get back, but I'm not willing for this—for *him*—to ruin whatever our future may be. I don't know what it will hold for us, but I do know one thing without a shadow of a doubt.

"I love you, Butterfly." Her breath shudders in her chest when I press my lips to her forehead. "I know telling you now doesn't fix anything, and I have a lot of work to do to make things right, but I need you to hear me say it."

It's not fair to her when I pull away and walk through the open doors behind her. No matter how much she may want to, I know she won't follow me any farther because she won't leave Paxton in his hospital room alone. Her unyielding devotion to my brother will work in my favor because I know someone will be by his side while I'm taking care of my family's lingering threat.

I'm halfway through the parking lot when I press my phone to my ear and a familiar voice picks up my call.

"Hey."

I don't waste any time. "I need your help."

FORTY
POSIE

IT'S BEEN seventy-two hours since my time protecting Paxton's secret came to an end and Rafferty left me alone in the hospital lobby. It feels longer because I haven't slept more than a handful of hours here and there over the past three days. Between taking care of Pax while he detoxes from the drugs and alcohol and worrying about Raff, sleep hasn't come easily to me. On top of that, I'm fucking emotionally exhausted. It's as if the past six years have finally caught up to me and I'm feeling everything we've been through all at once.

The doctors tried to keep Pax longer for observation, and when he denied them that, they had a doctor come in and talk to him about going to a rehabilitation center. I could tell there was a part of him that wanted to accept their help, but ultimately, he said no. I don't think he'll be able to think about the next steps in his recovery until he knows what is happening with Rafferty. The stress of the unknown is affecting him just as much as it is me.

Well, it's not entirely unknown. We both have a fairly good idea what he's out there doing, but neither of us have said it aloud. It's not exactly a topic easily woven into conversation. I know and understand why Rafferty thinks he needs to do this, but I worry about how it will weigh on his soul. Some acts are harder to live with than you originally think, and Raff's already lived through so much. I don't want this to be the thing that finally breaks him—the thing that finally lets the darkness consume him.

Pax had signed papers stating he was leaving the hospital against medical advice the morning after his brother disappeared, and an hour later we were walking into the empty firehouse. There was evidence that Raff had been there at some point during the night, but both cars were gone by the time we got there. I have to assume that Rome is driving one of them, and I take some comfort in that because at least he isn't alone.

I've texted and called him more times than I can count, but everything has gone unanswered. Same with my attempts to get in contact with Rome. The silence is deafening at this point and it's making my chest unbearably tight.

The cup of coffee I'm nursing in my hand as I walk back into the living room could be my fourth of the day or it could be my eighth. I've completely lost track at this point. I didn't even know how late it'd gotten until I saw the time on the coffeepot when I poured this cup.

Passing Pax, who lies on the leather sectional in nothing but his black and gray plaid boxers, I press my palm to his forehead. His skin is clammy and warm, but he's nowhere near as hot as he was hours ago.

"I think your fever broke," I tell him when his bloodshot eyes meet mine. "How are you feeling?"

I sit down on the opposite side of the L shaped couch. It's the same spot I've slept on since we got home. I didn't want to be too far away from Pax in case something happened, so I opted to sleep here instead of Raff's bed. The nurse at the hospital warned me about possible seizures before we left, and I've been worried about them ever since.

I don't want to get too optimistic, but it looks like he's finally turning a corner.

He pushes the blanket he'd been shivering under for the past two days farther down his legs and stiffly shakes his head. "Every single inch of my body hurts. I feel like I got run over by a train, but other than that, I'm *peachy*."

"I know you don't feel it, but you look and sound a lot better than you did this time yesterday." I'm not sure if he remembers or not, but between throwing up in a bowl I found in the kitchen, he was hallucinating. He thought I was his mom for almost four hours, and every time he'd call out to her, my heart broke a little more for him. I haven't brought it up, and I don't think I ever will. That's a sad memory he doesn't need to carry with him.

Eyes closing, he groans and turns his head into the pillow I'd brought down from his room. "If that's the case, I don't even want to know what I looked like yesterday because I caught a glimpse of myself in the mirror when I took a piss, and it wasn't pretty."

"You've looked better," I tease, enjoying this moment of levity. We haven't had this in a very long time. This is the first time I've heard any semblance of humor in his voice since I've been back. It gives me hope that the lighthearted boy I remember is still in there somewhere.

"You know what? Fuck off. You're not looking too hot either."

I was finally able to take a shower this morning when Pax was asleep, but I'd let my hair air-dry in a messy braid and didn't bother with makeup. The dark puffy circles under my eyes could still be seen through a pound of concealer, so I didn't even try to cover them. I'm wearing leggings and one of Rafferty's black hoodies that all but swallows me whole. The white socks that go up to my shins complete the glamorous look.

"That's fair," I concede, self-consciously smoothing the strands of hair that had fallen from my braid.

The corner of his mouth, the side with the two matching black hoops in his lip, pulls up in a half-hearted smile, but it quickly transitions into a grimace. I wait a minute for him to say something, but he remains silent, lost in his thoughts.

"What's going on in that head of yours?"

Eyes cracking open, he stares at me. "I'm just wondering how I let myself get to this point. It started with me just wanting to take the edge off. You know, just kinda numb myself from reality, but I lost control. And I hate that I did. I never want to get back to that low point, but I don't know how not to." He pauses, exhaling a long breath. "But I'm also ... relieved that I don't have to keep it a secret from Raff anymore. I should have told him sooner, and I'm sorry that I didn't. I know what keeping my secret did to you guys."

"You have to stop apologizing, Pax. That is something you *never* have to do for me. I knew what I was doing and what it would cost, and I still did it. Happily. It doesn't matter anymore anyway because we're all here now. Everything is going to be okay." I think I'm trying to manifest that last bit because the rock in my stomach is only growing heavier the longer Rafferty is gone.

Pax doesn't share my hopeful outlook. "I'm fairly certain my brother is out there somewhere getting his hands bloody on my behalf. Do you really think everything will be okay after that?"

There it is. The giant pink *homicidal* elephant in the room. Now that Raff knows what Adrian did, there is no way he's going to let him live. I don't blame him for wanting to eliminate his father himself, but I don't want him to put himself at risk in the process. Pax needs him here.

I need him.

I just got him back and I'm not ready to let him go.

"Adrian is in a guarded state prison. It's not like Rafferty can walk in there and sign him out for a field trip." I don't know who I'm trying to kid, or why I'm trying to gaslight myself into believing that's not exactly what he's doing. Maybe it's because if he gets caught, I'm going to have to visit the love of my life through bulletproof glass and that's a less than ideal situation.

"You know my brother. You've seen what he's capable of."

My stomach drops violently and a rush of anxiety washes over me. "Yeah... I do."

"P, WAKE UP."

Pax's alarmed voice pulls me from the fitful sleep I'd finally succumbed to, and instantly puts me on edge.

I fly into a sitting position so fast, my head spins. "What's wrong? What happened? Are you alright?" Like word-vomit, the questions fly out of my mouth. Through the dim light of the room, I peer at him with still blurry eyes. "Why are you dressed?"

"Rome texted me while you were asleep." He rounds the couch and grabs something off the floor. It lands at my feet with a clunk. Squinting, I find he's thrown my shoes to me. "We need to go."

FORTY-ONE
RAFFERTY

I GOT ELIJAH HILL, Zadie's father, his gig at the state prison for two reasons. One, so I could use Zadie to help manipulate Posie, and two, so I could have eyes on my father and get updates if I needed them. It was never my intention to use him to help break my father out of his confinement, but here we are. Desperate times and all that.

Turns out with Elijah's help and some assistance from a fairly reluctant warden, it wasn't as hard as I thought.

Dr. Hill secretly administered a medication that lowered Adrian's heartbeat so much, it made him appear like he was going into cardiac arrest. For appearances, Hill kept up *"life saving"* efforts until the warden okayed the entry of the ambulance to pick up the patient. If he didn't cooperate with me, information about his dirty dealings in his prison would have been aired on tomorrow's evening news. Before he could dial his lawyer's number and beg for help, the feds would have been up his ass and deep diving into his suspicious finances. He really thought he was getting away with blackmailing his prisoner's families and no one knew. It's amazing how little cash it takes for people to roll on their bosses.

The prison guard who helped push my unconscious and handcuffed father out on a gurney participates in Kason's fights on his free nights and was more than willing to play a role in tonight's events for a nice payday of his own.

It is moments just like these when it pays to have the connections I do. Trust me when I say I'm paying heavily for all of this to happen, but I know it will be worth every penny in the end.

On paper and on the security footage, it all looks legit. The paramedics come in and take over CPR, and an armed guard gets into the back of the ambulance with them to ride to the approved hospital. They leave, and on the way there, Adrian Blackwell officially codes and time of death is announced. He is then brought to the hospital morgue where he will later be cremated.

At least, that's what the story on the reports will say. What really happened was the paramedics administered medication to reverse what Dr. Hill had done, and fifteen minutes from the prison, away from any possible cameras, my father was swapped with the body of a John Doe. Rome was able to pull that one off with a call to his own connection at a morgue. This is exactly the kind of shit his family does for families like the Holloways, and he's gotten good at it in the last couple years. He deals with a more *nefarious* set of connections than I do on a typical day. He needs to make those relationships if he's going to be respected like his father is.

The paramedics and guard each took their bags of money and went on to deliver the body to the hospital morgue. All three know what will happen if they talk. I left a flash drive in each bag with the information I was able to gather on them in the short amount of time I had, and none of it was good. I consider it to be extra motivation for them to keep their mouths shut. I'll keep additional tabs on them just in case, but I doubt it'll be necessary. They're not stupid.

Rome and I loaded my father into the back of the car and

took off north to the housing development the Valentinos' real-estate company is building. This time next year it's going to be a suburban shitbox full of screaming kids and housewives, but until a nice family moves in, it will be my father's final resting place.

From the trunk of the SUV comes a sudden thud, and it has Rome's head turning in the passenger seat. "Someone's waking up."

"It's fine. Opening his eyes is about the only thing he can do right now." We'd tied his ankles and handcuffed his hands behind his back. The hood over his head keeps him from seeing and the gag in his mouth keeps him from talking. He's completely helpless and vulnerable, which is exactly how he made Pax feel. It's a small—*minuscule*—taste of what he put his child through.

Rome turns back in his seat but not before staring at me for a moment with skeptical eyes.

"What?"

"Nothing." He shrugs.

"Just spit it the fuck out," I growl, turning up the empty dark street of the new neighborhood. Ninety percent of the houses on this street are nothing but wood framing and poured foundations. "Are you having second thoughts?"

"What? Fuck, no. I *literally* just stole a dead body for you, and you're asking me this?"

I look between him and the dark road. "Then what is the problem? Why are you looking at me like that?"

The conflicted look on his face before answering is unmis-takable. "The operation you're building yourself is great and the amount of powerful people you have by the balls is impressive to say the least, but this isn't your gig, man. You use money and secrets to destroy lives. You don't take them." He pauses for a moment. "Did I ever tell you about the first time I killed some-

325

one? I was sixteen. My dad took me to a deal, and before we left the car, he gave me a revolver. He said it was just in case things went bad." Rome's upbringing couldn't have been more different from the other kids' we went to high school with. While the rest were learning how to sail their father's boats and were attending debutante balls, Rome was attending drug and weapon deals. He was learning how to survive the family business he is destined to take over. "Things went downhill so fast I could barely keep up with what was happening. This guy pointed his gun at my dad and before I knew what I was doing, I was pulling the trigger. I didn't think about it. Just ... *did it*. It wasn't until days later when the adrenaline faded that I fully comprehended I'd taken a life. I didn't regret it, I mean, he was going to kill my dad, but he was still a person. That's something that sticks with you, so I just want to make absolutely sure that you're ready for that. If you're not, I can pull the trigger for you. It'll be no skin off my back. Not anymore."

He wouldn't be asking me this if he knew the full reason I've decided to finally deal with my father. Rome knows when he should and shouldn't ask questions, and when I told him I was finally dealing with Dad, he simply said, *"What can I do to help?"* He's not dumb. He knows something has triggered this sudden response from me, but he's not prying for information. Even if he did, I wouldn't give it to him. Pax waited all this time to trust me with his secret, and I'm not going to betray him a mere three days later.

If the roles were reversed, I'd do the same for him in a heartbeat.

"I need to be the one who does it," I tell him, pulling to a stop in front of the house we'd chosen yesterday. We looked at his uncle's construction company's schedule and know it's due to get the concrete slab floors of its basement foundation poured tomorrow.

The team will show up in the morning none the wiser of what we've done to their construction site. They'll put the rebar down and pour the concrete over it. Just like that, my crime and all the evidence will be permanently entombed.

Keeping my headlights on so we're not out here in complete darkness, I cut the engine. Climbing from the car, I make my way to the trunk to open it.

Rome meets me there and we both stare at the bound and gagged man before us. He wears his ugly tan prison uniform and is barefoot. We'd removed his shoes when we transferred him into my trunk. On the off chance he was stupid enough to run, we didn't want to make it easy on him.

Adrian's hooded head jerks in our direction at the sound of our arrival. His chest and the rounded stomach he'd acquired in prison heave with anxious breaths.

I bet I'm the last person he expects to be here. He's always falsely assumed he had scared me into submission, and that I'd never try something like this. He doesn't know the only reasons for my compliance were both taken away. There's nothing stopping me anymore.

Jaw clenching so hard, I'm worried I'm going to crack a molar. I grab him by the collar of his shirt and forcibly drag him from the back of the car. His bound ankles stop him from being able to keep his balance and he lands with a harsh, satisfying thud in the dirt.

His strangled groan cuts through the quiet night air as he awkwardly rolls onto his back, but it's cut off when my boot presses into his throat. He freezes for a moment, his fear of the unknown making him turn rigid underneath my sole. This obedient state doesn't last long because his fight or flight response kicks in and he starts to struggle. Tied up, all he can manage to do is wiggle like a fucking worm in the dirt and mud.

It's a pathetic sight.

Keeping my foot firmly in place, I bend down and rip the hood from his head. It takes his eyes a second to register what he's seeing, but I know the second he realizes it's me. His eyes widen to the size of dinner plates and his mouth gapes around the gag.

"Miss me?" I ask, head cocking. "I decided it was time we had a family reunion."

Nodding at Rome, he takes Adrian by his arm and helps me haul him off the ground. He resists us the entire time we drag him across the lot. We reach the lowest side of the foundation wall that's already been built. The entire basement level has been dug into the earth and there are concrete walls surrounding the perimeter. We stop in front of the side that is only four feet or so deep, and I bend down to cut the duct tape around his ankles.

With his legs now unrestricted, I stand at his side and gesture with my chin toward the incomplete basement. "Jump."

His nostrils flare and a familiar anger reflects in his eyes.

"You're sorely mistaken if you think you have any fucking power or control here." A sinister grin pulls on my face when I point the end of my black switchblade to his throat. It's the same one I held on Posie, but it feels right using it on him. "It's my turn." Behind us, Rome easily jumps down. "Fucking jump."

With stiff, reluctant movements, he turns around and follows Rome. Only his descent isn't as graceful. With his hands still bound, he ultimately ends up tripping and crashing to his knees. My feet crash into the dirt right next to him, making him jump when I make the leap.

Adrian looks like the guy I used to consider my father, but now all I can see is the sadistic monster that's always lurked behind the mask. I see exactly who he is now and I'm ashamed of myself for missing it for so long.

Not bothering to wait for him to get to his feet, Rome and I drag him on his knees to the spot with the waiting shovels and tall piles of dirt. We were here until the sun started to rise this morning digging this hole. Since it's a Sunday, our activities have gone unnoticed by any construction workers. The storm that is brewing in the sky will wash away all the footsteps and signs of recently moved dirt. Bright and early tomorrow morning, they'll get back to their work and any traces of us will be long gone.

We drop him at the edge of his future grave and leave him in a hunched over heap.

Rome nods at me, silently telling me he's here if I need him, before climbing back up the wall to stand by the car and give me some time alone with the monster disguised as my father.

I pull the gag from Adrian's mouth, and let it hang around his thick neck.

He spits into the dirt before turning his head to look up at me. "You missed your old man so much you broke him out of jail, huh?"

The sound of his voice instantly puts me on edge. Unlike Pax, he didn't visit me in my dreams, and I had found a way to push my memories of him to the back of my mind. I focused more on Posie and my mother than I did Adrian, but hearing his voice has those ugly moments forced upon me in his office thundering to the surface. They're combined with the stomach-turning images I've been painting in my head since I learned what he did to my brother.

Just as the cocky grin splits his face, my fist slams into it. The bones of his nose crack under my knuckles. "Nope."

He falls to his side, and I yank him back up so I can do it again. It feels good. I envisioned doing this so many times before, but the crunch of his nose is more satisfying than I pictured it. I'd go to bed dreaming of bashing his head in with one of his expensive bookends weekly, and I never thought I'd get the chance to make him bleed.

His gushing broken nose and busted lip aren't enough to satiate my bloodthirst.

I want to see him suffer—to be in *agony* before he dies.

Holding him by the strands of his hair, I force him to look at me as I bite out, "I know what you did to Paxton. I know what you took from him." His sense of safety, his peace, and most importantly, his *innocence*. "What kind of man does that to his child?"

His bloody lips curl in a ghost of a smile for a second before it disappears and his chin lifts defiantly. "I have no idea what you're talking about. That kid was always a liar. You shouldn't believe a word that comes out of his mouth. He took after that pathetic mother of his."

Of course, he's going to deny it. I'd expect nothing less from him. He probably wants me to argue with him and come to the defense of my mother to buy him time so he can try to talk his way out of this. Letting that happen would be a waste of both of our time.

I lock eyes with him as I squat down in front of his kneeling form. "I'm going to kill you," I promise darkly. "I'm going to put you in the fucking ground for what you've done to my family."

"I don't know why you're blaming me for what your mother did to herself. You should be blaming that whore girlfriend of yours for taking that video. Had she minded her fucking business, your mother would still be alive."

"It was never Posie's fault. It was yours." The true and only villain in this story will always and forever be Adrian. That truth is so blatantly clear to me now. "Mom's death will only ever be on you, Adrian, and I want you to remember that during the final moments of your life." Standing, I hold him by the back of his shirt collar and lean him over the edge of the six-foot-deep hole. "While you suffocate on mouthfuls of dirt, you will regret ever laying a hand on Paxton. While your body is being crushed by the weight of the soil, you will realize that you only have yourself to blame. While you rot here, you will become nothing."

"You don't have it in you," he pants as he's forced to stare into the dark, cold abyss of his future grave. "You're not a killer."

"But you are." After his criminal treatment of his wife, and later his kids, he might as well have put the pills down Mom's throat himself. "You once said you were trying to raise me to be just like you. Congrats. You got your wish."

Rome's warning should have me concerned about how I will feel about myself when this is all said and done, but I'm not worried. Not for myself anyway. I know that I will be at peace with it and that I've done the right thing for my family. I can already feel the weight lifting from my shoulders as I stand on the brink.

My one concern is for the people I love the most and how they will be affected by what I'm doing. How will they look at me knowing I'm now a killer? Will it change me in their eyes? Can Posie still love me knowing what I've done? This isn't like any line I've crossed before with her. This is ending a life.

Not liking where my brain is heading, I shake off those thoughts and steady myself. *This has to happen. He can't live after what he did to Pax. You will find a way forward with Posie. You always do.*

"*You motherfucker!*" Adrian bellows as my grip loosens on his prison shirt. "No, no, no!"

"I'm sure my brother once begged you to stop too." Saying those words aloud makes my stomach roll and fury burn in my veins at the same time. "I'm going to ignore you just like you did him."

I'm about to let him fall face-first into the grave when the sound of car doors closing cuts through the air. Voices I can't quite make out quickly follow and movement in the beams of my car's headlight has my head turning.

"Where is he, Rome?" I hear her before I fully make out her figure. "Where the hell is he?" Posie demands with a little more force.

Rome throws his hands up as Pax and Posie push past him. "What the fuck, Pax? I didn't tell you where we were going to be you could *show up* here. The doc said you needed to keep your stress down and I was trying to be *helpful*. I mean, fuck, dude, your texts were starting to stress *me* out."

Pax ignores him and jumps down to where I am. He turns to help Posie, but she's got it covered. She lands gracefully on her feet before running to me.

"Well, look at that! It's the dirty whore herself," Adrian croaks when he recognizes her.

"Fuck you," Posie seethes, barely glancing at him before pinning me with her full attention.

"Get the hell out of here!" I yell at the pair as they approach. "You shouldn't be here."

Posie opens her mouth to argue but it's Pax that speaks up before her. "No. I'm not leaving. Not yet."

Adrian's cackle turns into a strangled sound as he chokes on some of the blood still pouring from his face. "Come to see your dear ol' dad off, son? Or maybe you're here to help me and put an end to this debauchery."

My skin crawls with disgust at the way he talks to him. "Shut the fuck up! You're not allowed to speak to him." I turn my head to look at my brother. He looks better than he did three days ago. He looks exhausted, like he's had a bad case of the flu, but otherwise the signs of his usual inebriated state are gone. I knew Posie would take care of him while I was away. "Pax, you need to leave. I don't want you to be here for this."

My brother stands his ground, and Posie looks between us with a terrified look on her face. "I don't want to be here either, but this is my only chance to get an answer. I need to know."

As she's always done, Posie shifts in front of him and acts

332

like a protective barrier between Adrian and Pax. "Are you sure?" she questions him.

"Let him ask," Adrian says. "I'm curious."

Everything in me screams that I shouldn't let this happen, and the look on Posie's face tells me she agrees, but if this is something Pax needs to get some sense of closure, should we deny him that?

Yanking Adrian back from the hole in the ground, I nod my head at my brother. "Make it fast. Then you both need to go."

Posie turns to face me as Pax pushes past her a couple steps. He keeps a healthy distance between us, refusing to get too close to the man who abused him for so many years.

There are so many emotions in Pax's eyes as he stares down at Adrian, it's impossible to pinpoint each one. His fingers create anxious fists at his sides and his breathing has quickened in pace. The silence between us all is heavy before he speaks.

"Why me?" he asks the man who was supposed to be his father—*his protector*—but ended up being the monster in his nightmares.

He doesn't have to clarify what he's asking. Everyone understands what he means. Adrian had two children but chose to do those horrific things to only one. I'd be lying if I said that question hadn't crossed my own mind a handful of times since I learned the truth. While he hurt me, Adrian never attempted anything like he did to Pax with me.

Like he's really thinking over his answer, Adrian's head cocks to the side. "Honestly?" he starts, not a single hint of denial in his voice this time. He's finally figuring out there's no point and he's going in the ground regardless. "I knew you wouldn't fight back."

The blood in my veins turns into liquid fire and it burns me as it floods through every inch of my body. My plan for him seems too *pleasant* now. If I had more time, I would be loading him back into my car and finding a place where I could skin him alive, but to ensure I don't get caught, I can't move to a second location. No matter how emotionally driven this is, I have to be smart about it.

The rage that is on Posie's face is something I've never seen before. It doesn't look natural on her. Meanwhile, the look on Pax's face is … empty. The emotions I'd seen reflected in his eyes have all but disappeared and he stands there like a statue. I couldn't even begin to guess what's going through his head.

His head lifts stiffly when he redirects his attention to me. "That's all I needed. You can do it now." Turning, he walks away.

"What? You're just going to let him do this?" Adrian fights against my hold as he yells at Pax's back, but I'm not going to let him go anywhere. "I'm your father! I'm the only goddamn parent you have left, and you're going to let him kill me?"

"You stopped being his father the second you laid a hand on him," I snarl, hauling him back to the edge. Glancing over my shoulder briefly, I find her still standing there. "Posie, I need you to go with Pax."

"Help me!" Adrian yells at her. "Don't just stand there, you useless cunt! Do something!"

I flip the blade in my hand and press the tip to the soft spot under his chin. "If you don't keep your fucking mouth shut, I'm going to cut out your tongue."

Refusing to look at him, Posie ignores his plea and name calling. Her gaze is still locked on me. The fury that had been there a moment ago is gone and the concern from before is firmly back in place. "Rafferty," she says my name calmly. There is no urgency or panic in her tone despite the situation. "I need you to stop for a second and look at me."

"No, I can't stop. This needs to happen."

I hear her footsteps move closer. My stomach rolls at the thought of her being near him. It's not safe for her here.

"Raff, please look at me."

The please is what finally has me turning to her. "I need to do this. He can't continue to breathe after what he's done. Prison isn't enough of a punishment. He would have gotten out in nine years, and then what? He just gets to continue on with his life? Fuck that. He needs to feel the same kind of pain he put him through." *The same kind of pain he put us through.*

"I'm not disagreeing with you on that. This is exactly what he deserves." She takes another small step forward. "But I just need you to look me in the eyes and tell me that you will be okay if you do this. Tell me that when you wake up tomorrow, you'll still be able to look at yourself in the mirror. You have to promise me you won't let this change you. If you can't do that, we need to come up with a different plan. I won't let him hurt you any more than he already has. He's done enough damage."

The same fears she has are the ones that have already run through my head. They're completely valid and her concern is more than understandable. She isn't here to stop me from taking a life, she's here to make sure that I will be okay after I do. Posie truly is exceptional. There's no one better out there for me. This just further proves to me that I can't live without her any longer. I need her in my life. *Forever.*

"The only thing I care about is whether or not you'll be able to look at me the same after." If she tells me she can't, I will take Rome up on his offer. I'm not going to jeopardize us again.

"Nothing you do will change the way I look at you or the way I feel about you. I'm not going anywhere. If this is what you need to do, I'll support you."

My hand tightens on Adrian's shirt. "I need to do this."

Of course, Adrian doesn't listen to my warning and opens his ugly mouth again. "No, you fucking don't! You don't have to do anything. Just let me go. We can pretend this never happened."

His begging falls on deaf ears.

"Okay." Posie nods once, fully accepting what is about to happen. "When you're finished, I'll be at home waiting for you."

Finally dropping her gaze, she glares at Adrian. "I hope he makes it hurt. You've earned a painful death."

"Fuck you," Adrian spits, lunging for her. My knife's blade pressing into his jugular has him freezing in place.

Posie turns halfway like she's going to leave but something has her thinking better of it. Spinning on her toes, she marches toward us. Her foot slams into Adrian's dick with unrestrained force. His scream fills the night, and he tries to double over from the pain. The sudden movement causes my blade to slice the skin on his neck.

Bending close, she gets right in his face as she seethes. "No, *fuck* you." The venom in her voice matches the raging fire in her brown eyes. For just a second, I recognize the chaos that storms beneath my skin etched in her features. This side of her is rare, and I can't help but like it.

Standing to her full height, she gives me one last look before leaving me with her blessing and support. Rome, who's moved from his place beside the car, helps her over the wall before switching places with her. Hands tucked in his black jacket pockets, he waits for my word.

I don't make another move until I hear Pax's car pulling away. With both of them gone, I can finally put an end to this.

"Hold him still," I order Rome.

My friend takes over for me, holding him in place while I move to kneel behind Adrian. With my free hand, I press down with my whole weight on his calf muscle to keep him still while I line the blade of my knife up just above his heel. The scream that escapes him when I slice through his Achilles tendon only lasts a split second before Rome shoves the gag back in his mouth.

Adrian fights us harder when I move on to his other leg. This cut isn't as clean as the last one, but I get the job done after a moment of struggle. He's crying and yelling in pain, but the sounds he makes only come out as pathetic choking noises.

"This will keep you from trying to climb out while we bury you alive," I explain when I move to stand before him again. "With each shovelful of dirt, your body will be crushed. Eventually, you won't be able to move your limbs and you're going to suffocate. While that happens, I want you to remember that's exactly how you made him feel. You can try and call for help, but just remember, the more you open your mouth, the quicker your lungs will fill with dirt." I pause, thinking that last sentence over. "Maybe that will be a good thing for you. It'll put you out of your misery sooner."

Reaching into his back pocket, Rome hands me the key to take off the handcuffs. I want to give him the false hope that he'll still be able to dig himself out before his chest is crushed and he runs out of air.

Rome steps back so I can be the one to push him in. Adrian tries to turn his head to look at me and his mouth opens around the gag like he's trying to say something. Hooking my finger around the torn fabric I tear it free from his mouth.

"I was too easy on you," he bites at me, already out of breath. "I should have beaten the fight out of you! Maybe then you'd have some fucking respect for me, and you wouldn't think you can get away with this!"

Till his very end, Adrian Blackwell has held fast to the idea that you only get respect through pain. The narcissist in him doesn't allow him to take any responsibility for his cruel actions. He doesn't understand he only has himself to blame for his early grave.

I couldn't save Paxton back then and I couldn't help my mom, but it gives me peace to know that I'm getting justice for them now.

"You're going to rot, Adrian." Hands on his back, I shove him. He lands at the bottom of the six-foot-deep cavern with a solid thud. The fall could have broken his neck right then and there, but the low moan that comes from the darkness tells me he's still breathing. Good. He needs to feel every agonizing second before his lungs give out.

"Ready?" Rome asks, handing me one of the shovels.

I nod at him. "Let's get this done. I need to go home."

She's waited almost six years for me already. I don't want to keep her waiting for me any longer.

FORTY-TWO
POSIE

THE SOUND of the shower turning on wakes me up.

I don't know how long I've been asleep, but a quick glance at the clock on his nightstand tells me it wasn't very long. After the silent and emotionally tense ride home, I sat on the couch with my cell phone in my hand until I was too tired to keep my eyes open. Pax had locked himself in his room the second we got back, so there was no reason for me to sleep on the couch tonight.

I'd knocked on his door a couple times to see if he was okay, and each time he answered through the wood. He told me he was fine, but I know he was lying. How can he possibly be fine after what his father told him tonight? He's going to need time to heal from the brutal honesty of Adrian's answer. I just hope he knows by now that both Rafferty and I are here to help him through it all, and that he doesn't have to do it alone.

Scrubbing the blurriness from my eyes, I push the door open to the en-suite bathroom. The entire room is made of black marble and chrome fixtures. It's dark and masculine. Just like Rafferty.

Inside the glass-walled walk-in shower, he stands under the

spray of water with his palms pressed to the marble and his head hanging to his chest. He doesn't hear me enter and his eyes remain closed. My heart sinks at the image.

Pulling the T-shirt I'd stolen from his dresser to wear to bed over my head, I drop it to the tile floor and step into the shower with him. I know he hears me now, but he still doesn't turn to look at me. That's okay. As long as he knows I'm here for him, he doesn't need to look at me now.

Stepping behind him, I wrap my arms around him and rest my hands on the strong muscles of his abdomen. He's stiff for only a second before I feel his chest expand as he pulls in a deep breath and slowly exhales it. Cheek resting against his back, I hold him tightly and try to somehow absorb some of the pain and trauma he's dealt with over the past few days.

I desperately want to take the guilt and blame he's feeling away but know that's something he'll need to do for himself. I'll remind him daily that it wasn't his fault he didn't know what was happening to Pax until he figures it out for himself.

There's a lot of healing that we all need to do. The good news is we get to do it together this time. We'll support and hold each other up until we can do it on our own two legs, and even then, we'll know we don't *have* to do it alone. That's what families do and that's what we are. A family. Always have been.

"I'm sorry," he whispers hoarsely, hand dropping from the wall so he can take hold of mine. He holds it against his chest in a grip that is borderline painful.

"Why are you apologizing to me?" He doesn't owe me an apology for what he did tonight. I already told him I supported his choice. Hell, there was a moment there after Adrian spoke to Pax that I considered being the one to push him into the deep grave. The only reason I didn't is because I knew Rafferty needed that closure more than I did.

"Because I blamed you for what happened. I blamed you and I *hurt* you. The things I did and said to you... *Fuck*!" The hand that is still on the wall curls into a fist and he slams his knuckles into the marble.

Releasing my hold from his torso, I twist around his tall frame so I'm directly in front of him. His chin is still pressed to his chest, and I take hold of his face, lifting it so he'll look at me. The spray of water drenches my hair, and it runs down my forehead and cheeks. My eyes blink when droplets stick on my lashes.

"What happened wasn't fair. To *any* of us. The way you treated me was … *awful,* but you didn't know. I lied to you, and you were reacting with the information you had. I can't blame you for that. It wasn't fair, but I understand why you did what you did." He tries to look away again and I force him to keep his head up. The walls he's built to keep everyone out are down and there's a vulnerability in his blue eyes that's rarely there. "If I don't blame you and can forgive you, then you need to forgive yourself." *For everything.*

He drops his forehead to mine and his hands hold either side of my neck in a gentle grasp. "Please just let me say it anyway. I need to."

"Okay."

His thumb slides back and forth on my jaw and I can't tell if he's doing it to comfort me or himself. "I'm so fucking sorry, Posie. Those words don't feel like they're enough, and they probably won't for a long time, but I'm going to keep saying them to you until they do."

My hands drop so I can grasp his sides. "They do mean something, Raff. They mean everything." I'd accepted a long time ago that he may never know the truth and we'd never find our way back together, but the fact that we've made it *here* is more than I could have allowed myself to hope for. "Those words mean we have a future, and that's all I want." *All I need.*

He pulls back and smooths the now wet strands of my hair off my face. "Good, because I have no intention of ever letting you go again. I lost you once and I refuse to do it again. You're fucking mine, Butterfly. I dare someone to try and take you from me."

I lay my hand over his heart, and like I'm engraving an unbreakable oath there, I make him a promise. "I'm not leaving you. I gave you my heart when I was fifteen years old, and even when you hated me, it still belonged to you. It always will." Then I tell him the three little words that are stronger and more powerful than *"I hate you"* will ever be. "I love you."

"Fuck, baby. Me too." Backing me out from under the spray, he presses my back to the cold wall on the other side of the large shower. Hands grabbing the back of my thighs, he lifts me up and I wrap my legs around him. Eye level with him, his blue gaze burns into mine. "I loved you even when I hated you. You are my heart, Posie Davenport."

The butterflies that erupt in my stomach are summoned by him when his lips crash into mine. This kiss feels different than the rest. This one signifies the start of a lifetime of more just like this. With our secrets and lies exposed, there's nothing left keeping us apart. For the first time, maybe ever, we're completely bare to one another.

I know now our story was never destined to be an easy one, but every heartache and lie was worth it in the end.

He groans, chest vibrating against mine when my tongue finds his. The tip of his cock nudges the back of my thigh, telling me he needs me as much as I do him.

"Take me to bed," I pant against his lips. We're both soaked and we'll need to change the sheets so we can sleep, but I don't care. "I want you."

Holding on to him, I lick and suck his neck while he turns off the water and carries me out of the shower. We leave a trail of water across the tile and the hardwood floor of his bedroom before we reach his king-sized bed. The dark charcoal sheets smell of him and the spicy scent wraps around me when my back hits the mattress.

Taking hold of my knees, he yanks my legs apart and the cool air hits my exposed pussy. My demand for him to touch me dies on my tongue when his lips close over my clit, and I momentarily lose the ability to bring air into my lungs.

"Shit!" I gasp, fingers pulling at the soft cotton sheets.

The long languid swipe of his tongue has my back arching off the bed and my toes curling. He doesn't need to do this, my body is ready for him, but he gets just as much pleasure out of this as I do. This is one of the few instances where I would classify Rafferty Wilde as *generous*.

One of his strong arms wraps around my thigh to keep me in place as he licks, sucks, and bites my sensitive flesh until I'm thrashing beneath him. His fingers sink into me and curl up toward that spot inside of me that he knows so well, and at the same time, his lips close on my clit again.

I pull a pillow over my face just in time to muffle the sounds he forces from my throat. Pax's room is right across the hall, and it feels insensitive for him to have to hear us in here after what happened.

I've just barely crashed back into my body after floating above it in ecstasy when he thrusts fully inside of me. He tears the pillow out of my grasp and takes hold of my face in a bruising touch.

He rears back before diving back just as deep as before. "Look at me," he orders. "Look at me and tell me you love me."

This is the easiest thing anyone's asked me to do. "I love you, Rafferty. Always have and always will."

The smile that pulls at his lips before they seal over mine makes my heart skip a beat, and I take joy in knowing I'm the only one who gets to see it. He saves his smiles and love for me, and they're both all I could ever want.

WE NEVER GOT AROUND to changing the sheets. We fell asleep tangled in each other with my head on his chest. Hours later, I woke up to him pulling a blanket over us, but I wasn't awake long. After the chaos and emotionally taxing events of the past four days, I was exhausted and couldn't keep my eyes open. I don't think I've ever slept as hard as I did last night.

The early afternoon sun nearly blinds me when my eyes do finally crack open. Groaning, I reach for Raff's pillow to throw over my head but stop when my fingers brush against paper.

What the hell? That wasn't there when we went to sleep last night.

One eye open and one still squeezed shut, I roll onto my stomach and reach across the half-empty bed for the paperwork. The lettering scrolled across it doesn't register in my brain for a solid ten seconds before a single word clicks.

Holy shit.

Like someone had shocked me with a live wire, I'm flying up into a sitting position and reading the document word for word. All evidence of exhaustion has completely vacated my system.

"I got it signed over to you. It's completely paid off and it's yours." Rafferty's voice comes from the doorway. I'm not sure when he appeared there or how long he's watched me scan over the updated deed to my father's house. "Henry will always have a home. You don't have to worry about that. We'll make whatever changes to it that still need to be done to make sure it's perfect for him and your aunt."

"Raff…" My throat is tight as I stare at him in disbelief. "I don't know what to say. Thank you."

He pushes off the doorframe and moves to sit on the end of the bed in front of me. He shoves his fingers through his hair, and the slightly wavy strands fall back to his forehead in a perfectly messy way.

"Don't fucking thank me. I never should have threatened to evict him in the first place. I'm just glad I can make it right now."

I fold the deed carefully before turning to place it on the nightstand. I freeze when I see the gold chain with the small key already lying there. There's only one thing a key that size would work on, and it's currently shackled around my throat.

"What..." I trail off, finding it concerning that I'm bothered at the prospect of him taking it off. It started off as a symbol of his absolute control over me, but at some point, I started to view it differently. It stopped being degrading. I'm not sure what it says about me that I'm upset at the idea of removing a literal *collar*, but I'm sure a psychiatrist would have a field day with it. "Do you want me to take it off?"

"Yes."

My stomach drops a little at his blunt answer.

"Unless I'm fucking you, I don't need you to wear it anymore," he explains, taking my hand in his and his fingers absentmindedly fiddle with mine. "I've already given you some-thing else to wear that marks you as mine. There will be no confusion from anyone when they see it. They'll know you're off-fucking-limits, and if they don't, my fist down their throat should do the trick."

Brows pulled in confusion, I shake my head at him. "What the hell are you talking—"

It's just then I realize his fingers are twisting a ring back and forth on my hand. *I don't wear rings.* Eyes snapping to where my left hand rests in my lap, I'm nearly *blinded* by the gigantic radi-ant-cut diamond sitting on my finger. I thought the ring Astor Banes's wife had was big, but Rafferty has somehow managed to outdo him.

I mean, of fucking course, he did.

I want to jump at him or scream *or something*, but instead I'm stuck frozen staring at the engagement ring. I'm not numb by any means. It's quite the opposite. I'm feeling so many things at once, my body has momentarily forgotten how to function.

"Rafferty…" I manage to choke out after a stunned minute.

He doesn't get on one knee, and I wouldn't expect him to. It's a move that is too traditional and rigid for him. Instead, he brings my left hand up and kisses my palm. "I'm not going to ask you anything because that insinuates there's a question at hand. This isn't a question. Not anymore." His gaze bores into mine and the intensity in those blue orbs all but steals my breath. "You're mine, Butterfly. That's just simple fucking fact. I want —*need*—to make you mine in every possible way because I'm not risking losing you again. I will legally bind you to me to ensure you stay with me. It's where you belong. We both know it."

Some will say this is fast and a rash decision. What they don't know is we've been slowly moving toward this inevitable point since we were kids. I didn't think I believed in fate, but now I think I do. We've been through hell and somehow managed to come out the other side *together*. If that isn't proof we are meant for each other, I don't know what is.

The best thing my mom ever did was leave me. It's because of her that Mollie took me in like she did. For that, I will forever be thankful to her for abandoning me.

She is the reason I met the one my very soul belongs to, and that is a debt I can never repay.

The breath I'd been holding escapes my parted lips in a slow shuddering exhale. "If this isn't a question, what do you want me to say?"

His request is simple. "Tell me you're mine."

"I'm yours."

For the rest of our lives, I'll never tell him truer words than those.

EPILOGUE
POSIE

One Month Later

I DON'T KNOW how parents do it. Just eight hours in a studio full of kids puts me on my ass. Exhausted, I collapse face down on the leather sectional and hug a pillow under my head. It's moments like these after my long shifts that I regret not taking Rafferty up on his offer. He told me I didn't need to work anymore. Since he officially moved me out of Zadie's apartment the day after he put his ring on my finger, I no longer have to worry about rent. And given he's the reason Zadie is without a roommate, he's agreed to pay my half on the apartment until the lease is up. It's not a big change for him seeing as he was already covering some of my rent to begin with.

He will always have more money than he knows what to do with, but I don't want to live solely off him. It doesn't feel right, and that's why I insisted on keeping my job at the ballet studio. There are days, like today, that are exhausting, but I also love it. I enjoy sharing my love of dance with those young minds. My

347

own dance future is still up in the air, and whether or not I'll end up back on stage is unknown, but until I figure it out, I'm happy at the studio.

My goal right now is to make it through the rest of this school year. Rafferty is graduating in the spring, and after he does, we're moving into the penthouse he's purchasing in downtown Seattle. It's a two-story place, and every wall is basically floor-to-ceiling windows with views of the water. It's over the top and lavish, but I wouldn't expect anything less from him.

He originally planned on selling the firehouse, but now with everything up in the air with Pax, he's decided to hold off until his brother has some kind of plan.

I wish I could say that Pax stayed sober after his encounter with Adrian, but that hasn't been the case. He lasted almost a week before he came home high, and he was so fucking upset with himself. I sat with him until he fell asleep, and then I stayed by his side the following two days while he detoxed again. He's been trying hard to stay clean, but he's fallen into a bit of a vicious cycle the past month. Raff and I are helping him as best we can and supporting him through it all. I'm proud of him for deciding he wants to be sober. That was a big step for him.

During the moments of clear-headedness over these weeks, he's made comments about the possibility of returning to school and getting his degree. It's those comments that have Rafferty holding off on selling this place.

Footsteps coming down the wooden stairs have my eyes opening.

"Hi."

"What are you doing?" Pax asks, making his way around the couch to sit across from me.

"My shift started at nine this morning. I really don't understand why parents would sign their five-year-old's up for early Saturday classes, but here we are." I roll onto my side and hold my head up with my hand so I can look at him while I talk. He's not sober. I can tell by the glassiness in his eyes. "How are you doing?"

I understand Adrian being dead doesn't magically erase the years of trauma he lived through, but I'd hoped knowing that his tormenter was gone would help him sleep a little bit better—that it would bring him a sliver of peace. He hasn't said a word about that night, and I haven't brought it up to him—to *either* of them —so I can only infer how he's feeling about it based on his actions and facial expressions. The latter has become hard to read lately as he draws further into himself, and that's why I can only assume he's been struggling. Which is more than under-standable.

His palms rub anxiously together, and he fidgets in his seat.

The nervous energy radiating off him instantly puts me on edge and I pull myself into a sitting position. "Pax?"

"I need your help."

The déjà vu hits me like a fucking semi-truck. We've been here before and my answer is the same as it was back then. "Name it."

What he's going to ask is a mystery to me, but there isn't any doubt in my mind that I'll do everything in my power to make it happen. For the Wilde boys, I will always drop everything and help them. That's a promise I made a long time ago.

Pulling his phone from his back pocket, he reaches across the dark wood coffee table to hand it to me. Glancing at the screen, there's a phone number already typed in. Someone just needs to hit the green dial button.

I look back at him, confused about what he needs me to do. "Whose number is this?"

His lips press into a thin line. "It's a rehab facility based in Oregon. It sounds like it could be a good fit for me. They focus not only on the addiction, but on the source. They have … trauma specialists on staff. Which is what I think I need." My heart hurts when his voice becomes a low whisper as he says the

349

last sentence. "I've already registered and set everything up. I just can't bring myself to make the last call."

The pride I feel for my best friend right now is indescribable. I could only hope for him that he would reach this point, and the fact that he's made these steps alone is amazing. He needed to decide when he was ready for more help, and he's finally reached that point.

I sit up straighter and clear my voice. He doesn't need me to cry happy tears for him right now. I'll save them for later. "What is the last call?"

"They send a car to come pick you up. They'll have a handler with them, and they'll stay with me during the flight there. From the airport, they'll take me directly to the facility."

"You don't want Rafferty or me to take you?" I can't help but ask. It goes against everything in me to let him face this alone.

His head shakes. "No, I think I need to do this part by myself." The ghost of a smile that forms on his face reminds me of the ones he used to wear before his world went so dark. "I'm ready to be sober—to be healthy. He told me I wouldn't fight back, and as long as I depend on these pills, I won't be able to fight to get my life back."

Adrian thought he'd broken his children, but he was wrong. They're strong despite what he did to them, and it's because of that he lost.

I hope Mollie is as proud of her boys as I am, and I hope she knows they're safe with me.

Fuck it. I let the tears fall from my eyes. Standing from the couch, I close the space between us and wrap my arms around him. He hugs me back just as tight and buries his face in my shoulder.

"I'm proud of you, Paxton."

New Year's Eve
Rafferty

THE WILDE CORPORATION has had an annual New Year's Eve party every year for the past fifty or so years. My grandfather decided it would be a good way to celebrate the successful year with the staff and shareholders. We rent out various venues around the city and people dress up like they're attending a movie premier in Hollywood or something. It's a lot of unnecessary fanfare, but it's tradition.

And Grandma Claire said I wasn't allowed to cancel it. She never had a leadership role at the company, and she's been retired for decades, but make no mistake, she still calls the shots on the holiday parties. It was a fight I didn't see myself winning so I let her have this one.

Standing on the outskirts of the gold and white decorated room, I try to keep to myself. I recognize many of the faces in this room as I was raised around many of them. It's an odd thought to know this time next year, I'll be their boss. I'd be lying if I said I didn't think I had a daunting task in front of me, but I also know I can do it. Grandpa showed me the ropes my entire life. I feel more ready to take it on than I ever did.

The weight of the past I've carried around with me has started to lift as pieces of my life fall back into place. I'm healing and Posie's the reason.

Every day I spend with her at my side, the anger and chaos that's burned inside of me lessens. The wounds that have been bleeding freely for so long are closing, and soon, we'll all bear matching scars. Those will never fade and that's okay. They're reminders of what we've survived.

Dressed in a white suit, Claire approaches with two glasses of champagne in her hands. "Hiding in a dark corner as usual, I see," she teases as she passes me the flute.

"Some habits die hard."

Her thin lips pull up in a grin before she takes a sip of her drink. "You don't have to be by yourself anymore, though. Where's my beautiful future granddaughter-in-law?"

Her use of the word *future* has me frowning. Every night, when her arms wrap around me and her head lays on my bare chest, I ask if we can get married. She laughs and tells me soon. She's enjoying being engaged, but I'm ready for her to have my last name. I would take her to city hall any time and get married in front of a random judge. I don't care about having an actual wedding. It's a glorified party with a specific color scheme. Posie wants to do something with our family and friends, and that's the only reason I haven't thrown her in the back of my car and hightailed it to city hall. Even if my patience is being severely tested, her happiness is the priority.

I lift my glass in the direction of where the human embodiment of my heart stands. Dressed in a short shimmery gold dress and her long hair curled, she looks absolutely stunning. While I struggle with small talk, she's easily chatting with one of the finance guys' wives. A smile grows on her pretty face, and it makes somewhere deep in my chest ache.

Fuck… The way I love this girl.

"I'm happy for you, Rafferty." Claire's boney hand grips my forearm. "This is exactly what your mother would have wanted for you."

"I know." In August, I couldn't have fathomed believing that, but now I understand it's the undeniable truth. She loved Posie like a daughter and she would love her even more knowing what she sacrificed for Paxton. I know I do.

"Now we just need to get Paxton better, and everything will be perfect."

Pax was the one who called Claire and admitted his struggle with the pills and alcohol. He did it on his way to the rehab facility in Oregon so she wouldn't worry about where he was for three months. Posie and I have gone down to visit him twice so far and are planning to go again in the next few weeks. He's doing really well and working his ass off. He doesn't see it yet, but one day he'll realize how strong he is.

"He's getting there," I tell her at the same time Posie's eyes lock with mine from across the room. "I'll catch up with you in a bit, Grandma."

Leaving my glass on a nearby table, I weave my way through the room to make it to her. I ignore the few people who call my name in an attempt to start up a conversation with me. If I'm going to be their boss, it's probably best they learn now that I'm not exactly cordial or approachable. It'll make it easier on us all if they do.

Posie's hand is already reaching out to me before I get to her, and as I pass her, my fingers intertwine with hers. I don't stop or slow down. I simply pull her with me toward the glass doors leading to the rooftop deck.

No one else is out here because it's too damn cold, but I don't care. The silence and her company are all I need right now. Leading her to the edge, we stare out over the city. From here, we can see the Space Needle and the various firework shows going off across the town.

"Oh, wow..." she murmurs, stepping forward to put her hands on the glass railing.

Knowing she's probably freezing, I take my black jacket off and slip it over her shoulders. Carefully pulling her hair free from the collar, I pull it to the side and expose her neck. Unable to stop myself, I dip my head and press my lips to her skin. The sigh of contentment has me smiling against her throat.

She leans her back into my front when I stand behind her and circle my arms around her waist. We stay like this, watching the fireworks light up the sky, for I don't know how long. It's these quiet moments that I like most. I let her calmness soak into me and allow it to center me.

Because it's become a habit at this point—tradition if you

will—to ask every night, I dip my head and whisper in her ear, "Can we get married now?"

I expect her to laugh at me and shake her head like she usually does, but this time she remains silent, attention still glued to the bright lights flashing in the sky. Those very lights reflect in her eyes when she turns her head to look up at me.

My heart all but stops when she nods her head and simply says, "Okay. Let's get married."

Not believing her, I take a step back so I can see her entire face. "Seriously?"

"Seriously. Let's get married."

"What happened to you wanting family and friends there?"

Her narrow shoulders shrug, and a breathtaking smile grows on dark-red lips. "We'll have a party another time, but this... This feels right. I want to marry you tonight. Just you and me."

Fingers tipping her chin up, I press my lips to hers. "Fucking finally," I murmur against them.

I have no idea where I'm going to find someone to marry us this late on New Year's Eve, but I'll figure it out.

For my Butterfly, I'll kidnap a priest if I have to.

The End.

Golden Wings &
PRETTY THINGS

KAYLEIGH KING

GOLDEN WINGS & PRETTY THINGS PREVIEW
INDIE CHAPTER 1

"Watch out!" is the only warning I get before ice-cold water splashes across my skin, stunning me out of the relaxed state I'd found myself in. The group erupts into laughter and cheers as I fly up into a sitting position on the large inflatable dock just in time to watch Callan's head resurface.

His perfectly straight teeth flash when he finds me gaping at him in shock. "Did I get you?"

This causes even more laughter from our friends, who either lie on the dock with me or float on smaller, colorful rafts all around us. Callan is the only one fully submerged in the frigid water. It may be July, but Lake Washington never gets much above sixty-five degrees.

I look down at my now waterlogged yellow bikini and back at my boyfriend. "Maybe just a little bit." It takes effort to keep my face pulled in a scowl, a smile and laugh fighting to the surface.

Callan sees right through it though. "Only a little bit?" His muscular arms, tan from spending our summer on the lake, glide with ease through the water. He stops just feet in front of me, his dark-blue eyes searching me over. "Show me where I missed.

I'm going to need to get there too," he taunts, his lips pulling into a smug smirk.

It's refreshing to see Callan like this. He's been so serious lately. I've tried asking him about it, but he's been cagey and vague with his answers. The desire to push him on it is strong, but when people pry me for information, it makes me want to punch them in the nose. So, I've tried my best to be patient.

He'll tell me when he's ready. Or at least I hope he will.

It's always been a toss-up with Callan. Since the beginning, it's felt like he's been holding back.

His hand wraps around my ankle, and with a harsh pull, he yanks me dangerously close to the edge. My nails dig into the surface to try and prevent him from pulling me farther. I have a feeling it's in vain though. My legs now dangle in the chilly water, making goose bumps dance across my skin.

"How about a quick dip, Indie?" Callan takes my other ankle in his grasp too. "Just so we can get all the places I missed."

"Don't you dare," I warn, my smile still threatening to escape no matter how much I don't want to get back in the lake. It took thirty minutes of lying in the sun to finally warm myself up after my brisk swim out here. Shore isn't far, forty feet at most, but it feels a lot farther when your muscles seize up from the icy water.

"Wouldn't dream of it. I promise." Callan lifts my foot out of the lake, bringing it to his mouth. He presses a kiss to the arch, his eyes locked with mine while he does.

It's a sweet moment he completely ruins by breaking his promise.

There's barely enough time for me to release a startled yelp before I'm fully submerged. The abrupt change in temperature is a shock to the system. My body stiffens and my chest aches.

It's only a few seconds I'm under, but it feels like minutes.

Not once do Callan's hands leave my body as he pulls me up and I surface, making a screeching sound. "*Holy shit!*" I shriek once I've sucked in a breath.

My boyfriend's laugh fills my ears while I shove the hair that's stuck to my forehead back. "Look how fast you get wet for me," he muses.

His hands flex on my hips and a shiver of anticipation shoots through me. It's been too long since we've slept together, and I miss being touched. In addition to his new evasive demeanor, he's been coming over less and less. When he does, he doesn't spend the night.

Since summer break started, he hasn't invited me over to his place on campus either. Before, there were times I spent two weeks there, not once returning to my own apartment. When we first got together almost six months ago, it was all heat. Didn't matter where we were, Callan's hands were on me, but now, I feel like I have to *work* to get him to show interest in me. And I'm starting to grow tired.

The red flags are basically glowing neon signs at this point.

I'm wary, but still pleased by his change in attitude now. I don't even care that our friends are five feet away from us, possibly eavesdropping.

"*Mmmhmm*," I agree, looping my arms around his neck, bringing our faces closer. "You got me wet, now what are you going to do about it?"

Callan's eyes flick to my lips, but where I should see desire reflected in them, all I find is contemplation.

Fuck this.

No longer waiting for him to make a move, I close the distance myself and test the waters.

I remember the first time Callan Banes kissed me. He literally swept me off my feet because he stole my ability to stand with a simple kiss. It was the epitome of making a girl weak in the knees. At the time, I thought that kiss was going to be my last first kiss.

Our kiss now confirms that I may have been wrong that night. Ever since then, I've been chasing that feeling like an addict chasing their first high. And now I'm starting to wonder if it's even worth it.

People sometimes describe kisses like a dance. There's passion and an elegant rhythm. The choreography should be exciting to perform. It feels taxing and boring now. Almost like it's a chore.

"Callan!" Hansen hollers from the dock I'd been yanked from, making Callan pull away. "Get your ass up here. I need a partner. Zadie and Lark think they have a chance against me in beer pong."

"Oh! I don't *think* anything," Zadie shouts back at Hansen from the hot-pink raft she sits on. "I *know*. I saw how you threw the ball last week at practice. We have this in the bag." Her hand points at the floating beer pong table, the various bracelets she wears chime every time she moves. "I'll bet you two hundred dollars right now that us *girls* can kick your ass six ways from Sunday."

Zadie Hill looks like a sweet little pixie, but she can verbally destroy the strongest of men. It's one of my favorite things to witness.

"Hey!" Hansen shouts at her. "Don't be a bitch."

"I'm not a bitch, I'm a fucking lady," Zadie hurls the ball in her lap at him. He catches it with ease, causing a scowl to form. "Stop talking and let's play."

Callan laughs, his handsome face pulling into a huge smile. "You're on, Hill." His quick kiss on my cheek feels like a dismissal as he pushes away from me without a second thought.

I stay there treading water, watching him swim away, not really sure what I'm waiting for him to do. Come back? Ask me to join? Just...*something.*

It's Lark, the stunning, soft-spoken blonde with the kind smile that yells over to me. Not my boyfriend. "Indie! Come on!" She motions to me with her hand. "We can take turns."

I think over her offer for all of two seconds before I shake my head at her. "No, it's okay," I lie. "You guys go ahead. I need to go inside and see if my mom called me back."

Not a complete lie. I have an event this weekend and need to make sure that everything is still okay on her end. When I told Mom my wish to participate in this competition, she dragged her feet on giving me her blessing. I'm counting down the days till I no longer need her permission.

For three years, I've squirreled away every loose piece of change and dollar bill I don't need to live so I can finally buy Jupiter from her. It's ridiculous that I would have to do such a thing when my dad gave me his beloved stallion as a gift when I was thirteen. The horse is rightfully mine, but when Dad died, my mom put her name on Jupiter's paperwork.

As long as she's the rightful owner of him, I need her permission for every event we participate in. It's just another way for her to keep me under her controlling thumb. Her new boyfriend isn't helping matters either.

Turning from my friends, I begin to swim back to the shore. I get no more than ten feet away when my name is called again.

This time it's Callan.

Treading water again, I look at the man I'm growing tired of wasting time on.

"I think my dad is working with that damn eagle again today," he warns from his place on the floating dock. His hand shields his eyes from the high afternoon sun as he squints at me. "It's never done anything, but I don't trust it. Just be careful."

"Oh," I nod once. "Okay."

With that, Callan turns his back on me. Confirming what I already know in my heart and making the disappointment I feel grow.

I don't chase after boys, but our story is the oldest one in the book. A popular upperclassman takes interest in the wide-eyed freshman. She's shy but loves that he takes her everywhere, showing her off. He introduces her to everyone like he's truly proud to have her at his side. She believes his whispered sweet nothings and false promises. She becomes swept up in him and thrives off the heat between them.

But what happens when it turns stone cold, and the sweet nothings become lies?

You discover it was all smoke and mirrors, and you're left clinging to something that never existed in the first place.

Chapter Two
Astor

Jealousy.

It's a peculiar emotion to experience when you're a man who's never wanted for anything. Yet I find that unbecoming shade of green working its way through my system more frequently as of late. It appears during the smallest moments, like now, watching the eagle soar up ahead.

I envy the bird of prey's freedom and ability to fly away from it all. His liberty is fleeting, but every second is priceless to him. I crave those own seconds for myself.

With a low whistle, I call the bird back to me. It's taken years and endless patience to get to this point, but he doesn't hesitate even a moment before swooping back toward the ground. The piece of rabbit leg I have in the leather pouch at my side keeps him coming back.

It's his reward.

Protected by a thick leather glove, he lands gracefully on my arm. He makes a low squawking sound, his yellow, ever-observant eyes looking for the treat he knows he's owed.

"Good boy," I praise, stroking a hand down his brown feathers before reattaching the leash to the leather straps around his ankles. It took us a long time to get here, but the contact no longer makes him uneasy. It wasn't an easy road, and I will forever carry scars on my hands and forearms as reminders of our progress.

The outcome has been more than worth it.

Taking his reward from me, he holds the piece of meat in his talons and eats happily as I carry him to the enclosure on the left side of the property. It's built in a dome shape, tight-knit black netting covering the whole structure. It's large enough the bird will never feel cooped up, and in the middle is a raised wooden building—almost like a small tree house—where he can escape the Washington rains.

Releasing the tied leash from his foot, I free him, lingering only a moment to watch him fly to a perch. His head nods once, as if he's bidding me farewell as I close the keypad-protected door behind me and head back toward my house.

The sound of boisterous laughter and yelling comes from the lake below, reminding me that I'll have another day of college kids in and out of my house. Early in the summer, I made the mistake of allowing Callan to have a few friends over. He has a house on campus he rents with a friend, but they wanted to swim in the lake my house sits on.

Had I known it was going to turn into a weekly event throughout the entire break, I would have rethought my original answer.

Especially had I known he would always bring *her* here.

I've never been one to deny myself what I want, but she is the exception. I've been forced to restrain my cravings for months—something that doesn't come naturally but it is required of me.

It would have been better had she never been put in my sights, but now that I know she exists, I can't seem to escape her.

Now is no different.

I enter through the tall glass backdoors of my home to find the main source of my growing jealousy standing in my kitchen.

The small triangles of her bikini cover little, revealing her sun-kissed skin. She doesn't hear me enter and her attention remains locked on the phone in her hand.

Even though I know I shouldn't, I take this moment to observe the girl who's unintentionally captured my attention.

She stands on a dish towel in an attempt to not get water on my hardwood floors, but it's not working. Small puddles are forming at her feet. A steady drip comes from her dark hair that doesn't quite reach her shoulders. I watch as a drop falls down her chest. My eyes follow the bead as it travels down her body, stopping only when it disappears into the waistband of her bright-yellow bottoms.

The unwelcome desire I feel for the girl rears its ugly head. My teeth clench in anger knowing that, without even trying, she's crawled under my skin. I'm even more infuriated by the fact I've allowed someone so unattainable to do so.

It's one thing to be jealous of another man, it's another thing entirely to be jealous of your own son.

And when I look at Indie Riverton, I'm uncontrollably envious that my son found her first and I'm angry he doesn't fully appreciate the prize he's obtained.

A siren whose song I must ignore.

She's a pretty thing that I'm aching to play with.

A toy that isn't mine to break.

Burying the ill-advised stirrings she causes, I focus on the resentment knowing I can't have her, and I clear my throat harshly.

Her amber eyes drift from the screen and noticeably widen when she finds me standing here. "Mr. Banes," she gasps. "I didn't see you there."

I shift forward a foot, hands behind my back. "You're dripping water on my floors."

She blinks slowly at me as if she's not understanding my remark. Finally, it clicks, and she quickly says, "*Crap*. I'm so sorry. I needed to check my phone, and I forgot to bring my towel up with me." Keeping her feet planted on the small towel, she reaches for the other dish towel that's folded neatly on the marble countertop. "I'll clean it up," she promises.

Before I can say another word, she squats down and wipes at the puddles on the hardwood. With each one she cleans, another appears from the water still escaping her drenched hair.

Shaking my head, I spin on my heels and head toward the laundry room where I know the housekeeper left a pile of fresh towels.

I return to find her on her hands and knees, a sight that makes my hands flex. Stepping closer, I dangle the towel off my fingertip in front of her face.

Indie's chin lifts, our eyes locking. The prettiest blush I've ever seen spreads across her face as her thin fingers wrap around the offering. "Thank you," she whispers with a sheepish smile.

I don't offer any reply or extend my hand to help her stand. I merely watch the way she nibbles on her bottom lip. It's a nervous tic I've seen her do many times. She does it when she's waiting for Callan to look at her or even acknowledge her. Her big doe-like eyes stare at him, silently pleading for him to remember that she's there, but he never does.

I've never been one to interfere with my son's personal life, and in truth, he's never responded well to hand-holding. He needs to make these mistakes so he can learn from them. He'll realize too late that he's fucked up. Though, I'm not convinced his retreat from her hasn't been methodically planned.

"Why are you in here?" I ask. "Shouldn't you be down there with the rest of them?" *With my son.*

Returning to her feet, Indie uses the towel to ring out the moisture from her hair. "I needed a break from the sun." She tells a lie better than most, but the falsehood is written in her amber eyes when she speaks. "And I've been waiting for my mom to get back to me all day about a show jumping event I have this

Sunday. She's out of town with her boyfriend, so getting a hold of her has been tricky."

Another thing I've noticed is she also rambles when she's nervous. It shouldn't please me as much as it does that I've caused such a reaction from her. It's not the reaction I desire, but then again, I shouldn't be craving a single thing from her.

"You turned down the spot on our equestrian team along with the scholarship that came with it, did you not?" It was an abuse of my power to look into her school records, but along with my jealousy, my curiosity was also piqued. "Why would you opt for a merit-based scholarship that covers less when you could have received a full ride?"

My question takes Indie by surprise. Her mouth opens and closes a couple of times before she finally finds her words. "I always forget you're the university president and know all this stuff about everyone."

"Not everyone."

Her mouth tilts in a playful smile. "So, I'm pretty special then, huh?"

"No." My correction comes with a terse edge, instantly killing her smile. "When my son is dating a fellow student, I tend to take an interest. I'm not fond of having strangers in my home to begin with, and Callan's judgment when it comes to the girls he brings home has been less than ideal."

After his senior year of high school, it went downhill fast and that is partially why I'm shocked he picked someone like Indie.

At the mention of dating Callan, Indie's face falls further, and her hands tighten around the white towel she's still holding. "*Right,* obviously." She nods. "That makes sense."

"Does mentioning my son's past conquests upset you?"

"Upset me? Not at all." Indie makes a scoffing noise before she can help it. It appears it comes as a surprise to even her by the way she covers her mouth. "I… I just mean, I know everyone has a past, and Callan is no different." She attempts to recover, but the damage has been done.

Silence falls between us when I don't offer a reply. Instead, I try to uncover the secrets she keeps guarded behind her pretty face.

She breaks it by answering my earlier question. "I'm good at what I do because of the horse I ride. We're a team, and if I can't compete with him, there's no point in me competing at all. My mom wouldn't allow me to bring him here to Seattle, and without her blessing, my hands were tied. I took the next best option the school offered me, which was the merit scholarship."

"I suppose that makes sense. It takes a long time to establish a bond with an animal, and once they're formed, they're not easily replaced."

Indie glances toward the backyard where I'd just been with the eagle. "I can't begin to imagine the kind of time it took you to bond with him. The patience alone to train an animal like him must have been intense. *How* exactly does one train a golden eagle?"

With her standing this close, I can't help my eyes from wandering across her tanned skin or my lungs from inhaling her. The sunscreen she wears smells of coconut and there's a light trail of freckles on her nose from spending her summer days lounging in my backyard.

"Training something is easy once you know what motivates them, Indie," I begin, my tone sounding darker than I intend it to, but her nearness is destroying my resolve.

Indie picks up on it and her teeth stop their nibbling on her bottom lip. Her eyes lock with mine and her breath shudders as the air suddenly shifts between us. She's looked at me before, but it's as if this is the first time she's truly allowing herself to *see* me.

"For the eagle, it's the promise of food. As long as I continue to reward him, he'll come when I call. Humans are just as easy.

They want money, power, or sex. Once you know which they desire, you can have them eating out of your hand just like the eagle does mine."

She stares up at me with her lips parted and chest rising faster than before. My own heart thuds against my chest and my mind fills with the filthy things I would do to her if she were my plaything.

Indie swallows hard, her throat bobbing. "Which one do you crave?" she boldly asks.

My hand reaches out and I push the wet strand of hair that sticks to her blushing cheek behind her ear. "I don't crave just one, I want all of them," I pause, my hand lingering longer on her skin than it should. "And I'll accept nothing less."

I'm already playing with fire and toeing the line that's been drawn in the sand.

To hell with it.

There are a million reasons to keep my distance, the biggest ones being Indie is Callan's girlfriend and a student at my university, but that doesn't stop me. *Can't* stop me.

Shifting forward another step, I bow my head. I'm not sure if she's even aware that she reacts and moves closer. Her chin tilts up toward me, further bridging the space between us. She's shorter than me by many inches, but we're close enough that I can feel her shaky breath across my chin.

"You would be just as easy," I tell her darkly, eyes cutting to her pink lips. "Once I figured out which reward you craved, I could make you just as obedient. Just like him, you'll come when I call." Even to me, I'm not sure if this is a threat or a promise. Maybe it's a mixture of both. "Just something to keep in mind." Searching for the resolve I originally entered the room with, I harden myself once more. "Please do bring a towel with you next time, Indie. I would hate to see you ruin my floors."

It's best for the both of us that I turn and leave before she can respond.

ACKNOWLEDGMENTS

This story… kicked my ass, but in the end I can truly say I wrote something I'm proud of, and I can only say that because you, my dear readers, were patient with me. I never planned on having to move the release date of this book as many times as I did, but *life* happens and some things are out of our control.

I knew that Posie and Rafferty's story needed to be handled with care and I needed all the extra time to do that. So THANK YOU READERS for sticking around and waiting for me.

My BETAS; Holy shit, this book wouldn't exist without you guys. Your constant messages of support and reassurance got me through this book. I doubted myself a lot writing this as you know, but you all made me believe I was writing a story worth telling. Thank you Aundi, Whitney, Kristy, Jaime & Carrie.

Greer, my best friend, my lifeline, my sounding board; Life's been really crazy these last five months and I've used you as a therapist more times than I can count. It's also probably more times than I should have. Oops… Sorry bout that. Also super sorry I f-ed up our co-write schedule and you've had to wait for me to get this book done before we can work on our next one together. Good news! We can finally start on our next secret project. I love you to death. Thank you for being my friend.

Cat, my angel baby, the Enid to my Wednesday, Kitchen; Watching you grow as a designer has been amazing, even if it means I have to share you with everyone now. You're taking book-world by storm and I'm so proud of you. The magic you create is one of a kind, and I'm lucky I get to work with you. I'm even luckier I get to call you a friend.

Bethany, my agent, thank you for getting my work out there in front of these important people. The audio deals and foreign translations are both things I never thought I'd be able to get, so thank you for making them happen.

To my editors Amanda and Ellie… are you guys both ready to fire me with these whack-ass deadlines? I pinky promise that I'm going to be changing my ways this year. Thank you for always fitting me into your schedules, and thank you for making my words pretty.

And to my puppy-dog Emme. You've been with me more than half of my life, and I'm so sad that I'm going to lose you soon. It breaks my heart you won't be my writing buddy keeping me company during my next book, but I know your sister Roux will be there to pick up the slack. Dogs should live forever.

ABOUT THE AUTHOR

USA Today Bestselling author Kayleigh King is a writer of contemporary and paranormal romance. She creates love stories that will stick with you, almost like they're haunting you. She's a Diet Coke and cold brew addict, sharing music is her love language, and she seriously lacks a filter. Anything she thinks, she usually says. And if she doesn't say it, her facial expressions will say it for her. Currently residing in Denver Colorado, you'll never find her on a snowboard since she avoids the snow like the plague.

Want to chat about books, music, or life in general? Make sure you join her Facebook reader group and follow her on Instagram. Her DMs are always open to her readers.

instagram.com/kayleighkingwrites

facebook.com/kayleighkingwrites

goodreads.com/kayleighkingwrites

tiktok.com/@kayleighkingauthor

amazon.com/author/kayleighkingwrites

ALSO BY KAYLEIGH KING

Fractured Rhymes

Golden Wings & Pretty Things

The Crimson Crown Duet

Bloody Kingdom

Midnight Queen

The White Wolf Prophecy Series

Wolf Bound

Soul Bound

Shadow Bound

Fire Bound

Standalone Books

Catching Lightning

Printed in Great Britain
by Amazon